The Peacebrokers

BY THE SAME AUTHOR
Walking Shadows
The Kinder Garden

THE PEACEBROKERS

Frederick Taylor

CENTURY

LONDON SYDNEY AUCKLAND JOHANNESBURG

First published in Great Britain in 1992 by
Random Century Group
20 Vauxhall Bridge Rd, London SW1V 2SA

Random Century South Africa (Pty) Ltd
PO Box 337, Bergvlei 2012, South Africa

Random Century Australia Pty Ltd
20 Alfred Street, Milsons Point, Sydney, NSW 2061
Australia

Random Century New Zealand Ltd
PO Box 40–086, Glenfield, Auckland 10
New Zealand

The catalogue data record for this book is available from the
British Library

Typeset by Pure Tech Corporation, Pondicherry, India

Printed and bound in Great Britain by
Mackays of Chatham PLC, Chatham, Kent

ISBN 0–7126–2914–9

I.M. Ann Louisa
1911–1991

I said I am awkward.
I said we make fools of our lives
For a little money and a coat . . .

John Ashbery
'Some Money'

Europe was moving into the year of peace, of freedom, of the retreat of fear. The East-West conflict, all that old-style treachery and death, had suddenly gone right out of fashion, along with junk bonds and unsafe sex.

This was the conspirators' greatest advantage. Like magicians or pickpockets, they knew how to divert the world's attention while they worked. And they were superb liars. Long ago, in a terrible time and place, they had learned to tell the truth—if they told it at all—only to each other . . .

GERMANY: A WINTER'S TALE

February 1989

ONE

HERE IN THE HARZ MOUNTAINS, where the border ran between the two Germanies like a long, poisoned wound, winter is often beautiful but always cruel.

On 24 February 1989, a Friday, a green Volvo bearing East German government number plates travelled along a lonely woodland track some ten miles east of the Iron Curtain. The earth cowered sullenly beneath its blanket of frost.

The Volvo kept up a good speed, undeterred by mud or ice, ruts or bumps. It was a large station-wagon, the top of the luxury range. Its driver, for his part, was also very big and powerful – a man nicknamed since his childhood 'Granit', German for that most massive, most unyielding of rocks. Eventually he brought the Volvo to its destination, a clearing occupied only by a squat state-issue forester's hut built in bald, grey cinderblock.

NO ACCESS WITHOUT PERMIT. FRONTIER AREA.

Granit didn't give a damn. He parked his Swedish status symbol smack in front of the sign, neatly blocking the exit for the two cars already there: a silver BMW registered in the West German city of Hamburg and a tiny, boxlike East German Trabant. He stood for a moment, as if savouring the bleak silence of the place. Then he clapped his gloved hands together, approached the hut and opened the door.

Because of his size, Granit had to duck through the entrance. Once inside he encountered a surprisingly cosy scene. The stove in the corner had been lit. Three large tumblers of schnapps had been placed ready on a table in the middle of the room. Two other men were waiting for him, and his arrival unleashed a wave of enthusiastic greetings. He bear-hugged each of them in turn, then both together. Then, even though they were all in their mid-fifties, the group traded playful punches, like adolescents meeting on a street corner. Jocular insults flew between them in a rapid guttural argot mixing old Berlin slang with a bizarre, garbled American-German language that was very much their own.

2

'Granit – welcome!'

'*Ach scheiss*, Banana. Still ugly as an Ivan's arse. But it's so good, yes, so good to see you again –'

'First gen-oo-ine Kinder-meeting in years, Granit. First gadawl-mighdy real meeting –'

'Gurkel, you beddabelieve –'

Granit took off his overcoat and laid it carefully – more carefully than he had parked his car – across the top of a rickety chair. Beneath the coat he wore a well-tailored Harris tweed jacket and razor-creased flannel slacks, the elegantly casual, 'English' look so popular with socially ambitious European businessmen – except that a tiny red and gold badge in his lapel proved his membership of the East German Socialist Unity Party. This was his civilian outfit. If this man had chosen to wear the uniform to which he was entitled, he would have been identifiable as a ranking general in the East German Ministry for State Security, the *Ministerium für Staatssicherheit*, more commonly known – and feared – as the *Stasi*.

'So, Granit, how is Comrade General Secretary Honecker, our great leader and teacher?' asked the taller of the two other men, switching back to standard German. He was rangy and skinny, with the scholarly stoop appropriate to a man who in the outside world lived by his pen. Sarcasm was his weapon of choice.

'Not so good. Digestive problems.'

'Oho. Maybe he's thinking of what Big Brother Gorbachev has in store for him. If I were Erich Honecker, I'd have butterflies in my stomach too. Iron ones with six-inch wings!'

Granit sat down heavily, reached for his glass of schnapps.

'You don't know how right you are, Banana. You just don't know,' he sighed.

Granit weighed close to two hundred and eighty pounds, most of it still muscle. Even as a boy he had been massive, despite the wretched diet during those hungry postwar years. Hence his nickname among the gang of war orphans known long ago, before the Iron Curtain divided Germany, as 'The Kinder'. In private, they all used their gang titles from that time: so, *Stasi* General Günther Albrecht was 'Granit'; the sardonic East Berlin writer Otmar Ziegler became 'Banana'; and the third member of the party, Hamburg businessman Jakob Brauer, the only West German present, answered

3

to 'Gurkel'. Of course, the outside world knew them only by their 'real' names and functions. But then, that was another story . . .

'Good times for the likes of you when Big Brother in Moscow decides to let the old warhorses go, eh?' Banana *alias* Ziegler pressed Granit. 'You're still in your prime. And you have an entire security apparatus at your disposal.'

'Forget it, Banana,' Granit said curtly.

'But Granit, the time is ripe for a strong man like you to step in and lick the GDR into shape . . . '

'Not me. I said *forget it.*'

Gurkel, also known as Brauer, showed no inclination to join in the banter. He sat quietly at the table, smoking and watching. When young he had been keen-eyed, fresh-faced, a charmer. Now, though he kept some semblance of those good looks, and though he sported the trendy weekend uniform of the fun-loving West – designer leather jacket, black turtleneck sweater, tailored jeans and hand-made loafers – the overall effect of the man was somehow sad. On closer inspection, his thinning sandy hair was peppered with grey. His eyes, though alert, were hooded with suspicion. There were bags under his eyes from too many late nights and too many ciga-rettes. A tracery of broken red veins scarred his cheeks and nose, the fruit of booze. Years since, hedonism for him had become habit, appetite had turned into addiction.

'That's enough,' Gurkel interrupted sharply. 'Let's hear why you called this meeting, Granit. I just drove all the way from Hamburg after a hard night . . . '

'Blonde, was she?' Banana asked with a laugh.

'Mostly.'

Granit nodded dismissively. 'Good to hear someone's enjoying themselves. Perhaps this will sober you up.' He solemnly poured more schnapps into each of their glasses. Then with dramatic deliberation he announced: 'I called you here to tell you that the Soviet-backed communist régime here in East Germany is finished. The Russians are about to ditch us.'

There was a long silence. Neither of the other men seemed to grasp his meaning. Then understanding dawned in Banana's eyes.

'Good Christ. We're really in the shit,' he murmured hoarsely. 'I can't believe what I'm hearing. Tell me you're joking, Granit . . . '

4

Gurkel took a drag on his tipped Virginia cigarette. 'You just love drama, don't you, Granit?' he said. 'Now be more specific. Explain.'

'The GDR as such has become . . . dispensable, so to say potentially an international bargaining counter. No one else knows this yet – *especially* not Comrade General Secretary Honecker. This comes straight from the innermost councils of the KGB, my friends. My information is as rare as an honest district secretary, and far more dangerous.'

Banana could hardly contain himself. 'But – but – *why*?'

'Simple. The Cold War has been ruinously expensive. The Kremlin is facing bankruptcy. Like any failing enterprise, the Soviet Union has decided to realise some of its assets.' Granit paused. 'To make *perestroika* work, Gorbachev desperately needs Western aid and investment. And let's be brutally frank, when we talk of Western cash these days, we mostly mean the almighty West German Deutschmark . . . '

Banana thumped the table with one bony fist. 'Those swine in the Kremlin are preparing to *sell* this country to West Germany! Seventeen million human beings auctioned like cattle! For what? MacDonald's and Coca-Cola! Miele and Mercedes!'

'Absolutely. It won't happen next month. Maybe not even next year. There's no definite timetable. But our dear GDR has definitely become expendable.'

Banana stared down at the tabletop for some time. '*Finita la commedia,*' he whispered. There was fear in his voice. '*And we're in deep shit. We've built everything on the assumption that East Germany will survive for our lifetime. If the GDR gets buried, so do we. For all the communist régime's faults, it has –* '

'Later, after we've saved our asses, you can write a nice fat book about the GDR and its faults,' Granit snapped. 'Right now we have to consider our plans for the big change that's coming. Listen: If we keep cool heads – and if we stand by each other, us against the rest of world – we'll survive and prosper. Just as we did when we were all orphans together.'

'But that was just after the war,' Gurkel reminded him. 'The world was devastated, chaotic, out of control. It was easy to hide. *Everyone* was hiding something – secrets, pasts, whole identities! These days, it's different. There are computers, expert police squads, nosy journalists.'

5

'I know that better than you!' Granit retorted. 'But I'm sure we can survive this. Banana is right about one thing. I control an entire security apparatus. True. At least until the GDR goes down the tubes. When I say *"Jump!"* –' Suddenly he made a little springing motion with the thick fingers of one massive hand 'No loyal East German citizen dares ask, how high?'

'That's not a survival plan. That's a boast.'

A dangerous glint came into Granit's gaze. 'Maybe. But don't forget, I'm the one who's protected all of you over the years, ever since you were still children. You want documents? I get them! Bank accounts? Jobs? Influence? You need someone got rid of? No problem! I've done everything for you Kinder, because the past we share transcends frontiers and ideologies. That's how we survived the orphanage, the war, and then defeat, starvation, the division of Germany . . . By staying true to each other, no matter the cost!' Granit eyeballed Banana. 'But for me, you'd have spent most of the past twenty years in jail with your fellow so-called dissidents. Instead, you're holding court in a nice villa in Griebnitzsee and taking regular trips abroad.' Next Gurkel got the gimlet stare. 'And you, Gurkel, you'd be in the gutter, clutching a schnapps bottle instead of crowing on top of your own little dung-heap as one of the most successful porn-distributors in Germany. All this because I've looked after you, put my loyalty to our tribe, above everything else. *Isn't that right . . ?'*

Banana bit his lip, overcome with emotion. Gurkel managed to stay cool. 'You can cut the sermonising, Granit. Let's hear your plan.'

'OK. And since you're so eager, I'll tell you your part first. I'm going to give you something to sell. And in order to sell it, you're going to get back in contact with Benno.'

'*Benno*?' Banana made a gesture of contempt. 'Contact Benno? But he's not one of us any more. He betrayed us. He chose the legit world.'

Granit ignored him. His attention was on Gurkel. 'I know you've kept in touch with that *Arschloch* Benno over the years. You're the only one of us who has. He advised you when you were getting your business started, back in the Sixties.'

'How the hell did you –'

'I know *everything*, Gurkel.'

6

Gurkel recovered quickly. 'We see each other now and then,' he conceded. 'I'm not as prejudiced as the rest of you. And Benno's been useful to me. But what does he have to do with any of this, for Christ's sake?'

'My plan needs a go-between. A go-between who'll also provide me with a patsy, and Benno fits both bills.'

'Are you serious? You may think Benno and me are pals – and so we are, up to a point – but he's no fool. I don't know what you have in mind, but he didn't get rich by mixing business with friendship. Getting him to trust me won't be easy.'

Granit cut in with a harsh laugh. 'Gurkel, of course he won't trust you. He doesn't have to. His distrust is built into the plan. But for reasons of his own, he'll buy what you're selling. I guarantee it!'

'I don't like the sound of this.' Gurkel lit another cigarette from the glowing stub of its predecessor. 'Jesus. You're not planning some weird revenge on Benno for his betrayal, are you? Not after all these years.'

'Nothing so trivial!' Granit barked. 'You heard what Banana said. We're all implicated up to our necks. I'm talking survival!' The big man's tone finally silenced even Gurkel. Granit let his message sink in, then glanced at his Rolex watch. 'It's time for me to call the Normannenstrasse on the car phone. In any case, there's some material in the car you need to see. It'll make your minds up – even yours, Gurkel. I'll bring it back with me presently. I'll be ten, fifteen minutes at the most.'

The Volvo's blow-heater roared expensively, keeping winter at bay while Granit settled down to make his phone call.

He noticed how the crowns of many pine trees outside were blackened and bald. The Western press wrote about pollution, about acid rain, about the need for a more environmentally-aware way of life. In the East, meanwhile, the newspapers listed only production increases, endless production increases. He sighed, picked up the handset from the dashboard, punched out his office number. East Germany had the worst telephone system west of Warsaw, but his organisation's communications functioned outside it.

'Hello, Captain Nitzschke?' he spoke quietly into the handset.

'Here, Comrade General.' Granit could read wary alertness in the man's voice.

7

'Some problems at the meeting,' Granit said. 'Nothing serious. Things will just take a bit longer, that's all. Tell our man in London that, will you, Nitzschke?'

'Very well, Comrade General.'

'Also . . . before you go home, get me the files on the . . . special immigrants . . . the D-2 category refugees. I'll be dropping by the office tonight, just briefly, and I want to look them over.' Granit paused, then added as if it were an afterthought: 'Nitzschke, this is one of those situations where you must not log the files out. I'll replace them personally when I've finished.'

'This is your wish . . . '

'It is. OK? Now, regarding that truck we discussed. Well, tomorrow night is the big night. Carry out a search at the petrol station I told you about, the one where it always fills up. I promise you, you'll get a big surprise.'

'Comrade General, we are referring to the Western truck with the . . . illustrated material.'

No initiative, Granit thought. 'That's right. On the Berlin-Hannover Autobahn,' he said. 'What other trucks have we discussed lately, for God's sake? And don't forget: the operation must be directed by you in person, exactly according to the instructions I gave you. Are you absolutely clear what you have to do?'

'Yes, Comrade General,' Nitzschke said miserably. 'So, do I report to you after I have searched the truck?'

But Granit had already hung up on him. He replaced the phone in its cradle on the dashboard, sighed, passed one hand over his eyes. Then he picked up the attaché case from the passenger seat and unzipped it. He handled the thick sheaf of papers inside lovingly.

Who said that he, Granit, had no creativity? Who said that those who laboured in the service of the Ministry for State Security were mere philistines?

'Sorry, Gurkel,' he whispered. Granit pictured the look on his friend's face if he had been able to witness this conversation. It was Gurkel's truck that was about to be searched. 'I just cost you around two hundred thousand Marks and a lot of grief. But,' he said to himself, and smiled, 'in the end you'll realise it was worth it. In the end.'

In the forester's hut, the two men waited in silence, stunned by what Granit had told them. Gurkel started to drum his fingers on the table. Banana glared at him.

'Sorry,' Gurkel said with a wry smile. 'Listen . . . do you believe what Granit says about East Germany's future?'

'Sure. It's logical, when you come to think of it. Anyway, why should he lie?'

'You trust him, then.'

'With my life. You know, after all this time, Gurkel, ideology apart, he –'

'I trust him too. He's behind the wheel. We are passengers. Trust is essential.' Taking advantage of the big man's absence, Gurkel poured himself another measure of liquor. 'But drivers have accidents,' he said. 'Their passengers are injured. Even killed . . . '

'Granit is a superb driver. The best.'

'Yes. If only we knew which nationality of car we're travelling in. And where we're going.'

'There's not much chance of Granit telling us at this stage.'

'Nor ever, maybe, Banana.'

'*Ach Scheiss*, Gurkel, maybe nor ever ever *ever*!'

TWO

'CHRISTMAS,' MICHAEL BLESSED said. 'I'll try to get out to Sydney for Christmas, Daisy.'

'That's a long time, Dad. It's only February now.'

'I know, love. But it may be the best I can do.'

'Promise?'

'Yes, I promise.'

'OK.'

Blessed wasn't sure which he hated more: when his ten-year-old daughter was heartbreakingly needy, or when she played the self-sufficient adult. That flat 'OK' had become her favourite defensive weapon since the divorce, since he had left her, eleven thousand miles away. Where had she learned it? From him? From Frances, his ex-wife? Or from Greg, Frances's lover?

'I'm sorry I'm so far away,' Blessed said. 'But it's for my work. You do understand that, don't you?'

'Yes.' A short, heavy pause. 'OK, Dad.'

She knows that's not really true, Blessed thought. *But we both need that white lie to cling to.*

'Darlene wants to say hi,' Daisy added quickly. 'She's sleeping over tonight. We're really best friends now.'

'Oh . . . all right. Darlene? Hello, Darlene. How are you?' A giggle. 'You're sleeping over at Daisy's house?' Another giggle. An encouraging whisper from Daisy, producing still more giggles. 'Nice to chat with you, Darlene. I'd like to talk to Daisy again. All right?'

A crackle. The return of Daisy. 'Hi, Dad. Darlene got the giggles.'

'Yeah. Well, sweetheart. Time to go, before this call bankrupts me. It's just so lovely to hear your voice. I love you very much. And I'm so proud you're doing well at school. Listen, I'll ring again in a week or so. Till then, lots of hugs and kisses.'

'OK, Dad.'

Blessed put the phone down, breathed out long and hard in an attempt to relieve the tightness in his chest. He felt weak, drained, as he always did after talking to his daughter. He reached for a

10

cigarette – yellow Gitanes, like Jean-Paul Belmondo in *Breathless*, a return to youth's risks, in a body approaching middle age.

Then again, what the hell? What was the point of doing the right thing? Twelve years of marriage, six years in Australia, a fine house, fame of a kind – a well-known byline, at least. *From Our Investigative Reporter – Michael Blessed.*

Then, within a year, no job, no marriage, no house . . .

From Our Pissed-off Pommie, Getting the Hell out of Here – Michael Blessed.

The only real problem was Daisy. New jobs, houses, even marriages, could be found. Smoking and drinking could be given up again when the stress passed, lungs and livers given a chance to heal. But there was only one Daisy in Blessed's life, and whatever he did she would still be at the opposite end of the earth in Sydney, New South Wales.

It was nine-thirty-one in the morning. Blessed was sitting at a table in the spare room of a pretty but cramped cottage in a village in the Brendon Hills, a hundred and fifty miles southwest of London. Although he had turned the place into his temporary home and this room into a makeshift office, the house was not his. It was a holiday cottage belonging to his half-sister. She was almost a decade older than he, the child of their father's first marriage – and her wealthy American husband. He was here for as long as he liked, but he was here by grace of others.

Looking out of the small, thick-silled window, Blessed could see from the ripples in the bank of snowdrops across the lane that the February wind was picking up. It might be ninety in the shade where Daisy was, but here a persistent northeasterly was keeping the West Country in the hard, bright grip of winter. He took a deep, grateful pull on his cigarette, stared guiltily at the chaos on his worktable. The sheet of paper in the portable printer attached to his laptop was starting to warp. It was a couple of days since the last time he'd slapped that *PRINT* button. So much for the novel he had been so determined to write when he got back to England.

Yet another working day that already felt less than promising. What the hell, let this be a chance to catch up on family. Blessed picked up the cordless phone, flipped it onto *TALK*, punched out a London number.

'Mum?'

11

'Michael. How are you?'

'Fine. I just rang to say hello.'

'Thank you, darling.'

There was always a lot of love combined with faint irony in his mother's voice. Blessed could see Gisela Blessed, née Meyer, in his mind's eye, her fine, well-preserved beauty framed by well-cut silver hair. Perhaps she had been contentedly listening to Mozart or – if she were in a sombre mood – a Mahler symphony. Perhaps it was long widowhood that had given her such self-reliance. Or . . . well, sometimes it was like talking to a German-born, sixty-five – year-old version of Daisy. Genes could defy the generation-gap and geography alike.

'I just spoke to Daisy . . . she's fine. A friend of hers is staying the night, anyway, she sent you her love. It's wonderful Daisy cares so much about her grandma, even though you haven't seen much of each other these past years . . . '

'You're upset, Michael. I can tell . . . but I'm very glad Daisy is well. Children are remarkably resilient. As long as she knows how you . . . we all . . . feel about her, and as long as you stay in regular contact. I know you won't be one of those fathers who lose touch with their children after divorce.'

This his mother said quite calmly. The pressure came with her next sentence.

'Have you thought what you will do now that the money from the divorce settlement has come through? You can't stay at your sister's cottage for ever.'

'I don't intend to. But Daphne really doesn't mind how long I stay here. She and Rockwell are in the States most of the time.' It was true. Fortunately for Blessed, his sister and her husband had bought this house as an investment rather than a home. But his mother didn't give up easily.

'A good two-bedroomed flat in London would be a wonderful investment,' she continued. 'Stability for you, and a place Daisy could call home when she comes to visit.'

As his mother spoke, Blessed saw a buzzard floating high above the cottage, riding the thermals.

'It's not what I want at the moment, Mum,' he said. 'I know what you're saying, but I only have enough capital for a deposit on a place. I'd be stuck with mortgage repayments.'

'I'm sure you would have no trouble finding a job with a news-paper once you were settled and in one place. The mortgage would be no problem. Everyone has one these days. It's not like when I was young, when people rented, Michael'

'Mum, I want to busk for a while, float free . . . ' The buzzard was swooping down below the line of the hill, out of sight. ' . . . enjoy my midlife crisis. I had twelve years as the responsible husband and father.'

There was a heavy silence.

'I might use some of the settlement money to visit Daisy next Christmas,' Blessed said, to change the subject. 'Or maybe I could fly her over here. She's old enough to travel alone . . . '

'She would love that. And the book? How's it going?'

'Pretty good,' Blessed lied. 'Rattling along.' He suddenly noticed that the blank paper in the printer was showing shrink marks where the damp had got to it.

'Wonderful. Well, darling, will you be in London soon?'

'Soon.'

'I look forward to that. As I said about the estate agents –'

'Listen, I'm taking a year off, Mum,' Blessed said, and decided to spell it out. 'No mortgage. No commitments. Maybe the book will work out, maybe it won't, but I want to give it a try. Naturally, I'll ring some old colleagues, see if I can get some freelance. And Daisy will be all right. She knows that wherever I am, that's her home. OK?'

'Of course.' His mother laughed. 'You are a stubborn man. Just like your father. And if I had not persuaded him to buy this flat when we came back to England, I would be a poor widow living in a bedsit with one old gas burner and a leaky roof that my landlord would refuse to fix. Maybe that's why I'm so keen to own bricks and mortar!'

'Sure, Mum. But don't worry about me. Really.'

'Ah well. Perhaps you are right, darling. For now you should stay where you are happiest. You have only been back from Australia for . . . two months? Three? I should stop pushing you into decisions.'

After they had said their goodbyes, Blessed put down the phone, stood up and stretched. Suddenly, for all his talk, this cottage on the edge of Exmoor seemed alien, impermanent. It was not *his*, in some profound way that had nothing to do with ownership or geography.

13

Even England felt alien. And his mother's reference to his father, who had died when Blessed was ten, had stirred up a hunger to explore, to return to the territory of childhood and see it through adult eyes. Maybe the high-windowed apartment in Hamburg where he had spent the first six years of his life with his father and mother was the only 'real' place he had ever experienced. He could still summon up an image of the sun playing on its cool, white walls, still smell the wax-and-turpentine smell of the oak floors, as if all it would take to recapture it all was an impulse trip, a joyride, not an impossible journey back through almost three decades.

Blessed stood up, stretched. He caught sight of himself in the little pine-framed mirror on the dresser. Lean, even features. A mouth whose definite line gave a hint of stubborn determination, offset by quizzical green eyes. Brown hair, and still plenty of it, thank God. Not bad for a '51 model, he decided – especially one that's had a bit of hammering lately. He had turned a little pale and gaunt since getting back from Australia, but maybe, when your tan faded, your true self showed through. Very European and interesting. All the same, he could certainly do with a haircut. And a shave.

Outside, the buzzard was hovering again. It had been joined by its mate. The area the pair kept returning to was a mile away, on the ridge up above the village church.

Blessed felt trapped in this place, in this moment. The phone calls this morning had brought too many conflicting emotions to the surface. He felt anger towards his ex-wife, guilt towards his daughter, an affectionate irritation towards his mother. The room felt too small to contain all that. Its confines stank to him of failure, of narrowness, of impasse.

Blessed went downstairs, began putting on his outdoor clothes.

The buzzards were still mewing high overhead. The animal sprawled on its side in the frosted hedge was an elderly vixen, winter-thin and bedraggled, her once fine coat of red fur patchy and rotten with mange. Her pinsharp teeth were bared in a final rictus of . . . pain or defiance? She hadn't been dead all that long.

There was a bullet-hole in the old lady's belly, he realised. Where the hindquarters met the rib-cage. Maybe she had cubs to feed and had been tempted to poke around some farmer's hencoops.

14

The risks a vixen takes for her young . . . the way even the meanest, loneliest death can reverberate through the world, force a story to be told . . .

Blessed looked down at the corpse for some time with a kind of cold fascination. Then he glanced back along the valley towards the church. A red hatchback, maybe a Volkswagen Golf, was parked down beside the church. It must have arrived there after he had begun to climb the hill, or he would have seen it earlier. Suddenly Blessed glimpsed a flash of reflected light, as if a lens – or a pair of lenses – had caught the pale sun. He waited. It happened again. He focused on the figure beside the car. It was probably a man, judging by the flat cap and overcoat, and those were definitely binoculars.

No question. He's looking up here, Blessed thought. Maybe he's studying those wheeling buzzards, though God knows they're a common enough sight. Or maybe he can see something that I can't. And why shouldn't a hardy tourist be out nature-watching on a bracing February day in Somerset? Has existence got so dull that you have to start manufacturing excitement?

It was time to get back to the cottage, to confront his sense of failure and futility. Time to face up to the rest of his life.

Blessed made a little bow of respect in the direction of the dead vixen. Then he set off back down the path towards the village church.

He had only gone about fifty yards when the tourist with the binoculars got back into his red car and started the engine. When Michael Blessed arrived at the strip of hardstanding beside the church, it was as if there had been no one there, not a soul.

15

THREE

THE SUN HAD SET an hour ago over the Berlin-Hannover Autobahn, bringing the temperature tumbling down below zero. The
truck's driver had filled up its tank. Then he had strolled into the
self-service cafeteria for a snack. All exactly as the general had
predicted.

The cold made Captain Nitzschke's face ache. He turned, caught
the imploring eye of one of the three undercover operatives he
had brought along for this job. This particular man, a stocky figure
with a goatee beard and hooded anorak, was rubbing his hands,
gently stamping his feet. It was freezing out here in the truck park.
But the general had said not to make a move until exactly two
minutes after the driver entered the cafeteria, and the general knew
best.

The second hand of Nitzschke's watch seemed to be made of
lead. Thirty seconds to go. He hated working away from Berlin.
He hated being home late. Jutta was the problem. She always gave
him a hard time when the general made him work at night. And this
time it was on a Saturday too . . . they had planned to go to the
swimming club dance. Before Nitzschke left the flat this evening,
Jutta had said she might go to the dance on her own. Someone
would see her home. Someone who had a normal job, who kept
normal hours.

What Jutta didn't understand was that no one argued with the
general. The rumours said that even the Minister himself rarely
argued with the general. This was why, when the general told
Nitzschke to remove documents from the department's confidential archives without logging them out, he had to obey. Removing
the documents was against the rules. But he had done it, as the
general had asked. It was, after all, the general who made the
rules. The general was God, Nitzschke's and Jutta's only protector,
the man who had got them a four-roomed flat in Pankow and access to the western-goods supermarket. Jutta liked all that, she
liked it fine! And unless he worked all the hours the general

16

demanded, there was no way Nitzschke could hold down such a good job in the *Stasi*. And no *Stasi* job, no privileges. It was as simple as that.

Nitzschke looked anxiously in the direction of the low, shabby cafeteria building. Like everything in this Autobahn rest area, it had been built in the Thirties by the Nazis, scarcely added to or repaired by the communist authorities since. The rest areas on Western Autobahns were like palaces in comparison. And they were *lit*. Here it was so gloomy that he could hardly tell which truck he was supposed to be investigating.

Nitzschke dammed the stream of disloyal thoughts bubbling through his mind, braced himself for action. The two minutes were up.

He nodded to each of the undercover men in his immediate vicinity, checked that the third was still in position at a window table inside the cafeteria, watching the driver.

A soft voice whispered, 'Let's go.' But the Goblin and his companion were already eagerly on their way. To keep their spirits up, Nitzschke had let slip that the truck might be carrying hardcore porno material. The prospect of a leisurely night back at headquarters perusing images rarely encountered in the First Workers' and Peasants' State on German Soil was enough to put a spring in these men's steps.

Taking care not to slip on the frosted cobbles or stumble in a pothole, Nitzschke hastened towards the truck. A Mercedes, it was the last in line, furthest from the cafeteria. Its panelled side carried the legend, 'QUICK-FOTO BRAUER' in huge, multicoloured letters. Beyond the vehicle, the dark expanse of the North German plain flowed to the horizon. A distant church seemed drowned. Frosted fields glistened in the moonlight like icebound lakes.

'Get to the rear. Wait by the loading doors,' Nitzschke hissed, following the general's instructions. 'I have to release the lock from up front.'

He hauled himself up onto the step below the cabin door and, holding on with one hand, used the other to take an icepick from his overcoat pocket. Without hesitation, he swung it back and smashed through the window – once, twice, a third time, until he had poked out a large hole around the original break. Nitzschke returned the icepick to his pocket, then reached in with his free hand for the inside door handle, to let himself in.

17

One minor irritation. Contrary to orders, Goblin was peering around the far corner of the truck, watching Nitzschke's efforts. Like a child, the captain thought irritably, and glowered at the man. A curious, ugly little child.

Making a mental note to have the man transferred at the earliest opportunity, Captain Nitzschke eased open the cabin door.

The explosion that followed blew the truck, Nitzschke and Goblin, into billions of component parts, spread all over the truck park of the Autobahn rest area, making the icy cobbles more treacherous still. The second undercover man – what was left of him – survived for about ten minutes. He screamed a great deal, but he never spoke again before he died.

The remaining member of Nitzschke's team, the lucky one who had been assigned to the window table in the cafeteria, was half-blinded by flying glass. The truck driver had just disappeared into the men's washroom when the explosion occurred. One witness reported seeing someone running towards a waiting car a short while later, but this evidence was quickly discounted by police.

The incident warranted a short item on that evening's West German TV news, the *Tagesschau*. The East Germans had refused to release any film, but a Western police helicopter hovering thirty kilometres away, just on its own side of the border, had managed to get pictures of the impressive flames and smoke, as well as of the traffic jam which resulted when the East German *Volkspolizei* sealed off the busy Autobahn in both directions. Afterwards, what most viewers recalled was not the image of the flames – this was standard disaster footage – but the haunting sight of thousands of pairs of headlights, one behind the other, stretching away eastwards as far as the camera's eye could see.

Early the following morning, 26 February, the East German News Agency ADN issued a statement. A truck carrying dangerous materials had been involved in a collision at a rest area on the Transit-Autobahn between Berlin (West) and the border with the Federal Republic. A major explosion had resulted, perhaps due to a fuel leak, and at least one unidentified driver had been killed. Safety experts were investigating.

The majority of West German papers reported the traffic jam. Some printed the picture of the headlights. Only a few carried the ADN statement, in their later editions.

It being a Sunday, there were no evening papers. Twenty-four hours later, when the dailies reached the street, the explosion was yesterday's news.

And then for almost three months, on the visible surface of things, there was silence.

MAY WHISPERS

May-June 1989

FOUR

'LISTEN, MIKE,' SAID THE pleasant but insistent American voice. 'Just three years ago, your sister and I paid forty-seven grand for this little slice of paradise. Any idea what it's worth now?'

'Surprise me, Rock.'

'OK. Last month an identical bijou property – but with a smaller garden and no central heating – went for a hundred and seventy-five. You know what that means, Mike? A tax-free gain of over forty thousand pounds a year! Try making that kind of money selling shoes! No wonder England's gone real estate crazy –'

There was a muffled electronic chirrup from the front hall. Rockwell Elliot broke off his monologue on property prices, frowned. But he sat tight in his favourite wingchair by the fire, waited for his wife to do phone answering duty.

Michael Blessed fished a cigarette from the pack on the coffee table, played it between his fingers.

'Please answer that, will you, Rock darling?' Daphne called from the kitchen.

'Shit. I just drove all the way from London through a typically quaint, English freak fucking hailstorm. In *May*.'

'Go *on*, before they ring off.'

'OK, OK . . . '

Blessed's brother-in-law put aside his half-full wine glass, loped into the hall and plucked the remote phone from its charger. 'Monkscombe three four five. Rock Elliot speaking.'

Blessed lit his cigarette, took a gulp of wine. When Rockwell and Daphne were here, it was their cottage, and by unspoken agreement their phone to answer. Out in the hall, Rockwell nodded, said 'Uh-huh', in that confident Ivy-League-lawyer way of his. Suddenly both his large, soft hands gripped the phone as if it had turned into a weapon. He laid the instrument down on the hall table and returned to the living room.

'It is for you, Michael,' he announced, mimicking the caller's foreign accent, his clipped, careful way of speaking. 'He will not

21

give his name. He says he must speak to you privately. You don't know him, though you will have heard talk of him. Maybe . . . '

There was a peal of laughter from the kitchen. 'It's Lord Lucan – invite him for dinner! No, wait, he's obviously foreign. How about Martin Bormann?'

Blessed made his way carefully over to the phone. He and Daphne had got through most of a bottle of Bulgarian pinot noir before Rockwell even got home.

He picked up the phone. 'Michael Blessed. Who am I speaking to?'

'My name is Klarfeld.'

'And what can I do for you?'

'Oh, something, I hope.' The German-accented voice was much as Rockwell had aped it, except that there was power, not prissiness, in the precision. 'First, Mr Blessed, you should know that I am calling from Berlin.'

'West?'

'Yes. West.'

'OK, Herr Klarfeld. Apparently you said I might know about you, but I'm sorry . . . '

'Don't worry. Your father certainly knew me well. Your half-sister Daphne knew me even better. Many, many years ago. Before you were born.'

'I see. Are you ready to tell me what this is about, Herr Klarfeld?'

'Of course. I know that you have lived in Australia. I see the experience has modified your English reticence,' the caller said with a laugh. 'So I will get to the point. You are a freelance journalist of some prominence, yes?'

'Not so much here. I suppose I was quite well known down in Sydney. For a while.'

'You're very modest. I have business associates in Australia, and they speak of you with respect – even a little healthy fear.'

'You're too kind. So this is business, is it?'

'I have a professional proposition for you, yes. I want you to come to West Berlin. At my expense, naturally, and as my guest.'

'*Now?*'

'No, no. Maybe a week, ten days' time. I'm leaving for Tunisia later tonight.'

'Lucky you. And what do you want from me when – if – I come to Berlin?'

22

'Ah . . . I want you to read something. Read it very carefully. And discuss it with me.'

'Listen, I need to know –'

'That's all I can say at the moment. If you decide to come – and I hope very much that you do, because I would like to meet Captain Blessed's son at last – then ring this number during office hours and a seat will be booked for you on a plane to Berlin. Do you have a pen and paper available?'

There was a Biro on the table, but no pad handy. Blessed peered into the gloom, located the list of 'useful numbers' Daphne had pinned to the wall. 'OK. Fire away,' he said, transferring his cigarette to his left hand and holding the pen poised over the space beneath the number of the local drains-clearing service.

Klarfeld slowly recited the digits of the Berlin number, country code, 030 prefix and all.

'Got that, Mr Blessed?'

'Yes.'

'Just read it back to me, please. To make sure you've taken it down correctly.'

Blessed obliged. 'Listen, what is it you want me to read?' he demanded, suddenly rebellious. 'And who are you exactly, anyway?'

'Your half-sister will know who I am – I believe you are at her vacation house.' Klarfeld sighed. 'Once you are here, I will explain everything, but now I must go. My plane leaves in two hours. Just . . . please . . . tell Daphne something, will you? Tell her . . . Benno sends his greetings and hopes you all have a nice weekend. Don't forget that name, all right? *Benno.*'

He hung up.

When Blessed returned to the living room, Rockwell was back in his chair, sipping wine.

'He hang up on you, Mike?'

'I suppose he did.'

'*Suppose* is pretty vague, Mike.' Rockwell grinned lazily. Though his handsome features were blandly humorous, his eyes were alert, searching. He had this way of putting leading questions in a very indirect way, and getting the answers he wanted. It was a skill that had stood him in very good stead in the real estate business.

'All right. I'll put you out of your misery, Rock.' Blessed sat down, reached for his wine. He raised his voice for Daphne's benefit. 'The man who rang just now sent his regards to you, Daff. Greetings from Benno, he said.'

Daphne appeared at the kitchen door, her eyes wide with surprise. Her face had been slightly flushed with booze. Now, all at once, her skin was pale; it seemed tight, almost translucent, like a much younger woman's.

She looks beautiful, Blessed thought. *My sister looks beautiful.*

'Benno?' Daphne said wonderingly. 'Are you absolutely sure?'

'Yup. He repeated the name, to make certain. He said you and Dad knew him a long time ago, before I was born.'

'Oh. Yes. But I haven't actually seen him since . . . it must have been the summer of 1957. Thirty-one years ago! He was about twenty then. In England on a sort of working holiday.'

'Hoho,' said her husband. 'Remarkably accurate placing. Dead sure of the chronology of that encounter, what?'

'Grow up, Rock,' she retorted with surprising sharpness. 'Grandpa Fiske died that Easter. I finally left that awful boarding school Mummy had insisted on sending me to. And in September, Dad and my stepmother and little Mike here moved back from Germany for good. A pretty significant year, don't you agree? Reason for me to be tolerably clear in my recollection?'

'Ouch. Forgive my levity, beloved.'

'I wonder how he knew I . . . we . . . were here,' Daphne said.

Rockwell shrugged his shoulders. With his free hand he was worrying at a hole in the old Arran sweater he always changed into the moment he arrived at the cottage. The sweater was Scotch House, of course. Ever since Blessed could remember, Rockwell had bought his sweaters from the Scotch House. So American of him. So bloody expensive.

'Wait a minute, sweetheart . . . ' he said. 'Klarfeld. Benno. Right? If it's the same guy, then we're talking about a very successful West German businessman. Real estate to publishing. Soup to nuts, everything based in West Berlin. It all computes . . . '

Rockwell switched his attention to Blessed. This was his hawk-ish, cut-the-shit-this-is-serious look.

'So, what did he want, Mike? What did he want from you?'

'He . . . he wants me to go to Berlin, all expenses paid, and read something.'

'*Read* something?'

'That's right.'

'*What*, for Christ's sake?'

'That's the trouble,' Blessed said, beginning to enjoy himself. 'I don't know. I was still trying to winkle it out of him when – as you so rightly guessed – the bugger put the phone down on me.'

There was a silence.

'How wonderful it would be to see Benno again,' Daphne said. 'He was one of those orphans – I told you about the child gang in Berlin, at the time of the airlift. They called themselves 'the Kinder'. They were real little brutes. Only Benno showed any human feeling. He . . . well, he saved my life.'

'And he hasn't done so badly for himself these past twenty years, either,' Rockwell commented drily.

Michael Blessed took a final drag on his cigarette, tossed it into the fire. Daphne looked at him reproachfully.

'Mike, do you have to smoke those bloody things?' she said. 'How long did you give them up for? Five years? Then you get divorced, and all of a sudden you're hooked again. You've got through at least a packet today.'

Blessed shrugged. 'I know. I know. To be a smoker is to be one of the lepers of the Eighties.'

'That's not the point. You know as well as I do that tobacco killed Dad. I worry it'll get you as well. I don't mean to nag, Mike darling, but we don't want to lose you . . .'

'Listen, Mike's had a shit-awful year,' Rockwell said mildly. 'A guy's got a right to his consolations, healthy and unhealthy.' He winked. 'I'll bet even Benno Klarfeld has vices. Tucked away. Somewhere.'

FIVE

IT WAS BENNO KLARFELD'S habit to avoid limousines, helicopters, all the conspicuous trappings of wealth. So, in Tunisia hc always travelled from the airport to his Hammamet villa in an ordinary cab. Preferably a well-aged Packard or Studebaker. He loved the rich, garlic and sweat scents of their interiors, the drivers' bright, darting eyes and harsh singsong voices, the way they treated their cars like a cross between a holy vessel and a pack-mule, praising and cursing, caressing and thrashing. He especially loved the way they tried to cheat him. It took him back to the wilder, more desperate, tragic and altogether more intense world of his postwar childhood in Berlin. Of course, Germany had since become rich, safe, sanitised. And why not? Like most of his countrymen, Benno Klarfeld would not have it any other way. But now and again it was good to take a break from that desirable bourgeois world . . .

The taxi driver was dispatched after a brief haggle. The time was after midnight. Benno Klarfeld rang the bell outside the villa. A couple of minutes later the caretaker, a Tunisian named Habib, appeared out of the darkness. Habib was in his thirties, stocky and barrel-chested, and he wore an electric-blue tracksuit, as if ready for anything. He peered suspiciously through the ornate grill of the courtyard gate. Klarfeld was expected, but it was, after all, the middle of the night. In a place for the transient rich like Hammamet, the even more transient poor were to be reckoned with.

As soon as Habib recognised him, he clapped his hands together. *'M'sieur Klarrfel'. Moment, s'il vous plait.'* He bustled back into the house, returned with a bunch of keys.

Klarfeld arrived with only carry-on luggage. Thanks to Habib, there would be a stack of immaculate linen shirts; freshly-pressed trousers ready and waiting; plus a selection of the cotton djellabas that were all he wore on the days he didn't go out shopping or socialising. The kitchen and bathroom would also be fully stocked.

Going straight through into his bedroom, Klarfeld shrugged off the light leather jacket he had worn for the journey from Berlin and

26

tossed it over a chair. He went to the window, which was already open for ventilation. In front of him lay the moonlit beach. The air was clear and briny. He inhaled it deeply, with childlike gratitude. There were still lights winking festively along the beach, sounds of shouting and laughter, the distant thump of electronically-regulated disco music in the cool of the North African night.

Habib came in with a tray. On it stood a decanter of single malt whisky – always Laphroaig, Klarfeld's favourite – a bottle of Malvern water and a tumbler. No ice. He set it down on the simple square table in the corner of the white-painted room.

'*On va dormir, M'sieur Klarrfel*'?' Habib asked.

'*Oui.*' This wasn't quite true, but after waiting up so late Habib deserved to get to bed.

Benno had bought this place overlooking the beach at Hammamet twelve years before, as a gift to his restless young wife, but they had spent only a few short periods here together. Two years later, after a party in Munich to celebrate the première of a fashionable new film, she had thrown herself from the balcony of its director's tenth-floor apartment. According to the autopsy, she had been under the influence of a huge dose of LSD – personally supplied, said rumours, by her host, with whom she had been conducting a crazy, hallucinogen-fuelled affair. Klarfeld had been in America at the time, on business. Before that, he had been in Kuwait. Before that, in Sydney, Australia. He had become bored with his wife by then, but he hadn't wanted her dead. He hadn't even been planning to divorce her, despite her infidelity. That wasn't his way.

So, why had he kept the villa? Was it because for a West Berliner, who spent so much of his life trapped hundreds of miles from the sea and surrounded by communist-ruled territory, a permanent bolt-hole on the coast was a luxury worth keeping? Or was it just for the pleasure of the taxi drive from the airport? For most of the year the retreat was left empty except for Habib. Sometimes Klarfeld lent it to friends and business acquaintances. But he always spent a week or so here around this time of year, before the full heat of summer fried the North African littoral and brought the tourist hordes. Usually he had company: the lover of the moment, one or two old friends. In a few days he would indeed no longer be alone here, but for now solitude was what he most desired. Time to think and to plan.

He took a shower. Afterwards, naked but for a small towel, he passed himself in the bedroom's full-length cheval mirror. Not so bad for a middle-aged millionaire, he thought, no matter what the doctors say about stress and high blood-pressure and 'type A' personalities. Receding hairline, compensated by a well-trimmed beard, dense and dark, touched here and there with silvery grey. Face barely lined. Chest broad and belly flat. Straight, strong legs that moved him around as efficiently as those of a man half his age. Klarfeld smiled wryly at his own reflection. Still the dark eyebrows that almost met in the middle and had led the other Kinder to dub him 'Gorilla' all those years ago. His eyebrows were the only thing about himself he had never been able to like.

Klarfeld entered the spacious closet, selected a freshly-laundered djellaba and slipped it on.

He next went into the living room. He removed a framed print from above the fireplace, turned the combination of the safe concealed behind it. From the safe he took out a light automatic pistol and a clip of ammunition. He checked the firing mechanism, loaded the clip, weighed the weapon briefly in his hand before returning to the bedroom. There he slid the gun under one of the pillows on his bed.

Klarfeld next fetched the overnight bag he had brought with him on the plane from Berlin. From inside it he produced a folder containing a xerox copy of a typed manuscript. This he slid into the drawer of the bedside table. After that, a copy of the business weekly *Wirtschaftswoche*, which he had been reading during the flight and which, along with a stiff whisky-and-Malvern, would lull him into a good night's sleep. Also, out came the small bottle of pills that helped control his blood pressure, his one concession to age and physicians. There remained just one more indispensable ritual of arrival. He took out a slightly faded black-and-white photograph mounted in a polished silver frame. Klarfeld placed it carefully beside the bed, angling it towards the pillow, where he would be able to see it when he awoke.

The photograph was of an extremely pretty girl in her teens. She wore a plain white blouse and a ribbon in her hair, in the style of the mid-1950s. She was smiling to the photographer's order. It was an ordinary studio portrait of that time, formal and unrevealing. Nevertheless, Klarfeld stared at it for some time, as if mesmerised.

The photograph was signed in black permanent ink by a careful schoolgirl's hand.

Always yours, the inscription read in English. *Love, Daphne*.

SIX

'YATES-DAVIES SPEAKING.' The voice was wary.

'Hello, John? It's Mike Blessed.'

'Right. Nice to hear from you! One of the crowd told me you'd come back from Downunder . . . ' Pause for a beat. 'Sorry about you and . . . '

'Frances. Her name was Frances.' Blessed forced a laugh. 'It still is, come to think of it.'

'Right.'

'How are you and Charlotte?' Blessed prided himself on his memory for names. It was something he worked on, for the moral advantage it gave him during conversations like these.

'Fine, touch wood . . . ups and downs, but we rub along . . . We've got an ankle-biter now too, you know. Answers to the name of Jack. He'll be having his first birthday soon . . . I'm altogether much more domesticated these days. I used to think of you as the respectable married bloke . . . sort of . . . but now I suppose the boot's on the other foot . . . '

John Yates-Davies was right. In the old days he had been the solid family man, and Yates-Davies and company had been the over-grown boys who drank too much and chased girls and rushed off to exotic places. Blessed felt a yearning to enjoy that same privilege, this time round as a deliberate choice.

'So, what are you doing back here in Blighty, Mike?' Yates-Davies continued. 'My same source – Eddie Deakins, actually – said you'd appeared briefly in the metrolops and then flashed off down to the country to write a book.'

'Correct. Well, I've done a fair amount of work on that, but I think I need a change of scene . . . I gather you're in charge of Europe for the *Bulletin* these days, and actually I was wondering if you'd consider some pieces about Germany.'

'Anything from you, Mike. But are you sure you wouldn't prefer to write about Australia? I mean, that's what you know, isn't it?'

'But I'm half-German, John. I spent a lot of my childhood there. I studied there . . . and I want to spend some time there, maybe a few months . . . back to my roots, so to speak. Listen, why don't I buy you lunch and we'll talk about it?'

'Fair enough. I can't promise anything, but what the hell.' There was a woman's voice in the background. Faintly irritated. Something like: What were these people doing, ringing him at home on a bank holiday? 'Mike, I have to go. Duty calls.'

'Thursday?'

'Sounds fine. Ring my secretary on Monday just to make sure, will you? Look forward to seeing you again.'

Blessed put the phone back on standby. He felt his body tingle, a surge of lightness in his chest. Excitement and fear, so intertwined as to be almost indistinguishable.

SEVEN

THE HOT NORTH AFRICAN breeze carried sand and salt invisibly, like gases. Benno Klarfeld felt their sting on his face. He wetted his lips, took a sip of his mineral water.

'I don't see how I can hurry Blessed,' he said. 'I don't see the necessity, anyway. Nothing can happen until I'm back in Berlin, and that's not for another four days.'

Gurkel stared down into the unnatural blue of the swimming pool.

'My people over there have taken an enormous risk. They badly need to know what's going on.'

'Push him too hard and we could lose him. If he's anything like his father, that is.'

'The project has to get moving,' Gurkel persisted. 'The people over there need action . . . '

'I know. We don't understand how tough it is for them with the *Stasi*. No one ever suffered like our fellow-countrymen in the East have suffered, et cetera et cetera.'

'It's easy for you to be sarcastic.'

'Easy? You forget what I – what we all – went through when we were young . . . But I won't let them down.' Just when Benno seemed to be softening, he jabbed an accusing finger at his friend. 'And you're drinking too damned much, Gurkel.'

Gurkel took another, defiant sip of his gin and tonic, realised he was already down to the ice and lemon. 'OK. But I'm under pressure. Pressure you don't know about.'

'Yes? If you have serious problems, why didn't you come to me before? What's a friend for?'

Gurkel shrugged.

Benno sighed. 'OK. What's the trouble? Business or politics?'

'Both.'

'Start with the business.'

Gurkel got to his feet. He was wearing a patterned cotton sweater, light slacks and blue deck shoes. The sweater had a hole in the front, the deck shoes were scuffed. He went to the table under the umbrella, poured himself another drink with casualness that masked intense concentration.

'My photo-development venture . . . you know, the agreement with the East German lab. Quite normal, everyone does it . . . '

Benno laughed. 'And no one talks about it. Everything from bath-towels to batteries, all quietly shipped back and forth over the dear old intra-German border. In public, the insults fly. In private, the filthy Western capitalists clink glasses with the bloodstained Eastern murderers. Money changes hands, and everyone is happy.'

'OK, OK. But it means I can undercut just about everybody. I got there first, I got the best deal, the use of the East Germans' best labs. Anyway, I now have serious problems.'

'Such as?'

'Such as, one of my trucks blew up on the Transit-Autobahn inside East German territory, and I don't think it was an accident.'

'You don't *think*, eh?'

'All right, I *know* it wasn't. The *Vopos* sent in an investigation team, claimed to have found no suspicious circumstances. Another dumb truck driver being careless with a cigarette, they said. Well, with those trucks that kind of accident's practically impossible, and in any case, the driver didn't smoke.'

'So why should the *Vopos* cover up?'

'One of two reasons. Because they were being bribed by one of my competitors. Or . . . '

'Yes. I have a feeling this is the interesting reason coming up, Gurkel.'

'. . . or, because someone inside the *Stasi* is out to get me.'

'Maybe their anti-pornography squad! Don't think I don't know what filth you smuggle around Europe in those happy-snaps trucks of yours! Did you forget to pay them their hard-currency bribes? Or are they getting greedy?'

Gurkel looked offended. 'I have an excellent working relationship with those people. No, they would never do a thing like this to me. It is more serious, Benno. You see, in the *Stasi* itself there is a struggle going on. Between the hard-liners and the reformers.'

'I know. Why do you think I agreed to handle the manuscript?'

'Of course . . . well, I'm worried that the hard-liners are targeting me, victimising me the go-between, maybe as a way of discrediting the reformists.'

33

Benno chuckled drily. 'Gurkel as hero. This is something I never thought I'd live to see.'

'You laugh, but you should have been a fly on the wall when I met my insurers last week. They were *not* pleased. They obviously think I'm in trouble with the Mafia.'

'They're right. In many ways, that's just what the *Stasi* has become. You know, its people call the organisation, *die Firma* – the firm. You like those gangster overtones?'

'I wish I had never got involved. Out of the goodness of my heart, I tried to help . . .'

Benno looked at his watch. 'Ah. Twelve. Habib will have lunch ready in fifteen minutes. Time for my swim.' He cast aside his robe and got to his feet, stood in his swimming trunks for a few moments, luxuriating in the feel of the sun on his body.

'Mr Fitness,' Gurkel murmured. 'You want to live for ever? No tobacco, no booze . . . no women . . .'

'Everything in its time, and in moderation. You're still living in the 1950s, Gurkel. We're all getting older. You should take a swim too.'

'Why? I get all the exercise I need at night. Girls can't resist me. They are drawn to me like moths to a flame.'

'Them and the *Stasi*, eh, Gurkel? The girls and the *Stasi* . . .'

Klarfeld dived into the pool.

The man with the headphones listening on the second storey of the nearby apartment block adjusted a knob or two, shook his head, yawned and relaxed. Conversation was unlikely while Klarfeld did his ten pre-lunch laps in the swimming pool.

The man in headphones took this opportunity to exchange the nearly full cassette for a fresh one; to adjust the directional mike so that it would also pick up the talk on the veranda above the pool, where even now Habib was laying out lobster salad for lunch. He noticed that Gurkel *alias* Jakob Brauer was returning to the gin bottle for a top-up while his friend did laps. Headphones smiled to himself. Another couple of hours and his shift would be over. Then, and only then, a glass of ice-cold Löwenbräu would slide down a treat. That was the good thing about foreign assignments. You got a chance to pamper yourself.

34

EIGHT

THE ATMOSPHERE IN THE Acland Arms these days was more like a
city winebar than a village pub. The stockbrokers and account
executives were down in full force for the weekend, determined to
enjoy their expensively acquired country retreats.

Rockwell and Blessed fetched pints of beer and claimed a corner
of the crowded room, next to a sign forbidding boots and overalls
in the bar.

'You're set on going to Berlin, aren't you?' Rockwell said without preamble. 'I mean, you made your mind up right away, isn't
that so?'

'Yes. I suppose you're right.'

'Daff's worried. I guess she has bad memories of the place.'

'I can understand that. To me, it's to do with rediscovery. Germany was my childhood. Happy on the whole. Mysterious, but
happy.'

Rockwell nodded. 'The fact is, Daff still sees you as her kid
brother. She worries. Dumb, I know, but there you are. Or . . . I
mean, I have my concerns too.'

'Yes?'

'Klarfeld. Watch yourself with him. I don't like it when a guy
like that behaves all coy and fucking secretive.'

'Maybe he's got some really interesting, exclusive project. Something he has to keep under wraps in case the competition run a
spoiler. It happens all the time.'

'Come on. What are we talking about? Some book, some magazine series? I mean, *he* approached *you*, not the other way around.'

'Klarfeld obviously thinks he and I can be of use to each other.
But he doesn't know me. Not yet. He's got every right to be cautious.' Blessed grinned. 'I'd say you're jealous. Because of the connection between him and Daphne, even if it was all those years ago.'

'You're full of shit, Michael,' Rockwell retorted pleasantly.

The disconcerting thing was that as Rockwell spoke, his gaze was
rarely on Blessed. His eyes were flitting around the crowd. This was

35

how he behaved. In restaurants and bars, at dinners and parties, even when he was supposed to be relaxing, Rockwell was always 'working the room', searching for prospective clients, contacts, clues, information. For his part, Blessed had not the slightest interest in anyone here. Apart from Daphne and Rockwell, he could think of maybe six people in the entire world he would have gone out of his way to talk to at this stage of his life . . . And maybe that was why Rock had made close to half a million dollars the previous year, while Blessed was on his uppers, scavenging for freelance and translation work, going to West Berlin to do a job he knew nothing about for a man he had never met.

Suddenly Rockwell spotted quarry. His hand was up, waving like a semaphore flag. He was beaming. Rockwell really knew how to flash the glad smile. At his college they must have offered beaming as a major.

'Jeremy! Hey, howya doing!' Rockwell bawled. He shot Blessed a sidelong glance. 'Advertising,' he muttered. 'Hot agency. His company's looking for prime office space, and we've got plenty of that on our hands at the moment. Just give me two minutes, Mike, OK?'

Rockwell's target was a second-homer in full seasonal uniform: sleeveless waxed-cotton jacket, Jermyn Street country shirt, pressed jeans and Hunter boots. He was lean and handsome, with the whipcord body of a sprinter and the eyes of a predator.

'Rockwell, hi . . . ' he drawled. The voice was minor public school overlaid with a patina of rockstar cool. 'Haven't seen you since our fireworks night bash. Where've you been hiding?'

'Back in the U.S. of A, Jeremy. I'm a travelling man – seems I do nothing else! Got to range farther on our foraging trips nowadays just to make the same money we did before the Crash. And I'll tell you, the she-wolf and the whelp still have expensive tastes.' Rockwell indicated Blessed. 'This, however, is Michael Blessed, my brother-in-law. Mike works for a living. He's a writer.'

'Oh yeah. Which shop?'

'I'm sorry –'

'Which agency?'

'I see. No, Rock's flattering me. I'm a jobbing freelancer. Journalism.'

'Right.' The light of interest in those hawklike eyes flickered and died.

'Mike's the creative one in our family,' Rockwell said. 'He just spent a few years down under in Australia, but he got sick of it. Isn't that right, Mike?'

'Something like that.'

Rockwell nodded enthusiastically. Then, even more enthusiastically, he clapped Jeremy on the shoulder. 'Good to see you. And talking of shops, are you still with Gannet, Spitt, Bollinger?'

'The silly sods made me Vice-Chairman in January, would you Adam-and-Eve it?' Jeremy's modesty did not convince. GSB had wanted a killer, and that's exactly what they'd hired.

'Hey. Terrific. Congratulations. Fat raise, stock options ... You'll really be in a position to watch the bank account grow, and why not?'

'If only. I've had to buy a pied-à-terre in town – endless dinners with clients, you know – and Jackie's spent what's left on a Genuine Georgian Orangerie. Size of a bloody aircraft hangar! Two years ago we blew ten grand on a Traditional Victorian Conservatory. Insisted she needed somewhere to air her dried flowers.'

'Dried flowers?'

'Yeah. But it was a passing phase, thank God. I'll tell you, at one point we couldn't move for slightly-foxed hydrangeas. Now, it's slightly sour lemons ...'

Rockwell chuckled comfortably, downed the rest of his beer. 'GSB still planning to expand?' he asked in the same cheery, casual manner.

'Full steam ahead. Unstoppable. Like Jackie.'

'Outgrowing Dean Street? GSB, I mean?'

'Quite possibly, yes.'

'Hah! Jeremy, we need to talk ... ' Rockwell stared comically into his empty pint-pot. 'Mike, lasso us some more drinks, will you?' he said, and slapped a ten-pound note into Blessed's hand. 'See if they have some of those panatella cigars too. What the hell, this is England. We can be tacky.'

'It's my round, Rock.'

'Nah. This session's on me.' Rockwell lowered his voice to a theatrical whisper. 'Don't tell Jeremy here, but actually it's been a pretty good year, Crash or no Crash. This is my treat.'

Blessed downed the rest of his beer, checked what Jeremy was having, made his way over to the bar, ordered three pints of

Poacher's Ale and the cigars. The landlady was pleasant but distant. She and her husband liked the newcomers' money, but they had nothing much to say to them.

After Blessed returned with the drinks, the guarded talk about locations and rents per square foot ebbed and flowed for a while. Jeremy drank his pint quickly. He kept smiling at a girl in the corner. After a while he moved off. He was due to talk to some local guy about getting a real, organic, free-range wild boar for a dinner-party they had planned. He'd promised Jackie.

'Bastard,' Rockwell remarked dispassionately once Jeremy was lost in the crush. 'And a philandering one to boot. You're no fool, Mike. You can guess what's going on. The lovely Jackie's hunkered down here with just a bunch of designer citrus fruit for company, desperately trying to live out the rural fantasy. Meanwhile, Monday to Friday, Jeremy's on the loose in the big city, screwing everything nubile within goosing-distance of Soho Square.'

'I did see him eyeing that brunette in the corner . . . anyway, how did it go with the square footage? Palatial new HQ lined up for his company . . ?'

'Oh yeah. Maybe. Advertising people lie a lot; you have to remember it's what they do for a living.'

Suddenly something occurred to Rockwell. He looked at Blessed in a concerned way.

'You *are* still coming over to the States at the end of the month for Josh's big day, aren't you? The kid's set great store by that.'

Blessed hesitated. Josh was his nephew, Daphne and Rockwell's twenty-year-old son, in his senior year at Middlebury College, Vermont. At Christmas when Josh had been over in England, Blessed had promised to fly to the States for the boy's graduation ceremony at the beginning of June. 'Absolutely. I can't let the kid down,' he said.

'But old Benno may not want you to. You think he got rich by letting his employees take vacations just whenever they wanted?'

'I'll insist.'

'You're a stalwart type, that's the truth, Mike,' Rockwell said, clapping him on the shoulder. 'If that's the way it is, I'll pick up the tab from Berlin. OK?'

'I'm not broke, Rock.'

'By my filthy capitalist standards you are.'

'Almost everybody is.'

'True. Listen, by my standards even I'm sailing a little too close to the wind . . . ' Rockwell downed the remains of his pint, patted Blessed on the shoulder in a fatherly way, as if to remind him there was twelve years between them. 'Good luck. Keep your feet on the ground. The cottage is yours whenever you need it. We're your family . . .'

'I know that.'

'Don't say anything to Daff about our conversation, OK?' Rockwell said casually as they made their way up the lane towards home. 'See, she's got this image of Benno Klarfeld as a kind of a cross between the Artful Dodger and Francis of Assisi. But he's a whole lot more complicated than she thinks, I'm damn sure of it.'

'Perhaps you could help her to get a more rounded view of Klarfeld.'

'Rockwell laughed glumly. We're talking childhood trauma here, Mike. And I know it would cause trouble if she thought I'd been warning you off him. So, please reveal nothing. Promise?'

'I'll be discreet.'

'Even if she asks a direct question?'

Blessed hesitated, then nodded. 'All right. If it's important to you.'

'I'm considering the power of first love, Mike,' Rockwell murmured as he slid the key into the front-door lock. 'You get older, smarter, richer, but there's nothing like the first time. Nothing in the world . . .'

NINE

THE EYES OF JESUS ON ONE WALL met the eyes of Karl Marx on the facing one. Between them, a leather-jacketed young man with a beard that could been seen as either Christlike or Marxlike, according to taste, sat swigging East German beer out of a bottle. There were twenty listeners crammed into the pastor's office, men and women equally represented, from scruffy beer-drinking students to respectable pensioners, who sipped lemon tea provided by the pastor's wife. All were East German citizens, all were listening with rapt attention to the man at the far end of the room.

'Here in the GDR we are privileged,' the speaker was saying. 'We have a unique opportunity to change two countries at once – our own *and* the capitalist West. Don't you see? After forty years of struggle, do any of us here want to throw away our positive achievements, to witness crude West German capitalism introduced here . . . ? No! There is a humane way, a middle way, in the tradition of the true German socialism that was driven underground by an unholy alliance of Nazi oppression and Stalinist treachery . . .'

Many in the room were nodding, young and old. The speaker, a tall, skinny man, known elsewhere as Banana, had a long lock of hair that kept tumbling over his forehead, to be brushed aside with a sweep of his hand.

'. . . Before, the Soviets were the oppressors. Now we have allies in Moscow! We must encourage the spirit of reform in this country, build bridges between the liberalisers in the Kremlin and the positive forces inside the government and the SED . . .'

Banana's mention of the ruling communist party brought the young man with the beard to his feet. 'Positive forces?' he growled. 'You see positive forces in the SED? My friend, with respect, all the positive forces – men such as yourself – were expelled from the Party long ago.'

The speaker nodded gravely. 'I understand – I try hard to understand – the feelings of your generation. You have seen only the betrayal of socialism on German soil. You were not there at the beginning, after the defeat of Hitler, when so much was noble, rich with hope for peace and a better tomorrow.'

'The Party bosses have forgotten that! See Honecker? Mielke? Where is the nobility in them?'

'There are allies inside the régime. I swear it.' The speaker fixed the young man with an intense stare. His voice dropped to a hoarse whisper. 'I know for sure. I know we are not alone. That is why we must keep pushing, in a spirit of constructive change – not to destroy socialism but to perfect it. There are individuals in the SED, even in the Politbüro . . . yes, even there, who will step forward when the time is ripe.'

There was a surprised silence, then a murmur of assent. The speaker looked at his watch. 'And now I must go,' he said. 'Thank you for listening to me. We are a small band within the Writers' Union, and we need all the support we can get from the Church and from students' organisations. There may be more expulsions from the Union before the year is out.'

The pastor, a man in his sixties dressed simply in a sweater and slacks, leaned over and shook the speaker's hand.

'We're glad to have you with us here,' the pastor said. 'We should begin to hold joint meetings – with your group, and with others. Discreetly. You know . . . '

The speaker, already putting on his raincoat, nodded and smiled. 'Definitely. The positive forces must unite. This is the decisive year. We all know that.'

A few minutes later, Banana emerged into the narrow alley beside the vicarage. He glanced quickly up and down, then set off towards the lights of a more peopled area a hundred yards or so to the left. He came out into the carefully restored 'Old Berlin' atmosphere of the Nikolaiviertel, the authorities' attempt to create a traditional tourist showcase in a city centre other- wise dominated by steel and concrete, sinister smoked glass and asbestos. After walking for a while through the near-deserted streets, he passed a bunch of drinkers outside the Alter Nuss- baum, the pub once favoured by turn-of-the-century bohemians. He moved away from the bright lights, eventually arriving at a small, dingy café close to the River Spree. The sign on the door said CLOSED, but Banana ignored it and walked straight inside.

General Abrecht of the *Stasi*, alias Granit, was seated at a corner table. He smiled, gestured for Banana to join him. There was schnapps waiting. Banana swallowed it in one gulp.

'Hey, Banana,' the big man said. 'Anyone would think you'd seen a corpse!'

'*Ach Scheiss*, Granit, but I have. The corpse of the Church, of Socialism, of everything.'

'Then I'd better get you another drink.' Granit had only to glance at the waitress, and she came running. There was something about him that commanded obedience. Or maybe the waitress was *Stasi* too. When she had gone to bring more schnapps, Granit leaned closer to Banana. 'Tell me simply, how do you rate your chances? Will you be able to do it?'

'My chances are excellent. I foresee no problems.'

'And how did they receive the main piece of news – about their Friends in High Places?'

'They swallowed it willingly,' Banana said. 'They have no strong leaders. They are still terrified of the power of the state. Most people in that room tonight *wanted* to believe that their revolution would be helped by a guardian angel from above. All in the best social democrat tradition – a wonderful omelette made without broken eggs. A student put up a bit of a fight right at the end, but he found no allies.'

'Ah. What did this student look like?'

Banana described the beer-drinking student with the beard.

Granit nodded. 'A good boy. Fresh out of training school. I sent him in there as your sparring-partner, to give you extra credibility. You'll come across him quite a bit in the months to come.'

Banana let the rest of the liquor burn its way down, began to relax. He was beyond surprise where the *Stasi*, and especially Granit, was concerned.

'The pastor asked me if we could arrange joint meetings,' he said. 'Give me a month and I'll be right where I need to be.'

'Where we *all* need you to be, Banana.'

The waitress reappeared with two more glasses of schnapps, plus the rest of the bottle. She was in her thirties, authentically puffy and tired-looking, but there was a telling precision about everything she did. Definitely *Stasi*, Banana thought. No ordinary, honest employee of a 'People's Own Dining and Refreshment Collective' ever snapped to quite so crisply.

42

'And how about Gurkel?' Banana asked.

'He got back from Tunisia this morning. Everything is OK, or so he believes. Personally, I think he and Benno may need a little help to keep everything going in the right direction.'

'Gurkel gets to sit by swimming pools in North Africa. I end up talking myself hoarse in draughty vicarages . . . '

'You are an intellectual. Intellectuals were not put on earth to have fun.' Granit turned to the waitress, who was cleaning glasses over by the counter. 'Isn't that right, Schröder?'

She shrugged. 'Some of them try, Comrade General. I don't think they're very good at it. And when they finally go West, they make a mess of their lives and end up even more miserable than before.'

'See? Schröder knows all about intellectuals. She is a member of a poetry and literary discussion circle in her neighbourhood out at Marzahn during her off-duty hours.'

Marzahn was a windswept concrete wilderness of modern high rise blocks on the eastern edge of the city. It had become a byword for bleak, modern living in a society which – officially – had outlawed unhappiness. Around two hundred thousand souls had been settled there since the mid-Seventies. Not all *Stasi* employees lived in fancy apartments or in specially protected districts.

'So, you are looking out for subversive poems from Marzahn, eh?' Banana jibed.

'I myself write nature stuff, very lyrical,' the waitress countered. 'And I mean every word.'

'Don't we all, Fräulein?'

'There is socialist poetry. There is also socialist lyricism.' the waitress said, poker-faced.

'Ease off. Schröder's sincere,' Granit agreed, heading off the potential dispute. 'In the case of the poetry circle, she confines herself to a watching brief. It's harmless – more like a way of sampling public opinion, really.'

'Crap. The fact is, even off-duty, you folk can't stop. You can't go to the bathroom without writing a report for *Stasi* files, eh?'

'Now, now. You're biting the hand –'

'Well, at least writers in the GDR are taken seriously enough to be persecuted,' Banana said with a sigh. 'Can you imagine the FBI reporting on a poetry circle in Jackson Heights? Or the English

43

Special Branch bothering with satirical verse in the East End? We are privileged.'

Granit smiled wryly. 'Oh, that you are, my precious scribbler. That you are – and always will be!'

TEN

THE RESTAURANT LOOKED OUT onto Kensington Church Street. And Kensington Church Street looked right back in.

That was the idea. A huge single pane of glass was all that divided the tables from the outside world. The owners of Kensington Place had discarded the idea of the eating-place as a private, intimate rendezvous. This was a large, expensive fishbowl where the famous and the would-be famous were guaranteed to see and be seen. Here a forty-year-old BBC 'youth programmer', in a lurex skirt that a teenager would have thought twice about wearing. There a famous photographer, *enfant terrible* of the Swinging Sixties, with his twin trademarks: greying one-day stubble and wine-stained designer rags. In the corner, a rockstar-turned-actor, lunching with a pop-promo whizzkid who was said to be in line for directing David Putnam's comeback movie. Eating as theatre. Cool meets coulis.

'Very nice sea bass.' Yates-Davies prodded the tender flesh before scooping another forkful. 'I mean, it's not as if the food's lousy here, unlike most trendy places. It feels well-cooked and . . . substantial . . .'

'Spoken like a true Englishman.' Blessed toyed with his own smoked chicken salad *à tiède*. He had made the mistake of eating on the train up from Somerset that morning. The full English breakfast – egg, bacon, sausage – why was it always so tempting? Why did it always turn out to be such a bad idea . . ?

Yates-Davies stared around balefully. Or so Blessed assumed from the curl of the thin lips between his well-trimmed moustache and his Velasquez beard, because the eyes were unreadable behind thick spectacles.

'That woman, though,' Yates-Davies nodded in the direction of the BBC's version of youth, 'is one of the few human beings on this earth that I actually hate.'

Blessed grinned. 'I knew you'd appreciate the crowd here, John . . . So, how's the *Bulletin*?'

45

'Flourishing. Doubled the circulation while you were in Australia. Change in the political wind over the past few years, you see. Good, lively writing mixed with stern, unbending Toryism. That's what today's punters want.'

'How . . . unbending is the line, actually?'

'Pretty much the straight Thatcher ticket on home issues, but when it comes to foreign reporting, our chaps can be as quirky and cosmopolitan as they like – though you'd be unlikely to get a piece in praising Castro or the Khmer Rouge. Unless it's *outstandingly* amusing. One has to draw the line somewhere.'

'Well, I don't think I'd go down too well on domestic issues, but I think I can fit the bill in other areas. Berlin's a very quirky city.'

'No "Divine Decadence", please. That's been done to death.'

'No way. I'm interested in Berlin as a laboratory. I mean, it always was as much a melting-pot as, say, New York or Melbourne, and in its way quite un-German . . . Now even more so, because of the Wall.'

'Yes.' Yates-Davies looked doubtful. 'What *is* there new to say about the Wall? I mean, how *are* we going to keep writing about the bloody thing for another x years? Some poor young sod got shot trying to hop across the other day, first one for ages, and you could hear the sigh of relief from every correspondent in Berlin. At last – decent Wall copy . . .'

'I'd like to make some comparisons between East and West. Two systems, two cultures. Music. Theatre. Galleries. Where the traditional culture and the Berlin counter-culture touch . . . I was there in the Seventies, at the tail end of the student revolt. I'd like to do a bit of "then and now" as well. Maybe look up some of the old radical leaders, see if they've turned to God, or drugs, or pyramid selling.'

'Sounds all right. Do me a good piece on the Arts first, OK? But plenty of anecdotes, colour. Enough zing to grab our man on the eight-fourteen to Canon Street.'

'I'll try.'

'I know it's not my business, but what will you do for other work, Mike? I'll tell you, what the *Bulletin* pays isn't going to cover much more than your phone bill.'

'Your concern is touching. Fortunately there's another possible source of income. An offer from a German publisher. Have you heard of a man called Benno Klarfeld?'

46

'Of course. He owns a stable of magazines, and then there's the book publishing. Low profile sort of bloke, not your brash West German type at all, but reckoned to be seriously loaded and . . . ah . . . well-connected . . . '

'Anything else about him I should know? I mean, is he on the level?'

There was a flicker of reaction, eyes invisible behind glasses but the reply was swift and bland. 'So far as anyone knows, yes.'

Blessed leaned forward and eyed Yates-Davies shrewdly. 'OK, John. Cards on the table. You've got contacts. I mean, you spent two years as a research fellow at St Anthony's, and we *all* know who recruits there. So, is there anything more to Klarfeld than that? I'm talking hanky-panky of the international sort.'

For the moment, Yates-Davies took an intense interest in what was left of his food. It was almost as if he hadn't heard Blessed's question. When he looked up, his expression had changed subtly, become both amused and guarded.

'How well do you know him?' he asked.

'Klarfeld? He's an old acquaintance of the family. From when my father was stationed in Berlin after the war.'

'And *you're* asking me . . .'

'If I ever met him, it was when I was very little. Far too young to remember. In those days Klarfeld was just a ragged-arsed orphan. Dad did him some good turns.'

'Well, your father chose the recipient of his charity very well indeed.'

'You're not answering my question. Come on, John. Out with it.'

Yates-Davies' eyes flickered round the nearby tables. The closest group was a loud bunch of film or advertising people who couldn't have heard a thing above their own self-regarding din.

'Klarfeld was, as they say, close to Intelligence circles. Back in the Sixties and Seventies. Since then, I wouldn't know. He always did a lot of travelling, East and West. He's got contacts, I'm sure. Listen, what kind of a proposition has he put to you?'

'Some kind of editing job, I think. He won't discuss the details. I haven't said a final yea or nay. Yet.'

'Well paid?'

'That I don't know. But I've got some money stashed away from the divorce settlement. Not a lot by some standards, but enough. I'm keen to get over there, John, that's the truth.'

47

'My God, a free spirit! The only unmortgaged man in London! Don't you feel you should get into the property market before it moves up again?'

'That's precisely what my mother said to me the other day.'

'Ah. *Touché*.'

Yates-Davies smiled for the first time. He had a wonderful smile that was all the better for its rarity value. It revealed boyish dimples and a gap in his front teeth. Women had fallen in love with him because of that smile. Blessed knew that for a fact, because they had told him so. Maybe they still did. Was there something irresistibly aphrodisiac about stern, unbending Toryism, Blessed wondered – or did the dimples explain everything?

'It's . . . an interesting time over there, plenty going on,' Yates-Davies murmured. 'Big changes. Which means lots of opportunities. And some risks. I'd imagine Klarfeld is up to something, but if so, he's not alone. If you're obliquely seeking advice on whether you should get involved or not, I'd say, it's up to you. Faint heart never won fair lady. It never got a big story either.'

'I don't know there is a big story. At the moment there's just a trip to Berlin.'

'Which gives me an idea,' Yates-Davies said. 'How were you planning to go to Berlin?'

'By air. The publisher's paying. That's the only firm thing about the whole business.'

'Why don't you take the train? Through the Iron Curtain, Warsaw Express, all that.'

'The journey's a bitch. I did it plenty of times in the Sixties and Seventies. Twenty-four hours straight, crawling through East Germany at a snail's pace in the middle of the bloody night, pig-faced border guards shaking you awake at two in the morning, sifting through your spare underwear . . .'

'Exactly. Germany still divided. Never mind *perestroika*: the Cold War lives! There's at least fifteen hundred words – no worries, as the Australians say. And you don't need to travel with the hoi-polloi like you did when you were a student. Hell, let Klarfeld buy you a first class ticket. He can certainly afford it.'

'I'll think it over.'

'I'll commit to one train-journey piece and one on the Arts, all right? I'm sure you'll do a good job, Mike,' Yates-Davies said. 'I saw some of your stuff from Australia, by the way. Terrific You were riding high down there. Why did you leave?'

Blessed had given up on his salad and lit a cigarette. He shrugged. 'Australia's not my country. This is. So is Germany. I told you, I'm half and half. Three-quarters, actually, because my father's mother was German too. I was born in Berlin, moved to Hamburg when I was just a few months old, spoke the language at home until I was five.'

He poured the remaining trickle of Californian Pouilly Fumé into Yates-Davies' empty glass. 'And how about another bottle of this stuff, John? I told you. I just got my divorce settlement through. This is my tab . . . '

The watcher was standing outside the post office almost on the corner of Kensington Church Street and the Bayswater Road. He checked the time as he saw Blessed and Yates-Davies emerge from the restaurant. He noted that they seemed on good terms, and that they shook hands.

The two men parted. As anticipated, Yates-Davies was heading north towards the Notting Hill Gate tube. Blessed was going south, in the direction that would eventually bring him out either into Hyde Park, if he took the cut-through, or straight on to Kensington High Street.

The watcher wandered casually off down the street after Blessed. He dawdled outside an antique shop while Blessed went into a restaurant-cum-delicatessen. He let his gaze sweep up and down the street, to confirm that he was the only operative following Blessed. Soon he was satisfied that this was so. It meant that the other side's people must be occupied elsewhere.

The boss would be very interested in this. This was something the watcher would have to report back to Berlin.

ELEVEN

BLESSED'S MOTHER POURED coffee into two delicate cups. At his urging she took an exploratory nibble at one of the handmade chocolate truffles on the low table between them.

'Delicious, Michael!' Gisela Blessed, née Meyer, spoke with the faintest trace of accent, so slight that it was hard to hear her German origins. 'You got these in London? Amazing!'

Blessed smiled. 'Clarke's of Ken. Church Street – down from where I had lunch. I got plenty, so you could enjoy them as a solitary vice when I've gone! But keep them in the fridge or they'll go soft.'

'Michael, I think you are glad to be back in London, in your old haunts. Soon you will wonder why you ever left.'

Blessed kept his eyes firmly fixed on the framed photograph of his parents on the mantlepiece. 'I like London very much, Mum. You know that.'

'So, what are you doing mouldering down there at Daphne and Rockwell's place in Somerset? It's morbid!'

His mother ran one slim hand through her well-cut, silver hair. At sixty-six, she showed few signs of age. Liver spots on the backs of her hands, which she was not vain enough to have removed. Lines etching deeper around the corners of her mouth.

'You're biased,' Blessed countered. 'You've been a city-dweller all your life, Mum. Königsberg, Berlin, Hamburg, London . . . You like pavement under your feet.'

'But a man like you needs distractions, contact, stimulation. And where will you . . . I mean, how many nice, single women are there tucked away in all that mud and muck?'

'Not many. But then, starting some wild love-affair was the last thing I was interested in when I got back from Australia.' Blessed paused before he continued. 'Actually, spending the winter down there has given me a chance to think. And I've decided I do need a dose of big-city life, after all.'

'Wonderful news! I will help you get together suitable lists from estate agents.'

50

'That's not –'

'But it's foolish to rent a flat these days! Mortgages are still no higher than you would expect to pay as a tenant.'

'But most people rent in Berlin, Mum.'

He had caught her out. The look Gisela gave him combined anguish with affection.

'Michael, I'm getting old,' she said at last. 'I don't like surprises. Now, tell me, are you planning to go and live there?'

'*You* lived there. With Dad, when he was in the military police. I was born there. I have relatives in Berlin – even though I haven't seen them since I was a child. I've visited there, studied there . . . '

'But Berlin these days is a *dead* place. It's nowhere for a middle-aged . . . sorry, but it's true . . . a middle-aged divorced man . . . '

'I don't know what is *somewhere* for me,' Blessed retorted, more harshly than he intended. 'And I doubt I shall be there for more than a few months. A few months thinking things over in the place I was born. Don't you understand?'

Gisela nodded reluctantly. 'Before the war, Berlin was a real city, where people could put down roots, bring up children, make their careers. Now it's just a zoo, a freakshow, full of crazies. Draft-dodgers, hippies, punks . . . West Berlin is nothing but a blind alley, the end of the road . . . '

'But there's something interesting about that too, surely?'

'It depends on your taste. I saw enough craziness between 1939 and 1945 to last me a lifetime. Michael, I worry about you getting depressed – spending all your money and ending up with nothing to show.'

'There's no reason –'

But Gisela hadn't finished. 'Michael, listen!' she continued, passionately, even angrily. 'I don't want you doing what your father did. He should have been providing a settled life for his family, securing all our futures – and instead he stayed on in Germany, playing those silly games!'

Blessed stared at his mother in astonishment. He knew that she was a woman of deep feelings, but she rarely showed them. And never before had she criticised his father, even by implication.

'What games?' he said. 'After he left the army, he moved to Hamburg and worked in business. OK. So now explain these games, Mother.'

51

'Well . . . they had to do with East and West. By the time you were a year or so old, I was keen to move to England. It was your father who insisted we stay. There were games he could not play in London.'

'I see. Import-export.' Blessed laughed out loud, everything about his father that had been mysterious was now so obvious to him. 'Classic cover. Was he involved in actual espionage?'

'It depends what you mean by that. I am pretty sure it was part of his job to screen East German defectors. There were lots of such people, of course – the border was relatively open in the early Fifties.'

'Is that all you can tell me?'

'We had one long night's discussion when he decided to take the job. After that, what was there to talk about? He was away no more than the average businessman, and he assured me there was no physical danger involved.'

'I never realised.'

'The company whose payroll he was on, I think it was a front for MI6,' Gisela said calmly. 'God knows, his salary was not at all generous, which tends to confirm that.'

'I never realised what Dad was up to,' Blessed repeated to himself. 'It was staring me in the face, and I never knew.'

'I didn't want you to know, Michael. Maybe if your father had been alive when you were older, he might have told you, but . . . well, when we were left alone, you and I, I didn't feel it was my place. Those were very confusing times for me, settling into a new country, hoping it would adopt me and you –'

'You wanted me to be really English, didn't you? You didn't want me following in my father's footsteps.'

Gisela nodded painfully. 'I wanted you to be happy. I adored your father. He was clever and brave, but he was not really a happy man, not ever. When we first fell in love, I thought I could change this part of him. That is love's delusion . . . '

Blessed urgently wanted a cigarette, but he knew how his mother hated tobacco after what it had done to his father's lungs.

Gisela got up, poured some more coffee. 'I have decided to be English, Michael. I love Hampstead. There are good patisseries here, excellent coffee and Torten. Just like home. I have no family left over there, as you know.'

'But Germany has changed, Mum.'

'True.'

'I want to write about those changes.'

'We are back to our phone conversation of the other day. You are a wonderful son, but you are stubborn, exactly like your father.'

'He was a good man. Not happy, but good.'

'Yes. Michael, how will you earn a living in Berlin?'

Blessed took a sip of coffee. He had let it go cold. 'John Yates-Davies has promised to take a couple of articles, maybe more. And do you remember Benno? Benno Klarfeld?'

Gisela looked at him sharply. 'Of course. He was the one . . . that gang after the war, the children who kidnapped Daphne . . . Benno was the one who helped rescue her.'

'He wants me to do something for him. He's a publisher, among other things. It's a perfect way of paying the rent while I'm in Berlin. There may even be real money in it.'

'Your father employed him for a while. In Hamburg,' Gisela said, 'as a messenger-cum-assistant. And I think he got Benno his first job on a magazine. Maybe you met him once or twice when you were tiny. You don't remember him?'

'No.'

'He was a complicated little boy. Secretive. He has done very well, so I've heard. Are you sure you will get along with him?'

'I don't know. But I'm going, you know. I fixed up a train ticket this afternoon, after lunch. I bought the chocolates, and then I marched into Thomas Cook's and booked the train.'

Gisela shook her head in resignation, got to her feet. 'Drink your coffee, Michael. I will go and fetch another of those truffles from the fridge. I believe the psychiatrists call this comfort eating, but I don't care. This is, thank God, a free country.'

TWELVE

THE SUDDENNESS, THE HURRY, were both essential ingredients of the coup that Michael Blessed had decided to mount. Lunch with Yates-Davies, ticket booked, confirmation to Benno Klarfeld's office in Berlin, all in the space of an afternoon. Hardly time to think. Like being called up at short notice. Yes, that was it: the feel of active service.

Blessed had spent the night back in Somerset. There wasn't much to do to the cottage – a local odd-job man (who now drove around in a van marked 'Garden and Property Maintenance') was paid to keep an eye on the place. But there had been the usual last-minute personal matters: Blessed's Australian tax return to be sent off; essential belongings to be sorted from inessentials. Finally, his farewells to the buzzards and the Acland Arms. Now he was off to his sister's flat in Mayfair. She and Rockwell had insisted that Michael spend tonight, his last in England, with them.

'To Mike, to the odyssey!' Daphne and Rockwell toasted him over dinner.

Blessed nodded. 'Back to the roots.'

'To Berlin. And to Benno.'

'Maybe to Benno, or maybe not. I've decided I'm not going because of Klarfeld but because I want to. I've got some money. And some freelance fixed up, so I'm not dependent on anyone.'

'Oh. But you'll see him, won't you?'

'Sure.'

'Good. I can't wait to hear what he's like these days.'

'Richer, that's for sure,' Rockwell chipped in. At the first mention of Klarfeld's name, he had pushed back his chair and left the room. He reappeared now with a clipping from the Wall Street Journal. 'Naturally, I have been extra vigilant these past few days. There you go.'

KLARFELD SELLS STAKE IN MAP AND GUIDE GIANT, the headline read. The article revealed that Benno Klarfeld's company's shares in Europe's largest travel publisher had just been sold for a rumoured $150 million, representing a 300% profit in less than three years.

Blessed whistled through his teeth. 'No wonder he offered to pay my fare to Berlin.'

'And no wonder you accepted. Read on.'

In German financial circles, the word is that Klarfeld plans to plough a great deal of his profit into a worldwide educational foundation, the article concluded. *The foundation's aim will be to improve the prospects of parentless children, especially in the slums of South America and the Middle East. Klarfeld himself was orphaned as a child and is known to have undergone hard times during the postwar period.*

'That's one way of describing life in the cellars with that gang,' said Daphne, who had been reading over her brother's shoulder. 'Good for him. Pity there's no picture.'

'I don't think he encourages photographs,' Rockwell said.

'Oh blimey, he's not some kind of Howard Hughes figure, is he?'

Rockwell shrugged.

'I'm sure he isn't, darling,' Daphne said. 'I mean, I know he was always quiet and kept himself to himself . . . '

'Secretive was the word my mother used,' Blessed said. 'A secretive little boy.'

'I never felt he was secretive with *me*,' Daphne retorted with sudden passion. 'As far as everyone else was concerned, though, he'd learned to be pretty careful what he did and said. The other kids were bad enough – then there were all these bloody child-molesters hanging around the ruins . . . '

'Hey, maybe he's a fag. Our Mike had better be careful!'

'Rock –'

'Joke. I happen to know he was married.'

'How did you find all this out?'

'I made it my business. I called a guy I know at the *Financial Times*. He gave me a whole bunch of information from their files.'

'I see. So, were they divorced, Benno and this wife of his?'

'She killed herself. '81, I think it was. She was fifteen years younger than Klarfeld, got in with a fast crowd, got to spending hubby's money on all the wrong things.'

'Children?'

Rockwell shook his head, then grinned wickedly. 'He's all alone in the world – except for twenty-seven bimbos, probably.'

'You're so gross sometimes, Rock,' Daphne said, and got to her feet. 'I knew you'd lower the tone. I'm going to fetch the coffee.'

'How was Gisela about your Berlin plans?' she said on her return, putting the coffee pot down on the table. 'She'd just got her son back, now she's losing him again.'

'Oh, she was OK. She wants me to buy a place in London, settle down. The trouble is, I could do with a little disturbance for a while . . .'

'We're lucky,' Daphne said. 'We'll see you next week. Rockwell says you're coming out to Josh's graduation.'

'That's right.'

She flashed her half-brother an affectionate smile. 'Thanks. You could easily have excused yourself, and Josh would have grinned and borne it, but . . . well, you know how it is for a young man of his age. He hero-worships you.'

'Yeah. For some weird reason,' Rockwell jibed. 'Uncle Mike the gipsy journalist! Josh thinks business sucks, see, and that I'm just a boring, workaholic old fart . . .'

'He's not that far wrong,' Daphne said with a sly grin.

'Hey! You know what? It's your fault Josh is such a spoilt brat!'

'Come on. He's a good kid, Rock,' Blessed put in.

'Listen, I pay twenty grand a year for him to study at one of the best colleges in the country. He gets to go skiing every winter weekend with all the latest equipment. And to drive around beautful Vermont in a nice little Subaru station wagon. Plus he jets across the Atlantic maybe twice a year. All courtesy of the parental pocket-book! Of course he's a good kid! Why the hell shouldn't he be?'

'You're a typical anal-retentive, Rockwell, did you know that?' Daphne said.

'Ah, don't hand me all that psychobabble . . . anal-attentive . . .'

'*Retentive*, my beloved old fart,' Daphne corrected him. She handed Rockwell his coffee, leaned over and kissed him on the forehead. 'And I'm sorry about what I said. You do work hard. And Josh does sometimes seem ungrateful.'

56

Rockwell grinned sheepishly. 'Hell, why are we talking about that kid anyway? This is Mike's evening.' He raised his coffee cup in a toast. 'To Mike,' he said. 'To good luck with the mysterious Herr Klarfeld. And to next week in America!'

THIRTEEN

'THESE SEATS ARE Forty-One F and Forty-Two F?' the German-accented voice demanded.

Blessed looked up from his *Independent*.

'Well, I'm Forty-One R. So I'd say you're right.'

The German turned, signalled down the centre aisle of the well-filled first-class carriage. He must have been thirty-four, thirty-five. His hair was modishly pony-tailed. He wore one ear-ring. His muscular body was covered in very upmarket leather and denim.

Without another word to Blessed, he lifted a smart leather briefcase and a leather dufflebag in turn and deposited them in the luggage rack.

Then the woman arrived. Dark, curly hair tumbling over her face, black motor-cycle jacket that probably cost more than most motorcycles, black leggings. She picked up her own holdall, heaved it up to join her companion's on the luggage rack. She was left with a red leather bag in the shape of a faintly grotesque human face.

Blessed knew from their clothes that they were both West Berliners. West Berliners of all classes, ages and sexes made such a fetish of leather that even in the Seventies, when he had studied there, it had stopped becoming a statement of politics, sexual orientation, or anything except general chic. 'Leather,' a friend of his once quipped, 'is the tweed of Berlin.'

When the woman sat down opposite him, Blessed got to examine – and appreciate – her. She had a wide, full mouth, the slightly almond-shaped eyes often found in German women from the eastern part of the country, and cheekbones that would keep breaking hearts until she was seventy. She wasn't classically beautiful, but she was very striking. And she exuded sexual magnetism.

This golden couple slid into the seats opposite Blessed. After settling down, the man stared impassively out at the crowds milling around the platform on Liverpool Street Station. She, by contrast, fizzed with mobile irritation, instantly opening a fresh packet of

58

cigarettes and looking for the ashtray. As she searched, she seemed to notice Blessed for the first time.

'So hard to find a smoking seat these days,' she said. 'The English have become like the Americans. They have turned the smoker into a criminal. This is not so in Berlin.'

Blessed nodded agreement, took out a cigarette himself. 'Berliners are slaves to nicotine. They blame the Wall Psychosis, but I don't buy that. I think they just like to smoke, the same way the Scandinavians like to get drunk or the Japanese to eat raw fish.'

She laughed throatily, lit her cigarette, then Blessed's.

'See, Wolfgang,' she said, digging her companion in the ribs. 'A non-puritanical Englishman. The first one on our whole trip, and now we're already on our way home.'

With a jolt, the train started to move away from the platform. Blessed tried to concentrate on his newspaper. He had been reading an article about *perestroika*. The liberalisation in the Soviet Union, reflected in Poland and Hungary, had so far not worked its way west into Czechoslovakia and, most crucially, East Germany. The GDR had even gone so far as to ban sales from its news-stands of the Soviet English-language paper *Moscow News*, for fear that the liberal ideas expressed in it would 'corrupt' East German citizens. Blessed pressed on with the long article until the writer concluded (via some padding about the revival of Prussian traditions) that the East German régime would hold out indefinitely. *The German masses are, as the history of this century proves, deeply unrebellious in the face of firm authority* . . . (the writer liked those kind of generalisations) . . . *and even if this were not so – if, buried deep in the German psyche could be found the spirit of a Hampden or a Mirabeau – still, there is the Soviet Union to be contended with. Even the most reformist Russians must feel safer with a hardline government ruling such a strategically important satellite.*

Hmmm. Suddenly Blessed lost interest in international affairs, returned to the tight little world of the railway carriage.

The woman with the cheekbones was saying something in German to Wolfgang. Something about how boring Cork Street had become these days. All safe stuff, art for soulless yuppies.

'*Ach*, Erika,' Wolfgang said. 'You are so idealistic. All art is for sale. And what do you mean, *safe*? All art that does not actually explode in your face is safe.'

59

Erika. Her name is Erika.

Blessed flipped through the rest of the foreign news section. Rumours of Soviet withdrawal from Afghanistan . . . pro-democracy demonstrations in Peking and other Chinese cities . . . He looked at his watch. It was shortly after eleven. Two hours to Harwich, six on the boat to the Hook of Holland, then the fourteen hour haul through Germany, across the Iron Curtain, to Berlin. For a moment he wished he had ignored Yates-Davies's suggestion and taken the plane. Then the woman with the cheekbones, Erika, stubbed out her cigarette and began to speak to him.

'You are going to Holland? Germany?'

'Berlin,' he said. 'You?'

'The same, of course. Where else is there to go once you get on this train? Berlin is the end of the line. Beyond that is only the commie void, the red wilderness.'

She laughed. Erika laughed easily. For all the attitude and the black leather, there was a freshness about her that appealed to Blessed. It didn't seem to do much for Wolfgang at the moment, though. He was still staring moodily out of the window, apparently gripped by suburbia's greenhouses, its chainlink fences, its washing hanging out to dry in the sunshine.

'We could have flown, of course,' Erika continued, 'but Wolfgang hates planes. So . . . here we are.'

Wolfgang shot her an irritated glance. *This Englishman is a stranger*, the look said. *Do you have to be so uncool as to tell him my life story?*

'Actually, train travel is more human,' Erika added. 'They say the soul travels on foot.'

Wolfgang sighed. Blessed was beginning to dislike him. Erika, he suspected, was chattering this way because she was lonely and hurt. Their stay in London had evidently been an unhappy one. She was looking for some distraction, an alternative to nearly twenty-four hours with Wolfgang, the human glacier.

'Business or pleasure?' Blessed asked Erika, partly because he genuinely wanted to know, but also out of a desire to further irritate her companion.

'Oh, business. Wolfgang's gallery represents some very interesting Berlin artists. This was a selling trip. Maybe buying too, we thought, but Cork Street was so boring. Even other places, in the East End and so, were not interesting . . . '

'This isn't so surprising in a country like England,' Wolfgang said, suddenly finding his tongue. 'Here history is a fairy-tale with nice costumes and a comforting moral. The ideal of the most radical citizen is a thatched cottage with birds singing. There are exceptions, but they only go to prove my point . . . ' He smiled slyly. 'Take Francis Bacon . . . spent time as a young man in Berlin . . . take Lucian Freud . . . grew up in Berlin . . . '

'David Hockney.'

Wolfgang shrugged. 'A skilled painter and decorator. Instead of a thatched cottage, he has his idyll in the sunshine of California. Always the English look for idylls, anything to avoid confronting modern political and sexual and industrial realities. If only the English were able to embrace the healthy urban neuroses, then they could begin to become interesting.'

'Absolutely,' said Blessed, dead-pan. 'Do you mind if I take notes?'

'Please?'

'I'd like to take notes.' Erika was trying not to laugh, Blessed saw with satisfaction. 'You see, this is part of what I'm going to Berlin for,' he explained. 'I'm a freelance journalist. One of the things I intend to write about is Art, with a capital 'A'. You seem to me like man of Art cap 'A' if ever I met one . . . '

During the journey from London to Harwich, Erika joined Blessed in an unspoken conspiracy to squeeze solemn verbiage from Wolfgang.

Blessed learned that Wolfgang managed a gallery (with Erika as his assistant) in the fashionable part of Kreuzberg. As opposed to Kreuzberg postal district 36, which was slums, *Autonomen* anarchists, and Turkish 'guestworkers', Wolfgang and Erika were Kreuzberg 61, an area thick with trendy temples to art and food.

It soon became clear that Erika and Wolfgang had been lovers for some time. Also, that their affair was disintegrating, their passion playing itself out in patronising boredom (for Wolfgang) and bewildered hurt (for Erika). Wolfgang lost few opportunities to demonstrate his knowledge and her ignorance. He was the expert. Often the conversation took a distinctly sour turn, and Blessed felt like an intruder.

Perhaps if Erika had not been so pretty, so full of life, and so eager for his company, Blessed might have made his excuses once he had gleaned some art copy for his piece in the *Bulletin*. But she was all those desirable things. And so he didn't.

They met up on the other side of Customs at Harwich, made their way together onto the ferry, grabbed a table in the first-class bar. A drink in the bar stretched to lunch in the restaurant. The six-hour crossing to the Hook of Holland passed in a comforting haze of plentiful food and even more plentiful wine. The transfer from the ferry onto the Berlin train was a bit of a blur.

Wolfgang dozed off somewhere around Utrecht, after a final, devastating burst of invective which included liberal quotations from the current German hero, Anselm Kiefer. It was then, with evening drawing on and with the compartment to themselves, that Erika and Blessed began to talk together like human beings.

'You have been a journalist in London?'

'Years ago. The last six years I was in Australia. Sydney.'

'Which paper?'

'One called the *National Tribune*. It was a political weekly.'

'I see. You like Australia?'

'Very much, in many ways. I like Australians. And the land is beautiful and mysterious. But . . . ' Blessed shrugged, 'many Europeans think it's a place with no problems. It's not.'

Erika nodded. 'An old girlfriend of mine, she and her man went out there. They wrote to me a few times from somewhere up by the Queensland border, I think. She talked of paradise. Endless beaches, endless sunshine, all-year surfing and swimming . . . ' Erika sighed. 'The letters stopped coming. Later, another acquaintance who visited Australia found out what happened. My girlfriend had become a member of some strange religious cult that lived in the forest, her man was a hopeless heroin addict. So much for paradise.'

'You know where you are with Berlin, eh? No one ever claimed Kreuzberg was heaven on earth!'

'You think like a Berliner!'

'I was born there.'

'What? Really?' Erika clapped her hands. 'That's amazing!'

'My father was an officer in the British Military Police. My mother was German. From Königsberg.'

62

'*Also. Du kannst Deutsch sprechen, oder . . .*'

'*Ach ja. Früher war ich ganz fliessend – als ich in Berlin studierte, weisst du – aber jetzt . . . na, ohne Übung vergisst man viel.*'

'*Kannst du aber ausgezeichnet, ganz ohne Akzent!*'

The conversation continued in German. Blessed learned that Erika had been born near Leipzig, in East Germany, brought to the West as a baby just before the Wall was built, and brought up in a small town close to the Iron Curtain. Twelve years ago, when she was seventeen, she had applied to art school in West Berlin, been accepted, and . . . well, it had been quite a change, from a staid community on the North German plain to the squats and *Polit-Kneipen* – 'political pubs' – of the half-city on the Spree . . .

'I went a little crazy,' Erika explained. 'I dropped out of art school, lived on the dole, took casual work in bars and places . . . then, two or three years ago, I decided to pull my life together. I put on my only good black dress, eventually got a job as a receptionist in a gallery . . . and there I met Wolfgang.'

'Successful, is it, his gallery?'

'Yes.' She leaned over confidentially. 'Actually, it is not really *his* gallery. It belongs to a group of investors. They bankroll him, trust him to find the right artists, buy the right works . . . and so far, Wolfgang has done very well. He gets commission as well as a salary. But one day he would like to really control his own gallery, totally, you know.'

'It all sounds comfortingly bourgeois.'

She lit yet another cigarette. 'Maybe.'

'I mean it. My brother-in-law buys and sells property on much the same basis, also using other people's money. What's the difference?'

'The pony tail?'

'And the leather. And the leather.'

The darkness came, and they slept too as the train rolled eastward over the plain. Around midnight, they reached the main station in Hanover, last major stop before the border. Beyond Braunschweig, Erika made a wry face, pointed out of the window as the train whizzed through a dimly-lit country station. In a few moments, the place was gone.

'That is where I grew up. Or where I failed to grow up, maybe.'

Then, two or three minutes later, came the border.

Nothing was different from the way Blessed remembered it. The echoing tannoys at Marienborn, on the East German side, where the train sat for what seemed like an hour. The sudden absence of western-style advertisements. The rudeness of the border guards in their ugly, badly-cut uniforms. The trained intensity of their stares as they looked from passport to traveller, back to passport, back to traveller, the requisite number of times. The seemingly endless ritual of checking under the train for escapees. Finally, the lurch as the train was released for its slow, stop-and-start journey through East Germany – three or so hours to cover the eighty miles to Berlin. Before the war, a simple, swift, city-to-city commute.

No, nothing had changed. This was how it had been in the Sixties and Seventies. But Blessed was surprised to realise that *he* had changed. As a student he had accepted all these inconveniences and minor humiliations, even found them 'special', interesting. Now, as a man in his late thirties who had travelled the world and discovered that there were more subtle troubles and humiliations, he found himself hating it, wanting to see it swept aside. The entire procedure was fake now, futile and life-destroying.

He said this, or something like it, to Erika – and to Wolfgang, who was now awake, watching everything with his habitual super-cool disinterest.

An elderly lady down the corridor was complaining loudly about the way they had searched her bag. Ridiculous! What would she be smuggling? She must be a westerner, Blessed thought. An East German pensioner returning from the West would never dare to complain, in case someone overheard them.

'All this border business is a necessary evil,' Wolfgang declared. 'We are prepared to put up with it. Our beloved hot-house of West Berlin would no longer be a hot-house if it weren't for this *cordon sanitaire*. As things stand, we have West Berlin to ourselves. Imagine, what if anyone, anyone at all, could come and live here, or visit as easily as going to Rome or Paris or . . . *was weiss ich* . . . Osnabrück . . ? As things stand, we are subsidised, no one works too hard, but a lot of people are rich. Only the weirdest people can stand it, so one meets only the weirdest people.' He formed his

64

hands into a megaphone and bellowed: 'Hurrah for the GDR! Hurray for East Germany!'

The conversation in the neighbouring compartments stopped for a long moment. A little later, a middle-aged man in a suit walked past, staring coldly at Wolfgang, who stared right back with solemn satisfaction.

'Hah!' he said when the man had gone. 'That one always flushes out the *Spiessbürger*. It's characteristic of the bourgeois that he has no sense of irony. Since art depends largely on irony, he therefore cannot understand art.'

Blessed wasn't at all sure whether he preferred the jokey Wolfgang to the humourless one. The only way out was to feign sleep. Soon feigning turned into the real thing.

When he opened his eyes, it was light. The train was edging along a tree-fringed lake at a steady twenty-five, thirty kilometres an hour. In the distance rose the familiar tower of the state-run Interhotel in Potsdam, which meant they would soon be arriving at the western boundary of West Berlin.

It was six-thirty. There was no sign of Erika and Wolfgang. Blessed, feeling unaccountably miffed, lit a cigarette and watched the Interhotel get closer. Soon he could see other landmarks – the dome of the old, bombed-out cathedral in the centre of the town; the town hall with its usual compliment of SED party slogans, fortunately illegible from the distance. The train rocked gently on, as if sharing its passengers' weariness.

The door of the compartment slid open, and there was Erika, a broad smile, and two plastic cups.

'Coffee. We shall soon be arriving at the Zoo Station. Over the Wall in maybe ten minutes. But why am I being the tourist guide? Of course you know that.'

Blessed sipped at his coffee – she had remembered he drank it black, without sugar.

'Thanks.'

'Are you doing anything tonight?' Erika asked.

'Tonight . . . no.'

'There is a Preview at the gallery. That's why we came back overnight. Everything was prepared before the trip, everything is ready. Would you like to come?'

'Well, yes.'

'Good.'

Wolfgang was standing in the doorway now, sallow and red-eyed. Blessed felt momentary concern for him, then realised he himself probably looked the same. Only Erika seemed perfect and well-rested. She was that kind of a woman.

'Michael is coming to the Preview tonight, as a member of the Press,' Erika announced.

'I have not invited the Press. You know me. I hate the Press.'

'All right, then he is invited as a friend.'

Blessed fancied something like a shadow of cruel amusement touched Wolfgang's square features. No, he decided once and for all, he really didn't like Wolfgang.

Then it was back to the affectless, who-gives-a-shit Andy Warhol stare. 'OK. Sure,' Wolfgang said softly. 'For your friends we have room enough, Erika. It is a big space. But today I think I should confine you to your apartment. In case you make any more friends.'

Erika pursed her lips, looked out of the window. They were passing very slowly through the no-man's-land on the East German side of the Wall, so slowly that it seemed that someone might call out '*Halt*!' at any moment. Blessed saw a green-uniformed Vopo guard watching them from a steel-and-concrete tower, his binoculars flashing in the early light. Then, quite suddenly, they were into West Berlin, suspended above a suburban shopping street crowded with bright shopfronts, billboards, cars and trucks going about their morning business.

'Welcome back,' said Erika. 'Welcome to the island-city, to the asylum. To the hot-house.'

66

FOURTEEN

BENNO KLARFELD'S OFFICE had booked Blessed into the huge, impersonally modern Hotel Berlin on the Lützowplatz. After taking his leave of Erika and Wolfgang, he commandeered a cab outside the Zoo station and travelled the last three-quarters of a mile or so in style.

When Blessed arrived, the lobby was full of Italian businessmen and their wives, fashionable, noisy and demanding. It took him another ten minutes or so to collect his key and his 'room passport' and make his way up to his room on the third floor. After a shower, he collapsed on the bed and stayed asleep until mid-afternoon, when the telephone at his bedside buzzed. It was Klarfeld's secretary, checking Blessed had arrived and asking him in perfect English if everything was OK. He said it was. She confirmed that Herr Klarfeld was expecting him the next morning at his home, which was some way from the centre of the city. A car would therefore pick Herr Blessed up from the Hotel Berlin at nine-thirty, if he could please be ready at that time.

So that's confirmed, he thought as he put down the phone. I'm a free man in Berlin until tomorrow at half past nine. I think God wants me to go to that gallery Preview.

It was now four-thirty. Blessed dressed in jeans, shirt and sports jacket, completing the ensemble with the R.M. Williams kangaroo-hide drover's boots he had bought in Sydney to see him through a European winter. Examining himself in the mirror, it seemed to him that his complexion was too healthy, his hair too neat, his look altogether un-Berlin. It was lucky that he smoked; this was at least some external evidence of fashionable degeneracy. He pictured Erika in her black motorcycle jacket and leggings, heard her wild laugh, wondered if she was interested in an early-middle-aged Englishman. Not a bad looking one, of course, but –

Coffee, he told himself firmly. *Coffee and something to fill the belly* . . .

Outside in the Lützowplatz, the afternoon sun shone down on the tiled-and-shrubbed park in the middle of the square. The traffic was light. West Berlin, almost the size of Paris but with only two million people, felt like an empty city. There were always places to park. Traffic jams were rare. Blessed stood for a few moments in front of the hotel and took his bearings. The East Berlin Television Tower jutted up over that way, which meant the Wall . . . Tiergarten and Reichstag building over there, via the bridge across the Landwehr Canal . . . then to the south Berlin-Schöneberg, and to the west, the Kurfürstendamm. The number 9 express bus for Tegel airport left from the other side of the square, on the corner of Schillstrasse and Kurfürstenstrasse. The nearest subway stations were the U-bahns at Wittenbergplatz or Nollendorfplatz. No cab rank so far as he could see. Fortunately, in Berlin you could always hail a cruising taxi; cabs were plentiful and not expensive. It was always Blessed's habit when arriving in a city to go through this routine. He called it, only half in jest, 'checking the exits'.

Blessed found himself a little café in the Tauentzienstrasse across the street from KaDeWe, the famous department store that was Berlin's equivalent to Harrods or Saks. There, watching the stream of customers, Blessed ate an excellent plate of ham and salad and drank a Schultheiss beer. Suddenly it was as if he had never left this place of his birth – and as if his father's ghost were at his side.

The strange thing was that Berlin had even been present when his father had been taken from him. He could remember vividly that Sunday afternoon in August 1961; his father, who had been sick for some time, getting up to join his mum and him, then ten years old, for Sunday lunch. Solemn adult conversation about the big crisis in Berlin, where the East Germans had started to build a wall . . . they were dividing the city. Then his father, pale and tired-looking, disappearing back upstairs to bed with the Sunday paper. Soon after, his mother rushing next door to fetch the neighbour, who was a nurse. His father's heavy, laboured breathing, a peek in the bed-room door revealing the neighbour frantically massaging his father's chest . . .

Some time later, after a long visit from the doctor, an ambulance took his father away. The last time Blessed saw him, his dad was lying on a stretcher, propped up on one elbow, just strong enough to grant him a little wave and a smile as the ambulancemen eased him up into the vehicle. Then the doors had closed between Michael and his father for ever.

That night, since Gisela was at the hospital, the neighbour stayed over, and Michael watched the black-and-white TV images of the Berlin crisis, American tanks facing Soviets across the newly-built barriers at Checkpoint Charlie. Grave discussion of nuclear war, of the End of the World. And with everything he had relied on and trusted collapsing all around him, Michael believed every word . . .

His father died early the next morning with Gisela at his side.

The crisis over Berlin ebbed. Incredibly, despite all the communists' attempts to strangle its economy and destroy its people's spirit, West Berlin survived as an island within communist-controlled East Germany. Twenty-eight years passed. But every time Blessed saw an image of Berlin, of the Wall, he would think of his father's laboured breathing, of the neighbour's slapping, sweating attempts at heart massage, and his mother's drawn face when she came home the next morning and told him: *Michael, you must be brave. I have bad news for you about daddy.*

He drained his beer and checked the time. Six-fifteen. The Preview was from seven onwards. On the wall of the café was an old print of Unter den Linden, with the Brandenburg Gate at the far end. No barbed wire, no breezeblock, no death-strips of swept sand. The memory of his father came back . . .

The place Wolfgang managed, the Galerie Schnittke, was in the hippest part of Kreuzberg 16. The show previewing tonight was a collection of huge canvases on the theme of *Deutscher Selbstmord* – 'German Suicide'.

Blessed was flattered to see Erika disentangle herself from a conversation on the far side of the room the moment she spotted him in the doorway. The gallery was a big, highceilinged hangar without windows or skylights. All surfaces were painted an identical aggressive, disorientating white. If there hadn't been several dozen people milling about, plus the great, square paintings, Blessed suspected that entering the place would have been like freefalling into a snowy void, an alternative universe of white.

'I'm so busy,' Erika said. 'But also, so glad you came. What do you think of the space?'

'Quite something.'

'You have heard of Jürgen Filbinger? These are his pictures. Wolfgang aims to take his next collection to New York.'

Blessed hadn't heard of Filbinger. His paintings were hard to ignore. The one he was looking at now showed a figure in a nineteenth-century army uniform sprawled in a scrubfringed ditch. Dimly in the background lay another figure. Blessed thought this figure was female and dressed in a riding-habit. It was all executed in realistic style, in stippled black-and-white to mimic the half-tone of newspaper photographs. The only touch of colour was a dribble of bright red in the bottom right hand corner, representing the blood coming from a wound in the man's head.

'See,' Erika said. 'This is Heinrich von Kleist, the romantic poet. He and his mistress killed themselves in a place outside Berlin in 1811. A suicide pact.'

'He wrote *The Marquis of O.*'

'Exactly. Then . . . ' Erika took his arm, hauled him through the crowd to another painting. This one was big – maybe eight feet by six. It showed a body in jeans and T-shirt that had evidently just been cut down after death by hanging. Again the sliver of blood the only touch of colour. ' . . . Andreas Baader, the Red Army Faction activist who was supposed to have killed himself in jail, but who knows?'

And on quickly to others . . . the exiled writer Kurt Tucholsky, pictured dead by his own hand against an imaginary jungle landscape representing his Brazilian refuge . . . Klaus Mann, unhappy son of the writer Thomas . . . Hermann Göring in his cell at Nuremberg . . . all with that touch of life-meaning-death, the telltale bloody red . . . and finally, twice the size of the rest, the pièce de résistance: Adolf Hitler and Eva Braun side by side on their couch in the bunker – she still upright, he knocked off to one side by the force of the bullet that had ended his life when he had held a pistol in his mouth and pulled the trigger.

'This one is the trouble . . . and the publicity . . . ' Erika said. 'Some say that an artist should not paint themes like this. What do you think?'

Blessed hesitated. It was well crafted. And the effect was grotesque and intimidating. But this was a political and emotional minefield that for the moment he was reluctant to enter. 'It depends on the painter's motives, I think.'

'If they can be known!' Blessed turned, and there stood Wolfgang, in black suit and black turtleneck. 'You think they can be
known?' Wolfgang demanded in English.

'Painters often talk about their work. Just as writers discuss their
books.'

'But I am saying, you think it matters what the apparent motives
are? I mean, if Filbinger were a Nazi, I personally would not want
to show him, but part of the reason why we bother to look at his
paintings is to work out the whole complex of factors that lie
beneath the apparent motives! Otherwise, why don't we just ask the
painter to appear on TV and *tell* us why he does these things?'

Blessed was still staring up at the painting of Adolf and Eva, dead
in their bunker. There was something touchingly domestic about the
painting, actually, but nothing whatsoever that could be seen as
Nazi.

'From what I can feel about the artist's motives, I don't think I
want to argue,' he said.

Wolfgang laughed. 'A pity, in a way.' He switched to German.
'Erika, I think Jürgen is wilting a little. He needs a drink.' Then he
moved away through the throng, broad-shouldered, as smooth and
strong in his movements as a competition swimmer.

Jürgen Filbinger had been surrounded by a fashionably-dressed
crowd, but he himself was balding, myopically mild-mannered,
undistinguished looking. He wore a chainstore zipper jacket and
cheap trousers.

'He doesn't look as if he could paint something like that,' Blessed
said. 'Just the scale of it . . . '

'He's a lot tougher than he looks. And he has plenty of help. A
small factory of assistants. I'll get you and him some wine. Follow
me. You might get to touch the hem of the great man's garment.'

Blessed didn't actually meet Filbinger. This was because
everyone around Filbinger was pressing in towards him, and doing
all the talking. The artist's only words that Blessed heard were a
mumbled 'thank you' when Erika handed him his drink. Then she
was called away by Wolfgang to meet a potential customer.

About twenty minutes later, Blessed was on his second glass of
wine and talking with a young musician from America who had
moved to Berlin the previous autumn and was in love with the place.
His name was Boris – or so he said. He must have been in his early

71

twenties, bleach-blond à la David Bowie, wore a purple silk suit and a badge that was a parody of the anti-nuclear button popular in the early Eighties. It consisted of a smiling face and the legend: *Arbeit? Nein Danke!* – 'Work? No thanks!' This was apparently a hot item among the local *jeunesse dorée*, who delighted in spitting in the face of the postwar German work ethic.

'You have to realise, Germany has been up more blind alleys than just about any nation.' The American who called himself Boris jabbed a finger in the direction of dead Kleist. 'Romantic nationalism.' Tucholsky. 'The Weimar Republic, all that high-risk libertarian democracy.' Adolf and Eva. 'And . . . yeah, well, I guess we know about that one . . . '

Boris was just getting on to a rave about the local music scene. The neo-punks and skinhead bands were getting big in the East. And had Blessed heard of the famous West Berlin avantgarde band *Einstürzende Neubauten* – 'Collapsing New Buildings' – whose stage act was played on construction machinery like jackhammers and such, it was a-fucking-mazing . . .

Out of the corner of his eye, Blessed could see Erika, and, close by her, Wolfgang. In fact, Wolfgang seemed to have her pinned to the wall, and she was looking unhappy. As for Wolfgang, he was more animated than Blessed had ever seen him – really angry and contemptuous, not just posing – and he was talking, talking, talking . . .

Blessed asked the American where he lived. Over close by the Wall, he said proudly, deep in guestworker territory. Little Turkey. There was a house that had been under occupation for about three years now – the guy who'd organised the original occupation was a former member of *Kommune II*. Did Blessed know about *Kommune II*?

'I was studying in Berlin at the time.' Blessed sighed. 'It ended in tears.'

Boris looked a little crestfallen at not being able to go into his *Kommune II* routine. 'It's *the* place to be,' he said after a while. 'Nobody works. Everybody hangs loose. It's kind of a suspended reality. Like West Berlin itself.'

Blessed had the growing impression that the conditioning factor in Boris's life might well be the regular allowance cheque that was – perhaps even now – waiting cosily for him, care of the American Express office.

Suddenly he felt tired. There were things to think about, and at nine-thirty Benno Klarfeld's car would be arriving at the Hotel Berlin.

'Nice to meet you,' Blessed told Boris, and edged away. A check round the room, which was starting to empty, showed no sign of Erika and Wolfgang. Jürgen Filbinger was still silent, still surrounded by fans.

Wolfgang suddenly walked in through the street entrance, as if he had just gone out for fresh air. Blessed made his way over to him.

'I have to go now. Thanks for the invite,' he said. Wolfgang nodded. 'Is . . . Erika around? I'd like to say goodbye.'

Wolfgang stared around in a comedy of searching, then shrugged wordlessly.

'Fuck off, Wolfgang,' Blessed said in English, and headed for the street. He knew where the gallery was now. He would drop by on Erika some other time. No panic.

He had gone about fifty yards in the direction of the U-bahn station when he heard a voice call out his name. He turned on his heel, and there was Erika waving from the open door of the gallery. He walked back with what he hoped was not indecent haste.

'I looked for you,' he told her. 'Wanted to say thanks. It was very interesting. I think I can do something with it.'

She nodded. Looking more closely in the light of the street-lamp, he realised that her make-up was smudged, her eyes a little pink. She had been crying.

'Are you OK?' he said.

'Things are not good between me and Wolfgang, as I think you realised even on the train.'

'You seemed to be having a row earlier on. I mean, at the Preview.'

'It happens all the time these days. All the time.'

'I'm sorry. What are you going to do?'

'Try freedom. Maybe . . . Do you have a pencil, and something I can write on?'

'Sure.'

When Blessed produced the implements, she scribbled down her phone number.

'Give me a ring. Let me know how things go with your job, and everything . . . ' She smiled sourly. 'Listen, this was a bad evening . . . I think this is the end for Wolfgang and me, you know. I mean, what I'm trying to say is, perhaps both you and I will be lonely this week . . . '

'I suppose that's true.'

Raising herself on tiptoe, Erika gave Blessed a little peck on the cheek. Then she turned and ran back into the Galerie Schnittke to help Wolfgang's guests appreciate all those expensive German suicides.

FIFTEEN

KLARFELD SENT AN ORDINARY Mercedes taxi for Blessed. The driver headed out onto the Avus, the motorway link between Berlin's centre and the prosperous lakeside suburbs in the southwest of the city. He turned off over the Wannseebrücke. Luxurious villas lined the neat, leafy streets; there were boat-trailers in almost every drive-way.

'*Das wär' es*,' the driver announced at last, pulling in by a pair of high wrought-iron gates.

Blessed emerged onto the sandy roadway. He had put on a clean white shirt this morning; otherwise he was wearing the same outfit he had worn to the Preview last night – sports jacket, jeans, his well-worn Australian boots. On the other side of the gates, the drive sloped gently down to Klarfeld's house, a big, mock-Tyrolean villa of a type commonly found in the older, richer Berlin suburbs. The house was surrounded by smooth expanses of lawn, beyond which sparkled the slate-blue waters of the lake, only just visible through tiny gaps in a screen of trees. The sun was already beginning to burn.

Blessed tried the gate. Locked, of course. Almost immediately, there was a buzzing sound and it clicked free. He had gone just a few steps down the drive when he saw someone approaching from the direction of the house.

It was a casually-dressed man in his fifties, bearded, thinning on top, average height and strong build. He was smiling.

They met, shook hands.

'Benno Klarfeld,' the man said.

'Michael Blessed.'

Klarfeld was still holding on to Blessed's hand. 'You . . . I know this is maybe a boringly predictable thing to say . . . but you look very much like your father.' His English was excellent.

Blessed shrugged, smiled by way of a reply. Klarfeld didn't look like a millionaire to him. The clothes were good, the beard neatly trimmed, the tan recent. There was a great deal of strength in this

75

man's presence. But there was no arrogance, no assumption of superiority. Only the eyes were very bright and watchful. And Klarfeld's eyebrows were very thick, almost meeting in the middle, which gave him an intense, almost frowning look.

'Welcome, anyway,' Klarfeld said, finally letting go of his hand. 'It's a pleasure to meet you at last. Your father was one of the most important people in my life. Come on. I'll show you around a little.'

Blessed followed him down a stone path that skirted the lawn. They passed the door of the house, continued until they reached a stand of trees. From here they could see clearly out over the lake. The opposite bank was less than a hundred yards away. It was green, forested, with only a thin scattering of buildings.

'We're on the western bank of the Stölpchensee,' Klarfeld explained. 'This small lake is part of a chain of lakes and canals that loop round to connect the Wannsee to the Havel. Over there . . . ' he pointed to the opposite bank. ' . . . after a while you reach the Teltow Canal and East German territory.' He indicated the water going south. 'That way, to the Griebnitzsee – which is also East German territorial waters. Before the Wall went up, of course, one could take a boat-trip right around. It's very pretty . . . '

'This is the end of the line. Real borderland. Don't you feel hemmed in here?'

Klarfeld gave a typical Berliner's shrug. 'Well, for one thing it's quiet,' he said. 'Except when the GIs get going on the firing range over by the Dreilinden border-crossing. And it's beautiful. One cannot see the barriers and the barbed-wire. They're further down, towards Potsdam, or to be more precise, Potsdam-Babelsberg. You know Babelsberg?'

'I've wandered around there. I spent a few days in Potsdam researching for my thesis, back in the Seventies.'

'I know.'

Blessed let that one pass. He could sense the way he was being tested. 'Defa – the East German state film studios – are there. They used to be the old Ufa film studios, where they made those classic films in the Twenties and Thirties. In those days, Babelsberg was the German Hollywood.'

'Quite right. And many of the famous Ufa stars had houses on the water around here, close to the studios. If Babelsberg was the

76

German Hollywood, the lakeside suburbs were the German Beverly Hills.'

Blessed smiled. 'I'd never have taken you for a romantic, Herr Klarfeld.'

'Please call me Benno. If I may call you Michael.'

'Of course.'

'Coffee?'

'OK.'

'Let's go into the boathouse and make ourselves comfortable. We have a lot to discuss.'

On the outside the boathouse was a simple, green-painted shed on the water's edge, with steps running down to a mooring. Its interior came as a surprise: the building had been cleverly transformed into a comfortable office-cum-flat, with a desk facing the water, a couple of leather-covered easy chairs, a television on a low table, and a bed in the corner. Klarfeld motioned for Blessed to take a seat, went over to a phone, punched out an extension number.

'Frau Smilovici? Coffee, please.'

'Mind if I smoke?' Blessed asked.

Klarfeld gestured in the direction of the table, where there was an ashtray. 'I gave up five years ago, when my doctor started muttering about blood pressure and my heart and all that, but I understand the attraction. I had, of course, been smoking since the age of eight, maybe nine . . . you know, in the streets, we youngsters . . . ' He hesitated. 'How much do you know about the Kinder, Michael?'

'A bit. My sister and mother talk about those days sometimes. Usually when we get onto the subject of my father.'

'Only your sister really knows what it was like. After the war. In the ruins and cellars of Berlin. She had an . . . an enforced experience of that life.'

'It's given her an incredibly strong attachment to you,' Blessed said. 'Sometimes her husband, Rockwell, cracks jokes about the old days and "Saint Benno", but she's deadly serious. When did you last see each other?'

'Daphne and I? It would have been 1958. I was over in England for that summer, on a training course.'

Blessed had found the ashtray, lit his cigarette. He finally sat down. 'Did you see my father on that trip?'

'In London. He treated me to lunch at a pub on the river. Beer and steak-and-kidney pie. It was our last meeting.'

'Yes.' *Here goes*, Blessed thought. *What have I got lose?* 'I gather you worked for the same company as my father. But that company was a front for British Intelligence. Did you work for SIS too?'

If he had expected to catch Klarfeld off guard, he was disappointed. The older man made a faint, almost nostalgic little grimace.

'The company was undoubtedly British financed,' he said. 'It also made a profit. And yes, your father got me the job, and yes, I suppose ultimately I was working for British Intelligence. I ran messages. I was fifteen, sixteen. By the time I was in my early twenties – when I came to England for the course – the company had passed into German hands.' Klarfeld smiled wryly. 'I should have known better than to invite a journalist in for coffee. Impossible to tell who is interviewing whom.'

There was a buzz at the door. Klarfeld called out, '*Herein!*'

The woman who came in was in her early forties, tall, handsome in a bony, slavic way. She was dressed in jeans and a cotton top and carrying a silver tray with coffee things.

'Frau Smilovici, thank you,' Klarfeld said as she put it down on the table between himself and Blessed. 'This is Michael Blessed, the young English writer I told you about.'

Frau Smilovici nodded, granted Blessed a distinctly wary glance, then returned her attention to Klarfeld. 'Will you want lunch?' She asked in slightly-accented German.

Klarfeld shook his head. Frau Smilovici glided back out of the boathouse as quietly as she had entered it.

'She's been with me for five years,' Klarfeld said when she had gone. He was on his feet, pouring coffee. 'A widow. Yugoslav by birth. Her son also lives here, but most of the time he is away at college. In Kassel. Engineering. Frau Smilovici cooks – wonderfully – and looks after the place when I'm away on business trips, which happens only too often. But we're getting ahead of ourselves. Do you mind if I take us back forty years and fill in some background?'

'Please. It's one of the reasons I'm here.'

Klarfeld handed him his cup of black coffee. 'The Kinder were a gang of orphaned boys, aged between say, eight, and fourteen when the war ended. Like most Berlin kids, we had become hardened survivors in a very tough city. The different thing about us was that, when the collapse of the Third Reich came and the entire of Berlin was in chaos, we rose up and took over the orphanage. It became a centre for crime – theft, robbery, drug-running – with the boys mainly acting as couriers. Also, we were part of a big scam to defraud the Allied rations office. The kids were registered in empty orphanages. That way, several lots of rations could be drawn per child, and the extra sold on the black market. You're with me?'

Blessed nodded. 'Amazing that children could do this.'

'Amazing? You should have lived through what we lived through!' Klarfeld's eyes gleamed briefly. Mockery and anger mixed. 'And the thing is, it bred an extraordinary solidarity, an absolute trust in the gang and the safety it represented. We were all each other had. We trusted no one else. The Nazis had been pigs – hunting down kids to serve in their army towards the end, hanging boys hardly older than ourselves from lampposts. And the Allies . . . well, we had seen Russian soldiers rape and burn and steal . . . '

'I think I understand,' Blessed murmured.

Klarfeld shrugged. 'It's difficult to talk about such things. It's even harder to explain to someone who wasn't there . . . ' he said. 'On the one hand, our hideout was warm, close, lots of affection. Those young people in the Sixties who tried to found communes were aiming for the same thing. The difference was that those kids were mostly from prosperous bourgeois backgrounds, trying to escape the very economic miracle that enabled them to experiment in that way – whereas we Kinder were forced by hunger, by distrust of the adult world . . . ' He sighed softly. 'But, of course, like the experiments of the 1960s, it went sour. For me, this happened when the Kinder organised the kidnap of Daphne and planned to kill her. Then I rebelled. I was terrified, and I hated myself for betraying my fellow-Kinder, but I couldn't go on that way. I had to help Daphne to safety, which meant ratting on my friends and transferring my loyalty to the adult world.'

'Daphne insists that she owes you her life.'

'That's not strictly true. Actually, my attempt to help Daphne escape failed. We were caught just short of our goal and taken back to the hideout. If it hadn't been for your father's persistence,

Daphne and I would probably both have been killed. Your father found out where the Kinder were holding us. He came and got us.'

Klarfeld closed his eyes for a moment, took a couple of deep breaths. Then he half turned and gazed for a few moments out of the big window overlooking the Stölpchensee. It was an unexpected sequence of reactions. This man, Blessed realised, was the creation of an almost superhuman self-control. Maybe this was how Klarfeld had learned to be even when his name was just Benno and he was a small, orphaned boy who had learned how to survive in a world of defeat and death, rape and starvation.

'You must be wondering why I'm telling you this,' Klarfeld said.

'I suppose I am.'

Klarfeld chose his words carefully. 'Well, it's because . . . the offer I want to make to you . . . I mean, the project we might work together on . . . is based entirely on trust. Trust between you and me. Trust that the source who provided me with the material which is the basis of this project can be relied upon absolutely.'

Blessed was lighting up his second cigarette of the meeting. 'Is this connected with Intelligence work? Forgive my abruptness, but I think I have a right to know where I stand.'

'I'm doing this on my own account,' Klarfeld assured him. 'That's all I can say at the moment.' He looked at his watch. 'I'm afraid we can only spend one hour together today. This afternoon I have a business meeting that just could not be postponed. I am winding down my business affairs, selling off some assets, but there is some way to go before I can really take things easier . . . '

'You're picking up the tab. We'll keep to your schedule.'

Klarfeld nodded. 'I'll be brief. After your sister was rescued and restored to her family, I was, so to speak, adopted by your father. A place was found in a school, a foster-family provided, very kind people. I lost touch with the other members of the gang. Except for one, who had been my special friend.' Klarfeld sighed. 'The thing was, I had broken the rules by collaborating with the enemy, the adult world. This meant that from that time I was excommunicated, so to speak, by the other Kinder.'

'Weren't they found homes and families too?'

'Oh no.' Klarfeld shook his head. 'They got away, re-formed under a new leader, a tough, resourceful boy nicknamed "Granit". The gang went underground for at least two more years, still operating various criminal schemes. Anyway, this special friend and I continued to see each other without the rest of the gang's knowledge . . . and not so long afterwards the gang was broken up – some of the older Kinder were arrested for selling drugs.'

'*Plus ça change.*'

'Indeed. Anyway, my friend, who by this time was fifteen or so, managed to get a job . . . I helped him set up a business back in the Sixties . . . then we drifted apart . . . until a few weeks ago, when he came back into my life, with a proposition. Some contacts in East Germany had persuaded him to smuggle some important material out to the West . . . '

There was the sound of rain on the window panes. Sudden showers were typical of Berlin in summer. Klarfeld got to his feet, went over to the cupboard in the corner, opened a drawer. He returned to the table carrying a thick plastic folder.

'This is why I asked you to come to Berlin, Michael,' he said, placing the folder on the table. He tapped it with his index finger. 'These are memoirs, but no ordinary memoirs. They are the recollections and revelations of a man who for years has been – and still is – one of the most powerful figures in East Germany. A member of the ruling SED for thirty years, a candidate member of the Central Committee of the Party, and a general in the *Stasi*. You know what the *Stasi* is?'

Blessed nodded. Another match, another cigarette. 'The Ministry for State Security. The East German secret police. Like the KGB.'

'Absolutely. And, like the KGB, it doesn't just spy on its own citizens. The *Stasi* is also very active in foreign espionage. In fact, it prides itself – with some justice – on being one of the most efficient secret services in the world, maybe second only to the Israeli *Mossad*. It's often called upon by the Russians to carry out difficult missions, and over the years has achieved a deep penetration of the West German government and business worlds. It is well known that at least one aide to a West German Chancellor – Günther Guillaume, who worked for Willy Brandt – was a *Stasi* man. Others have been uncovered in quite senior positions. Such . . . 'moles' is the term English spywriters use, isn't it? . . . such deep-cover agents are still in place in prominent positions in Bonn and other places.'

81

'I'm beginning to see. So, this is rather like the English book, *Spycatcher* – except from an East German point of view. Interesting.'

'Oh, a lot more than just "interesting". Of course, the details about *Stasi* methods and organisation would be sensational enough, but our *Stasi* general gives away more. He goes in great detail and with apparent frankness into the fraud that the communist bosses have been perpetrating for years – demanding that the East German people make endless sacrifices for "real existing socialism", as they call it, allowing the cities to turn into dilapidated industrial hells, the land to be polluted, and forcing East German citizens to live in cramped, jerry-built flats . . . while themselves living like kings and princes.'

'Surely that's what everyone's always suspected?'

'Yes. But our *Stasi* general gives chapter and verse. Stories about the Party bigwigs' houses, limousines, private yachts and hunting-lodges, beautifully furnished at enormous public expense – and their Swiss bank accounts too.'

'Ah. Now you're talking.'

'Our *Stasi* general is not alone in his disillusion. There's growing unrest on the other side of the Wall. East Germany is a pressure-cooker with the lid rammed on tight. The people have had enough of being bossed around, of not being able to travel, of going without the basic amenities. In the present political climate, this material is extremely subversive. Revolutionary, in fact. It could tip the balance towards radical change in the GDR . . . '

'The final straw. So, do you want me to evaluate this material as a journalist? Do you want me to write about this general?'

'Not yet. When the story is ready to break, you can have it as an exclusive. When we're good and ready.' Klarfeld was very much the publisher now, the stern proprietor. 'But at this point what I want from you is something else. You speak German. I want you to translate this manuscript into English.'

'I see. Looks like a fair amount of work.'

'It's an easy read. You'll have no problems.'

'That may be true. But what about the general's *Stasi* colleagues? How will they feel?'

Klarfeld smiled in wry acknowledgement. 'I'll be frank. If the *Stasi* finds out we have these memoirs, there's not much they won't do to prevent publication.'

82

'But how would they find out? Through your source?'

'No. I trust him. But you understand, he has acquired this manuscript through contacts in the East, and they may not be quite as reliable as he is.'

Blessed grunted sceptically. He picked up the manuscript. 'I'd like to take a look?'

'Of course. I have a couple of phone calls to make. So long as that won't disturb you . . . '

'Are you serious? I've spent half my waking life in open-plan offices. I could carry on reading through the Third World War if need be.'

Klarfeld went over to the phone, punched out a number. Within moments he was engaged in a rapid-fire conversation with a secretary, discussing the agenda for the afternoon's meeting. It seemed to concern a new series of guidebooks to Eastern Europe.

Meanwhile, Blessed opened up the manuscript. The title page, typed in neat, square gothic, read *FAILURE OF A REVOLUTION* and was subtitled *Memoirs of a Stasi General*. He turned to the first page of the work itself.

I was born in the working-class district of Prenzlauer Berg in 1931. Mine was the lost generation, brainwashed, exploited, and then betrayed by Nazism. When Hitler's mad fantasy collapsed in 1945, in a tidal wave of blood and suffering, my world was shattered too. I determined, like millions of other Germans, that this must never happen again.

In the first few years after the war, I was apolitical. But I gradually came to some political awareness, recovered my early idealism. Comparing the developments in the Soviet Zone with what was happening in the western sectors of Berlin and the rest of occupied Germany, I came to the conclusion that only communism could ensure that Germany was never again infected with the lethal bacillus of fascism. This was why, in 1951 I became an official in the SED's Free German Youth. It was also why – and this my readers may find harder to swallow – two years later I entered the so-called 'Institute for Scientific Research' in East Berlin, a place whose innocent-sounding name concealed the fact that it was a training-school for the notorious Main Bureau for Enlightenment of the East German Ministry of State Security, already known and feared as the 'Stasi'.

There had recently been rioting on the streets of East Berlin. I genuinely believed this had been a western-financed plot to over-throw the first socialist state on German soil and that an efficient secret police apparatus was needed in order protect the fledgling GDR from such capitalist machinations. This was the first of my many illusions. The second was that the leaders of the East German state cared anything about the working class, anything at all . . .

Blessed leafed on. Through the Fifties. Missions in West Germany. Involvement in black-marketeering between East and West, from which the *Stasi* took its hard-currency cut. Blackmail of western politicians and businessmen. The building of the Wall. The Prague Spring . . . the author's first inklings of disillusionment, not strong enough to stop him from ploughing on for another twenty years, rising in rank and power . . . leading on to the revelations about the luxurious palaces, the home-grown Bardot blondes invited to lavish parties at remote hunting-lodges – while the hypocritical communist leadership exhorted the people to yet more sacrifices in the interests of socialism, peace, and solid, family virtues . . .

Blessed looked up. Klarfeld had finished with his phone calls. 'If it's genuine, this manuscript will cause an awful lot of shit to hit a very big fan,' Blessed said. 'Have you met this general? Do you know his name?'

'No. But the general is willing to come forward at publication time, to stand up and be counted. Until then, he insists on complete anonymity. He's still working inside the *Stasi* apparatus, remember. If his superiors got wind of this, they could act drastically to ensure its – and *his* – suppression. Do you follow me?'

'Yes. Now the big question: why hire me for this job? Why me specifically? Your company must be stuffed with bilingual editors who could handle this job with complete confidentiality.'

'They could handle the job. But with complete confidentiality? That's the problem. No German can be guaranteed free of the *Stasi's* influence . . . the *Stasi* network in the West runs into thousands, maybe tens of thousands, both full-time "officers on special assignment" and "unofficial employees", many in the media and politics . . . You, however, are my friend Captain Blessed's son. And you have been in Australia all these years. You are *clean*, Michael – a man as clean as you is very hard to find!'

'I'm flattered.'

84

'Oh, I'm telling the simple truth. Now, money: thirty thousand marks on signature, thirty thousand on delivery. Standard contract, which will not mention the details of the project. Also, a daily subsistence rate, to be agreed, up to a maximum of four months. A two per cent royalty on the English language edition, plus exclusive rights to break the story – and you'll be given an exclusive interview with the *Stasi* general when he decides to go public.'

'That's extremely generous. You can deliver those last things?'

'The people close to the general have agreed in principle. I can near as damn it guarantee you'll get your interview.' Klarfeld glanced at his watch. 'I'm not asking you to make your mind up now. In fact, I'd prefer it if you didn't. The room at the Hotel Berlin is yours for another couple of nights. And here's some good will . . . '

Klarfeld went over to the drawer of the table by the window, took out an envelope.

'One thousand marks. What the Americans call "walking out money". It's yours, job or no job. Now I have to go. Tomorrow I'm keeping completely free. I would like to spend the entire day with you, whatever we decide.' Klarfeld could see the incredulity on Blessed's face. 'This is too much, eh? Maybe too good to be true? Well, I tell you that when I want something, I pay well for it. No one who gives me what I want goes short. I'm after justice, truth, and a bestseller, and I think this project gives me all three.'

Blessed accepted the money. He felt like a child taking sweets from an uncle, one who smiled all the time but could all the same be wicked.

SIXTEEN

HIS JACKBOOTS WERE POLISHED like mirrors. The medals of the Karl-Marx and Scharnhorst Orders festooned the breast of his impeccably-tailored, olive-green general's uniform. At ten a.m. precisely, General Albrecht, *alias* Granit, presented himself at the largest of the forty-one buildings that made up the Normannen-strasse complex. A young adjutant showed him up to the boss's office.

The second most powerful man in East Germany was seated at his huge mahogany desk at the far end of the room. He did not look up when Granit entered.

Granit waited, eyes straight ahead.

Armeegeneral Erich Mielke made a final annotation, closed the file and pushed it to one side. He got nimbly to his feet – even at eighty-two, as a non-smoker and teetotaller who swam every morning without fail, he was in good condition. He moved out from behind his desk, beckoned for Granit to join him by the window.

'Fuck that bastard Gorbachev,' snarled the old man who for thirty years had been Minister of State Security and supreme commander of the *Stasi*. 'Damn him to hell – him and all his smooth-talking liberal backsliders with their soft, clean hands! I'd rather deal with a killer like old Joe Stalin any day. Stalin liquidated his enemies, protected his friends! Gorbachev does the exact opposite!'

Mielke's face had turned pink. The high colour had spread even under the thin hair plastered back over his age-mottled skull.

Granit nodded earnestly. 'He's not making our job any easier,' he conceded.

'Don't talk to me about easy jobs,' Mielke growled. 'You know I personally killed two men back in '31. A pair of Nazi cops who were working against the Party. They were outside the Babylon movie theatre in the Scheunenviertel one night in August. I shot them both, in the back.' Mielke squinted down an imaginary barrel, recoiled twice, smiled grimly. 'And I escaped abroad. With Soviet papers. See? We knew our enemies, we knew our friends, and we acted accordingly.'

'Heroic days, Comrade Minister.'

Mielke nodded energetically. '*That* was revolution, *that* was class-struggle! Now we're supposed to throw away all the achievements we won with ours and our friends' blood because there's the occasional shortage of tractor parts, because our industry needs a little overhaul, because our young people do not find the clothes in the shops sufficiently *chic* ... ' Mielke spat out the word as if it were poison, then continued: 'We communists survived Hitler. We survived Bonn's revanchist plots by building the Anti-fascist Protection Wall. And we made our own, socialist economic miracle in this republic ... ' His voice dropped to a low, thick whisper. 'But now ... now we're supposed to sit by meekly while CIA-sponsored so-called priests and publicity-crazy so-called "dissidents" destroy everything we've spent forty years building ... '

Mielke got to his feet, made his way to the window. For some time he looked out in silence. Then he swung round and fixed Granit with a cold, inquisitorial stare. 'Are you on my side, Albrecht? Really?' the Minister rasped.

'Comrade Minister, my loyalty is total.'

'Are you with me, with this republic of ours, to the bitter end?'

'Absolutely, Comrade Minister.'

Mielke's pale, almost slavic eyes didn't leave Granit's for a second. '*Then why are you protecting the subversive writer Otmar Ziegler – codename "Banana"? Are you a secret sympathiser with the dissidents, another closet counter-revolutionary, or what*?'

There was a split-second more silence than felt strictly comfortable. Granit had been caught off balance. A torrent of thoughts poured through his brain. Overruling them all was one simple, tried and trusted imperative that had governed the life of this man and those of the men he had grown up with since they were barely old enough to walk or talk. That imperative was: *lie quickly, and lie well.*

'Otmar Ziegler has served us faithfully,' Granit said formally. 'I do not understand your objection, Comrade Minister.'

'Served *us*? Did you see that interview he gave to West German television last week?'

'Comrade Minister, if it hadn't been him, it would have been someone else. Someone saying much the same things, but not one of our people. Ziegler reports *everything* back to me. He has been an unofficial employee of my section for many years now, enormously useful.'

Mielke pursed his fleshy lips, like a schoolmaster receiving a pupil's flimsy excuse. 'He's going too far.'

'Comrade Minister, he *has* to be outspoken. Otherwise he would lose all credibility in opposition circles. For the same reason, we have to arrest him from time to time. Also, this gives me a chance to meet with him and debrief him without arousing suspicion . . .'

Ominous silence. *Could someone in the Section have been reporting to Mielke's office? Or had the old bastard got Granit's place bugged? Shit, but if Mielke had any idea of the true relationship between Granit and not only Banana but at least two dozen other of his* Stasi *Section's extremely well-paid and privileged 'unofficial employees', then Granit was finished. And all the ex-Kinder from the orphanage were blown apart, washed up, dead men . . .*

'These are appallingly difficult times, Comrade Minister,' Granit pressed on, controlling every muscle in his face, every nerve in his body to give the impression of faintly amused but respectful calm. 'We have to do things that we would never have considered a year, two years ago. We have to ride the tiger, and to ride the tiger we must be on its back – inside its brain, to be more precise – '

'I know that, you idiot!' Mielke barked. 'But does that include passing damaging material to the West? I refer to these general's memoirs! You think I don't know what you've been up to? You think I don't know what *all* my people are up to!'

'The Memoirs are a plant,' Granit said easily.

Mielke is a skilled interrogator, he thought. The child in him, the frightened orphan, surfaced to haunt Granit. *Surely he's never going to fall for this. Surely by now he will have noticed the sweat forming on my brow.*

'Explain.' Mielke hissed. 'Carefully. Talk yourself out of trouble, Albrecht.'

'Comrade Minister, we *want* the material to be published in the West,' Granit declared. 'Because it will blow up in the publisher's face! At the right time, the memoirs will be revealed as a plot by Western Intelligence. When this happens, the West will look stupid. Not only that, but our own population – who of course watch these things on West German television – will tend to distrust any future "revelations".' Granit coughed discreetly. 'Even, or should I say, *precisely*, the revelations that are actually . . . one must admit this, Comrade Minister . . . actually *true* . . . '

'Explain. I said *explain*, Albrecht. How will you discredit these defamations?'

Mielke's eyes were still slits, but he had relaxed slightly. Maybe Granit was getting through to him. Mielke had somehow managed to connect Banana alias Ziegler with the general's memoirs, but maybe that was as far as it went. Maybe the Minister knew nothing about the wider conspiracy. Maybe everything would be OK. Just keep smiling and lying, Granit told himself. As ever ever ever.

'The translator of the supposed *Stasi* general's memoirs . . . ' Granit began carefully ' . . . the translator is an English journalist with family connections to both MI6 and the CIA. The German publisher who has commissioned him was formerly of MI6 and latterly of the BND. We chose them both with enormous care. They publish the *Stasi* general's memoirs with a fanfare – we immediately and crushingly blow their cover, identifying the entire thing as a fabrication by Western intelligence. So!' He snapped his huge, thick fingers. 'The memoirs – and much other anti-socialist propaganda besides – are totally discredited!'

Mielke suddenly lumbered back to his desk, sat down heavily in his leather-padded swivel chair. He punched a button on the console in front of him.

'Tea. With lemon. For me and General Albrecht,' he ordered.

Granit breathed a little easier. All was not yet safe – nothing ever was with Mielke – but the immediate crisis was over.

'Sit down.' Mielke indicated the chair opposite his desk. 'Describe the details of this plan. The English journalist interests me especially. Explain how you intend to control him, ensure he doesn't step out of line.'

Mielke licked his lips, smiled for the first time. There was something distinctly prurient about that lip-licking and that smile. The Minister loved to hunt at his country estate and display his trophies for all to see. In fact, the People's Own Meat Collective of Erfurt was rumoured to receive orders to thaw out quantities of frozen hares, to bolster the Comrade Minister's public image as a prolific slaughterer of wildlife. But Mielke's real pleasure, his ruling passion, was for knowledge and the power it gave him. Omniscience was this old communist's personal, absolute pornography, his solitary delight.

'So far he's been good as gold, Comrade Minister.'

'But you must have contingency plans. Has he debts? Is it girls? Boys? Or have you some other hold over him? There's always an angle. Always.'

'In his case, there are several. The man has been an investigative reporter in Australia – quite well known there, in fact – but recently returned to Europe following a divorce.'

'Children?'

'One daughter. Still in Australia. Likewise ex-wife.'

'Ah. Money?'

'Not much. All this knits together. Loneliness, lack of money, a certain remnant of former idealism.' Granit smiled. 'He is that perfect target: an intelligent grown-up who is still roaming the world looking for a father figure.'

'Ah,' Mielke breathed, clapping his hands together with pleasure. 'Now *that*, Albrecht, is what I really like to hear . . . '

SEVENTEEN

BLESSED AMBLED DOWN the long, featureless hotel corridor to fetch a beer from the automat. Three bored French teenagers were playing a game of chicken with the shoeshine machine next to the lift, daring each other to wait until the very last moment before they whipped their gleaming-white sneakers away from the black-impregnated brushes.

He wondered why Klarfeld had chosen the Hotel Berlin for him. A kind of wry joke? Because it was so big, so impersonal, so resolutely unfashionable, that no cruising *Stasi* watcher would ever pick Blessed out the way they might at the Kempinski or the Hotel am Kurfürstendamm?

Back in his room, Blessed kicked off his shoes and sprawled on the king-size bed. Apart from the muted thrum of traffic outside on the Lützowplatz, the place was quiet. He took his first swallow of expensive beer. Immediately he came to his first realisation: that it wasn't actually he, Michael Blessed, who was being given time to think but Benno Klarfeld. Michael Blessed was hooked, hot to trot, eager to share the danger, and Klarfeld knew it.

Close on the heels of this initial epiphany came a second, which was that Blessed felt intensely lonely.

Blessed took his wallet out of his pocket, found the scrap of paper that Erika had slipped to him as he left the Preview at the Galerie Schnittke. He prayed she and Wolfgang hadn't made up since last night. He put the beer bottle down on the bedside table and began to dial her number.

Erika was waiting in the street doorway of the turn-of-the century apartment block where she lived. As soon as the taxi stopped, she ran out. She was wearing her usual leggings, ankle-boots and motorcycle jacket.

'How was the meeting?' she panted, clambering into the back seat beside Blessed. It seemed natural that she spoke in German.

'I'd like to take on the project,' Blessed said. 'But I think he still has to make his mind up. I'll know tomorrow. How about you? What's the story with Wolfgang?'

'I returned to fetch my things this morning. That's *it*. No more Wolfgang, no more Galerie Schnittke. *Ende. Schluss. Finito.*'

Erika giggled, gave Blessed's hand a quick squeeze. Long enough to be friendly, he thought, but not so long that he got the wrong idea.

'What will you do? For money, I mean,' Blessed asked.

She tossed her hair, which she had combed back and out. The punk look tonight. Kicking over all the traces. 'I have some savings. In Berlin no one worries about all that stuff, anyway! I'm a free woman. Anything is possible. It's only when you break out of a lousy relationship that you realise how much it was dragging you down. You know?'

'Yes, I think I do.'

There was something almost feverish about Erika tonight. Blessed knew all those feelings. Horror and relief, sadness and euphoria, adding up to a determination to get out there and grab some life before the realities closed in. The classic symptoms of the end of a love affair.

'I thought we could eat first,' Blessed said. 'Then you could keep your side of the bargain and show me some of Berlin.'

'All of it. I'll show you all of it.'

'The man I saw today gave me very generous expenses. I think we should spend them.'

'That asshole Wolfgang said you were just a poor freelancer. But I knew better. Well, then we shall start with oysters and champagne!'

'Great.'

'And pasta. I know a place.' Erika switched to English. 'This restaurant makes the best fettucini outside Rome city limits.' She gave him another of her pecks on the cheek. 'Trust me.'

Erika got her oysters and champagne. And she was right about the fettucini. Blessed paid in cash, peeling the fifty-mark notes from the roll with exaggerated delight, like an old-fashioned black-marketeer showing his mistress a good time. Erika laughed so loud and long that she turned almost every head in the trattoria.

92

From there they walked back towards Kreuzberg, taking in the balmy evening air, stopping at cafés for refreshers. In one or two, Erika nodded to people she knew, but she showed no desire to talk to them or introduce them to Blessed, whom she was already calling 'my Englishman'. They drifted into the badder lands of Kreuzberg 36, past Turkish clubs where *Gastarbeiter* played cards, drank fiery liquors and thick coffee and stared at the passing women.

They ducked down into a basement where 'Happenings' were advertised, watched a woman, naked except for a pair of men's boxer shorts, sing snatches of Brecht and Elvis Presley before smearing herself with Vaseline and finally insulting a doll at enormous, richly invective length. Some time after midnight, they arrived at a club called simply 'HIER'. Erika dragged Blessed past the six-foot tall blond transvestite on the door, who looked at him very strangely. 'His name is Steffi. He knows me!' she explained. They emerged through the entrance tunnel into a chamber filled with phenomenally loud German rap music and wall-to-wall beautiful people of every possible sex. More who seemed to know Erika drifted by. She and Blessed even spoke to some of them, though little could be heard above the din. Almost everyone wore black. As a clean-looking Englishman, Blessed was generally agreed to get the freak award of the evening. He also got pretty drunk as the effects of the dinner wore off and the power of the alcohol wore on.

They left some time around two. Blessed knew he had to be breakfasted and dressed by nine-thirty, and he really didn't care. It was only a ten-minute walk back to Erika's apartment block, and the night still felt as if it was unique, unrepeatable, to be lingered over.

Erika lived in one of the fortunate flats that was situated directly on the street rather than in a dark *Hinterhof* or backyard, where the rooms were dark and cold and the rents correspondingly lower. A friend had found it for her – a friend of Wolfgang's to be strictly accurate – and she got it at an affordable rent because, although this was not a bad street, the building was not in the best condition. The stairs were wooden, the stairwells and halls painted in peeling browns and yellows, old-fashioned colours. There was a very faint smell of damp, but no holes in the ceilings or windows. It compared well with the room he had lived in as a student here in the Seventies. Erika's flat was one of three on the second-floor landing. One had remained unlet for the past few months, she explained. The other was inhabited by a couple of men who she thought were gay. They were certainly very quiet. She giggled. Maybe they were busy . . .

'Coffee,' she said, fumbling for her key. 'We can't send you back without coffee in your bloodstream. You have a very very very important meeting first thing with a wonderful man whose wonderful expenses we have just spent.'

The key was found and inserted into the lock, the ancient, flimsy-looking door opened inwards. Erika's apartment was just a big living room with high windows. A bedroom was off to the left, a kitchenette in a hollow against the wall to the right. Before she drew the curtains, the living room was bathed in the glow from the streetlamps.

Erika ducked into the kitchenette, returned with a virgin bottle of German-made *Gorbatschow* vodka. Smiling, she held it up for Blessed's inspection. 'The Russian government is trying to sue this company for using their President's name in vain. I can't think why. Meanwhile, for us a little *glasnost*, a little freedom.' She opened the bottle, poured a tot each for herself and Blessed. 'A nightcap. To chase the coffee down. Or is it the other way round?'

They touched glasses in a toast to their, and everybody's, personal *glasnost*. A gulp of the clear, fiery vodka was almost sobering. Almost.

'Now, take off your jacket,' Erika said. 'Relax. I won't be a moment.'

She went back into the kitchenette and began to grind coffee, preparatory to brewing up in a sleek little espresso machine. Blessed was impressed, despite himself. None of your London bedsit Nescafé and Bailey's here. Or had things simply changed since the Seventies, when he had last been in an unmarried young woman's room with no idea how the evening was going to end? Was it all fresh-ground coffee and nice spirits in Earl's Court these days as well?

The room was plainly but tastefully furnished. Some flea-market junk of the better sort: a charmingly cracked oriental statue of a fluteplayer; a sturdy-looking Wilhelmine table; Wiener-Werkstatt-type bentwood chairs. A reproduction print of the huge dance-frieze by Edvard Münch from the Neue Nationalgalerie in the Potsdamer Strasse, covered most of one wall. The sofa, dressed up with a patchy velvet throw, looked temptingly comfortable, as if it should have been crowded with purring cats. It was there that Blessed decided to take his ease while the coffee was brewing.

'This is all surprisingly domestic,' he said when Erika re-emerged with the coffee.

'Maybe a reaction to Wolfgang's place – all steel and austere minimalism there, of course. That's why I needed my own environment to be relaxing, undemanding.' She gazed round the room as if seeing it through new eyes. 'Now, maybe, I'll alter this room again. Make it wilder, less cosy. But not immediately. First I'll probably take off somewhere for a while, get some perspective on things.'

'That's exactly why I left Australia after my divorce. You get too close . . . '

Erika nodded solemnly. 'To get away from a man like Wolfgang, that's what you need. He . . . he shatters one's confidence, you know . . . ' Her eyes had been sparkling with slightly drunken excitement. Now she seemed frightened, vulnerable. The dramatic change in her mood caught Blessed by surprise.

'Did Wolfgang always belittle you, make you feel stupid?' he asked.

'Not at the beginning . . . I think he wanted to parade me around'. Erika shrugged. 'But . . . I don't want to talk about Wolfgang. It's so hard to explain how he operates. I want to start again. I want to be *free*. So let's talk about something else.'

Blessed was glad to oblige. Helped by the vodka, he told Erika the story of his father, his sister and the Kinder. She was an appreciative audience, a listener as well as a talker.

Suddenly, however, she looked at her watch. 'Michael . . . this has been wonderful. But actually I am very tired all of a sudden. I think everything is catching up with me. We must meet again. In the meantime . . . '

Blessed nodded, hiding a stab of disappointment. 'I understand. Soon, I hope. I'm staying in Berlin for a while, job or no job. But if Klarfeld comes through, I'll have more expenses to spend.'

He found himself wanting to reach out and touch her, but he also knew it would be wrong – for himself, yes, because he was still confused about what he really wanted from this encounter, but mainly for Erika's sake. *She's in a more fragile state than she chooses to let on*, he thought. *Slowly does it, if – God knows – at all. Let things develop at their own pace.*

At first it sounded as if some giant claw were scrabbling at the windows. Then Blessed realised that someone was throwing gravel up from the street. Erika tensed, swallowed hard. Her eyes were frightened.

'Shit,' she murmured. 'Oh shit oh shit.'

Then a drunken voice boomed up from the street. '*E-r-r- eeee-ka! E-rrr-ee-k-a! Mach' doch auf. Lass mich 'rein. Ich will dir sprechen. Ich bin so very, very sorry . . .*'

The last part of the delivery, in its plaintive switch to English, made Erika bite her lip with pained disgust. Blessed realised that this was the rejected Wolfgang, returned to haunt her first night of freedom.

'Always the same,' Erika said softly. 'A year of sneers, then suddenly – when you no longer want them – they turn into sad little boys who want their mummies. *Nicht zu glauben*,' she said through gritted teeth. Unbelievable. '*Einfach nicht zu glauben.*'

Another hefty quantity of road-surfacing struck the windowpane. '*Errreeeka! C'mon! I just wanna talk! I'll stay here until you let me in! Believe me! Erika! Erika?*'

Blessed stood up. 'I'll get rid of him.'

'*No!*' Erika shook her head. Her voice was low, urgent. 'Even if you got rid of him for now, he would not stay away once he knew you had been here alone with me. He would find a chance to come back when I was alone. He is . . . let's just say there are things you don't know about Wolfgang, that I can't tell you, but it would not be good for you to get involved with him. OK?'

'For Christ's sake –' Blessed was just one slug of Gorbatschow short of not giving a damn for tomorrow or what would happen when the appalling Wolfgang returned. He could feel himself swaying gently, so he sat down again. 'For Christ's sake . . . '

'*Erika! Lass' mich 'rein! Du blöde sau, das gibt's nicht, so was . . .*'

Erika reached over and stroked Blessed's hand. 'He'll go,' she whispered. 'We'll ignore him. He'll think I've gone off to spend the night with a girlfriend, something like that. In the end he'll go home to his austerity and his pretentiousness. Just so long as he doesn't know you're here. Please. We have a whole bottle of good vodka to share, Michael, and I'm no longer tired. Let Wolfgang rave down there in the street all he wants. No one will take any notice of him. He's just a nuisance factor, as they say.'

'Nuisance is the right word.'

Erika was very close to Blessed. 'See,' she said. 'We're trapped in this place. You, me, and our friend Gorbatschow.' She laughed throatily. Blessed could feel a strange, infectious excitement emanating from her. 'Now I don't want you to go', she said. 'Maybe I didn't, even before he arrived. Wolfgang, poor Wolfgang, has forced my hand.'

Hell, Blessed thought. *Unless I'm very much mistaken, this woman can look after herself.* 'I wanted you from the moment I set eyes on you. In the train,' he said.

'I know. And everything that has happened has pushed us together. But let's not be too hasty. First more vodka.'

Erika's words may have been cautious, but before she pulled away from him to retrieve the vodka, she kissed Blessed full on the lips.

EIGHTEEN

BLESSED WAS AIRLIFTED out of unconsciousness by a pinching, nipping sensation in the area of his navel. He stirred, grunted. The feeling moved down towards his groin.

'What?' he half-opened his eyes. 'What?'

The door of the bedroom was ajar. Light was pouring in from high windows. Erika . . . he thought dreamily . . . Erika's apartment . . . There was cool air playing on Blessed's naked chest. Forcing his eyelids fully apart, he looked down. The bedclothes had been thrown back. Sprawled on the foot of the bed was the ivory-white, naked body of Erika. She was lying on her belly, with one hand encircling his lazily tumescent cock, running the sharp-nailed fingers of the other over his skin, all the while making little bites on his lower belly. He grunted again, half in surprise, half in pleasure. She looked up briefly, smiled, then returned her attention to his groin.

'Good morning, Herr Blessed,' she greeted him, patting his cock. Her other hand went down and cupped his balls. 'You look well. The good thing about vodka is that there are few after-effects. *Gorbatschow* is good for you. You may not remember, but you were busy last night . . . '

'Oh God, yes.' Some images had started to drift back: of clothes discarded on the living room rug, of him pulling her down onto him on the sofa, of making love frontways, backways, up and down; of bellies, breasts, thighs, buttocks, pale and soft and endlessly pleasurable. 'I'd never have thought it possible,' Blessed said.

'Ah, but it was.' Erika was still addressing his cock. 'You fell asleep eventually, but not before everyone concerned was satisfied.'

'A miracle.' Blessed was hardening now. She was starting to lubricate his tip with saliva.

'I don't believe in miracles,' Erika murmured. 'Miracles only happen once, and I want it again and again . . . '

Still massaging him, Erika reached over to the half-open drawer beside the bed, delicately produced a rubber sheath, which she unrolled over his cock with an intense, gentle concentration.

98

'Of course. I was a faithfully married man for such a long time . . . '

'But no longer. This is 1989, Herr Blessed. And this is Berlin.'

She sat up abruptly. She was now looking straight into his eyes. Her lips were slightly parted, showing even teeth and a darting pink tongue. Blessed could see full breasts with their nipples rosy and erect, a superbly-sculpted, lithe body, thighs slowly parting.

Oh Jesus Jesus Jesus . . .

Erika slid forward onto him. As he eased into her, she placed his hands on her breasts, tossed back her head and began to respond to his thrusts, to do her part to take them where they both wanted to go . . .

Only a lot later did Blessed think to look at his watch. It was after eight.

'Christ. My meeting.'

Erika placed a cool, calming hand on his belly. 'Don't worry. I called a cab before I woke you up. It's booked for half past. Twenty minutes to your hotel. Forty minutes to shower and change. Sound OK?'

'Who's the miracle now?' Blessed kissed her on the cheek. 'Thanks.'

'It was nothing.'

He dressed quickly, refusing her offer of coffee. The cab appeared in the street right on time, tooted its horn.

Blessed quickly checked the street, then waved to the taxi driver. 'Well, no Wolfgang, at least,' he remarked, turning back into the room.

'I don't know when he went,' Erika said. 'I was pre-occupied with other things.'

Blessed went through to the living room, picked up his jacket from the chair where he had left it the previous night before coffee, *Gorbatschow* and Wolfgang had intervened.

The taxi had just slapped his horn for the second time.

'I have to go,' he said. 'I'll ring.'

She thought about that, nodded. 'The love-making was beautiful. We will see each other, enjoy each other again soon. But I'll need my freedom and I may be a little hard to deal with sometimes . . . Do you understand?'

'Yes. Oh, yes.'

'Really? You don't mind?'

'No. I have a few things to sort out myself. I'll be away for a few days in the States next week, then there'll be work to do. Let's be easy on each other.'

She stepped forward and gave him one of her chaste little kisses, just as she had at the start of last evening.

'*Tschüss.*'

So simple. So calm. Who would dream of the reckless pleasure they had given each other that night and this morning?

'*Auf Wiedersehen*, Erika,' he suggested gently. Until the next time.

She nodded solemnly, like a little girl. 'Yes. Definitely. *Auf Wiedersehen*, Michael.'

Her face was at the window as he climbed into the cab. She blew him a kiss.

The cabby grinned in lewd appreciation.

'Hotel Berlin, please,' Blessed said.

'You're staying there? Foreign?'

Blessed nodded. 'English.'

'*Sprichst aber gut deutsch.* And you're a lucky tourist to score in Berlin. Go on, tell me your secret . . . '

NINETEEN

'So. That's fine about the trip to America for your nephew's graduation,' Klarfeld said. 'I don't want to sound uncaring, but it's best that it's so soon. You can get it out of the way . . . '

'I understand. Anyway, I'll move into the boathouse tomorrow morning, and give the manuscript a first read-through before I leave for New York.'

'Excellent. This is the perfect place for you, Michael. It will save you money, and it's quiet.'

'You're very kind.'

'Actually, if you'd put up a fight I would have had to insist. Security reasons.' Klarfeld smiled broadly.

Blessed also got the sense of a lonely man, a man who wanted someone to come home to.

'I can look for a place of my own after I've finished the translation. If I decide to stay on in Berlin.'

'No pressure.'

There was a pause. Blessed lit a cigarette, briefly considered where to put his laptop, his printer, all the other essentials. There in the corner. A great view to the other bank. He was lucky to be offered this beautiful boathouse as a place to live . . . and also indebted. If it hadn't been for Klarfeld's connection with his father and Daphne, he would have thought twice about accepting. And even so, it would be advisable to make it clear from the start that indebtedness only stretched so far.

Blessed got to his feet, walked to the window and stretched. Erika had been right about the vodka. His head was surprisingly clear. He felt far better than he had any right to this morning. He turned on his heel. 'It's good to be back in history,' he said.

'I don't get your meaning.'

'I spent six years in Australia. A backwater. The place feels outside the mainstream, away from where everything's happening. In Europe – and especially in Berlin – one's aware of the tide of history, of where it arose and, perhaps, where it's going . . . '

Klarfeld wagged a finger in mock accusation. 'Didn't we already discuss the perils of Cold War romanticism?'

'It's interesting. You can't deny it.'

'Old Chinese proverb: Heaven save us from the curse of living in interesting times. Personally, I think Australia is wonderful. I adore the place. As a nation, we Germans are tired of history.' Klarfeld looked at his watch. 'Twelve-thirty. Frau Smilovici will have lunch ready in half an hour. Why don't we have a glass of something? To celebrate our partnership.'

'OK. A cold beer would be great.'

'For me too, I think.'

Klarfeld went over to the fridge, opened it and produced two bottles of Berliner Kindl.

'I want to try to fit in as much journalism as I can. When exactly do you need the *Stasi* general's memoirs?' Blessed asked.

'September. In time for the Frankfurt Book Fair the next month. So long as you can guarantee the manuscript will be ready it's up to you how you organise your time. As for other journalistic work, why not? It will do no harm. Also . . . well, a few pieces appearing under your byline in the British press will explain your presence in Berlin.'

Blessed accepted his glass of beer. 'I suppose they will.'

'I don't *suppose* so. I *know*. Berlin is a small town in some ways. Just in case anyone starts asking, you can say you're here to do some freelancing, write a book, and you're staying with me as an old family friend.'

'OK by me. All OK by me.'

'*Prost!*'

'Cheers.'

'After lunch, we might go down the lake in the boat, prowl as close as we can to the border. A little bit of the Iron Curtain for dessert, eh? In case you are still hungry for history!'

It was eight when Blessed got back to the Hotel Berlin, and the restaurant was serving dinner. His face was flushed from the sun reflecting off the water of the Wannsee during their trip in Klarfeld's speedboat. It had been quite a day, and Blessed needed to tell someone. He rang Erika's number the moment he got up to his room. He let it go for about a dozen rings, then replaced it, tried again.

By the time Blessed went to bed just before midnight, he had tried Erika six or seven times without success. Was she reconciled with Wolfgang, despite all that vehement renunciation? Had she just gone out to see a friend? Was she roaming the bars, looking for another lover?

Hadn't Erika warned him she might be difficult?

Blessed knew he had no right to be possessive or jealous. He hardly knew her. This was the city, and this was the way the natives dealt with sex. This was about high risk, take-your-knocks relationships. It was about freedom – for him as well as for Erika.

This is why I came here, he told himself as he sought unconsciousness. This is why I came to Berlin, to the city of my father's life – and symbol of his death.

TWENTY

THERE HAD BEEN A nine-hour flight via Frankfurt. Then a five-hour drive from New York followed by a short night's sleep at the old inn, on the Breadloaf campus. Today, a hair-raising spin down the winding Route 125 to Middlebury and a pre–graduation lunch at the River Run restaurant.

Afterwards, in front of the main building of the hundred-and-fifty-year-old college, an open-air Commencement address that seemed to go on forever. There were no seats available by the time the Elliots and Blessed arrived, and certainly no shade. But now, at last, here was young Josh Elliot, safely graduated *cum laude*, capped and gowned, running the gauntlet between faculty members, grinning like a treeful of cheshire cats. And here was his uncle Michael Blessed, trying through a mist of exhaustion to grin right back with some kind of conviction.

'Hey, this man's a BA. Give him a drink,' Rockwell was saying, holding out a cup of punch. Daphne was unsuccessfully struggling to hold back her tears.

Blessed congratulated his nephew. 'Good on you, Josh. Welcome to what passes for the real world.'

He put out his hand. Josh grabbed it with his free one, downed some of the weak punch with the other. Champagne cork-popping was conspicuously absent from the celebrations. This was a very American, middle-class family affair. None of your Oxbridge Moët marauders around these parts.

It was time to get out of the way, make way for other families. The stream of newly-graduated students just kept coming. There was a constant flow of welcoming committees eager to glad-hand their boys and girls. Josh took his little group of supporters and set off across the grass to nowhere in particular, greeting other kids as he went, exchanging banter, acknowledging smiles and congratulations.

All of a sudden, a willowy young blonde appeared from out of nowhere, embraced Josh and gave him a big, smacking kiss. He rocked on his heels, then turned to his parents and Blessed.

'This,' Josh said, 'is Diane Kelly. She never kissed me like that before, I swear it! Diane, you know my dad, Rockwell, and my mom, Daphne . . . this is my uncle, the one I told you about – Michael Blessed.'

Diane Kelly was gorgeous: perfect fair skin, tall, eyes of that startling cornflower blue that he had only ever seen this side of the Atlantic.

'Nice to meet yet another of Josh's fellow-students ,' Blessed said.

Josh let out a joyful guffaw. 'C'mon, Mike . . . Diane's on the faculty! She's my creative writing teacher!'

'My mistake.'

She flashed him a dazzling smile. 'You can mistake me for a college senior any time.'

Meanwhile, Josh had turned to his parents. 'Hey, Mum and Dad! Remember Diane from the Parents' Weekend last year . . . '

'Well, yes,' Daphne said. 'But I'd forgotten she was practically the same age as you.'

'Jesus, Daff. I remember Diane even if you don't,' Rockwell put in. He flashed his most charming grin. 'She and I spent a good deal of the evening discussing the Freudian symbolism in the novels of Tom Clancy. Miss Kelly here taught me a thing or two about what makes the military-industrial complex tick, I'll tell you.'

Blessed lit a cigarette in a mildly defiant way. Not only did middle-class Americans not seem to drink in public, but smoking was taboo too. 'Glad to meet you anyway,' he said to Diane Kelly. 'I know Josh enjoyed your course a lot.'

'Diane's been published, you know that?' Josh contributed. 'She has a collection of short stories out with . . . ' He frowned, turned to Diane with an embarassed smile. 'Ah, who was it again?'

She cited a company Blessed had never heard of. Its name had a strongly western-mystical flavour, something to do with spirits and horses. 'They publish out of Santa Fe. You know how it is. You have to start somewhere . . . ' She gave a wry shrug. 'They got me some review coverage. I'm aiming for one of the New York houses for my novel. When I finish it . . . '

Just then, a friend of Josh turned up and took him to one side. Soon they were eagerly discussing some project they had in mind for the long summer to come. Daphne and Rockwell had already

105

been swept into conversation with people they knew from a previous Middlebury junket.

'You're the journalist, right?' Diane said. 'From Australia. Josh told me – well, the whole class, in fact – about you. He brought along some articles you'd written about Australian politics. They were wonderful, if I may say so.'

'You may indeed. In fact, you can say that kind of thing as often as you like.'

'Still uncovering the sins of the mighty in places with wonderful aboriginal names?'

Blessed shook his head. 'Not any more. I'm back in Europe. Based in Berlin at the moment.'

'Oh. I didn't know that. I only taught Josh during his junior year, of course.'

'And did you give him good grades?'

'Sure. Mostly B's. An A or two. He's smart, full of ideas, and he writes pretty well. I wish I'd been able to give him more A's ... Trouble is, despite his British background, he's pretty much like his American friends: hot on "creativity" but not so eager to slog through the reading list. I guess I sound like an old fuddy-duddy ... '

'Not a bit,' Michael laughed, still wondering at this glorious creature – Emily Dickinson meets Kim Basinger. 'Couldn't agree more. Reading other authors sharpens the bullshit-detector. It's the only way young writers can get to realise how much of what they think is stunningly original has already been said, often over and over. One man's "creativity" is another's cliché ... Anyway, he seems very keen on you.' Blessed smiled. 'Despite your stuffiness and authoritarian tendencies.'

'I think he was at one time, yes.' Diane said, effortlessly fielding the hint. 'You know how these things are. I felt the same way – for six months or so – about the man who taught the Elizabethan playwrights when I was at Wellesley. Ten years later, ask me about Beaumont and Fletcher and I confess I'm a little shaky. Ask me about Bill Krankenpfeil's baby-blue eyes and there's still total recall.'

'Well, in Josh's case his reaction is perfectly understandable.'

'Hey. This is a *lot* of flattery in a *very* short time. Josh also said uncle Michael was a family man!'

'I'm divorced. That's the other thing that happened since Josh's junior year.'

106

'Ah.' She nodded sympathetically, sighed.

'You too. I can tell from your reaction.'

'It only lasted three years or so. One of those college-romance-turns-sour things.' Diane made a face. 'He worked in an office to put me through graduate school. Trouble was, this office of his was a fashion magazine. He met an awful lot of beautiful young women in the normal course of his work. And he slept with most of them – only one at a time, I gather, but still . . . '

'I'm sorry.'

'So was I at the time. I'm not now.'

There was nothing self-consciously brave or fake-mature in the way she expressed herself. She seemed to mean it.

Then Josh was back, with a girl of his own age in tow. A pretty, intense-looking brunette wearing a huge pair of sunglasses with a reproduction of the Hollywood sign ranged along the top of the rims.

'Uncle Mike,' Josh said. 'This is Parker Glossop, known as Glossie. She was also in my creative writing class, a star thereof. And she's off to California to film school in the fall.'

Glossie effortlessly took her place centre stage, as if born to it. 'I want to learn every aspect,' she assured everyone. 'I mean, of course, what I really want to do is write, but you have to have acquired some production skills to get people to take you seriously . . . '

And soon they were into the big discussion about which particular twenty-year-old had just gotten X-hundred thousand bucks for his/her first film script: every ambitious college graduate's fantasy this year. Diane showed polite interest, but it was clear to Blessed at least that she didn't really approve or care. He realised how much he liked her, and there was a tiny but real stab of disappointment when Rockwell swung by to remind him and Josh that they were due back at the Breadloaf campus for a post-graduation barbecue in just a while.

Blessed felt a fizz of real cheer when Diane said that she too had been invited up to the cookout on the mountain campus. She'd been considering passing on it, but maybe she'd come after all. It was such a beautiful day . . .

'I think you should join the party, if only for the sake of these misguided children,' Blessed said. He glanced in the direction of Josh and Glossie. They were still chattering about the lures of

107

California. 'Definitely. As you can see, there are still plenty of young souls to be saved.'

'Who said I was in the business of salvation?'

'Aren't all teachers? Secretly.'

She smiled, with a hint of challenge in her eyes. 'Don't bet on it,' she said. 'You can think it, Uncle Michael, but just don't bet on it.'

Later Blessed recalled that there might have been someone sitting in a stationery workman's truck, maybe a hundred yards or so from where they were all drinking and eating and talking, talking, in the cool of that Vermont June evening.

He also remembered the pickup he and Diane Kelly saw the next morning when they arrived at the parking lot by the beginning of the Robert Frost Trail. It was white, a Nissan, quite new, with nothing in the back so far as they could see. A big, black Suburban four-wheel-drive stood at the far end of the lot. Neither Blessed nor Diane paid either vehicle much attention. This was his second and final morning up at Breadloaf; she had offered to take him on the Frost trail before he drove back to Connecticut with Rockwell and Daphne.

At the barbecue, Blessed had found out that Diane Kelly was twenty-seven years old. More interestingly, she was leaving the college at the end of this semester – her post was untenured – and instead of plunging straight into the academic job market she planned to give herself a year to finish her novel – a historical fiction based on a meeting between the opium-eating English poet De Quincy and the French decadent, Baudelaire. She had a room fixed up in London, handy for the British Library, and would also be going over to the Bibliothèque Nationale in Paris to do some research there.

'Frost lived down the road a bit. Near Ripton. Farmed and wrote,' Diane explained as they crossed a bridge over a stream and set off up the first part of the carefully-landscaped trail. 'These round here were his woods, his mountains. Of course, not like this neat tourist trail ... Frost got very grumpy and in his old age, hankered for some real old-fashioned Yankee misery in the face of all the relentless feelgood niceness that was seeping in from the West. He'd have hated us spoiled-brat tourists, if he'd lived to see us.'

'And you? How are you dealing with the human race at the moment?' Blessed asked.

Diane just laughed. Her response had the touch of evasion about it. She took Blessed by the arm and led him up a steep part of the track that climbed higher above the spring-fed river. 'See, the point about the Robert Frost Trail is, you stop here and there at your designated places and in those places they have kindly printed a poem or a bit of a poem. Now somewhere on the trail is one you'll know – Some say the world will end in fire / Some say in ice / From what I've tasted of desire / I hold with those who favour fire . . . '

Blessed saw her move ahead of him. Her legs were long and tanned. She moved gracefully, with a kind of sensual power.

'Lead on,' he said. 'Sounds right in tune with my mood.'

It was a half-hour or so later. They had gone round in a loop and were slowly beginning to head back towards the river, across the other side of which lay the parking lot. The sun was starting to burn the dew off the grass. Blessed saw a flash of lenses among the trees ahead, and his mind went back to that almost-forgotten incident in Somerset, when he had seen the figure staring up at him from the church.

'I think someone may be watching us,' he said to Diane.

'Yes?' Her tone was only a little incredulous. 'Why?'

'I don't know. A peeping Tom, maybe. Let's just stand here and see what he does.'

'You're serious, aren't you?'

'Absolutely. I'm going to stare up there, hard, and watch for his – or her – reaction.'

Blessed lit a cigarette and they waited. He kept looking right towards where he had seen the gleam of the lenses. No one up there could be in any doubt that he'd been spotted.

At last it happened. The sound of a distant footfall among dry branches. Then a male figure broke onto the path a couple of hundred yards below them, moving away fast. All they could tell from behind was that the man was about five feet ten, wearing jeans, a baseball cap, a sleeveless woollen jacket. There was a pair of binoculars bobbing around his neck as he ran.

Blessed dropped his cigarette, hastily ground it with his heel. 'I'm going after him.'

'Michael –'

But Blessed was already breaking into a run, shouting, 'Hey, you!'

The track was still slightly muddy, and it went steeply down hill towards the river. Blessed, in sneakers, was able to move with reasonable speed and assurance, but the man ahead was possibly younger, certainly fitter, and had a good start on him. Nevertheless, Blessed felt that he was gaining. But was he gaining fast enough? It was only about a quarter of a mile back to the car park. Soon the sweat was soaking his denim shirt and his legs were aching. The river came into view, crossed by a wooden bridge, and after that a fork, giving a choice of routes back to the car park.

The man Blessed was chasing, moving at a swift lope, thudded across the bridge, swerved to take the right fork, and in doing so stumbled. He righted himself quickly, got back on his feet and pressed on, but in the meantime Blessed had made fifty yards on him. At the worst, even if the guy made it to his car, he might get a look at him, Blessed thought. Maybe he was just some local voyeur.'

The right fork took the path around by a rivulet. Blessed recognised this as the way they had come when starting the trail earlier that morning. Just around the corner were some rocks that would make a good place to sit in the sun. After that, just a couple of hundred yards to the vehicles. He snatched a deep breath, forced his arms and legs to move faster round the bend . . .

The man he ran into was big. He was standing with his back to Blessed, hands on his hips and feet apart, square in the middle of the path, right on the curve.

There was no way Blessed could have avoided him. The collision was quick and heavy. Blessed's head, bowed forward as he ran, hit the big man square between the shoulder-blades, and his neck felt like it snapped. They both went down heavily. Blessed found himself rolling back onto the path and looking up at a woman's face. It wasn't Diane. This woman was quite dark, wearing shorts and a sweatshirt, and saying over and over in a strong New York accent: 'Gary, this is crazy. Gary, y'hear me? Crazy . . . '

Blessed clambered to his feet. His vision was blurred. Dimly he saw Diane arrive, heard her talking to the dark-haired woman. He heard an engine starting up down in the car park, the tear of tyres on gravel as his quarry's vehicle pulled away.

As it happened, Gary and Tania Dershovitz had a thermos of black coffee with them, and they were of a forgiving nature.

Gary helped Blessed to his feet and sat him down on a rock. 'I think you're the one who came off worst, pal,' he said with a sympathetic laugh. 'I weigh two hundred and twenty pounds. Just can't seem to lose it.'

He and Tania were up for the long weekend. They had been around the trail and were sitting on the rocks by the stream, just gently canoodling, when this guy had come racing past as if the cops were after him. Gary had stepped out onto the path and was staring after him when Blessed careered around the corner and hit him from the back. The rest was history.

'I think he might have been some kind of voyeur,' Blessed explained. 'He was watching Diane and me from up in the woods, and when I faced him out he made a run for it. A confession of guilt, you might say.'

'He had glasses. I remember he had tinted glasses,' Tania said helpfully. She had her hair tied up with a little gipsy kerchief.

'Did he look like he was from round here?'

'He was white, if that's any help . . . '

'Which car in the lot is yours?'

'The Suburban.'

'OK. So he was driving the pickup.'

'It was new,' Diane said. 'Smarter than most you see around here.' She smiled in anticipation of her next revelation. 'And I am here to tell you, it had Connecticut license-plates.'

Blessed looked at his watch, cursed under his breath. 'Which reminds me. I'm due back at the campus in twenty minutes. We have a four-hour drive ahead of us, back to Greenwich.'

'The woods are lovely, dark, and deep / But I have promises to keep / And miles to go before I sleep / And miles to go before I sleep,' recited Tania shyly.

Blessed sighed. 'Jesus. Old man Frost had a line for *every* occasion.'

They said their farewells while Rockwell and Daphne waited in the ready-packed station-wagon. Josh had already disappeared back to

111

Middlebury with his friends. There were parties all day, all week, and the young in pursuit of pleasure are not sentimental.

'It's been great,' Blessed said. 'My brains are scrambled, but it's been great.'

'Michael,' Diane said, 'what are you *really* up to? I mean, that guy with the binoculars, are we talking about a redneck voyeur or something entirely more sinister? You seemed to be half-expecting him. Is it to do with your work in Berlin?'

'It could be,' Blessed conceded. 'I really haven't a clue.'

'You don't seem that naïve to me.'

'Diane – all I can tell you is that I'm not a spy. Got that? What I'm involved in is a freelance journalistic project . . . and yes, it's sensitive. I mean, there are people who will not like what's going to happen as a result of this job.' He shrugged his shoulders. 'On the positive side, it looks like no one was intending me – us – physical harm. We could be dead and buried back there in Frost's beloved woods. God knows, they had the chance.'

Diane nodded slowly. 'I guess you're right. Listen . . . I told you about my trip to Europe. Well, I'll be in England at the end of next month. We could . . . well . . . I mean, I don't intend to cloister myself in the library right away . . . '

Her hesitation was touching. Blessed gladly eased her off the hook. 'By all means drop by Berlin,' he said. 'If you like.'

'Worth the risk, you think?'

'Depends which one you're talking about. I can't offer guarantees on any front – but I'd love to see you.'

'I think I may take a chance.'

'You have my number. Until mid-September at least. If anything changes, I'll let you know.'

'Promise?'

'Promise.'

They shook hands.

Daphne was thrilled with the romantic developments she had observed from the car, and as Rockwell negotiated the twisting highway back away from Breadloaf, she eagerly cross-questioned him. Blessed put up with his sister's goodnatured interest, and mentioned Diane's European plans.

'Terrific. She's a great kid,' Rockwell said. 'Stunning, too. Give yourself a break. Get to know her.' He laughed heartily. 'I mean, first get rid of all those Fräuleins you got hanging around the place . . . '

TWENTY-ONE

BLESSED'S PASSION FOR NEW YORK was still as intense as ever, but it had necessary limits. He compared it to an affair – first falling for a louche, exciting lover, then slowly witnessing the adored one go crazy, become life-threateningly violent – while he struggled to keep the good feelings alive.

He had first visited in the late 1960s, as a teenager, not long after Daphne and Rockwell had married. In those days, when Rockwell was starting out in real estate and Daphne was working as a secretary at an advertising agency, Blessed had slept on the sofa at their tiny apartment in the upper Eighties. Central Park was just a block away, the Metropolitan and MOMA within walking distance. While they were both at work, he had cruised the city alone, browsing through Brentano's and Doubleday, catching the sweat and the noise of the garment district, getting to know the Village dives, daring the sleaze of Hell's Kitchen and Times Square. In the evenings he and the Elliots would go to Chinatown, or Little Italy, dine cheaply and well in friendly family-run restaurants. Of course, even in those days there was risk involved when you walked the streets. New York had felt pleasantly on the edge, intense, going somewhere. Now, in the late 1980s, it had tipped over the edge. But how could he desert his beloved? The seductive shapes still stood: the Chrysler building, the Empire State, the Flatiron, soaring into a copper-and marble sky. Grand Central Station was no less magical, just deeply tarnished by its increased population of resident crazies and panhandlers.

Since Blessed's plane didn't leave until the early evening, Rockwell generously offered to buy him lunch. Toting his one travel bag, Blessed joined him on the train into Grand Central from Greenwich. He deposited the bag uptown at his brother-in-law's office, then ambled off to revisit his favourite haunts. Around noon, Blessed began heading reluctantly back, to tear Daphne's workaholic husband away from his desk.

114

The offices of Elliot, Birnbaum were on two floors of a building around 52nd and Park. Elegant green carpets, a sweeping staircase – installed since Blessed's last visit – roomy, oak-panelled offices.

Rockwell and his partner, Jim Birnbaum, were the frontmen, but the real, and mostly unseen power, in the business belonged to the Dracoulis family. The Athens-based Greek shipping magnates bankrolled the real estate portfolio which the firm of Elliot, Birnbaum had been administering for almost ten years now. Stavros and Apostoulos Dracoulis, and Stavros's tough, clever daughter, Elli – all of whom had seats on the board – were known collectively simply as 'The Family'. When they descended on the office, it was like a royal visit. Blessed had been there for one such occasion. It was possibly the only time he had seen his brother-in-law show fear. If Rockwell failed to produce the goods, then the Dracoulis organisation could drop him, and Rockwell knew it. He wouldn't go broke, he had some capital and investments of his own and he was a smart operator, but he would go from the major league to the very minor in one short, steep tumble.

'Nice morning in the juicy old Apple?' Rockwell said, emerging from his office.

'As ever. There's more street traders. Where do they get that stuff? Books, china, videos . . . '

'Ask not.' Rockwell looked at his watch. 'Twelve-thirty already. You're checking in at five, right? Let's go for the taste of Tokyo . . . you know Hatsuhana?'

'Not yet.'

'Remiss of you, dear boy. So remiss. C'mon. It's not far.'

Ten minutes later they were perched at the crowded sushi bar, watching the chef slicing raw fish. 'Slicing', of course, couldn't justly describe the process. It was a performance, part-ballet, part meditation, part sculptural miracle, performed with a knife as sharp as a laser-beam.

'These guys train for years to do this,' Rockwell said. 'It's practically a religion. The most tempting one I've encountered, anyway.' He picked up a menu. 'I'd suggest you join me in a huge platter of mixed sushi – tuna, yellowtail, all the best stuff.'

'Sounds fine.'

'We'll wash it down with a couple of Sapporos. I don't usually touch alcohol at lunch, but what the hell. I don't see Mike off back to Berlin every day of the week.'

115

The beers came quickly. Blessed raised his glass. 'To Josh,' he toasted.

'To Josh. Right.' Rockwell took a sip of his Sapporo. 'And how about you, Mike?'

'I'm fine too.'

'How's Berlin? I know we talked about this with Daff, but . . . *entre nous*, as they say . . . '

Blessed decided to open up a little. 'Berlin is terrific,' he said. 'And mysterious. I'm pretty sure, for instance, that someone is unhappy – or at least very curious – about my job with Klarfeld.'

'Oh yeah. Tell me more.'

Blessed quietly told Rockwell about the watcher in Somerset, the watcher in Vermont. And Benno Klarfeld's gentle warnings. He didn't describe the exact subject-matter of the general's memoirs.

'The material is politically very damaging to the East German régime,' Blessed explained. 'Some people over there may not be too keen on seeing it published.'

Rockwell grunted. 'And in the West?'

'What do you mean?'

'Listen, there are people here who *like* the Cold War. Who – and here's your paradox – don't want the hardliners in places like East Germany undermined, in case it deals one more blow, maybe the final, mortal one, to the old East-West confrontation. The bad guys in the CIA and the Pentagon and the arms companies are shit-scared of that happening, because then there'll be no bogey-man anymore . . . ' Rockwell looked shrewdly at Blessed. 'I don't know how damaging this stuff you're talking about actually is. Can you give me an idea?'

'In the context, very damaging. It has legs. People are prepared to do things because of it.'

'Mike, I'm concerned about you, you know that. I don't want you hurt.'

'I'd have thought that if anyone wanted to hurt me, they could have done that by now. Christ knows, they've had their chances.'

'Maybe. But these people have their own agendas. It's probably not you they're after. Maybe Benno Klarfeld, or someone else connected with this piece of business.'

The platter arrived. Neat, modernist blocks of raw fish, loglike sashimi on the side, high voltage Japanese mustard glowing greenly in its pot. The two men began to eat.

116

'I'll be in Germany later this summer, you know,' Rockwell said after a while. 'That's why I'm pumping you in this ruthless fashion.' He glanced around, lowered his voice. 'The real interest in Germany will be to see some of the money guys in Frankfurt. The Family are interested in checking out investment opportunities in Eastern Europe. And even though Berlin's not technically on my itinerary – I mean, whatever you say, there's no actual action there at the moment – I'll try to stop over there at some point.'

'It'll be good to see you. What are you going to be looking for in the East?'

'First of all, real estate. Co-ownership schemes and such. OK. And there are specific industries the Family might profit from taking a share in: Polish shipyards, Bulgarian tourism, Czech auto building. The commies are quietly liberalising their laws for foreign investors, making it easier to re-export profits.'

'The fruits of *glasnost*.'

'Absolutely. But I'll tell you, if the Soviet bloc is starting to open up, it's because they're all deep in the financial crap, including the USSR itself. That's what'll really catalyse change in the East, more than any number of damaging revelations.' Rockwell sought out the last remaining sliver of yellowtail, hauled it through the mustard. 'All the same, it's kind of interesting to know that the sort of waste material you just mentioned is just about to hit the fan. Very interesting indeed. Thanks.'

'Can I take that as approval?' Blessed asked sardonically.

Rockwell laughed. 'It doesn't matter if I approve or not, Mike. I know the signs when I see them. You're hooked, boy – hooked on what you see as your own little corner of the Great Game.'

'It *is* interesting.'

'It's a jungle – luxuriant, hot, risky. But so long as you don't do anything really dumb, you'll probably be OK.' Rockwell was working his front teeth with a toothpick. 'One big thing in your favour is, you don't shoot from the lip. Don't think I haven't noticed that after an hour of sitting in this place, you know all my plans and I know zero about yours. It's the journalist's technique.'

'Worse than that. It's my temperament.'

'Worse, Mike? No! *Better*! You never had to learn it, so you'll never forget it. Now, you said you're doing mainstream journalism as well as this mysterious stuff. We've got another hour before the limo leaves. Tell me about it.'

'I've started with the Art scene. Cap "A".'

'In which case, you'd better have another beer. Cap "B". Don't worry. You've got all night on that plane to sleep it off . . . '

TWENTY-TWO

OF COURSE, AS AN ORPHANED CHILD of working-class parents, for a while I was far too interested in the issue which also concerned the vast majority of other Germans during the immediate post war period: physical survival. I befriended soldiers of all nationalities, I hustled, and I stole. In fact, it was getting caught after just one such escapade in the winter of 1949-50 – just after the creation of the West and East German states – that brought me into close contact with the newly-established Deutsche Volkspolizei. This police force was, in fact, already becoming the de facto army of the new communist government of the Soviet Zone of Germany . . .

Blessed's master plan had been to crack the style of the piece, and get a couple of chapters under his belt before he considered taking out time for the freelance articles, but things weren't turning out according to calculations.

Blessed noted his spot in the manuscript of the *Stasi* general's memoirs, got to his feet. He lit a cigarette and began to pace restlessly around the boathouse. It was a dull, showery afternoon outside, uninviting, but he couldn't stay still, and he couldn't stay here. He eyed the phone on his desk. Finally he picked it up, dialled, waited. No reply.

Erika. Not a word for five days. She had said she needed freedom, but this was carrying it to extremes, wasn't it?

Blessed cursed himself for putting himself back in thrall to a woman. At the same time, he went over to the door, took his raincoat off its hook. Within moments he had locked the door behind him and was off up the path towards the gates. Frau Smilovici's face appeared briefly in an upstairs window as he passed the house. She gave him a little smile and a wave. Klarfeld was away for a couple of days in Hamburg.

From Chausseestrasse, a number 18 bus took him the couple of kilometres to Wannsee S-bahn station. The weather had kept the boaters and bathers away. The gardens of the pubs along the lake

119

opposite the station were empty, and there was no queue at the ticket window inside.

Wannsee – Nikolassee – Schlachtensee – Mexikoplatz – Zehlendorf . . . The old S-bahn car rattled over the long, wooded stretches of the Berlin outskirts. Kids in waterproof anoraks had brought their bikes onto the train. Then into the city proper. At Yorckstrasse Blessed changed to the U-bahn for the short hop to Mehringdamm. From there he could walk to Erika's flat.

When Blessed reached the third-floor landing, there was not a sound except the squeak of his footfall on the floorboards. He stopped, rang Erika's doorbell. He could hear himself breathing. No answer. He rang again.

After the fourth ring, Blessed tried the door of the flat where, Erika said, the two gay men lived. Nothing there, either. And the third flat was empty. He moved down to the next landing and struck lucky. The door opened on a short chain, a pair of rheumy eyes peered out. The old lady must have been in her eighties.

'Yes?' she said in German. 'I don't want to buy anything. Really, believe me . . . '

'Don't worry.' Blessed essayed a glassy smile. 'I'm looking for Erika . . . The young woman upstairs. I've been trying to ring her for days.'

The old lady smiled back. 'She is pretty. She has lots of friends . . . but at the moment she is away.'

'Yes? For long?'

'I don't know. Maybe for good. These young people, they come, and then they go. I last saw her four, five days ago.' She paused for a beat. Her timing was superb. 'She was carrying a big bag and she took a taxi.'

'Is the landlord on the premises? Or a janitor?'

'The janitor is Herr Hildebrandt. In the Hinterhof, fourth floor, apartment three. He will know.'

Blessed thanked her, descended to the ground floor, emerged into the courtyard. Further back was the Hinterhof, and the inner building housing more flats. It wasn't hard to find the one the old lady had indicated, and Blessed's run of luck continued. Someone answered immediately he pushed the doorbell.

It was one of those minor but vividly embarrassing moments. When the door to apartment three opened, a small figure appeared in the doorway. Blessed was about to ask for the child's father when he looked down and saw that the face staring up at him belonged to a middle-aged man – a fifty-year-old inhabiting a twelve-year-old's body. The little man was wearing carpet slippers and a cardigan and carrying a copy of the tabloid newspaper, *B-Z.*

'Herr Hildebrandt?'

The little man nodded. 'Yes. How can I help you?' he said in a comically deep voice, a voice that went with someone twice his size.

'I . . . I'm looking for one of your tenants. Fräulein Winter. Erika Winter.'

'Ah. And what would you want with her?'

The other curious feature of Herr Hildebrandt was his eyes, which were dark and huge, like a marmoset's. Blessed found them unsettling. And for such a small human being, Herr Hildebrandt exuded cool self-assurance in large quantities.

'She's a friend. I've been trying to ring her without success, I happened to be in the area, and . . . well, I just wanted to know . . . Listen, has she moved? And if so, is there a forwarding address?'

Suddenly Herr Hildebrandt smiled. For an instant his face looked as young as his body. In some way known only to himself, Herr Hildebrandt was enjoying himself.

'No. She hasn't moved,' he said then. 'She has gone away for a while.'

'Did she say why?' Blessed knew he was being played for a fool but didn't much care.

Herr Hildebrandt shrugged his bony shoulders. 'Family trouble, something like that, I don't know. I didn't ask her.'

'I see.'

'Do you? Tell me your name, please.'

'Blessed. Michael Blessed.'

'Ah. The Englishman. I thought so. I have something for you. *Augenblick, bitte.*'

Herr Hildebrandt shuffled back into his tiny apartment. From the threshold Blessed could see a bare living room, with a cheap sofa and table. A television set was on, with the volume at a low setting, showing a Tom and Jerry cartoon. Jerry looked extraordinarily like Herr Hildebrandt, come to think of it.

121

'*Bitteschön*,' Herr Hildebrandt said when he re-appeared. He was holding out an envelope towards Blessed. 'First Fräulein Winter paid her rent in advance. Then she gave me this for you.'

Blessed took it. 'Thanks.'

'It's nothing. Really. The life of a janitor is full and rich. One is constantly performing little acts of kindness.'

With that, Herr Hildebrandt laughed, said an *Auf Wiedersehen*, and closed the door on Blessed, leaving him standing out on the landing with Erika's letter.

Blessed put on the light on the stairwell, opened the envelope. Inside was a handwritten note, no date.

Dear Michael,

This is hard for me as well as for you, but I did warn you that I needed to get away and find myself. Well, on impulse I rang a friend – not in Berlin – told her about me and Wolfgang, and also about you, and asked if I could just come and stay for a few weeks until I felt clearer. She said yes, and so off I went.

I would like very much to see you when I come back to Berlin in three (?) four (?) or more (?) weeks. It was a very good time we spent together, in bed and out, and I like you very much. If you want to, just go to my apartment, write your phone number down and slip it under the door so that it will be waiting for me when I return. Very romantic!

Yours with love
Erika

Blessed carefully pocketed the letter. Erika wanted what she wanted, no more or less. And . . . this was the goddamned trouble . . . he was going straight back over to her apartment. And he was going to write his phone number down on a little bit of paper. And he was going to put it under her door.

So that it would be waiting for Erika when she returned. All just as she said.

TWENTY-THREE

THE WESTERN TOURISTS WERE OUT in force on Unter den Linden. Some were staring in their usual puzzled way at the stone-washed jeans in the windows of the Textile House of the GDR, or inspecting the Fifties-style pottery on display at the Bulgarian Trade Centre. Most were drifting steadily towards the crash barriers on the eastern side of the Brandenburg Gate. There they could spend a happy quarter-hour taking pictures of the tourists on the western side taking pictures of them. It was a game that barely involved the East German natives at all, but no one seemed to mind.

Granit turned away from the window. 'Another day in paradise,' he said drily.

'And all's well,' retorted Gurkel, raising his schnapps glass and downing a hearty draught.

'So far!' the third voice said.

The other two exchanged grins. 'The pessimist, Wonder. Always the pessimist,' said Gurkel.

The dwarf figure in the corner was also holding a glass of schnapps, but it had hardly been touched. 'What if Blessed tells Benno everything? The girl, Wolfgang, the meeting with me, "Herr Hilde brandt" . . . '

Granit frowned. 'He hasn't talked about it to Benno, Wonder. We *know* he hasn't.'

'True. So far. But he might.'

'Why should he?'

'Because he might get lonely. Because he might become angry. Because he might be even more of a fool than you take him for.'

'OK, OK. And so what?' Granit shrugged. 'We change things if necessary, play them differently. After all, why shouldn't our young Mr Blessed have a little girlfriend on the side while he's in Berlin? He's a nice-looking boy, she's a pretty girl . . . Benno would understand that if he found out about it.'

123

'Maybe ... but you know when I saw that Blessed yesterday, so much like the kepten his father ... and when I thought of Benno ... ' The little man was suddenly lost for words.

Granit's features softened. Wordlessly he touched him on the shoulder with one huge hand. His tenderness was surprising.

'Maybe I can forgive Blessed,' the little man continued. 'But never Benno. He betrayed us Kinder all those years ago, and he'll do it again if he gets the chance. Benno's one of nature's collaborators.'

'Don't forget – we're using Benno this time, not the other way round,' Granit reminded him. 'Now, I've set the big Kinder-Meeting for mid-August,' he said, returning to business. 'I'll be sending out invitations through the usual channels. Naturally I can't discuss the details at the moment.'

The two other men nodded to indicate that they understood his caution. This small office suite overlooking Unter den Linden belonged to one of Granit's *Stasi* front companies. On the plus side, its position close to the border was highly convenient for both Gurkel and 'Herr Hildebrandt', when, as now, they needed to cross over from the West at short notice. The minus was, there existed the likelihood that someone – possibly Western Intelligence, equally possibly Minister Mielke, who was famous for his distrust of his underlings – had by now managed to have this room bugged. As a consequence, they had agreed that simple references could be made to the Kinder and the old days, because after all, who could make head or tale of those stories anyway? But current Kinder-business, or criminal acts past and present, could only be discussed when they were safely in the West, or in some place that had been secured against surveillance, such as the forester's hut in the border district, where they had met in February.

'That'll be good,' the Wonder said finally. 'Good to see everyone. August. There's still time for a lot of changes, my friends, a lot of surprises.'

Granit had returned to the window. From there he could see the distant Wall, and across the top of it he could make out one of the battered, castellated towers of the Reichstag building, just inside West Berlin. It was hard to believe that one day all this might change. Everything out there at this moment looked so permanent, he thought, so impregnably solid, as solid – that was the phrase –

as life itself. Except, of course, that belief in life's particular solidity was also an illusion. The saddest and most foolish of all.

'Oh yes,' Granit said. 'Many more surprises for everyone, everywhere.'

TWENTY-FOUR

IT CAME AS A BIG SHOCK, even to a boy like me, who had grown up on the streets, to realise that under the GDR's 'Real Existing Socialism' the old rules still applied and that power, if anything, was even more of an aphrodisiac. In the West, it was the bloated capitalist with his young mistress on his arm; in the East, where all that had been 'abolished', it was the Volksarmee general or the Politbüro bigwig squiring his Bardot lookalike to the Opera Grill or getting her into tight shorts for a weekend sailing party on the Potsdam lakes ...

Blessed's fingers moved smoothly and easily over the keys of his laptop. So long as he didn't think of Erika, he was OK. So long as he didn't think of her long legs wrapping themselves around him, her full lips hungry for his. Maybe it was the *Stasi* general's talk of sex that was to blame. Sex got in everywhere.

All Blessed could tell himself was: maybe I've lost a girl, but I've gained a part in history. Because Benno Klarfeld was right – these memoirs were going to help make an earthquake, in East and West, but especially in the East.

My first real experience of this came when I was a lowly 'OIBE', Blessed continued to translate. 'OIBE' was *Stasi* jargon for 'Officer on Special Assignment'. *I was called to a weekend briefing get-together at a Stasi vacation colony up on the Mecklenburg coast. There were some very attractive women there who had been operating in the West – and some of us, at least, were goodlooking young men. But the colonels and majors, many of them middle-aged and ugly, had no trouble getting companions for the night. The word was, the women didn't keep their highly-valued jobs unless they were willing to sleep with 'the Chief' ...*

There was a perfunctory knock on the door. A moment later, Klarfeld burst into the boathouse. He acknowledged Blessed's presence with a mere wave of the hand, dashed directly to the television set.

'Benno? Are you OK?'

126

'One moment!' Klarfeld said. He snapped on the TV.

The midday news was starting. The newsreader said they were going straight to the border between Hungary and Austria.

'Watch this!' Klarfeld murmured, transfixed.

On screen, a young couple in casual clothes were standing by a frontier marker on the Hungarian side. They were carrying canvas grip bags. Then the camera moved away from them, maybe fifty yards, to a Hungarian border guard. He seemed to be deliberately ignoring the couple. The camera pulled back. Suddenly the couple started running across no-man's-land towards Austria. Flash to the guard, who was still doing nothing. Now to another camera's point of view, on the Austrian side. The young couple had arrived there and were being congratulated by a small but noisily triumphant crowd.

The announcer's voice intervened at last. It explained that the young couple were supposedly East German, 'tourists' in Hungary. They had just left Hungarian territory for Austria without any officials attempting to stop them. Hungary, for years the most liberal of the East Bloc countries, had already begun to dismantle its border fortifications. Now its government had decided to stop enforcing its exit-visa requirements . . . So any East German in Hungary who took a deep breath and legged it for the West was pretty much guaranteed to get through.

Now the camera switched to a miserable-looking East German spokesman, consulted just minutes ago at his office in East Berlin. The man, a grey *apparatchik*, was doing his best to brazen things out in the way that only government press spokesmen know how.

The East German official said everything that could be expected. He said he couldn't believe that a fraternal state such as the Hungarian Socialist Republic would do such a thing. He said that the negligence of individuals must be responsible. He said that the GDR's embassy in Budapest was seeking urgent clarification of the matter. Rest assured, he promised grimly, that any East German citizens who abused 'socialist hospitality' in this criminal fashion would be severely punished!

Blessed and Klarfeld watched in silence. No explanations were needed for them to gauge the full significance of this event. What they, and the commentator, and the po-faced East German spokesman realised was that the Iron Curtain had begun to collapse. For forty years, its barbed wire and minefields and guard-towers had scarred Europe from the Baltic to the Danube. For East Germany especially, the existence of this lethal barrier had been a life-and-death issue – without it, the artificial, Russian-founded and controlled state on German soil would long ago have lost its brightest, best-educated citizens to prosperous, free West Germany. That was why the Berlin Wall had been built in 1961, to close off the last escape route. But once one communist country took down its section of the curtain, the East Bloc was no longer sealed tight – the border defences might still be in place in Czechoslovakia and East Germany, but now the people of those countries could go *round* them.

The news moved on to the next story. Klarfeld turned off the television. For a moment neither of the men spoke.

'You know what this means?' Klarfeld said then. 'The cage is opening. Those timid little birds over in the East don't yet know they're free. It will take time until the fact really sinks in. Weeks, even months. But soon enough they'll realise that *nothing* – nothing at all – is actually holding them in . . . '

'And all hell will break loose. There'll be a stampede to the West.'

'Precisely.' Klarfeld got to his feet, paced around restlessly, then turned to face Blessed. 'And you had better keep working very hard, Michael. Because if things continue to develop at this pace, then our *Stasi* general could decide to go public with his memoirs sooner – maybe much sooner – than we ever thought.'

THE SUMMER OF THE STASI

July-August 1989

TWENTY-FIVE

THE EDGE OF THE INDOOR swimming-pool was inlaid with marble. The high, frosted windows let in light but ensured privacy. From his lounger beside the water, Erich Honecker asked if either guest would like tea, or perhaps freshly-squeezed juice, from imported fruits.

'Thank you, yes, Comrade General Secretary.' Granit said. 'An orange juice.'

Mielke declined the invitation.

Honecker signalled to the aide waiting by the door to the pool annexe. 'Orange juice for General Albrecht. For me, more mineral water.'

The East German leader's accent betrayed his origins in the Saar, the westernmost part of the old Germany, bordering on France, where he had been born seventy-six years ago, the son of a miner. His bespectacled face was drawn and pasty, with an unhealthy yellow tinge.

Granit studied that face, trying to read its mood. The huge billboard portraits that accompanied the metres-high slogans such as WITH THE AID OF THE DECISIONS OF THE XIV. CONGRESS OF THE SED WE SHALL INCREASE PRODUCTIVITY AND PROSPERITY were retouched to take twenty years off Honecker's age; they plumped out his cheeks and lent him a look of fatherly authority. Observing him now, Granit thought Honecker resembled a retired undertaker, a sick old man coming to the comfortless realisation that he would soon be needing one of the caskets he had so long reserved for others. Nevertheless, Honecker's toughness and cunning were not be underestimated. This man might be old and sick now, but after the war he had ruthlessly clawed his way to the top. It was Honecker, they said, who had personally ordered guards to 'shoot to kill' on the border between East and West Germany.

'The Comrade General Secretary is well?' Granit asked with careful politeness.

'The years of struggle and service have taken their toll. They say I must have an operation. I tell them I have no time, that our Republic needs my whole attention . . . '

'You have to be fit by October, for the Fortieth Anniversary Celebrations, Erich,' Minister Mielke said. 'I recommend you have the surgeons do their work this summer. This will give you plenty of time to recover before the festivities.'

'We, the generation that fought to create the GDR, are all getting old,' Honecker grumbled. 'What is your age, General Albrecht?'

'Fifty-six, Comrade General Secretary.'

'See?' Honecker appealed to Mielke. 'When you and I were already involved in the underground struggle against Hitler, Albrecht was still in nappies! When the victorious Red Army gave us the chance to establish a socialist state on German soil, he was hardly old enough to shave!'

'Albrecht was an orphan,' Mielke said. 'When he was eighteen, he and some other boys were arrested for black-marketeering. His intelligent demeanour and fine physique attracted the attention of the political official attached to the police unit concerned. He graduated from our training school with the highest honours. From ragged proletarian orphan to stalwart upholder of socialism! What a success story for our GDR!'

The orange juice and mineral water arrived. The aide returned to his place by the door.

Honecker's expression was suddenly alert. 'I tell you, in our year of triumph – when we celebrate four decades of Real Existing Socialism on German Soil – our enemies will be working tirelessly to undermine us. Exploiting the confusion since Gorbachev embarked on his reforms in the USSR, counter-revolutionary forces have become active once more . . . Our first problem is the local government elections. There's talk that they were rigged . . . '

'Erich, I'm liaising with young Egon Krenz,' Mielke interrupted. 'He'll make sure the vote sticks, don't worry.'

'If so, why are these dissidents being allowed to mar our Republic's anniversary year?' Honecker demanded with a hint of petulance.

'We're walking a tightrope,' Mielke said. 'If we crack down on internal dissent in a crude way, we attract bad publicity in the West *and* in Moscow. Comrade Gorbachev is impatient at what he sees as our unwillingness to introduce reforms here. So . . . '

131

'So, *what*? If you can't stop subversion, why are you Minister for State Security?'

'But that's why I brought along General Albrecht,' Mielke explained smoothly. 'His section is particularly concerned with foreign transactions . . . comings and goings, hard currency movements, all highly secret. His people have spread their net wide over these past years. We can use their contacts abroad and in West Germany to discredit the opposition. Don't you see, Erich? When subversives are jailed or beaten up, they become martyrs. When they are shown to be corrupt tools of western Intelligence, they are disempowered, and at the same time our state's credibility is enhanced. Two birds with one stone!'

Honecker gloomily sipped his mineral water. His voice was a hard monotone. 'Let's hear the details, General Albrecht.'

'Certainly, Comrade General Secretary,' Granit said. 'We begin a long time ago, in the Fifties. Not here in Berlin, but in London . . . '

They emerged into the sunlight in front of the General Secretary's villa. All was tranquillity in the Party bosses' ghetto of Wandlitz. Mielke's and Granit's personal limousines were waiting in the turning-space. Mielke's chauffeur sprang to open the passenger door, but the Minister motioned for him to wait. The two *Stasi* generals moved out into the immaculately-tended garden, putting a distance between themselves and the building.

'Honecker was impressed,' Mielke said.

'I'm glad. I'm confident he'll be even more impressed by the time we've finished.'

'Glad to hear it. You'd better deliver the goods, that's all I can say.'

Beyond the high wall that surrounded the villa's garden, there were other villas, all new and built to the highest specifications. Wandlitz, in the old days a leafy, middle-class commuter suburb, was now the exclusive preserve of East Germany's communist élite, of Politbüro and Central Committee members, ministers and heads of state corporations. Mielke himself lived close by. Fine woods and ornamental brickwork graced his and the other SED bosses' homes. Foreign-built cars were parked in their driveways. In the centre of the 'village' stood a western-style supermarket where all kinds of imported goods unavailable elsewhere in the country, from compact-disc players to caviar, from perfumes to polo-shirts, could be bought with 'soft' East German marks – though only to the privileged inhabitants of Wandlitz. In fact, as if in ironic mimicry of the wall that surrounded the GDR, there was a wall all around the settlement – though in this case to keep the East German public *out*, so that they would never see how their socialist masters lived. There were checkpoints on all roads leading into Wandlitz. The leaders' paradise was a mere half-hour by escorted limousine from the government and party offices in East Berlin, but a world away from the shabbiness and brown-coal filth, the shortages and the queues of most East Germans' daily lives.

Granit spoke again. 'My section needs more buildings, Comrade Minister. More safe houses, more places where we can entertain western business contacts.'

'Our Ministry has plenty. They are at your disposal.'

'But it's a question of credibility – and confidentiality. Technically, to satisfy our criteria, such places should belong to front companies of ours. I'd like to continue requisitioning the appropriate buildings . . . '

Mielke looked sharply at the big man. 'You'll give me – and Erich – what we want, won't you, Albrecht? A major propaganda setback for the West?'

'Word of honour, Comrade Minister.'

'That's all I need to hear.' Mielke looked at his watch. 'Submit a detailed proposal regarding those properties and I'll see what I can do.'

'I have a list ready for your approval.' Granit reached into the pocket of his coat and handed Mielke a folded sheet of paper. 'The properties have been chosen very carefully. There won't be any problems, I promise you. We move quietly and discreetly, as one must do in this age of increased openness,' he said, without a flicker of irony. 'We're stuck with *glasnost*, like it or not.'

While Granit waited, Mielke glanced through the typewritten details. Finally the Minister laughed harshly. 'Ach, Albrecht. For an old communist fighter like me, this pussyfooting seems unnatural. Property law? Corporate structures? What's the world coming to! In the early days, if it was necessary to build socialism, we took what we wanted. Think about the consequences later, that was the motto! Don't you feel nostalgic, Albrecht, for those days?'

'I was seventeen, living in a cellar on lung-soup and dry bread, when the Party first took power, Comrade Minister,' Granit said smoothly. 'Nostalgia? I don't think so. I *like* socialist order, socialist legality. So long as it doesn't get in our way . . . '

Mielke grunted, took out a pen, put his signature at the bottom of Granit's list.

'My authorisation,' he said, handing the document back. 'You can have your properties, Albrecht.' He began to move towards the waiting car. 'In fact, if you pull off this operation with these so-called 'memoirs' and keep Erich Honecker happy, you can have anything – anything you damned well want.'

TWENTY-SIX

SINCE BLESSED'S RETURN from America, the weeks had drifted past like a school term, regular and relatively featureless. The piece he had written about the Opening at Wolfgang's gallery had been accepted by the *Bulletin* and printed this last week. The pattern was straightforward. Most days he started work at nine, broke at one. Lunch was a salad at his worktable. Then it was back to the memoirs until early evening. He usually ate dinner up at the house if Benno Klarfeld was about; otherwise Frau Smilovici brought him a tray in here. She could cook German, Italian, and pungent, spicy Yugoslav. Some evenings Blessed stayed here. Others he went walking, even to a film. On a couple of occasions Klarfeld had accompanied him. Relations were warm, easy. Discussions were of politics and the old days in Berlin, of Blessed's father – whom Klarfeld had clearly hero-worshipped as a boy – and sometimes of Daphne and Rockwell.

Only one thing marked out this particular domesticity from others: shortly after Blessed came back, Klarfeld showed him a place in the house, behind a clock, where he kept a gun. It was a small automatic, provided with a clip of ten shells. If Klarfeld was away, and for any reason Blessed felt nervous, he should take this and keep it in the boathouse, his host told him. The weapon was simply, matter-of-factly, offered and its workings explained. More than twenty years ago at school, Blessed had reluctantly submitted to military training in the CCF. He had assumed he would never use it, done his best to forget it the moment he walked out of the school gates for the last time. That, as they say, was then. This was now.

It was two in the afternoon. Back to work.

In 1958 I was sent on my first assignment to West Germany. Infiltrated over the still-open border with West Berlin, I was to deliver sums of money to various agents of ours in the grimy industrial towns of the Ruhr Area, ex-members of the now-banned German Communist Party. It didn't take me long to realise that they

135

were not really spies at all but charity cases. Small potatoes, dull people, a futile, routine operation. So unglamourous, so altogether worthy, so much not what I had expected . . .

The phone rang. Blessed started, stood up, got to it on the third ring.

'Hello.' He never gave his name.

'Oh, hello. It was the right number.'

'I'm sorry?'

'You don't know who this is?'

Well, yes. Suddenly he did. 'Erika.'

'At last. That realisation took some time, Michael. I obviously made less impression on you than I thought.' The throaty laugh was just as he remembered. 'I returned this morning from the beautiful south and found your phone number waiting for me under the door. Very exciting.'

'Why didn't you ring before you went? If I hadn't tracked down Herr Hildebrandt, I wouldn't have known what you were up to. And you wouldn't have got my phone number.'

'I considered ringing you first. Then I thought, if he really cares, he will come to the apartment block, and he will make enquiries . . . '

Blessed eased himself into a chair by the window. It was a fine day. A sailing boat was making its way up the lake, heading north towards the Havel. Its crew, a man, a women and a child, were wearing matching yellow T-shirts.

'Where did you go?' he asked. 'Or is it a state secret?'

'Oh no. It is no secret, state or otherwise. I went to München.' Erika sighed gently. 'You know, after you and I spent the night together, I called a girlfriend who lives down there – she has a wonderful little apartment in Schwabing. We discussed the end of my relationship with Wolfgang and so on. She said: pack your bags immediately, get away from all that gloom and pretension in grey old Berlin, come down and stay with me . . . And that is just what I did!'

'Well, you sound cheerful, I'll say that. Benefits of the alpine air, the Weisswurst and that well-known Bavarian insouciance –'

'Ach, you're mocking me, Englishman.'

'Sure I am. We should meet,' he said.

'Oh yes. This past month I've had time to think. I've made a free decision to see you. It's been . . . ' Erika paused. 'I want to make love *now*. Shall I come to where you are?'

'No. No, that's difficult. I'll grab a cab and be with you in an hour or so.'

'Oh, please.'

Decision made, Blessed thought. 'An hour,' he repeated. 'No longer than an hour, I promise you.'

Erika answered the door wearing a red silk robe. As she pulled Blessed into the room, it fell open to reveal that underneath she was naked except for a silver crucifix at her throat. She drew his fingers down between her legs, to prove that she was already damp with arousal.

Soon they were both naked. They tumbled onto the sofa as one. There they rutted like animals – or strangers – he hard and thrusting, ruthlessly furthering his own pleasure, while she wrapped her limbs around him, rocking and writhing, pulling him into her to the very last inch, squeezing the sperm from him. They both came within minutes.

After they had lain still for a while, Erika laughed softly.

'I waited a month for this. For you.'

'There was no one in München?'

'No one like this.'

'That's an interesting answer –'

But Erika had already slid from the sofa. She padded into the kitchen. Blessed heard her humming to herself as she opened the refrigerator. Glasses clinked. A cork popped.

'*Voilà!*' Erika re-appeared, brandishing a bottle and two glasses.

'How do you think of these things?'

'It's a special occasion.' She filled two glasses with champagne, knelt beside Blessed and handed him one. 'Soon there will not be so many opportunities for lazy, sexy afternoons. Tomorrow I start a temporary job.'

'Oh yes? Where will you be working?'

'At a gallery off the Ku-Damm. Just for the next two weeks, filling in for a friend who is going on holiday. I've been networking, as the Americans say. With any luck, I should be able to get temporary work of that kind right through to the autumn.' Erika took a sip of champagne. 'How's your job going?'

137

'The translation? Pretty good. Dull stuff,' he said, conscious of how smoothly the lie slid from his lips, and curiously excited by that fact. 'The article on the opening at Wolfgang's place went down well, by the way. It was published last week. Next time we meet, I'll bring it with me for you to read.'

'Wonderful,' she said, absently stroking his chest with her free hand.

'I should be writing something else for the *Bulletin* . . . maybe a comparative piece about what they're doing in the East. Music, painting, what passes for an avant-garde over there.'

'I know people on both sides of the Wall. I'll do what I can. I'll be busy these next weeks, though. I suppose we'll both be busy.'

'You're right. Not too many sexy afternoons. So we'd better enjoy this one.'

Blessed reached over, eased Erika forward towards his still-full champagne glass, lowered it and delicately dipped the tip of her left breast into the cold liquid. She shivered with pleasure and shock. He licked the wine from her erect nipple, savouring the taste on his tongue.

Erika moaned softly. 'Come into the bedroom. It's more comfortable, more intimate. We have a lot to do before we get back to work.'

TWENTY-SEVEN

'IT'S A TECHNICALITY, REALLY,' the young man said pleasantly. He had introduced himself as Herr Dittfürth.

Escher, the director of VEB Storage Collective/Berlin Centre, had been alone in his office, working late, when the two men had rung the street bell and invited themselves in. Dittfürth and his colleague, Herr Vorster, claimed to be from the Ministry of Foreign Trade – even produced documents to that effect – but Escher was no fool. He hadn't worked his way to a senior job like this, in charge of a major import-export and distribution group – close to the government district, slap by the Wall – without having an instinct for which way the wind was blowing.

Escher ran a plump hand through his thinning hair. 'I don't call it a technicality when some know-nothing stranger is brought in over my head,' he said. 'I've been in charge here since 1976. I've been a member of the Party for thirty-one years –'

'We're all members of the Party here, all subject to the same voluntarily chosen disciplines, Comrade Escher,' Vorster said, switching to the formal SED mode of address. 'All the more reason to do as we're told, eh?'

Dittfürth was all smiles and we-can-work-this-out charm, but there was something about his friend that was blunter, harder . . . deadlier.

'It's a question of re-organisation,' Dittfürth continued. 'Things are being decentralised. You'll be left to do what you do best – which is to run the warehouse. The new group general-director will liaise with the new authorities. You'll hardly ever see him. But he'll take all sorts of burdens from your shoulders.'

'Wait a minute. New authorities? What new authorities?'

'Ah yes. Another technicality. The warehouse will no longer be attached to the Ministry of Foreign Trade. Instead, it will become part of an independent new State Corporation. But you don't need to worry about that . . . '

'Why was I given no warning? How can a thing like this happen?' Escher's palms were sweating. Oh, he knew the smell of this one, all

139

right. This would be a completely different set-up. His new bosses would be keen-eyed, ruthless, not like the cosy bumblers from the old ministry. 'What if I protest to the Deputy Minister!' Escher blustered, playing for time. 'I know him well! We used to go hunting together . . . '

'Better you just do your job, keep your head down,' smiled Herr Dittfürth. 'Far better.' He reached into his case and produced a stapled sheaf of documents. 'Please sign these in the places indicated.'

'I can't. You don't understand. I'm responsible for this entire organisation, the building, everything! Have you any idea of the turnover involved? Of the strategic nature of the site alone? Of the value of the equipment we keep here? I have special status. I report direct to the Foreign Trade Ministry, always have done!'

'Not any more,' Vorster said.

'All changed,' Dittfürth chimed in.

Vorster bared his teeth. With a shock, Escher realised the man was smiling. 'You see, comrade, there have been too many irregularities over the years. Goods mislaid, later surfacing on the black market. As the man in charge, you have attracted notice to yourself, and . . . well, if we decided on a full investigation, things could get very hard for you.'

'This is outrageous!'

'You have a western car, a Golf. You own a holiday home on the Baltic. It's in your wife's name, strangely enough. And wouldn't you agree that it's unusual for a man in your position to have quite so much money in the bank? Especially in so many different accounts, under so many different names . . . '

Dittfürth nodded solemnly. 'After so many years of loyal service, it would be regrettable it all this were to come to light. Don't you think so, Comrade Escher?'

Escher said nothing.

Dittfürth brought Escher's attention back to the document he had shown him a few minutes before. 'This is the authorisation, changing the status of this storage collective. You can read it if you absolutely insist. But the main thing you have to do is sign it at the end. I should mention that your signature will render you subject to secret-bearer status.'

140

Vorster laughed like a child tormenting a small animal. 'It will also ensure that you stay out of jail and collect your pension in two years time. All right?'

Escher nodded slowly.

Dittfürth looked at the clock on the wall of the manager's office, clucked impatiently. 'On second thoughts, don't bother reading the paper before you sign it,' he said. 'You've kept us waiting long enough, Comrade Escher, and we're busy men.'

It was eleven on a Thursday morning, and Willi Kovács was sitting out on his terrace, drinking cold Thuringian wine with his wife. This was not unusual for them these days. Three months ago he had applied to emigrate from the GDR. For three months now he hadn't worked in the state film or theatre industries. His membership of the key theatrical clubs and Academy of Arts had been withdrawn. So, there was nothing much else to do but drink.

Kovács' wife Lotte heard the knocking at the front door and went to answer. Lotte was his third wife, twenty-five years younger than himself, and quite a lot less drunk.

She was pale when she re-appeared, followed by two men in suits.

'These gentlemen are from the Ministry of State Security,' Lotte announced. She lowered herself into her rattan chair carefully, like an invalid, and looked away.

Kovács stood up, almost knocking over his half-full glass of wine.

'So. The gentlemen of the *Stasi*,' he said. 'I've been expecting you for months. Ever since I filed my emigration request . . . '

The taller of the two, lean-faced with close-together eyes, shrugged. 'As such, a private citizen's emigration request does not concern us.'

'Oh, sure. So why are you here?' The wine made Kovács bold.

'Because of your position as a leader of culture in this country, what you choose to do and where you choose to go is the concern of the republic's government, a matter of state security.'

The other one spoke now. He was balding, plump, mid-thirties, more diffident. 'I saw you in *The Miracle of Michael and Michaela*. That was in '72, eh? You played the District Secretary. Then, yes, there was the Western film you did with Dean Jones. Time flies. I have to admit, I always liked you.'

'You're a fine actor, Herr Kovács,' his friend said. 'But not such a fine citizen.'

141

The *Stasi* man gestured at the well-built, two-storey house, with its four bedrooms and guest suite, its acre of garden with views of the lake, its sauna hut. No wretched Trabi or Wartburg parked in the drive here; instead a three-year-old BMW for the master of the house and a little Fiat for the wife.

Kovács held up his fine profile, gave them the noble-but-strong look that had indeed made his reputation when he had played the District Secretary in love, in *The Miracle of Michael and Michaela*.

'Can I offer you a drink, gentlemen?' he said. 'Is this going to take long?'

They exchanged looks. The diffident one said, 'Depends what you mean by long.'

'Couldn't accept a drink,' the other asserted, shaking his narrow head. 'Not after what you've done to the GDR. After twenty years of luxury, recognition . . . ' He glanced at Lotte, who wore imported make-up, whose hands were soft, whose long legs were pampered, made even more desirable, by a cotton mini-dress and high-quality, flesh-tinted pantyhose, also probably from the West.

'Listen, is this an interrogation?' Kovács said. 'Does my wife need to be here?'

'No. To both questions. I mean, this isn't an interrogation, and she doesn't need to be here. In fact, I think it might be better for all of us if she wasn't.'

'Willi, really –' Lotte pouted.

'It's OK, Lotte,' Kovács murmured. 'Go start getting lunch. I can handle this.'

She tossed her long blonde hair, strode back into the house, followed by both the *Stasi* men's admiring eyes.

'Disgrace or no disgrace, you're a pretty lucky guy, Herr Kovács,' the diffident one said. He paused, smiled. 'Shall we tell you the good news first?'

Kovács could feel the way they were setting him up. First the subtle, indirect humiliation in front of his young wife. Now the real thing.

'Up to you.'

'All right. The good news it is. Herr Kovács, in my briefcase I have an emigration permit, made out in the name of you and Frau Kovács, enabling you to travel anywhere in the world, anywhere at all, with immediate effect. You can take everything you own . . . almost.'

Kovács swallowed hard. He was working now to maintain his cool.

'I can't believe what I'm hearing,' he said.

'Is that so?' said narrow-face. 'Very well . . . ' He flipped open his cheap plastic briefcase, held up a document that bore the seal of the State Council of the German Democratic Republic. 'Do you know how important you have to be to get one of these?'

Kovács nodded. 'Yes.'

'Good. Now we're talking.'

'You . . . you said the good news first.'

'I'm sorry?' Narrow-face seemed almost to have forgotten there was anything else. Then he nodded. He nodded slowly, at some length, and the nod became a little grimmer each time. 'Oh yes. The . . . *bad* news.'

The diffident one took over. 'See, there's a problem. Something to be overcome before you leave.' He seemed almost embarrassed. 'I don't know how to say this, Herr Kovács, and as I mentioned I really like your acting, but . . . Well, the tax office has re-opened your file, you see, and . . . '

'And *what*?' Kovács was genuinely angry. Say what you like, but he had always done all that stuff by the book. No sneaking in hard-currency income, no fancy footwork on trips abroad – when there had still been the trips abroad – and no concealment of assets. This was outrageous!

'Well . . . they reckon you've fraudulently concealed a lot of income. I mean, we've tried to reason with them, but they're after your neck. There's talk of prosecution . . . '

'This is impossible.'

'That's what I said! But they insist you owe them . . . something close to a million marks!' The diffident one laughed incredulously.

'But I don't have a million marks.'

'Right.' Diffident looked at his colleague. 'That's just what I said, didn't I, Jürgen?' Then back to Kovács, who was hunched in his chair, like a statue of some troubled god. 'I mean, that's why our Ministry's become involved. We've offered ourselves as honest brokers. Because we're aware of your status as a well-known actor, we're eager to sort all this out in a way that will cause the least damage – both to the GDR and to you.'

'I told you. I don't *have* a million marks.'

Diffident nodded. 'No.' He looked back at the house, still nodding. 'But you've got something that the authorities might accept in lieu of a million,' he said then. He lifted a chubby hand, gestured at the luxurious buildings, the sauna hut, the acre of land, the priceless views. 'You see, Herr Kovács, you've got all *this*.'

Narrow-face came back into the game. 'Just a simple signature on a straightforward legal document,' he said. 'We've brought it with us! You assign this place to the authorities named in this paper, and you're a free man. You could be strolling down the Kurfürstendamm this time tomorrow. You could be taking a plane to Hamburg, or Helsinki, or to Hollywood!'

'And if I don't sign?'

'The tax people are dead set on prosecuting you, Herr Kovács. It's all we can do to hold them back. You know how seriously our government treats economic crimes . . . '

'Why don't you just take the goddamned place away from me! Why go through this charade?'

Diffident drew himself up to his full height. He looked hurt, he really did. '*Take* your house? Then it wouldn't belong to anyone. Haven't you heard of socialist legality, Herr Kovács? Don't you know there are property laws in the German Democratic Republic?'

The operatives in white tunics had said they were from the Babelsberg Welfare Department. They had arrived twenty minutes ago, given old Frau Tischler just enough time to pack some clothes, a couple of nighties, a few of her most treasured possessions. They kept insisting that everything else would be sent on to her at the old people's home in Potsdam.

'It's a beautiful place, where you're going,' the short one kept repeating. 'Just beautiful. You've earned a rest, Grandma. Everything will be taken care of. Don't worry.'

This was Frau Tischler's eighty-sixth summer, her fortieth as a tenant in this state-owned villa. She had hoped to stay here after her husband died. But these men had medical papers saying she was senile, unable to look after herself any more, that she must go to a home.

The door to her balcony was still open. Frau Tischler shuffled over to it and looked out across the water. Her legs were stiff, her heart weak, and sometimes she got confused, but she could still see

144

well enough to make out the watchtowers on the far shore of the Havel, where West Berlin began. She also noted the men impatiently checking the time. There was the short, talkative one, and the silent, fair-haired one – quite good-looking, but with cold blue eyes – and they made her flesh creep.

'I'm the last tenant in the entire building. This place will be empty when I'm gone. You know that?' she said.

'Is that so?'

'You know perfectly well, young man. You people know everything!'

'If only, Granny. If only.'

She hated the way he spoke to her. Frau Tischler turned stiffly.

'*I know you*,' she said with sudden vehemence. There was nothing confused about the way she fixed him with her gaze. 'You and your friend aren't welfare workers at all. You're *Stasi*. I can smell it, just like I could smell the Gestapo in the old days. What will you do with this building after you've winkled me out? Turn it into a prison, like you've done with the rest of the country?'

The short one's smile became a little fixed. The old were always humoured in the GDR. They could say what they liked, they could travel to the West. They could stay over there if they wanted, because the East German state was grateful to get rid of unproductive mouths.

'C'mon, Granny,' the short one said. 'Let's make it easy on ourselves, shall we? I'm from the Welfare. We both are. Look . . . my white coat here . . . you wanna see my papers again?'

Ignoring him, she moved painfully out onto the balcony and gazed out across the blue-grey waters of the Havel to breathe in the fresh spring air one more time. One last time. To her right she saw the peeling facade of another of these once grand turn-of-the-century villas, all expropriated and turned into flats after the war. Along the way, part-hidden by trees, was the neighbouring house. The inhabitants of one of those flats had put out their washing this morning, and Frau Tischler could see it drying in the garden: underwear and sheets the colour of cement, drab nylon shirts, East German-made stonewashed jeans. She knew the people: a couple of teachers and their little girl. They would be out at work now. Should she cry for help anyway, call out and say: 'The *Stasi* has come to take me – help me!' Of course not. There was nothing to be done. *There was never anything to be done.*

145

The short one had followed her out onto the balcony. She could tell he was becoming nervous.

'You know who used to live in this villa before the war?' Frau Tischler said. 'Before the State took everything? A millionaire! He owned a department store in Berlin. His chauffeur would drive him into the city every day except Sunday. His wife was an actress, so beautiful . . . I remember there used to be parties. Everyone in town talked about those parties . . . 'She sighed. 'I know it was wicked, a few having so much while ordinary working people had nothing, but . . . '

'Well, the party's over, Granny. For them, and now for you too.'

Frau Tischler looked at the neat little row of pots lined against the whitewashed wall, positioned to catch the afternoon sun. The tomato plants were young. Just a week since she had spent an entire afternoon transplanting them, bedding them comfortably for their summer's growth. It had not been easy, with her arthritis, her back, her need to rest so often, but she had managed it. Frau Tischler felt a surge of defiance that went beyond all reason, that overcame the effects of almost sixty years of authoritarian rule, first Nazi, then communist. *Why should she leave her home, everything she loved? Why did she have to do this just because these awful men said so*?

'No,' Frau Tischler said sharply. 'You can't make me leave if I don't want! I'll talk to someone! Herr Vietinghoff at number 27 works for the Welfare – the *real* Welfare. And he's a Party member! We'll wait until he comes home . . . '

Frau Tischler's voice was trembling with emotion. Her eyes, set deep between wizened folds of skin, were bright with hostility and pride.

The short one stepped aside and the blond one came forward. He produced a phial and a hypodermic from his tunic pocket.

'Something to help you relax, Granny,' the blond one said. He had a soft voice, like a hypnotist. She hated him even more than the short one. 'You're upset. It's understandable . . . '

'*No!*'

After the tranquilliser had taken effect, they fetched a wheelchair and trundled the old lady down to the East-German-made Barkas ambulance that was parked unobtrusively outside in the street. Once she was safely stashed in the back, they returned to the villa, gathered up a few of her belongings and sealed the doors.

146

When they got back to the ambulance, they settled into the cab and took a smoke-break. The short one kept taking quick, short drags on his cigarette, obviously upset.

'Shit,' he said. 'This is not my idea of a nice job.'

The blond one shrugged. 'Comes with the territory, as they say.'

'Have you an idea what they intend to do with this mausoleum now we've emptied it?'

The blond one shook his head. 'Nope. But the general must have big plans. I hcard the builders and decorators are due in next week.'

'Maybe he's gonna give it to one of his girlfriends.' The short one cheered up, started to forget the old lady's defiance. The subject of sex never failed to lift his spirits. 'A sex-palace with a river view, eh? If this was the West, a house like this on the water would be worth a goddamned fortune. Same goes for all these places round here. Every single one of them.'

TWENTY-EIGHT

FROM TEN THOUSAND FEET UP, even the pollution that cursed the land looked beautiful, like a drifting gossamer veil cast across the fine and the ugly alike.

They had left Schönefeld airport half an hour earlier – just the pair of them and a pilot in a speedy little Russian-built six-seater – and had kept to a steady southwest course. Ten minutes ago they had overflown the quaint university town of Wittenberg, birthplace of the great religious reformer, Martin Luther. Now, across the other side of the Dübener Heide, the picture down there was dramatically different. They had passed over one man's gate to heaven, were now granted a god's-eye view of a nation's road to hell.

A major river snaked across their flightpath. Granit identified it as the Saale. Slow-moving barges were visible on the stretches where it flowed through open country. The vessels were large carriers, but from this perspective they were tiny toys – or like microscopic creatures moving along a sluggish, infected bloodstream. Directly below the plane lay the dirty industrial town of Merseburg. Its sprawling factories seemed to fight for position beside the river like giant creatures at a crowded watering place.

'They call this district "the poisoned triangle",' Granit observed coolly. He pointed out of the window for his passenger's benefit. 'Bitterfeld-Halle-Merseburg . . . Along the Mulde to the Saale, both rivers feeding into the poor old Elbe . . . In Bitterfeld there's the brown-coal industries, in Merseburg the Leuna Works, the biggest chemical plant in Eastern Europe – all pre-war technology, no anti-pollution filters, nobody giving a shit where the waste runs off to . . . Not much of a salesman, am I?'

His companion smiled politely. When Dr Hans Bästli replied, it was in the cosy singsong accent of Zürich, his home city. 'I know the GDR's heartlands are in bad shape,' he said. 'But they're not where we're heading, are they?'

Granit shook his head. 'Oh no. Don't worry. Our destination is another hundred kilometres on. Away into fairytale Thuringia, where the cattle's bells tinkle on the hillsides, where the rustics glow with pure vitality, where Goethe and Schiller found their paradise . . . Thank God, the GDR is not all brown coal and acid rain – as you will find out very soon.'

'I'm on tenterhooks,' Bästli answered wryly. 'After all these months.'

'For this, Herr Bästli, you have had to wait, it's true. Until now, when you have proved your credentials.' Granit paused deliberately. 'Almost.'

The plane taxied into position by the airfield administration building, cut its engines. The propellers were still turning as the door opened and Granit climbed out. Today he was wearing a dark wool suit, white shirt, Italian silk tie. Bästli almost stumbled and fell as he jumped down after him. He was no athlete, and he was encumbered by a briefcase – an accessory the Swiss lawyer carried as if it were an integral organ, a natural outcropping of his body.

'Welcome to *Komputron*'s airfield, Herr Bästli,' Granit said.

A uniformed *Stasi* officer had emerged from the admin building. He saluted Granit.'The Comrade General's car is on its way.'

'I see you employ only the best security staff, General,' Bästli said. He laughed softly at his own satirical little jest. He spoke quietly and precisely, in a way that inspired trust, despite his bad jokes. And the international legal firm of Bästli & Fichte was a byword for discretion, at its base in Zürich and among clients from Peking to Peshawar, Baghdad to East Berlin.

Granit smiled. The limousine he had ordered, one of his favoured Volvos with tinted windows, was approaching along the tarmac. Within moments, he and Herr Bästli had settled into the well-upholstered rear seat, the glass barrier between them and the driver ensuring privacy. They began moving towards the gates of the airfield, and beyond.

The limousine travelled along a bumpy, cobbled service road, eventually joining a highway. The signs said Weimar one way, Erfurt the other. They headed for Weimar.

Soon the Volvo passed through a small town. Many of the buildings were old, some of them beautiful, but their facades were peeling and cracked, their windows and doors unpainted. Housewives hurried through the streets, clutching shopping bags of provisions from dishevelled HO shops whose monotone storefront signs read simply MEAT or GROCERIES.

The sky was leaden, the clouds grey. Bästli observed everything keenly. The faces of the people he could see from the car were grey too. Grey, he thought, grey is the colour of communism, not red. Can you imagine, though – comrades saluting the Grey Flag? Greeting the glorious Grey Army? Composing a heroic opera entitled *The East is Grey?*

'I know what you're thinking,' Granit murmured. 'You're thinking, if this little town was in Bavaria, or the Bernese Oberland . . . '

Bästli shrugged. 'I don't know how you can let your country's treasures rot like this.'

'Things will change,' Granit said. 'Things *are* changing. And the people I represent are in the forefront of that progress.'

Bästli said nothing more. The feasibility studies had been done, the initial payments made. It was not his job to make political or aesthetic judgements, merely to verify that the information was correct.

They left the town, entered a thickly-forested area. Ten minutes later, the limousine slowed and turned off the highway onto a road marked as a cul-de-sac. It was surprisingly wide and well-surfaced. A little further on, a sign said RESTRICTED AREA. UNAUTH-ORISED ENTRY FORBIDDEN. Another quarter of a mile or so, a high, wide pair of security gates swung open smoothly at their approach and closed behind them when they were through.

The buildings inside the gates were modern, clean. There were flowerbeds to greet the visitor. The East German flag, black-red-gold with the distinctive compass-and-mallet-in-cornsheaves design at its heart, flew on a tall pole. The main building bore a sign with the collective's name: VEB ELEKTRONIK-KOMBINAT 'KOM-PUTRON'. And underneath that, a quote from Honecker's speech at a recent SED party congress, proclaiming the GDR's position at the forefront of the electronic age.

'Even when it comes to the silicon chip, your Comrade General Secretary is an expert, eh?'

'I told you things *are* changing in the GDR. I didn't say they *had*.'

They both laughed. The limousine stopped outside the main building. An overweight man in a white coat was hurrying towards them.

150

When they emerged from the limousine, Granit, who towered over both him and Bästli, took each man by an arm and propelled them gently together: 'Herr Bästli, this is Herr Doktor Prinz, the manager of VEB Elektronik-Kombinat "Komputron".'

Bästli and the East German shook hands. Then Prinz turned to Granit.

'Comrade General . . . ' he began.

'Around here, Herr Albrecht will do, don't you think? Herr Bästli is Swiss. He will feel more comfortable with simple titles.'

'Of course. Anyway, welcome. Everything is ready. I had in mind to begin with coffee in my office. While getting a technical overview . . . '

'Herr Bästli isn't interested in the technical aspect. He just wants to *see*. Straight to the electronics section, I think. We're due back in Berlin in two hours.'

'Comrade . . . I mean, Herr Albrecht . . . '

'The electronics, Prinz!'

'Fine.'

Granit led Bästli and Prinz across the yard towards the long, low factory buildings. Bästli could not fail to notice new Mercedes trucks with western numberplates parked by the loading-bays, alongside the homely W-50 dinosaurs produced at the GDR's Ludwigsfelde truck plant. The Mercedes were marked with a logo showing a stylised roll of film and the name: QUICK-FOTO BRAUER KG.

'The western trucks are for the photographic business,' Granit explained. 'Our big western-currency earner. And our second port of call.'

There was a checkpoint at the entrance to the factory. The guards knew Granit and factory-director Prinz, but they examined everyone's documents all the same. 'Your papers, Comrade General . . . Comrade factory-director . . . '

There were graceful potted plants in the lobby. The assembly workers were functioning as small teams in pleasant surroundings instead of in drab, regimented masses. The atmosphere was serious without being solemn, hardworking without seeming driven. This was much more like a western factory than any other he had seen in the Eastern Bloc. Everyone looked up briefly as Granit entered, then returned to their work. The workforce had been primed for a visit from the proprietor.

'We buy our chips from Taiwan at competitive prices.' Granit winked. 'Our friends in Red China might object if they knew ... but of course we launder the stuff through Malaysia first ... '

'The rest of the technology is home-grown,' Prinz put in, eager to remind them of his presence. 'Naturally, we've taken our lead from certain American and Japanese products.'

Granit nodded. 'The electronic surveillance equipment we make here is cheap and effective, as good as you'll find anywhere in the world. This is one of the few areas in which the GDR has managed to stay up with the leaders. Of course, we have a ready made market in the Ministry for State Security and in various departments of the Volkspolizei. Plus there's our allies ... '

'Hard-currency export potential?'

'Absolutely. Once the market frees up. And it will.'

Bästli recorded that in a leather-bound notebook.

'You will see many oriental faces in the assembly shops,' Granit continued. 'Vietnamese.'

Prinz tuned in again. 'We use a lot of such guestworkers for the precision circuit-assembly work. Women. They're deft and meticulous. Isn't that true of all Asiatics? Also, they speak hardly any German, they have no social lives outside their own little community ... and, most useful of all, they have no idea what the devices they make are used for.'

Twenty minutes later, they emerged into the open air. Granit led Bästli the three or four hundred yards to the photo-development lab. Their documents were checked again before they were allowed to enter.

Bästli queried, 'For the electronic bugs and the West German happy-snaps, you have the same level of security?'

Granit shrugged. 'Of course, we know the West is aware of what we do here, but it's good to keep them guessing just a little.'

Inside were rows of computerised machines for the development of colour film, for cutting, drying, sorting. Its sophistication seemed equal to that of a plant in the West. Successions of the banal everyday images we choose to record – families, trees, dogs – kept rolling off with a smoothness and speed that was almost surreal.

'So. Quick-Foto Brauer. Fine,' Bästli said. He looked at his watch. In itself none of this was new or interesting. Then a door

152

opened to his right and a pair of men in white overalls emerged, pushing a trolley. A glimpse through the open door revealed another work-area and – more significantly – two uniformed guards at a desk.

There was a sign above the door saying 'Only Authorised Personnel. Show Passes.' He frowned. 'Happy-snaps?'

Prinz was looking intensely worried. Granit, on the other hand appeared unconcerned. 'Not part of the main business,' he said. 'Government work. Established contracts. Very nice, but not directly relevant to the future economics of the business.' With that, he steered Bästli away.

After a perfunctory cup of bitter Nicaraguan coffee in Doktor Prinz's office, they took their leave. As they walked back towards the waiting limousine, Granit was genial.

'This place is a goldmine,' he said. 'Because of the government work, we've got the most up-to-date equipment. We can compete with any equivalent plant in the West – at a fraction of the price.'

Bästli nodded. 'With the *Stasi*, one is guaranteed quality. That's what makes this place attractive in a country where – I'll be frank – standards are generally not high.'

When they arrived at the car, Bästli took a last look around. 'But I could not choose to live here,' he said.

'You don't have to, Herr Bästli. All you have to know is that this place is one of the few really good greenfield sites in the GDR. Nothing like it in the whole East Bloc, in fact. Fifty acres, which means plenty of room to expand. Latest technology. Excellent communications.'

They climbed back into the limousine.

'None of this really matters,' Bästli said to Granit as the car pulled away. '*So long as the title to the land is indisputable.* And the airfield has to be included in our property portfolio. Factories come and go, but land always holds its value.'

'What you do with the site in future is up to you. Make that clear to your clients.'

'Of course.'

Granit smiled. 'The legal moves are complete,' he said. 'I promise you there will be no difficulties over the ownership.' He glanced sideways at Bästli. Suddenly, though he was still smiling, there was nothing easygoing in his tone. 'So. I've taken my risks. I've prepared everything, and it hasn't been easy. Now it's time for your clients to put up – or shut up. That's what we agreed at the last meeting. Any problems?'

Bästli stroked the soft leather of the briefcase on his lap. 'There are no problems.'

The electronically-operated gates swung open. They emerged onto the approach-road again.

'You'll sign the final papers.'

'Yes . . . yes.'

'Good,' Granit growled. 'We'll fulfil our side of the bargain. But I warn you again, Herr Bästli – if a word of what I have told you gets out, or if you try any funny business, you and your clients will learn what else the *Stasi* is good at.' He settled back into the upholstery, his eyes half-closed, like a carnivore at rest after a good meal. 'And I don't mean processing happy-snaps.'

TWENTY-NINE

THERE WAS NO ONE ELSE in the café at the Nationalgalerie but the fashionably surly young woman behind the counter and the manager of the tiny art bookshop to which the café provided access. Erika was on her second coffee. Blessed was already on his third cigarette.

'Of course, you have to keep your freedom, I can see that,' he was saying.

'You're sure?' Erika looked at him in exaggerated surprise.

'Sure. You had a year with Wolfgang . . . '

'One year, three months, twenty-three days. I worked it out the other day in an idle moment.'

'OK . . . and I had twelve years of marriage. We neither of us need a ball and chain. I'd just like to know if you're seeing someone else on a regular basis, that's all.'

'On a regular basis? No, no.'

'What does that mean?' Blessed tried to look amused, tried to keep it light.

She squeezed his hand. 'I see friends. Sometimes men friends, a man friend, girl friends, a girl friend, a mixture of the two . . . No one like you, I tell you honestly. And that's *all* I am prepared to say.'

'Fine.'

'Mike, we meet twice a week. The sex is *wonderful*. This is healthy for both of us . . . '

'I know, I know.'

'And you have your work.' Erika shrugged. 'How is it going, your mysterious translation?'

'Very well. I'm ahead of schedule.' He ground his cigarette out into the ashtray, caught himself reaching for another. He slid it back and returned the pack to his coat pocket. 'I owe the *Bulletin* an article. They'll think I've disappeared off the face of the earth.'

'You know what, Mike?' Erika said suddenly.

'What?'

'You look like you could do with some *fun*. The really simple, old-fashioned kind.'

'You could be right. But where?'

'Where everything old-fashioned happens. The East. Where the lemonade still tastes like real lemonade, the beer like real beer . . . '

'And the coffee like mud.'

'Exactly. There's a party tomorrow night in East Berlin. Prenzlauer Berg. At the flat of an artist named Klaus Hammerschmidt. He's a terrific guy, does huge, doomy oils full of sex-and-death imagery. He's also very big in dissident circles. One of the leaders of the current protests.'

'Sound very interesting. And what makes you break your rule?'

Erika coloured slightly. 'My rule?'

'That'll make three times we've met this week. I mean, I don't want us to overdo it.'

'See what happens when I try to cheer you up? You use the opportunity to make me feel bad! I had been thinking of going on my own – Klaus doesn't like Wolfgang at all, so no danger the bastard would be there – but I decided to invite you. Well, let's say this is a one-off, Mike, eh? You want to come, or not?'

'Sure. Of course I do.'

'OK. I tell you, this scene at Klaus's is definitely shabby-chic. And we had better eat somewhere on the way. It's always wise to line your stomach well before going to one of Klaus's parties. This is a hard-drinking crowd, I tell you. Work hard, protest hard, play hard!'

THIRTY

THE CHINESE ARMOURED VEHICLE bears the red star symbol of the People's Liberation Army. It rumbles forward, heading across the empty no-man's-land on its side of the square towards the makeshift barriers.

. . . Cut to the students waiting behind the barricade. They carry improvised weapons – sticks, iron bars, maybe knives, it's hard to tell – and there is anguished resolution etched in their fresh young faces. All those in the square say they are ready to die. One of them has already declared this to the world.

. . . Cut to the first of the armoured vehicles, halted by the crowds, tipped over, set fire. Visions of the crew being hauled out and beaten, as the masses who days before had celebrated peace wreak vengeance on the servants of oppression.

. . . Cut to the now world-famous image of the tank, the young man with the flag blocking its way.

. . . Cut to the horror of dawn, the crowds fleeing the tanks, the gunfire, the screams piercing the morning around Tiananmen Square.

. . . Cut . . .

Granit activated the remote, killing the stream of images. The lighting in the windowless room had been dimmed. He turned to Otmar Ziegler, also known as Banana.

'You see?' he said. 'You see what can go wrong? We put this sequence together, courtesy of CNN and NBC. Of course, viewers in this country will never get to see any of it . . . '

Banana nodded. 'Our Politbüro just sent the Chinese a congratulatory telegram! Our heartiest best wishes to you for slaughtering your own people! I mean, even the Albanians haven't gone that far. Have those senile old bastards in the Palace of the Republic here completely lost contact with reality? Is it the asbestos in the panelling, maybe?'

'Oh, it gets worse, my friend,' Granit said. 'The latest is, yes, the latest is, they're sending young Egon Krenz over to Peking to deliver our felicitations in person.'

157

'*Eck*,' Banana chuckled. 'I bet the Chinese didn't realise it was the Year of the Horse!'

Jokes about Krenz's equine appearance were ten a penny, but this was one of the better ones, and Granit guffawed along with his friend. The youngest member of the Politbüro – the only one under fifty-five, in fact – Egon Krenz had long been head of the Party's youth movement, the Free German Youth. He was a shifty timeserver. He was also, however, the Politbüro's liaison with the security forces, and therefore a man to be watched as well as mocked.

Granit went over to the video machine, removed the previous cassette and inserted another. Retreating until he was back at Banana's side, he pointed the remote-control and the monitor screen flickered into life once more.

Now they were back in Europe, in a large hall filled with people, some seated and some standing, most of them young. A speaker was addressing the crowd.

'That's the Dresden student leader, Grau.' Banana said. 'And that, I think, is the students' union building. Where did you get this film?'

Granit laughed but didn't answer the question. 'It's Grau, yes,' he agreed. 'This is one of the university protest meetings. About the doctoring of the local election results.' He pressed a switch. This time a vigil in the open air. A couple of hundred protestors with banners protesting at the election fraud. 'Leipzig,' Granit explained. On to another meeting, inside a church. 'East Berlin. And no, don't bother to ask me where the camera is, or how our people got it in there . . . '

'Why are you showing me all this?'

Granit froze the final image. 'To encourage you. We have people in all these places. We can deal with most of the problems you might come up against. As you progress through the ranks of the opposition, they will all be on your side. Softly, softly is the motto. We don't want an East German Tiananmen Square.'

'The difference is, our army would never fire on the people.'

'Maybe not. But the Feliks Dzierzynski Regiment would. Without compunction. Unlike the rest of the *Stasi*, the Dzierzynski people are totally committed to the régime. They're Mielke's fallback, his praetorian guard, and they'll do anything they're told. Such as – for instance – rounding up the leaders of the opposition in all the major cities and sticking them in concentration camps.'

'Are you serious?'

'Never more so, Banana. You have to realise that, like the Chinese leaders, the Stalinist diehards around Honecker are desperate men, and they still have their hands on the levers of power.' Granit was staring at the freeze-framed image on the screen. Perhaps not entirely coincidentally, when Granit had stopped it the camera had just caught the face of the bearded young man who had heckled Banana at the vicarage meeting months before. 'You see,' he continued, 'nothing is certain. You learn that in this business. That's why we need our fall-guys. Like Benno. Like Blessed. Until things are past the point of no return. Until Honecker, Mielke and the others have been stripped of all power.'

'Which *will* happen.'

'Probably.' Granit looked at his watch. 'You're under arrest for another seventeen hours. The plan is, you and the others taken in at the demonstration will be released tomorrow around noon, in plenty of time for the evening's revels. In the meantime, we have a lot of homework to do. I want us to look through all the video material I have here. Then I want us discuss – little by little, face by face, personality by personality – how you see your way forward over the next weeks and months.'

'OK.'

'You seem reluctant.'

'You never told me this was going to be such hard work.'

'*Hard work*?' Granit snorted. 'This is *nothing*! You wait until things really start moving. But . . . ' He wagged one massive finger. 'There's a reward. You survive. And you prosper. Instead of going to jail. Or dying. Is that a deal?'

'Put like that, I suppose it is. It's just disappointing. Forty years ago, there was idealism, however wrongheaded – now there's just survival.'

'You're learning, Banana. At last, you're learning.'

THIRTY-ONE

KLAUS HAMMERSCHMIDT HAD pockmarked skin. He was balding, with a walrus moustache and yellow nicotine-stained teeth. In that first moment when Hammerschmidt opened the door, Blessed wondered how he had such a reputation as a womaniser. Erika had gleefully recounted Hammerschmidt's colourful lovelife all through their pre-party dinner at the Haus Warschau fish restaurant in the Karl-Marx Allée. Then their host smiled, a broad, warm grin that transformed his ugly face. Suddenly he was a mixture of Puck and every girl's favourite uncle. Ah yes. That smile, plus his talent, would get Klaus Hammerschmidt an awful long way, Blessed realised.

'Hey, Erika!' Hammerschmidt grabbed her in a bear-hug. 'You got rid of that pretentious asshole Wolfgang at last! Congratulations!' Hammerschmidt looked past her to Blessed, put on a mock-crestfallen look. 'And immediately you get yourself a new boyfriend! Where does that leave a poor old bastard like me, who's been waiting his turn for so long . . . '

'This is Mike Blessed,' Erika said. 'He's English. A journalist. But he was born in Berlin, of a German mother. Isn't that romantic?'

Hammerschmidt smiled wolfishly. 'Maybe. There are people I know who were born in Berlin of German mothers and foreign fathers, and their stories are far from romantic.'

Erika wagged a chiding finger. 'Klaus –'

The next moment, a hairy paw was extended to Blessed – Hammerschmidt's hands were what most people would think of as a worker's rather than an artist's – and the grin returned.

'Excuse my sense of humour,' Hammerschmidt said. 'Also, I am already drunk. Welcome.'

'Call me Mike.'

'Call me Klaus. Call me Mickey Mouse if you like. Just come in and enjoy . . . '

The flat was big by East Berlin standards, sparsely furnished and untidy. It looked as though Klaus spent most of his time in his

160

studio – or out on the streets. Inside, a couple of dozen Bohemian types were munching goodies from Poland and Hungary and drinking beer and wine from the kind of unreliable, semi-absorbent paper cups Blessed hadn't seen in the West since the Sixties. The young tended to the all-black chic of the West, the older ones to an artificial-fibre shagginess. Almost everyone in the room was smoking, and talking as if their lives depended on it.

'There's extra reason for this celebration,' Hammerschmidt explained. 'Several of our people just got out of jail. They were held after the last big demonstration, you know. Including my friend Ziegler here . . . Hey, Otmar!'

A tall, thin man with spectacles halfturned, a quizzical smile on his gaunt, intelligent face. He was in his mid-fifties.

'*Ach*, Klaus. You drunk already?'

'You should meet our Englishman here,' Hammerschmidt said, ignoring the jibe. 'He's a journalist. Erika brought him. You know Erika? She used to work for that prick Wolfgang Langenhagen over in Kreuzberg, but now she's a free woman . . . '

Hammerschmidt had this way of starting what appeared to be a dialogue and just keeping going, what with explanations and elaborations and little tangents and stories that happened to occur to him, so that the apparent partner in the conversation rarely had a chance to say anything. It was not so much egotism, Blessed decided, as a kind of anxiety to explain.

Blessed had heard Ziegler's name before. A novelist? Political theorist? Both? Hadn't he been expelled from the East German ruling party a few years back?

For the next hour, though, he circulated. It was well into evening before he was given a chance to confirm his half-remembered details. Ziegler, now slightly flushed with drink, eventually loped over to where Erika and Blessed were standing.

'I know of your ex-boss, Langenhagen,' he told Erika by way of introduction. 'Though I never met him. Once when they let me go to West Berlin to talk about my books, I was taken to his gallery by someone from my western publishers. What was it called, Langenhagen's gallery?'

'Schnittke. The Galerie Schnittke. But at the moment I'd rather forget it.'

'Ah. Not a happy parting.'

161

'No.'

Ziegler turned to Blessed. 'And you, Herr Blessed? What are you doing in Berlin? The usual journalistic voyeurism – West meets East . . . '

Blessed patted his pocket where his little Japanese helpmate nestled. 'Do you mind if I switch on my cassette recorder?'

'Why not? I'm not going to say anything I haven't already said in public twenty times. Anyway, first I want to know why you're here.'

'For the reasons you named, I suppose. Voyeurism. Though I have family connections to the place as well, if that's an excuse.'

'Extenuating circumstances, certainly. But you don't have a German name.'

'My father was an officer in the British Army of Occupation after the war. My mother was . . . is . . . German.'

Ziegler's eyes, behind their lenses, seemed to flicker. He was looking down on Blessed – at about six-four, he had several inches' advantage over the Englishman – with a naked curiosity that was as unexpected as it was unnerving.

'I was an orphan then,' Ziegler said at last. 'The British were the second-softest touches. After the Americans. Then came the Russians – very unpredictable, sometimes they would shower you with sweets, at others chase you the length of the street with a bayonet – and last of all the French.' He smiled, revealing surprisingly good teeth. 'If I hadn't become a communist, I would have gone to America, no question.'

'Why did you become a communist, Herr Ziegler?'

'There seemed no alternative. In many ways, there still doesn't.'

'But you're fighting the system here?'

'Of course. More than ever. Because now, after all this time, there is a chance of real reform. What we have here is not what we set out to build forty years ago. But what we have is still so much better than the soulless, drugs-and-consumerism ethic that rules the West.'

'Klaus was telling me that you've just spent some time in jail?'

'An occupational hazard. Eight of us were taken in for protesting against the way the régime faked the local election results.'

'And how long did you spend inside?'

'Six days.'

'Solitary confinement?'

162

Ziegler nodded. 'And no, they didn't torture us. There were some interrogation sessions, some vague threats of expulsion from the GDR . . . '

'That's something most GDR citizens would give their right arm for, of course.'

Ziegler chuckled wryly. 'I'm amazed they haven't chucked me out of the country before now. I must be the East German government's token dissident, the exception that proves the rule.' He assumed the expression of a stern communist bureaucrat, wagged a premonitory finger. *'See! You say we allow no freedom of expression in our Republic, but that man Ziegler is still running around free! And earning a fortune from hard-currency royalties!'* The pantomime ended. A shadow of regret passed over Ziegler's bony features. 'As you probably know, I haven't had a book published here in the GDR for ten years or so, but in the West it's been a different story.'

'I remember something else. You were a member of the ruling party, the SED, but they expelled you.'

'Yes,' Ziegler said quietly, 'they certainly did that. After twenty-five years. The swine.'

'You're bitter? But the SED was always an authoritarian, Marxist-Leninist party.'

'In the early days we hoped to bring about a synthesis. Don't forget that the name of the SED means "Socialist Unity Party". It was created by a merger between the Communist and the Social-Democratic Party in the Russian Zone.'

'Come on, Herr Ziegler. That was a forced merger, a shotgun marriage!'

'Not entirely! The experience of fascism was still fresh in people's memories. There were many in the Social-Democratic Party who honestly believed they should combine with the Communists to prevent any repetition of what happened in 1933, when a divided Left allowed Hitler into power.'

Erika began questioning Ziegler, revealing that she knew about the politics of the East, past and present.

'So,' she said, 'do you see yourself in the tradition of a critic working from inside the system – kind of a loyal opposition, like Robert Havemann, or Stefan Heym? You want to change the GDR in order to save it?'

163

'Sure. Most of us under the Democratic Action umbrella are eager to preserve – in fact to revitalise – what's best about the socialist structures we've built up here since 1945 . . . '

Hammerschmidt arrived with red wine for Erika and Blessed, beer for himself and Ziegler.

'Oh sure, maybe,' he interrupted. 'You're a hopeless idealist, Otmar. How many times do I have to tell you? Out there on the streets the people just want a car, a decent flat, and a video recorder. And the little things . . . like being able to find fresh fruit and vegetables, or to buy the exact pair of shoes you want when you go to the shop . . . '

'Klaus –'

Hammerschmidt took a hefty swig of beer, ploughed on. 'The system is not just tyrannical,' he insisted. 'It's also laughably inefficient. You know what I heard? When there's suddenly lemons in supply, it's only because Honecker's niece complained about not being able to make a hot toddy for her husband's cold. If the people feel that your kind of reforms are just going to mean more of the same, then they're going to treat your "revitalised socialist structures" with the same contempt they feel for the present régime!'

Ziegler had been tapping his foot restlessly during Hammerschmidt's monologue. 'Oh yes?' he snorted. 'So why are they out on the streets in this city? In Leipzig? Are they calling for more lemons? Is it: Give us video recorders or death? No! They want more freedom of speech and travel, more democracy, more real socialism.'

'They might want that today, but you wait! Unless the people are offered a genuine alternative, they'll reject everything good about this country along with the bad. Otmar, I'm –'

Hammerschmidt never finished his sentence. One of the younger guests, a woman, had answered the door. So involved was Hammerschmidt in his argument with Ziegler that he hadn't even heard the bell. It was when the woman yelled '*Stasi!*' that he paused, swung round.

Three men had burst into the apartment. One had gone straight into the bedroom. The other two appeared in the living room.

'What the hell is this?' Hammerschmidt growled.

'We're searching this place.' The speaker was the taller of the two men. He was in his late twenties, good-looking, cocky,

164

dressed in the unofficial uniform of the *Stasi* plainclothes: leather jacket, jeans, dazzling white socks, his loafers cut low to expose them to the best advantage. He pointed to the far window. 'Everybody line up over there, and we'll see what we find, eh?'

Hammerschmidt folded his arms. 'Go ahead. The place is enough of a mess already,' he said.

Others were less calm. The woman who had answered the door looked close to a breakdown. Ziegler's fists were clenched. He wore a look of furious indignation.

As for Blessed, he had slipped his tape recorder into his trouser pocket the moment the two policemen entered the room. The tape was still running. He stood nonchalantly with his hands in his pockets, his right one on the wipe button of the machine.

'Over there!' the taller *Stasi* man repeated. 'Any more trouble and we'll take you all in. I wouldn't mind getting some of you bastards on your own, I'll tell you.'

The guests began to shuffle back towards the windows, some muttering and cursing under their breath, but obedient all the same. Habit? Genuine fear? Blessed followed. When he reached the window, he turned and saw that Ziegler had stood his ground. He towered above the *Stasi* man, and the gaze that swept his chosen victim was coldly contemptuous. For the first time, Blessed recognised Otmar Ziegler as a genuinely formidable man of power and understood why he was already one of the most respected opposition leaders. He brought with him an aura of . . . invulnerability was the word that sprang to mind. People wanted to feed off that strength, have it on their side.

'Move,' the *Stasi* man rasped. 'Unless you want to go back inside.'

'Your colleagues already had me inside, Comrade officer,' Ziegler said, 'For almost a week. This is a legal gathering of citizens of the German Democratic Republic. A Friday-night party, a get-together of Berlin's artistic community. Nothing and nobody here to concern you, except . . . '

'Listen, you bastard –'

' . . . Except the presence of an influential foreign journalist. This,' Ziegler continued, indicating Blessed, 'is Mr Michael Blessed of the London *Times*. He's a friend, here to talk about Art. You know Art, Comrade officer? But, instead of getting an article about Art – a field in which our Republic can be justly proud – Mr Blessed gets to witness an act of outrageous police brutality.' He paused. 'You make me sick. And when your superiors see Mr Blessed's article, they'll be even sicker.'

The *Stasi* man swaggered over to Blessed. 'Name,' he demanded.

'Michael Blessed.' Blessed took his hands out of his pockets for long enough to find and hand over both his passport and his NUJ card. 'To confirm this, ring the Foreign Press Club. Or alternatively the London *Bulletin*. Ask to speak to John Yates- Davies, European Editor.'

The *Stasi* man stared at him suspiciously. 'Not *The Times*? Ziegler there said *The Times*. *The Times* is the organ of the English government. What is this *Bulletin* newspaper?'

'It's not a paper, it's a weekly magazine. Like *Time* or *Newsweek*. Or in West Germany, *Der Spiegel*.'

The man looked at Blessed steadily for several moments. Then he turned abruptly to his assistant. 'Let's see their identity cards and residence permits. That's all.' Back to face Blessed, 'This is a routine check. There are provocateurs at work in our major cities, aiming to disrupt the celebrations of our Republic's fortieth anniversary. Outsiders, mostly. West Berliners . . . ' He glanced in the direction of Erika, whose well-finished jacket and expensive jewellery marked her out.

'She's with me, officer,' Blessed said. On cue he felt the tape on his pocket-recorder run to its end, click and be still. This had been a risk, but by Christ it had been perfect.

The *Stasi* men stayed no more than another five minutes. They gave Erika no trouble. Most of their time was taken up being routinely tough with the one non-Berliner in the group, a friend of Hammerschmidt's up on a visit from Dresden, who had to prove that he had a job in the Saxon capital (he did: as a teacher of fine art) and that he hadn't tried to move illegally to East Berlin. But there was an air in all this of saving face, of an ill-judged project abandoned.

All the same, Hammerschmidt looked shaken when the Stasi people had left. Everyone had rediscovered their drinks, bolted them down, and were looking for refills. Blessed felt like doing the same, but it was after eleven-thirty. He had only a twenty-four hour visa, which ran out at midnight. Usually the guards at the Friedrichstrasse, used to Western drunks rolling home late, gave you twenty minutes to half an hour's grace, but with this full tape of subversive material, and the *Stasi* on extra alert against subversives, it might be unwise to challenge fate.

'Erika,' he said. 'We have to go. Even now we might not make it.'

'Get a private cab,' Ziegler suggested, grateful for the distraction of someone else's problems. 'Illegal, of course, but the government's given up trying to control them. They'll be cruising around, looking for hard-currency business. Just tell the driver your problem and he'll get you to the border-crossing on time. So long as you cross his palm with Westmarks or dollars.'

'Thanks. Good to meet you,' Blessed said. 'I'll write this up, I warn you. With a few name-changes to protect the innocent . . .'

Ziegler held his gaze. 'OK. But box clever, eh? For me, it's not so bad to go to jail. I'm an old communist, and I'm known outside this country. They daren't mistreat me too badly. Others here are less privileged. Be careful about quoting them in traceable form.'

'I will. I hope we meet again. You did a good job with that *Stasi* man.'

'Bluff is my strong suit,' Ziegler said simply. 'The authorities' weakness is that they wish to be repressive and to be loved at the same time. They haven't realised this is impossible.'

'Promise a proper interview later this summer?'

'If I'm available.'

Hammerschmidt insisted on escorting them down onto the street. He said it was because he couldn't bear to let go of Erika, but Blessed knew better. The artist's eyes checked the street the moment they emerged. And he knew a private cab when he saw one. Before Blessed or Erika had time to sort out what was going on, Hammerschmidt had flagged down an unmarked Trabant, established that it was available for hire, and agreed a fair price in Westmarks. He sent them on their way with a bellowed 'good luck!' that was probably intended as much for the benefit of any *Stasi* watchers as for his departing guests.

The driver was a schoolteacher from Köpenick who came moonlighting in the city at weekends with his shabby little two-stroke car. He was saving up to build a holiday home for himself and his family, and the *valuta* came in useful. He pushed the car to the limits of its feeble performance.

In exchange for laughably small sum in Westmarks, Blessed and Erika arrived at the westward-bound entrance to the Friedrichstrasse checkpoint at eight past midnight, where they joined a substantial queue of returning tourists and revellers who had also only just made the deadline. They got back through the barrier with no trouble. The final problem to be dealt with tonight was a perfectly normal drunk – who threw up only a couple of feet from Blessed's shoes. The bored *Vopos* patrolling the platform bundled the man onto the westbound S-bahn train when it arrived. Among the tourists, the duty-free smugglers, the separated family members and the other wanderers between two worlds, the drunk collapsed into oblivion. He was still snoring loudly when Blessed and Erika left the train at the Zoo Station. Blessed glanced one last time at the passengers stepping around him. For all they knew, or cared, the man would choke on his vomit. Welcome to the West, he thought – where freedom and indifference are so hard to tell apart.

Later they stopped for a nightcap at HIER – Stefan, the transvestite doorman, now greeted Blessed with a friendly leer and a roll of his heavily-kohled eyes. Blessed told Erika he had the makings of a good article for the *Bulletin*.

'The *Stasi* hasn't been known to mount raids à la Gestapo for a long time,' she remarked with a yawn followed by a gulp of vodka – Gorbatschow, naturally, in memory of their first night together. 'Mostly, they are more subtle, monitoring and entrapping . . . you know.'

'Maybe they're scared.'

'Maybe.' Erika's tumbler was empty. She closed her eyes for a moment. The noise, the crowd, seemed suddenly to have got to her. Reaching over, she brazenly slid one heavily-ringed hand onto Blessed's lap and gave his cock a slow, insistent squeeze. 'No more explanations, no more theories. I want *action* . . . '

Blessed downed his own *Gorbatschow*. 'My dear. Absolutely,' he said with a laugh. 'Let's just hope Stefan lets me out of here, though. With a hard-on like this passing by him, he might just get jealous.'

Erika's hand was still working gently on Blessed in the darkness. He was so hard now that it was sweetly painful, almost unbearably so.

'Stop,' Blessed murmured. 'I'll scarcely be able to walk out that door. Really.'

'I told you, Englishman. Don't worry about Stefan. Any trouble and I'll scratch his eyes out.'

THIRTY-TWO

BLESSED CHECKED THE ORDER of the pages, secured them with a paperclip. Two thousand ironic, Orwellian words about the sinister-farcical raid on Klaus Hammerschmidt's flat two days earlier. To-morrow, Monday, first thing he would take these pages up to the house and use Benno Klarfeld's transmitter to fax the article through to Yates-Davies at the *Bulletin*.

The inevitable cigarette, reward for a job well done. Maybe a beer too, as was his habit at the end of a working day. Frau Smilovici kept his fridge well stocked. Blessed eased the top off the bottle of cold Berliner Kindl, lifted it in silent salute to Hammerschmidt, Ziegler, and to all the rest of them, and drank gratefully.

The lake was crowded with sailing boats and trippers. On the oppo-site bank Blessed could see West Berliners out for a Sunday stroll in the woods, stopping at that nice, old fashioned woodland pub, almost lost among the maze of paths. Klarfeld had taken Blessed over there one evening for beer and *Kasseler Rippchen*, chops of cold smoked ham. Garish lanterns provided light. The garden was filled with laughter, along the with the scent of pine needles, the tang of beer and cigarettes wafting on the breeze – a working man's heaven where any treat was deserved; where precisely those things the doctors said were bad turned out, after all, to be the best.

Blessed felt very much at home. He had three articles for the *Bulletin* under his belt. He had reached halfway point in the general's manuscript. And the *Stasi* had had him right where they needed, that night at Hammerschmidt's flat, but they hadn't known it. Another toast . . . to the memoirs . . .

The phone rang. Aha. Maybe Erika. They had spent a sensational night together on Friday, after the East Berlin party. Such physical ease between a man and a woman as Blessed had rarely experi-enced. Worth waiting thirty-eight years for – even if the whole affair ended tomorrow. Or maybe it was Klarfeld, who was in Düsseldorf, attending a weekend get-together of guidebook publish-ers. He often called to check everything was OK.

170

Blessed put down the beer bottle, picked up the phone. *'Hallo.'*
Nothing.
'Hallo? Wer ist das?'
A click. Street sounds.
'Hallo . . . ' Blessed repeated.
A child's voice. Kids fooling around from a phone booth? Blessed prepared to slam down the phone. Wait a minute. The words were English. Listen . . .
'This is yours, Darlene. Now you have to swap that lolly for one of those coins, see? That's how it's played.'
Blessed recognised the Australian accent, half-knew the voice. 'Lolly' was Aussie slang for a sweet. A little girl's laugh. Another voice:
'That's not fair! That means you get five lollies and I only get one. Daisy Blessed, you are such a cheat . . .'
'Hi, Daisy,' Blessed said with a laugh.
'Darlene, I am not a cheat! This is how the game's played!'
The voice moved off, as if Daisy had moved away from the phone. It was still there, but fainter. 'Daisy? Daisy?' Blessed repeated, an edge of irritation in his voice. 'Stop playing games, darling. Speak to me!'
Fainter, now louder: *'Cheat, cheat, cheat!'*
'Don't do this to your dad, Daisy!'
Click. Silence.
Blessed carefully replaced the phone in its cradle. His heart was beating small explosions. He could feel the artery in his neck pulse as if it were threatening to burst away from him. His body suddenly felt too hot, too uncomfortable for his skin to contain.
Oh Jesus. What the hell is going on?
His first thoughts were, how did they know he was here, specifically now and specifically here? This was a separate connection that bypassed the two lines up in Klarfeld's house. Somehow they knew that this number would get him and only him . . .
Blessed dialled the house in Sydney that had once been his but now belonged to his ex-wife.
He let the number ring for a full minute. He could picture every detail of the scene eleven thousand miles away: the phone on the sill of the big picture window overlooking the Pittwater, where – like here – you could chat and watch the boats, except that there

was also usually a show of lorikeets, kookaburras, warbling Australian magpies. It was winter there, so it might be raining or overcast. Or perhaps one of those clear Australian winter days, when the sky was like thin blue paper and out in the waterside suburbs sounds carried for miles. Voices. The sounds of children playing.

Blessed cursed, killed the connection, thought wildly for a moment. Then he dialled again, another Sydney number, and waited.

A dozen rings. Then a sleepy voice: 'Hello.'

'Bill?'

'Yeah. Speaking. Whoosat? Do you know it's the middle of the bloody night?'

Of course. Ten-hour time-difference. Two or three a.m. in Australia. 'Jesus, Bill. I'm sorry. This is Mike Blessed.'

Slightly cautious but friendly. 'Mike . . . well, gee, what's this about? You OK, mate?'

'Sort of.' Bill Lindop's familiar slow drawl focused Blessed. Lindop had worked with him for three years, lived in the same suburb, they'd socialised. 'Where's Daisy? Do you know where Daisy is?'

'Eh . . . '

'Come on, Bill, your Gail sees Frances practically every day. You're just two streets away . . . is Daisy all right, that's all I want to know. I tried to ring Frances just now, and there was no answer.'

Someone was muttering sleepily in the background.

'Hang on a minute, Mike. I'll have a word with Gail.'

A few moments later, Lindop returned. 'Gail says Frances and wossisname . . . Greg . . . have gone to the Snow. Skiing at Jindabyne, private lodge, no less. With Daisy. Gail says they went five days ago, and they'll be back on Wednesday. I mean, I don't have their number down there . . . '

'What about Darlene? Did she go to the Snow too? You know Darlene?'

'Er, yeah. That's that little red-haired kid of the Callaghans, isn't it?' Another consultation with Gail. She was big in the PTA and the Neighbourhood Watch. She knew everyone's everyday movements, particularly if they had kids. 'Gail says she saw Darlene yesterday. Definitely. Kid seemed fine.'

'Thanks. I don't know how to explain this. I just had reason to . . . you know . . . '

'Yeah, Mike. I sort of get what you're going through. Tough being over there and away from the family. And we all miss you at the rag. Listen, Gail and me still see Frances but we don't, like *socialise* as such, you know . . . '

Blessed had confirmed two things. That Daisy was unharmed, and that the tape of his daughter and her friend – because a tape it must have been – was at least five days old. He wanted to laugh, he wanted to cry. He took a deep breath and said: 'Don't worry, Bill. I miss Daisy, but everything else is fine. I'm in Berlin, on a job.'

'Oh yeah? Cabaret. All that.'

Blessed recalled now that Bill Lindop did, in his lazy way, love to talk. It took him another few minutes to get Bill – wide awake now, poor guy – off the phone.

Blessed, in a fog, returned to the forgotten bottle of beer. It had lost its taste. A half hour or so passed until a measure of calm returned.

So they're on to me, Blessed thought. *And whatever they have in mind, it doesn't include anything so crude or obvious as arresting me, or doing me violence. Oh, they're clever. Daisy. You see they know about Daisy . . . which means they probably know everything there is to know about Michael Blessed . . . every thing he cares about, everything . . .*

Again, Blessed checked his watch, jotted down the time of the call, forced himself to keep listening.

This was the fourth call in twenty-four sleepless hours . . .

'*You can comb Petula if you like. If I can have the top bunk.*'

'*No. That's my bed. You never let me have your bed when I sleep over at your place.*'

'*I want it.*'

'*But it's my house, Darlene!*'

'*I don't care. I want the top bunk.*'

'*All right. I'm going to the Snow next week anyway. With my mum. And Greg . . .*'

Click. Silence.

'Listen, you must want something,' Blessed said. 'Tell me what it is.'

Silence. But still the faint, buzzing rush of an open line.

'Speak to me,' Blessed persisted. 'Who *are* you?'

His grip on the phone tightened. This time there was a human being breathing, live, on the other end of the line. A moment later, someone spoke.

'All right, Michael Blessed, the joke is over. Quite a good one, eh?' The man's voice was mocking, the English almost perfect, but slightly stilted and German-accented. *Choke* for "joke". *Kvite* instead of "quite". 'The wonders of technology make even the humblest home accessible. And our network is worldwide, as we have just proved to you!'

'Listen. If there's something you want, say what it is.'

'Something we *want*? Maybe you think we object to what you are doing? Oh no, Mr Blessed. Please, continue. You are *doing* exactly what we want. But just remember, we are *watching* and *listening*! Goodbye!'

Click. Silence.

A half-hour later, Blessed saw Benno Klarfeld's chauffeur-driven Mercedes coming down the drive. He gave Klarfeld a few minutes, then dialled his private number.

'Benno. Hello.'

'Michael. You don't waste time. I am exactly five and a quarter minutes back from Düsseldorf, and there you are on the line. How are you?'

'I need to talk to you. There's been a development while you've been away.'

'You are OK? What –'

'Nothing violent, nothing physical. Just get yourself down here, will you, and I'll explain.'

Blessed had made notes on the four calls. When Klarfeld arrived, he took him through the calls, citing time and content.

'Surely *Stasi*,' Blessed concluded.

Klarfeld shrugged his shoulders. 'It's possible. Whoever did it obviously used a bugging device to record your daughter playing at home. It's a way of showing their power, you're right. They didn't threaten you or warn you?'

'Nope. The guy acted very satirical. He congratulated me on doing just what they wanted. But he wanted me to know they were listening and watching . . . ' Blessed, pacing the room, caught sight of himself in the long mirror by the door, realised he hadn't combed his hair this morning. 'I mean, don't think I haven't had threatening

174

phone calls before. When I did some work on the links between the Sydney police and the drug barons, I got plenty. I went unlisted and a day later they started again . . . but it didn't really get to me. It was part of the job. Expected.'

'They made threats but did nothing.'

'Yes. But this crowd don't even make threats. It's actually much creepier, in a strange kind of way, you know that?'

'I suppose.' Klarfeld sighed. 'I'm sorry I was away. You must have had a lousy twenty-four hours.' He looked up at Blessed, motioned for him to stop pacing. 'OK, stand still. And tell me, do you want to pull out? You won't suffer financially. I don't think they are after your family, but nevertheless I would understand if you were not prepared to take that risk.'

Blessed, hands in his pockets and rocking on his heels, met Klarfeld's steady, grey-blue eyes. No mixed message there as far as he could see.

'I don't want to give up,' he said eventually. 'I don't even think that's the answer. The *Stasi* had me the other day, you see, and they let me go. Isn't that odd?'

Blessed told Klarfeld about the party, glossing over his relationship with Erika – she became 'someone I met at a gallery opening' – describing his conversation with Hammerschmidt and Ziegler, the story of the taperecorder, the way Ziegler had faced down the *Stasi* when they raided the apartment.

'You know anything about Otmar Ziegler?' Blessed asked Klarfeld.

'Of course. A dissident communist. His book *Shame on You, Comrade Z* was banned in East Germany in the late 1970s but sold very well in the West. Ziegler has always walked a tightrope between the Party and the opposition. Protected, I think, by his high international profile and his contacts in the West. He was one of several protesters arrested about ten days ago, held for some time and then released. That was quite a party you were at. The martyrs' return!'

'I faxed my copy into the *Bulletin* this morning.'

Klarfeld grinned. 'A pro to the last.'

'Life goes on. But the point is, those recordings of my daughter were made at least a week ago. So it can't have been my activities in the East that provoked this. It must definitely have to do with the memoirs. But why reveal that they're watching me and my family?'

'Maybe they're biding their time. The *Stasi* is not stupid. And like the rest of East German society, it's divided between conservatives and radicals.' Klarfeld paused thoughtfully. 'Maybe . . . may-be the group your caller represents – who can tell which side they're on? – is waiting to see how the political situation develops. By putting pressure on you now – on *us*, in fact – they are in a sense staking their claim, softening us up.'

'Well, they sure as hell knocked me off balance,' Blessed admitted. 'You don't know who to trust, that's the thing. And once you're in that situation, they've got you where they want you.'

'Or they think they have,' Klarfeld chided him gently. 'That's to our advantage, don't you see? They *think* they have . . . '

THIRTY-THREE

IN THE CORNER OF THE TAPROOM, two men huddled in bitter argument. It was a big, modern, East Berlin workers' pub. The vertical surfaces were all kitschy tile friezes displaying the joys of proletarian leisure, while the tables and counters were operating-theatre aluminium. The two men had agreed to meet here precisely because this was not their kind of place, because no one would know them. But still they took no risks, and growled and hissed in heavy whispers.

'I don't know how you can say this,' muttered Otmar Ziegler. 'I know I repeat myself, but –'

'I'm just asking you to take a back seat for a few weeks until the situation is clear. You can continue to address demonstrations, to write, but . . . ' Klaus Hammerschmidt took a deep breath. ' . . . But I *can't* support you for the chairmanship. In fact, I have to oppose you. At the committee meeting tonight, I shall present my suspicions, my evidence . . . '

Ziegler slapped the table with his hand. His gaunt features were tight with rage. 'After all these years! You think I work for the *Stasi*!'

'That's not what I said. I said, I *think* the *Stasi* is getting information through you, Otmar! OK say I believe your denial. But what if you're being bugged? Or Magda? Or that girl you see down in Eichwalde once a week? What if they're being used, blackmailed? The fact is, you're the *only* source the leaks can be coming from.'

Ziegler was staring into the middle distance. Only the white skin stretched over his bony knuckles betrayed his continuing anger. 'Impossible,' he hissed. '*Impossible.*'

Hammerschmidt shook his head slowly. His homely, good-natured face was set in an expression of solemn determination. This time the joker of the dissident scene was utterly serious.

'I can't help it, Otmar,' he said softly. 'If only I could! But does the chairmanship matter? Your power is out on the streets, and in your books and articles, not in committee work!'

Ziegler chewed his lip, pulled on his beer. Then he looked at Hammerschmidt calmly and directly.

'All right. If that's what the committee decides, I'll go along with them. The important thing is, we stop the haemorrhaging of information to the *Stasi*. And the only way I can prove it isn't me is if I step back and the leaks continue. Isn't that right?'

'Right.' Hammerschmidt touched his old friend's hand.

Ziegler stood up abruptly. 'It's going to be a long meeting, I think. Can you just give me two minutes to phone Magda? I'll tell her not to wait up. Otherwise she'll worry.'

'Of course. There's a phone in the back, on the way out to the toilets.'

The skinhead gang was waiting for them in the dimly-lit alley alongside the *Staatsoper*, through which tourists and East Berliners alike might take a shortcut through to the Nikolaiviertel.

Ziegler swivelled round to check for a way of flight – but there were even more of them coming up behind from the direction of Unter den Linden: Shorn heads like penitents, cutoff jeans, steel-capped boots and vicious chains; close up, you could see the tattooed swastikas on the kids' knuckles and foreheads, the sick messages of hate burned into young, healthy flesh. Nine, ten of them altogether – all big boys, broad and muscular.

The really terrifying thing was their silence. No threats, no insults. No hint of the flimsy, improvised *casus belli* that usually provides an excuse, however flimsy, for a street attack . . . They say to fear a pack of wild dogs not when they bark or howl but when they advance precisely like this . . . *in the concentrated, silent way of the predator* . . .

Within moments, the attackers sprang at them. Several of them pushed Ziegler against the wall, started pummelling and kicking him. He was taller than any of them, but thin and almost forty years their senior.

At least Ziegler managed to stay on his feet for a while Hammerschmidt fared far worse. Chunkily-built but none too fit, the painter also had six of them against his one. Almost immediately, he doubled up from an initial boot in the groin. As he crumpled, a wheezing groan echoed along the cobbled alleyway. Fists, knees, kicks drove him to the hard ground within moments. Hammersch-

178

midt lay there writhing, his hair and face already a mass of blood. Briefly he managed to mouth, in a helpless voice slewed through broken teeth: 'Ot-maarrr . . . '

Then a strange thing happened: The biggest of the skinheads, the one who had been concentrating on Hammerschmidt, suddenly bellowed: "ENOUGH!". The attack on Ziegler ceased.

But in the same moment, the skinhead leader reached down with one meaty hand, his face twisted in a grimace of hatred, and grabbed the motionless Hammerschmidt by his blood-matted hair. He hauled the head up until it was a good twelve inches off the ground – and then, just as abruptly, he let it drop . . .

The shell of Hammerschmidt's cranium hit the unyielding cobbles with a reverberating, liquid crack.

Someone must have called the cops. They came quickly, from the police station on the corner of Wallstrasse and Domstrasse. Many witnesses described how the two victims were found a few minutes later.

Ziegler, the tall man who had mocked so much, written such clever, satirical books was still crouched by the wall with his hands over his head, obviously catatonic with terror. Hammerschmidt, the bold, dissident artist, just lay still, chillingly still on those slimy cobbles, face up and limp arms outstretched. An unlucky bather floating home on a tide of his own blood.

THIRTY-FOUR

'OF COURSE I'VE TRIED,' Blessed said. 'There's no one at Ziegler's house. I managed to speak to Hammerschmidt's ex-wife – or one of them, I should say. He's still in a coma. The chances of his ever coming out of it are narrowing by the day.'

'Oh shit, Mike, he was a good guy.' Erika reached over and retrieved the wine bottle from the bedside table, topped up both their glasses. I don't know Ziegler. I don't care about him. But Klaus was something special.'

'I don't believe those kids attacked them by chance.'

She sighed. 'Maybe you're right.'

'What if it has something to do with what happened at the party? When the *Stasi* raided Hammerschmidt's flat . . . I mean, what if it has to do with *me*?'

Erika started. 'You? Why you? You wrote a funny article, that's all.'

'I don't know why me.' Even Blessed knew it sounded pretty unconvincing. Erika was on him like a hawk that's spotted movement.

'Don't give me that. Why should you be so afraid? Listen, what are you *really* up to in Berlin, Mike?'

'I told you, it's a translating assignment.'

'Yes? Over there in your boathouse beside the lake. You tell me all about it, but have I ever visited? I introduce you to people. Do you do me the same favour? No!'

Blessed tensed. He had brought a bottle of light red from Baden with him tonight. Expensive but delicious. He gulped some down hard, pulled back. Why was he so suspicious? Erika had never asked him the details of what he was doing. No Mata Hari pillow-interrogations. Only now, when she was worried and confused, had the subject surfaced. And in any case, he been the one to bring it up.

'It's confidential,' Blessed said. 'The publisher doesn't want anyone to know about it, that's all. You'll see why when it's published. And that'll be in the none-too-distant future.'

They lay in silence for some time, barely touching. The shock of the all-but-death of Klaus Hammerschmidt had taken the wildness from their sexual relationship. Tonight their lovemaking had been gentle, an exchange of comfort. For the first time in months, Blessed had remembered what it is to be married, where sex is a lot, but not everything. Even though he and Erika still saw each other only twice a week, there was a regularity, a predictability. The mutual territory seemed to have been mapped out, established. He had stopped asking questions now. She had never really asked any in the first place . . .

'I'm sorry I got angry with you,' Erika said softly. 'It's only that the world seems suddenly so terrible. Whatever the reason why those skinheads attacked Hammerschmidt and Ziegler, the world is a terrible place tonight. So, I am tired. For once I am tired.'

Blessed had never known her look so vulnerable, so sad. Not even when she had been so hurt by the split with Wolfgang. At that moment, he wanted to tell her about everything: the general's memoirs, the watchers, the horror of the tapes played over the phone. But he kept his silence. He just took Erika in his arms and held her, until it was time to get up and go home.

THIRTY-FIVE

THE PHONE CALL CAME at around four that Friday afternoon, at the boathouse. The weather had changed, and it was raining outside. Blessed was back in a light sweater and jeans.

'Yes.'

'Mike.'

'Rock! Nice surprise.'

'Yeah. Listen, I have to be quick. I'm in Frankfurt, and I'm calling between meetings. How would you like some visitors this weekend?'

'Plural?'

'Daphne's with me on this trip. Listen, we thought we'd hop on a plane, come and see brother Mike . . . and old Saint Benno.'

'Well, that's great. I'm working my ass off, but maybe it wouldn't be a bad idea to take a break. Benno's here, as it happens. He got back from Paris this morning.'

'I'll get my office to book us into Kempinski's or wherever. You have a word with Klarfeld, tell him he's coming out for dinner tomorrow night with us and that's definite. Don't take no for an answer. Daff will kill me if she doesn't get to see Benno after all these years.' Rockwell laughed knowingly. 'Anyway, you never know when the real estate in Berlin and Eastern Europe might open up. You have to think ahead. It might do no harm to pick that cunning bastard Klarfeld's brains, if he'll allow it . . . '

'Why bother with dinner? Why not just call the entire weekend a meeting?'

No response to that gibe. Rockwell joked about everything, except business. 'Right. Now, I gotta go. We'll give you a call when we arrive tomorrow, OK? Bye, Mike.'

After Rockwell had hung up, Blessed rang Klarfeld's personal number up at the house.

'I see,' Klarfeld said when he heard the news. 'I see . . . '

Blessed was surprised at the vagueness of the man's response. 'Rockwell thought you'd be pleased. So did I, to be honest.'

182

Klarfeld was silent for one more moment. 'I am pleased. Extraordinarily pleased. But also surprised – and I thought nothing would ever surprise me again . . . you realise how long it is since I last saw your sister?'

'So you're OK about our getting together?'

'There are some things . . . dinner is definite, but to make the daytime free I must make some arrangements. How are the general's memoirs?'

'Fine. Ahead of schedule, in fact. He's just describing Minister Mielke's hunting-lodge.'

'Let's take the whole day off tomorrow, OK?' Klarfeld was easy now, if still slightly distracted, mentally re-arranging some complicated schedule as he spoke. He laughed. 'Come on, Mr Blessed. Let's show these people the town. The general can wait!'

The relationships were defined as soon as the four of them met in the lobby of the Bristol-Kempinski. For Rockwell from Klarfeld, a stiff handshake; for Daphne an embrace. Talk of how good she looked, how wonderful to see her again.

Then the surprise – which Klarfeld had kept even from Blessed. They emerged from the hotel, were led around the corner into the Fasanenstrasse, and there a large Mercedes limousine was waiting. Soon they were settled in the back with a chilled bottle of French champagne, heading off on a grand tour of West Berlin, courtesy of Klarfeld. "Saint Benno" was out to prove he was no ascetic.

All the same, it was not an uncomplicated day. Klarfeld was punctiliously polite, but clearly it was only Daphne he was interested in: talking to her, showing her round the city she had not seen for more than thirty years.

In a subtle, never-stated way, Blessed was left to be Rockwell's companion. Rockwell seemed to accept this. There was a self-effacing, almost complaisant quality to Blessed's brother-in-law that rarely showed itself.

They stopped at the Brandenburg Gate, then at the viewing platform on the Potsdamer Platz, criss-crossing the Tiergarten before heading out to the border at Dreilinden. There they were treated to the bizarre sight of a camping site ground on the former Berlin Autobahn. Tents and caravans spread across the decaying concrete slabs of what had once been one of the busiest highways in Europe.

183

Lunch was at an open-air restaurant in the Grunewald. Then the limousine took them to the landing-stage opposite the Pfaueninsel, the 'Peacock Island'. From here they took the short boat trip to this strange and beautiful island, shaped like the flamboyant bird, where the 18th-century Prussian kings had built themselves gardens and eccentric pleasure-palaces. Here, for an hour or an afternoon, the visitors could wander, forget there was a Wall, and dream themselves back to that time . . . until they saw the barbed wire out on the lake; the warning signs and patrol boats announcing where Prussian monarchs' fantasy ended and the German Democratic Republic began.

Daphne was in wonderful form, laughing and joking like a teenager. At one point, walking along a sandy lakeside track on the Pfaueninsel, she flung one arm around Klarfeld's shoulder, one around Rockwell's, and posed like an old-fashioned Hollywood vamp.

'At last!' she proclaimed. 'The two most important men in my life meet! Can you believe it?' She made a face at Blessed, who was preparing to take a photograph. 'I know there are really three, Mike, including you.'

Rockwell grinned in his easy way. Klarfeld also, Blessed realised, looked happy – as opposed to amused, or wryly content with things, or any of the other approximations of happiness which had seemed to be the best that Klarfeld could manage. There was a spring in his step.

And so there was the photograph, with the pines and the blue waters of the lake behind them, Rockwell with his Aquascutum raincoat over his arm, Daphne looking forty-five going on twenty in a suede jacket and jeans, Klarfeld beaming impishly to camera, the years and the millions fallen away to reveal the boy beneath.

Just a few minutes later, Blessed saw the other side of Klarfeld. They had returned to the landing-stage. Daphne was in the ladies' room of the ferry office, Klarfeld had gone to fetch some souvenirs she had asked for. Blessed and Rockwell were standing talking about nothing special when, for some reason, Blessed felt an urge to turn round. Klarfeld had returned and was standing ten feet or so behind them, levelling a gaze at Rockwell's back: a cold-eyed, measuring stare.

184

He looked away immediately, caught out. Rockwell, for his part, couldn't have noticed. Moments later, Daphne re-emerged. The ferry came. They headed back towards the far bank with the other tourists and made their way over to the waiting limousine.

'Back to the city,' Klarfeld announced, once more the jolly tour-guide. 'To the Charlottenburg Palace, and then change for dinner. We must stay fit, so before we eat there will be a compulsory stroll through the Tiergarten . . . '

Rockwell looked around. Klarfeld and Daphne were fifty yards behind, supposedly looking at trees, deep in conversation.

'Well, it's great for her,' he said. 'I mean, I work all the time, don't usually take her on business trips. This is very special. A chance to talk about the past . . . '

Blessed nodded. 'Saint Benno looks like he's won a major prize too.'

'You getting on well?' Rockwell said, moving ahead between the rows of chestnut trees. Before the war, the chestnuts in the Tiergarten, planted on the order of the old Prussian kings, had been famous for their age; during the hungry, cold times of the late 1940s, most had been cut down for firewood, and their replacements were only just starting to reach a respectable size. 'You and Benno get along, I mean?'

'Oh, yes. When I see him, that is. He's away a lot on business. Mostly I'm working.'

'No diversions?' Rockwell laughed. 'I thought this town was full of diversions . . . most of them blonde . . . '

It was an invitation for Blessed to talk, and he was inclined to take his brother-in-law up on it. He had never felt able to discuss Erika with Klarfeld.

'Brunette, actually,' he confessed. 'Her name's Erika. I met her on the train coming over. We see each other a couple of times a week. Once she took me over to East Berlin. To a dissident party.'

'Small "p"?'

'Yeah. Not like "Communist Party", if that's what you're getting at.'

Rockwell walked on a little further. 'Took you East, did she? Know what she was doing?'

'It was the party where we were shaken down by the *Stasi*. I wrote an article for the *Bulletin* about it, faxed you and Daff a copy.'

185

'Right. Daff mentioned it. I was away on a trip, by the time I got back it had disappeared. I guess Josh stole it for his personal archive.'

'It doesn't matter. The point is what happened later. Two of the people I met at the party were attacked in the street in East Berlin. One is still in a coma. To some people, the attack had *Stasi* written all over it.'

'Now I begin to understand. Sounds . . . interesting.'

They walked on a little further. The wind had changed direction. There was a faint smell of brown-coal pollution drifting over from the East.

'*Stasi*, you reckon? Fuck the *Stasi*,' Rockwell hissed then. Have you ever considered Saint Benno as the guy behind it all?'

'*Benno*?'

'Sure. You were happily ensconced in the English countryside, letting your wounds heal, generally getting your shit together. He called up, brought you here, hooked you into this scheme of his. He's got you under his roof. He might have plans you don't know about. In fact, he might – just might – be setting you up.'

'Listen, there are things I don't know about Klarfeld, but look at him with Daphne, for Christ's sake. Think what he owes our family – '

'You get cynical as you get older, Mike. You realise that people slice their loyalties into bits and ration them – some to this cause, that person, some to another . . . I'm sure Klarfeld's affection for Daff and you is genuine. But if his long-term interests are not compatible with yours – I might say, ours – then who knows what he'll do – is already doing . . . '

'This is a hell of a lecture, Rock. On no evidence, what's more.'

Rockwell nodded. 'Maybe I'm wrong about Klarfeld. But . . . hell, Mike, I'm going to tell you something.' He looked round as if to check that Daphne and Klarfeld were still out of ear-shot. 'OK, you know I did a stint in Thailand? Back in the Sixties.'

'Yes, of course. The Peace Corps.'

'That was the start. Later . . . listen, I haven't told this to too many people . . . later I worked for the CIA in Bangkok. Regular trips to Kuala Lumpur and Singapore.'

'Singapore was where you met Daff. She was a secretary at the British High Commission.'

186

'Correct. I was acting as a courier, taking stuff from my boss to hers.'

'I don't much like the sound of this. Anyway, and?'

'I was young, looking for thrills. But, of course, I kissed the company goodbye when I wed your sister. Too weird. No job for a family man. So, we returned to the US. I got into real estate law. The rest, as they say, is history. But you get an instinct, and it never leaves you. That's why I've been worried about Benno Klarfeld, and this trip confirms it. He's playing both sides against the middle, believe me.'

'Oh yes? You're sure you've left the Company?' Blessed asked. He was smiling, but he was only half-joking, and Rockwell knew it.

'Mike, it's like having been to Harvard or Oxford. Wherever you go, you keep meeting fellow-graduates. And you kind of keep learning, picking up this tidbit and that . . . '

'All right. Well, naturally I've thought about Klarfeld. And the thing is, what does he have to gain? There's usually a fairly obvious angle, but I can't see one here. He's rich. He's not what I'd call a happy man in the conventional sense, but he's found some kind of way of living that suits him. Why would he play games?'

Rockwell took Blessed's arm. Klarfeld and Daphne were waving, indicating they would be coming over in a moment. He started talking quickly, urgently. 'I don't know why. But I'll tell you, with the Cold War just a fading memory, we could find ourselves in a new era that'll be more hazardous than ever. Much, much more so. I told you, I talk to people from the intelligence-gathering community. I'm thinking of making investments, and they know the inside track. Their feeling is, the Russians can't hold on to their empire. Eastern Europe is up for grabs. This means big opportunities, big risks, with the emphasis on the risks.'

Blessed glanced at Rockwell. His brother-in-law's normally relaxed features were grim. He was staring into the middle distance with something close to bitterness.

'You OK, Rock?'

'Sure. Sure.' Rockwell was watching Daphne and Klarfeld's approach. 'I have a lot on my mind. 1989 is shaping up to be a year of surprises – not all of them necessarily nice ones. And I guess I'm just tired. I'm looking forward to taking a week or two off this

187

summer. Just hang around the house. Take the boat out. Forget the whole damned thing.'

'I never thought I'd hear *you* of all people talk like that. You're the original workaholic.'

'Right. But I'm fifty, Mike, and I'm starting to feel it. One day maybe I'll tell you all about my life. Not just the easy bits but the hard bits as well.'

'I'll hold you to that.'

'Fine. And don't forget, you do the right thing with that Diane Kelly. She is coming, isn't she? Well, I'll tell you, she's the only human being in this town over the next few weeks you're going to be able to trust. That's my last piece of free advice to you, Mike.' Rockwell smiled briefly in his old, sardonic way. 'You want any more counselling, I charge by the hour.'

Daphne and Klarfeld swept towards them. 'We've been catching up on more than thirty years of history,' Daphne said to Rockwell. 'This is an awful bore for you and Mike, darling. But it's just one day in so long . . . and now we're with you again, aren't we, Benno?'

'Of course.' Klarfeld made a little bow. 'At your disposal. Our table is for eight o'clock, and we have precisely fifteen minutes to make it to the restaurant.'

The meal, German cooking at the Ax Bax with a celebrity crowd, was not important. What was evidently important was that Klarfeld and Daphne were together again. Blessed enjoyed their spark. Everyone made an attempt to draw Rockwell into the fun, but without success, even after they got onto the third bottle of wine. Oh, he talked. He cross-questioned Klarfeld about investment prospects hereabouts, cracked a joke or two, but he was on auto-pilot it seemed, going through the motions. Beneath the social facade Blessed sensed a quality that was solemn, even elegiac.

A new Daphne. A new Benno Klarfeld. And certainly a new Rockwell.

As Rockwell had so truly said, 1989 was turning into a year of surprises.

THIRTY-SIX

BLESSED WAS DOING some interviews in the meanest part of Kreuzberg 36, close to the Wall. It was early evening and still warm, even for August. He'd worked on the memoirs until lunchtime, arriving here around three for his investigation into the hearts and minds of the Kreuzberg *Szene*. For four hours he had been wandering its notorious demi-monde of squatters, anarchists and all-round alternative humans. So far, so bad . . .

The kid standing opposite him in the centre of this one-room hovel was about nineteen, wearing a sleeveless denim jacket and cut-off T-shirt to show his tattooed muscles. His hair was shaved at the sides, knotted into a pigtail at the back. His face was scarred from a recent fight. He was taking swigs from a bottle of beer that he held in his left hand. In his right he held a six-inch knife. It was pointed at Blessed.

'You got cash, credit cards?' the boy repeated, as if it was a catechism, a mantra, and jabbed the knife dramatically in Blessed's direction. Blessed recognised the kind of gesture that was certainly theatrical but, unfortunately, not necessarily fake. 'Or you leave 'em at home when you come slumming?'

The girl was completely shaven-skulled. She had a tiny death's-head printed in the centre of her forehead, like a third eye. She was even younger than the boy with the knife, pale, with bad skin. She wore a crucifix at her throat.

'*Ach*, Johnnie, siddown. Stop this shit,' she said in a bored voice. She returned her attention to Blessed. 'Fifty marks.'

'I don't pay for interviews.'

She shrugged. The boy, very drunk, was still waving his knife, but now in a less specific way.

During the stand-off, Blessed looked around. The room was damp, peeling wallpaper, nothing in the way of decoration. There was a bed in the corner, foetid and rank. The corridor of the abandoned block provided no relief, as he had found on the way in. It was paved in faeces and urine.

189

'Why did you come to Berlin? It's a simple question. No pressure.'

She pointed to Johnnie, who had now sat down on the floor and was morosely drinking his beer, staring at Blessed as if he was a not especially interesting insect.

'He didn't want to go to the *Bundeswehr*. You know, to the army.'

'Army, army! *Heil!*' Johnnie bellowed. His right arm shot up in a parody of a Nazi salute. He laughed, in a kind of convulsive, damp-mouthed way that was close to sobbing.

'That's not a bad reason. Where do you come from?'

She looked him suspiciously. 'Why do you want to know that? Are you a journalist or a social worker? Or a cop?'

'A journalist.' Blessed sighed, showing her his press card. Her expression didn't change. He knew he shouldn't but he fished a twenty-mark note out of his pocket. 'Here. Just get yourself and Johnnie something to eat. Now, where are you from?'

'Osnabrück.'

'You come from Osnabrück?'

'Sure.'

Catholic, middle Germany. The equivalent of Chipping Norton, or Dubuque. Blessed wrote it down. He gestured to indicate the state of the decaying apartment block they were in. 'This is a terrible place to live.'

'You reckon, yeah. Ever been to Osnabrück?'

Blessed shook his head. And suddenly he'd had enough. He'd visited a couple of other squatter communes, one organised, political, the other just a bunch of kids who didn't earn enough to get decent flats. He'd thought twice about it when one of the previous crowd had mentioned this building, the worst of the lot, but he'd chanced his arm and come across Johnnie and . . . he still didn't know what to call her.

'What's your name?' Blessed asked gently. 'Just . . . whatever it is that you like to be called, OK?'

'Doll,' she said in English, and smiled, showing surprisingly even teeth. 'Broken doll.'

Johnnie threw his empty beer-bottle. It smashed against the wall. He started to struggle to his feet, mumbling threats. Blessed's mind was made up. He backed out of the room and headed for the stairs.

Once outside in the street, Blessed took a few breaths of what passed for fresh air, lit a cigarette. A bunch of Arab-looking kids were kicking a ball against the wall of the block where Johnnie and

Doll lived. Opposite, an old lady sat out on her balcony, facing west into the warmth of the setting sun. She was wearing a cotton dress and she had it hitched up above her knees. Her legs were parted, exposing dough-white thighs to the sun in what might have been thought a shameless fashion, but her beatific smile disarmed the world. She was just an animal seeking comfort.

Blessed smiled to himself. Someone had sprayed one of the *Autonomen* anarchists' slogans on the wall below her: LEGAL, IL-LEGAL, SCHEISSEGAL! — roughly translatable as 'Legit, non-legit, who gives a shit!'. He ducked past the kids, made it to the corner. From there he set off briskly westward, careful to steer round the fizzing mounds of dogshit that were a feature of dog-loving but lac-kadaisical Kreuzberg 61. He needed a drink, but he was tired of the *Szene*, its anger and its suspicions, its forms of understandable but exhausting madness. Kreuzberg was still a working-class district, he thought. Surely there would be somewhere where you could have a quiet beer and mind your own business, where your haircut and the shoes you wore weren't judged as a punishable political statement?

There was. A tacky-looking but pretty clean place a couple of streets away, clientele an acceptable mixture of the local proletariat and students. A gruff, sharp-tongued barman of the typical Berlin *Kneipe* sort. Noisy pinball machines and a huge, blaring television. Blessed couldn't hear himself think, but then again, he didn't necessarily want to.

The barman was talking to one of his regulars. '*Die da drüben,*' he was saying – 'them over there', meaning on the other side of the Wall – 'they're going crazy, and I don't blame them. Out in the streets. Hammering the cops. Something's got to give. That Ho-necker's got nothing to offer. Hell, they watch our TV. That's the difference between East Germany and Russia or Bulgaria or wher-ever. They want to know, they tune in to our TV. Then they know what's really going on, and they know that what their own govern-ment says is full of shit . . . '

The barman looked up. On cue, the giant TV had erupted into the signature tune and titles for the evening news. Blessed turned so he could see. Sure enough, footage of crowds filling a square in Leip-zig, East Germany's radical second city. Speakers on improvised platforms. Individuals struggling with police in riot gear. Plain-clothes *Stasi* snatching supposed ringleaders.

191

The voiceover came in:

'Today, more demonstrations in the GDR, the biggest in Leipzig, where twenty thousand protested against continued emigration restrictions. There were also calls for free elections. Elsewhere in the city, some opposition groups agreed to combine into an umbrella group under the name "Democratic Action". A well-known dissident writer, Otmar Ziegler, was elected its first Chairman. Ten days ago, Ziegler survived an apparently random skinhead attack in which his fellow-dissident, Klaus Hammerschmidt, was beaten into a coma. Hammerschmidt is not expected to recover, and sources here say that only political considerations have caused the East German authorities to keep him on a life-support machine. Ziegler fights on, however. After today's vote, he becomes the most important single figure in the growing opposition to the Honecker régime . . . '

Cut to a room. Bad videotape. People shuffling around, unused to being filmed. Then close-up of a gaunt, bespectacled face, still puffy and bruised. Pull away. He had his arm in a sling. Yes, that was Ziegler all right, showing evidence of the injuries inflicted during that mysterious attack. But alive. Unlike the amiable, and unlucky, Klaus Hammerschmidt. And talking and talking to camera – about justice and change and renewal, about a middle way between untrammelled capitalism and unreconstructed Stalinism – surrounded by grave, respectful faces.

Ziegler. A hero with the scars to prove it.

Blessed gulped down his beer, ordered another. He had notes at home! No question, every paper was going to be trying to get an interview with Ziegler tonight, frantically gathering material for the inevitable profiles. Well, Blessed – by coincidence or otherwise – had an entire tape-recording of material, only a fraction of which he had used for the article on the *Stasi* raid the previous month. After all, at that time Ziegler had been just one dissident among many.

It was back to the boathouse now, to work through the night if necessary.

He and his tape recorder had captured Otmar Ziegler unguarded and unadorned, before Ziegler made the political big-time. He had interviewed him the way no one else would get him again. And tomorrow Yates-Davies and the Bulletin would have him too.

Setup or no setup, Blessed thought wryly, these were rich pickings.

THIRTY-SEVEN

GRANIT THANKED THE AIDE who had brought him the video cassette, dismissed him from the room.

The big man paced his office restlessly, like a caged animal. Or an expectant parent. Then he sighed, went over to the video machine, inserted the cassette the aide had delivered. He punched the play button on the remote, waited for the high-definition twenty-four-inch screen to come to life.

Granit smiled as he watched a tape of Otmar Ziegler *alias* Banana going through his well-rehearsed liberal-reformist spiel at the Leipzig meeting. Terrific. Christ, the *Stasi* didn't even need to put spy-cameras in these goddamned places these days: the Western news cameramen were there to record it all for them.

'This is a historic opportunity,' Banana was saying. 'The best of the East, the best of the West. These things are within our grasp! And there are those, even in the government and the Party who know that the distortions of Stalinism must be corrected, who realise that this opportunity cannot be ignored . . . '

Click. Very nice. Absolutely as planned. And why not? The Kinder had killed to get Banana where he was now, and he'd better have his role word-perfect, or everyone else in the tribe would want to know why not.

Granit tossed the remote onto the desk. He wandered over to the cupboard in the corner of his office, fished out a bottle of Jack Daniels and poured himself a generous measure of the precious Tennessee whiskey. It was time for a small celebration. Minister Mielke had given him everything he wanted. Bästli was co-operating beautifully. Even Blessed was proceeding just as programmed, girl or no girl. Now Banana had pulled off the ultimate confidence-trick.

He raised the tumbler in one meaty fist. *Prost Banana alias Ziegler. Good for you!*

Granit took a hefty sip of whiskey, savoured this moment of triumph, his placing of the first really crucial piece into position on the chess-board of the future.

193

THIRTY-EIGHT

THEY HAD BEEN OUT for a Turkish kebab dinner, gone drinking in the usual Kreuzberg hangouts. Then back to Erika's flat, for Gorbatschow and what would inevitably follow.

Blessed broached his news before they were even through the door.

'I'm going to be a part-time tourist guide for a couple of days,' he announced.

Erika, slightly unsteady with drink, managed to slip her key into the lock and turn it. 'Oh yes,' she said, pushing open the door. 'More visitors?'

Blessed followed her into the living room, flopped on the sofa. 'An American. A university teacher. I met her at my nephew's graduation. She told me she was coming over to Europe for a while and said she might drop by.' He shrugged. 'Well, I got a card from her today. She's coming to Berlin for the weekend. I'm going to take Saturday off to show her around.'

Erika smiled. 'Don't worry. I don't want to meet her.'

'It's not –'

'I don't care if it is. Remember? We agreed about that. In any case, I already have a full diary over the weekend.'

Erika turned on her heel, disappeared into the kitchen. There was soon the familiar, homely snarl of the coffee-grinder, followed by the clink of bottle and glass.

'I tried to get an interview with Ziegler today,' he called through from the living room. 'He's very busy, but we've pencilled in a time next week. Want to come along?'

Back with the Gorbatschow, Erika frowned. 'Maybe. When?'

'Tuesday around six. At the church in the Nikolaiviertel where Democratic Action first started out. We could go out afterwards. I'll take you to the Palast-Hotel and fill you up with Crimean champagne. We can watch the call-girls while the *Stasi* look through their peepholes and watch us.'

'What peepholes? Erika frowned. 'Do they have peepholes?'

194

Too late, Blessed remembered he had read about the peepholes existing in the bar of the Palast-Hotel in the general's memoirs.

'That's what they say,' he answered quickly. 'That's the gossip.'

Erika shrugged. 'Well, I'm working in Charlottenburg until five. I was going to see a film, but I can do that another night.'

'Take your time. Meet me at the church. Before, if you can make it. Otherwise, if you don't mind waiting . . . '

'No. I don't mind at all.' She tossed her hair, took a big gulp of vodka. 'There will be interesting people to talk to, I'm sure.'

THIRTY-NINE

'I'M NEARLY THERE, Diane.' Blessed said. 'Only forty manuscript pages to go. And two weeks ahead of schedule.'

'Plus you've published five articles, with another to come. Congratulations. If you were a student of mine, you'd be loaded down with honours.'

'If I were a student of yours, I wouldn't have the nerve to invite you out in the first place.'

Diane Kelly laughed, took a sip of coffee. She had arrived in Berlin late the previous night, and Blessed had joined her for breakfast at her hotel, a homely little establishment off the Kurfürstenstrasse. His impressions were mixed. Away from the States, Diane was every bit as warm and funny – and even more desirable, in designer jeans and a Mexican blouse, but a little more reticent. Perhaps she just was eager not to appear new-world-naive, untutored in European ways.

'Is it all right to go to the East?' she said. 'I mean . . . '

'Fine. I'm back and forth all the time, when I'm not working on the manuscript.'

'No more signs of . . . anyone?'

'Listen, I'm still in one piece . . . '

'OK, OK. Just checking. Take me through the Iron Curtain, please.'

'Absolutely. The plan is, first we glance at the bits in the middle . . . '

'Oh. I know that's where everybody goes. The old centre of Berlin. This is our only full day together. So let's avoid the tourist traps, please, Mike.'

'Ha! One or two of those. But then out on the S-bahn to the Müggelsee lake. It's pretty out there, one of the places where all the ordinary East Berliners go at weekends to relax. Simple, of course, with little stands where you can get an old-fashioned sausage and a bag of *pommes frites*, you know –'

'French fries. In English-type English, "chips". See, I'm already becoming accustomed to the local usages.'

It was peak season for tourists, the twenty-ninth anniversary of the building of the Wall. The wait at the Friedrichstrasse checkpoint was long and stifling. Once through, they walked to the 'Museum Island', crossed the bridge over the Kupfergraben, strolled into the turn-of-the-century Pergamon Museum to snatch a glance at the famous Pergamon Altar, dedicated to Zeus and Athena almost two hundred years before Christ and – apart from the Elgin Marbles in London – one of the most spectacular examples of archaeological theft in Europe.

And they talked. Diane enthusiastically described her research plans. By Christmas she should be ready to plough on with her novel.

'I've never had all this time just to write,' Diane said. 'How does it feel? How do you organise yourself? I guess I'll get a laptop word processor just like yours. They're not hard to deal with, are they?'

'No. Even the manuals are in English-English – as opposed to the Japanese version – these days.'

'Any problems, I'll call you.'

Diane wanted know all about his laptop and his working methods. He knew it was a little ego-trip, but it made him feel good. *She* made him feel good.

And he told her about Benno, about his own father, his fascination with Berlin. The memoirs he continued to skate over. They were controversial, political, was all he said.

At midday they took the S-bahn out to the Müggelsee. They lunched late, in an almost-deserted garden restaurant, on sausage and spicy *Puszta-Salat* and warm East German beer. From there they walked along the side of the lake, grateful for the cooling breeze off the water, to the bathing beach. They saw relatively few other pleasure-seekers. In the GDR there was full employment, as its government so keenly wanted you to know, and in the GDR its citizens worked regular hours, with everything in its place. Only here and there did they spot occasional hedonists: families on their summer holidays, schoolchildren out bathing and walking, even a few who looked as though they *never* had anything to do except please themselves.

197

They walked right round to the smaller lake, the Kleiner Müggel-see, stopped for more refreshments. It would be dusk soon. Before returning to West Berlin for dinner, Blessed wanted to take Diane on a final wander through the Berlin Municipal Forest, picking up the westbound S-bahn back at Rahnsdorf station, in the middle of the woods.

Just as they left the inhabited places behind, just as they began to make their way through the woods towards Rahnsdorf, they found the skinheads waiting for them.

There were six of them, loosely grouped about twenty yards ahead, not exactly blocking the path but making it narrow, hardly wide enough for a child to pass. Two were smoking cigarettes, each standing with his free hand jammed in his jeans pockets. The big-gest, about nineteen, six feet three and at least fourteen stone, was one of the smokers. At first, as Blessed and Diane approached, he seemed self-absorbed, paying no attention at all. Then, when they were within ten yards or so, he dropped his half-smoked cigarette and crushed it under his boot-heel in the soft sand. The movement worked like a signal.

Blessed quickly glanced behind. Two more skinheads coming up to the rear, cutting off his and Diane's retreat. They had no choice but to keep going, rely on cunning, speed, and – dammit – *luck*.

'*Prepare to run like hell*,' he whispered to Diane, giving her a squeeze on the arm.

'OK.' Her voice was steady.

They drew level.

'*Wessis*,' the big one growled. He had yellowish slits for eyes. On his forearm he had a tattoo of a scorpion striking. '*Scheiss-Wessis*. West-shit.'

Hammerschmidt. Blessed kept thinking of poor Hammerschmidt, still in a coma in hospital. He saw in his mind's eye the news footage of Ziegler, still scarred and bandaged. He eased Diane through ahead of him.

The big skinhead licked his lips. 'Money. *Valuta*. West-money . . . '

'*Run!*' Blessed hissed.

But they stood no chance. The big one grabbed his arm as he passed, like a kid with a stick of candy. Held it in one huge hand and spun Blessed round to face him. Blessed saw a gleaming pink forehead coming to meet his own face as the skinhead leader butted

198

him like a bull. Everything slipped out of focus, and within moments he was face-down on the ground, his mouth eating sand. He felt several of them pile on top of him, crushing him down further into the earth, all yelling and whooping, continuing to pummel him. He felt hands searching his jacket, his trouser pockets, and all the time that snarling, chanting voice: '*Scheiss-Wessi! Scheiss-Wessi!*'.

Blessed felt his nostrils and mouth filling up with fine sand, making breathing impossible. The veins in his head threatened to explode, and as the oxygen flow to his brain slowed down, reality became thin and dark, and the voices and the blows mercifully but also dangerously detached. With this unshiftable ton of weight on top of him, there was nothing Blessed could do.

He found himself expecting to die.

Blessed came back slowly. It took a moment or two until he realised that he could breathe at all, that the pressure had gone. He broke into a spasm of coughing – blood, sand and spit. He began choking on his saliva.

Oh dear God. Diane . . .

Blessed rolled over into his side, raised himself onto one elbow. At first he could see nothing. Then he shook the sand from his eyes and saw a figure looming above him, looking down.

'Bastard,' he mumbled, too weak to fend off the assailant.

But the figure knelt down beside him and started brushing sand from his eyes, nose, mouth, hair – with gentle fingers.

'Are you all right? Oh God, Mike. There were so many of them.'

Diane's hair was awry, her make-up smudged, but she seemed unhurt.

'Jesus. What happened?' Blessed spat out the last of the dirt from his mouth. 'They went away. I can't believe it.'

'They were just after money, thank God.'

'I was sure they were going to kill us . . . rape you, or God knows what.'

She shook her head. 'They got my bag, though. I didn't put up much of a fight. What's the point of dying for a bunch of traveller's cheques?'

Blessed was incredulous. 'I was sure . . . ' He climbed slowly, unsteadily to his feet, realised he still had the use of his limbs.

His wallet lay on the ground about ten feet away. A little further on, his passport.

'The cash has gone,' Blessed reported. 'But they left the credit cards. Not much use for them in East Berlin. Unless they fancy having their tattoos removed and trying to get served dinner at the Palast-Hotel.' He laughed with an edge of hysteria. 'It was a robbery, would you believe it, just a robbery . . . '

They walked on for a bit. Just round the bend, they found Diane's bag. Again, the skin-heads had stolen the cash – about fifty West marks and a hundred US dollars – but they'd left her passport and all the plastic.

And, of course, they'd left the East German currency they had changed at Friedrichstrasse Station. No one wanted that.

'So much for your "ordinary East Germans",' Diane said. 'Give me the decadent West anytime.'

Blessed shrugged. 'First the Robert Frost Trail, and now this. I'm surprised you're willing to walk another step through the woods with me. But if you can bear it, let's press on and catch our train for the border. Dinner's entirely on me. The damage-limitation operation starts here.'

In the event, they got some money from the all-night *Wechselstube* at the Zoo Station and Blessed cleaned up in the washroom. Dinner was at Bocca in the Kurfürstenstrasse, where his bruises garnered a few stares. They strolled back to Diane's hotel in the August heat. Distant shrills and squeals from the Tiergarten carried through the night air.

'A nightcap?' Diane said. 'And . . . ' She hesitated. 'I mean just that. Is it old-fashioned of me to say that I hardly know you?'

'No. No, of course it isn't.'

She smiled with such shy sweetness that Blessed couldn't possibly not join her for a goodnight drink. In fact, it was quite nice not to feel pressure, he thought.

They had a couple of brandies in the little bar. Then a delicate peck on the cheek, an agreement to meet late the following afternoon, after Blessed had cranked out another few pages of the memoirs. He left shortly after midnight, feeling about sixteen and a half, and enjoying it.

As he walked towards the taxi-stand on the corner of Landgrafenstrasse, Blessed automatically began a long-habitual routine, feeling in his pockets for coins and keys. The keys were not immediately apparent. Blessed stopped under a streetlamp, checked again – no keys in his trousers. Then he remembered. Yesterday, for safety's sake, hadn't he slipped them both – the little silvery key to the security gate, the older brass one to the boathouse – into the inner breast pocket of his jacket? Blessed began going through all its pockets, cursing to himself in a mixture of English and German.

The skinheads had done him over thoroughly. He had been close to unconsciousness towards the end. *Shit*, Blessed thought with dawning horror. *I have got to get back to boathouse. Fast.*

FORTY

THE CAB DEPOSITED Blessed by the security gate at the top of Klarfeld's drive. He had no choice but to find the buzzer in the dark, wait for someone to come and open up.

It was several minutes before a figure appeared out of the night. Klarfeld. Moving slowly and carefully. The torch went on at the last possible moment, dazzling Blessed, who involuntarily threw up his hands to shield his eyes.

'Stay right . . . Oh, it's you, Michael.' Klarfeld's voice echoed through the clear air. He lowered his torch. 'Your face . . . are you OK?'

'I'll tell you in a few minutes,' Blessed said. 'Just let me in.'

'Sure. One moment . . . '

Blessed realised there was a reason for the delay. Klarfeld was slipping the gun he kept in the house back into his waistband.

Klarfeld unlocked the gate. Blessed asked him for the torch, which he handed over without comment, and set off down the drive towards the boathouse.

Something about the air, the smell, hinted to Blessed that he had been right. He arrived at the boathouse. The door was already flung wide open. He eased in slowly, cautiously, until he could be sure there was no one still there. Only the damage remained. Drawers had been pulled out of the desk and their contents dumped on the floor. His laptop had been stomped on, the VDU smashed. The stack of translated pages was missing. The box of computer disks containing the memoirs had gone too.

The people who had done this had been professionals. They had carried out their task quickly and quietly. How had they managed to get past the house without attracting attention? It occurred to Blessed that they might easily have come across from the East German side by boat.

Klarfeld had followed Blessed to the boathouse. 'To think I made jokes about your careful writerly habits,' he said softly. 'Forgive me, Michael.'

'It's all right. This is hardly the kind of disaster I usually try to anticipate. Fire. Flood. That's more the kind of thing . . . Anyway, Benno, if you could get my duplicate set of disks out of the safe?' He lit a cigarette. 'And I'll need a new, compatible machine. Providing you can have your people express one over this morning we should have hard copy of the memoirs again by the end of the day.'

'No problem.'

'This is a new situation, Benno. I think we need to talk.'

'We do. That we do.' Klarfeld sighed. 'I have a few things to tell you. A few things I probably should have told you some time ago.'

They cracked a bottle of Asbacher Uralt in Klarfeld's upstairs study. The room was comfortingly secure in its feel – all Brazilian leather chairs and solid, imported teak. There were several original Zille drawings of Berlin street-urchins framed on the wall, a particularly eerie Max Beckmann self-portrait over the fireplace.

'The connections are hard to ignore,' Blessed finished his story. 'Erika led me to Ziegler/Hammerschmidt – which brought the skinheads on the scene . . .' He shrugged, drank some coffee, waited for the older man to comment.

'I suppose you should have told me about all this before,' Klarfeld said. 'Or maybe I should have asked you more about who you were seeing. But the damage – if damage it is – has been done.'

'Do you think that Erika was – is – a *Stasi* agent?'

Klarfeld hesitated. 'I honestly don't know. If she was, then they were onto us a long way back, since before you came to Berlin. It would have taken real knowledge to set up the meeting on the train. Very precise knowledge of your intentions and movements. This information leads me to rethink certain fundamentals . . .'

'Are you implying that we've been set up?'

'Not . . . necessarily. It's just that more people – more *factors* – may be involved than I thought.'

'Nothing much fazes you, does it?'

Klarfeld looked at Blessed calmly. 'I learned very early on that the world is a dangerous place. We discussed this right at the beginning of our relationship. If one makes plans with the assumption that there are dangers, one is rarely surprised when they appear.' He paused. 'What do you propose to do about Erika?'

203

Blessed was surprised at the intensity of the feelings that flooded over him. 'I – I guess I'd better ease off on that relationship,' he said. His difficulty must have been obvious, but Klarfeld remained impassive. 'At least until after the memoirs are finished. After that . . . '

Klarfeld nodded. 'After that, it's up to you.'

'I'll give her the impression that disaster has struck, that I have to catch up on a whole lot of lost work.'

'Fine.'

'I'm seeing Diane again tomorrow.' He looked at his watch. 'I mean, tonight.'

'When does she leave Berlin?'

'Monday. She's flying on to Paris to check out the *Bibliothèque Nationale*.'

'Right,' Klarfeld said. 'Now, for the moment. They'll think they've bought themselves time by destroying the translation. I doubt they wll cancel their surveillance operation altogether, but they may relax it somewhat . . . '

'I was planning to take Diane to the *Berliner Ensemble* tonight. East Berlin. Should I brazen it out?'

Klarfeld shook his head. 'Take her somewhere else. Anywhere. Stay away from the East until you've finished work on the memoirs. It's not so long now.'

'I was also planning to cover the big dissident rock concert out at Lichtenberg next week.'

Klarfeld's tone was suddenly sharp. 'Michael, I'm no longer just offering you advice. This is an order. I don't need more trouble. I need those memoirs, and I need them soon. OK?'

Their gazes met. Eventually Blessed nodded. 'Sure. You're paying the bills, you make the rules. After tonight, it's head down and stay home.'

Klarfeld seemed to soften. He got to his feet. 'When you have loved, and lost, you . . . you look for it again and often you do stupid, stupid things, make yourself vulnerable . . . ' He was standing half-turned away so that Blessed couldn't see the expression on his face, but his voice was thick with emotion. 'One day, perhaps you'll really know what I mean. One day.'

FORTY-ONE

THE MERCEDES TRUCK with QUICK-FOTO BRAUER in large letters on its side pulled off the highway, waited briefly at the depot gate while its driver's documents were checked. Then the truck was waved through. It rumbled across a concrete yard, docked alongside the low warehouse building. The whole process took barely a minute.

Labourers in white overalls bearing the BRAUER-FOTO motif were already waiting by the rear doors of the truck when they were unlocked. Cartons were passed to them and taken into the building.

One operative, a short, fat, red-haired man in a white coat that marked him out as a foreman, watched and exhorted, made notes on a clipboard. When the unloading work was over, he followed the labourers into the storage room, told them to take their lunch break. This left him alone. Slipping his clipboard under his arm, he prowled the rows of cartons, counting, checking.

When he reached a certain point, he squinted at the label on one carton. It was addressed to FOTO BRAUER – SUPERSERVICE. The foreman picked it up and carried it out of the room.

The boss's office was just across the yard in an undistinguished square building, the size of a couple of caravans lashed together. Apart from the smart seven-series BMW parked in the assigned space, there was no other indication of luxury, though QUICK-FOTO BRAUER was known as an extremely profitable concern. The foreman marched in, ignoring the secretary at the reception desk, knocked on the door marked G. BRAUER and walked straight in.

'Chief, the superservice batch. Only one today,' he said, placing the carton carefully on the desk.

Günther Brauer alias Gurkel looked up from his work. 'Fine.' This was routine, and yet also not routine. 'Time for your lunch now, eh?'

'Yes, chief.'

'See you Tuesday. I'll be away on business until then.'

When the foreman had left, Gurkel closed the file he had been pretending to check. He took a paperknife and opened the carton. Inside were brightly-coloured and numbered paper wallets containing film and prints, apparently identical to all the others that returned from the labs in East Germany, and passed back through the depot en route to the outlets that had taken the original film-processing orders. At this time of year, when the snap-taking masses were on holiday in their hordes, the number of cartons that went through the depot every day climbed into the hundreds, the number of individual wallets into the tens of thousands.

Gurkel selected only seven of the wallets in the carton. A very observant eye might have noticed an apparently accidental red smudge on each packet, in the bottom left-hand corner of the label identifying the recipient.

The seven wallets went into a steel-reinforced attaché case, which Gurkel locked. Next he reached into the drawer of his desk, took out his passport, slipped it into the inside pocket of his jacket.

Gurkel would leave the carton for the foreman to deal with when he returned from lunch.

The foreman believed that the 'Superservice' prints Gurkel removed were so outrageously pornographic that they could be handled by no one but the chief. The foreman got paid extremely well for keeping his mouth shut. Hush money. And fear money. Because the foreman also knew that Gurkel had powerful, ruthless friends.

This procedure had been going on now for five years.

Until this spring. Granit's announcement at the meeting at the forester's hut in February had changed everything. Previously, the foreman had been right in his assumption about the pornography. Now he was unwittingly involved in the production of something very different. To some, more desirable than pornography. More secret, certainly. And far more dangerous.

Gurkel picked up the steel briefcase. It contained not photographs but the latest batch of micofiche copies made by Granit from the *Stasi's* most secret files. To the big man and Gurkel, they were collectively known as "the insurance".

On his way out of the building, Gurkel blew his secretary a kiss, wished her a good weekend. No, he wouldn't be back in the office today.

His BMW was waiting outside. He knew it had a full tank of petrol, although even that wouldn't get him to where he was going. He put the attaché case down on the front-passenger seat, selected a tape and slid it into the deck.

This was his routine. The expensive music system was playing digitally-enhanced Glenn Miller – to remind Gurkel of the old days, the postwar days of GIs and their Fräuleins, of 'jitterbug strictly forbidden', of hunger-rations and feverish excitement. Within a few minutes Gurkel was out on the Autobahn, cruising southbound out of Hamburg at an untroubled hundred and forty kilometres an hour.

The big car had almost a thousand kilometres to cover before it rested, in the VIP parking bunker beneath a Zürich bank. And even after that business had been concluded, Gurkel's journey wasn't over. By the morning he had to be back in North Germany.

This weekend was special: it was the weekend of the big Kinder-Meeting, when Granit had promised to tell all, to make everything ab-so-lutely clear . . . .

FORTY-TWO

'DOES IT MATTER?' Blessed with a shrug. 'They think they've cooked our goose. I'm not about to disabuse them. Listen, Diane, I just want to finish, get the money, and get out . . . '

They were drinking coffee in the bar at Tegel Airport, waiting for Diane's Paris flight to be called. Along the narrow concourse in front of them, crowds of tourists and businessmen browsed in the souvenir shops, debating whether to make that last-minute purchase, perhaps an innocuous, fluffy Berlin bear, or one of those wearable political statements – a black T-shirt with the outlines of the city sectors in red on the chest. *Were any of those waiting and wandering actually watching him*? The fat man in shorts over by the news stand, hadn't he glanced over here just a little too often for it to be a coincidence? And what about the blonde woman at a nearby table? She'd finished her drink at least fifteen minutes ago, seemed to have no bag, no belongings. Maybe they were just intrigued by his facial injuries.

Diane Kelly glanced up at the departures screen. 'Out of where? Berlin?'

'Out of Benno Klarfeld's boathouse. And out of this kind of work.'

Last night he had decided that he owed her an explanation. So, he had told her the story of Benno, of the *Stasi* general's memoirs, of the itch that had brought him back to Berlin. He had told her about everything – except Erika.

'Disillusioned?' Diane asked.

'In a way,' Blessed said. 'When I started this project, I thought that first it would put my career back on the up, second that I'd be helping right a historical wrong.'

'Well, maybe that was correct.'

'Maybe. If all goes well with the memoirs, and they break big, and I get exclusive access, as Klarfeld promised . . . which could lead to lusher pastures than the *Bulletin* . . . Success, in other words. The only question is, do I want it?'

'Success is what everybody wants, Michael.'

'That's a very American thing to say.'

'I know,' Diane answered with a small shrug. 'I can't escape the society I grew up in. Success equals meaning to us. America is a society where people are creating and recreating themselves all the time. Success has become the only yardstick that makes any sense. Prominence. Fame. Money . . . '

'Along with violence. Death. Betrayal.'

'Yes. Those things too. Nobody said life was uncomplicated.'

Blessed nodded slowly. 'Listen, I don't know if I'll stay on in Berlin, but I'll certainly give myself a break and come to London this autumn. How would you feel about that?'

'Great.' Diane paused, checked the departures screen again. 'So long as you really are out of all this. See, I think that incident over at the . . . whatever that lake was called . . . got to me more than I'd care to admit.'

'I can understand that.'

'Yes. You're a very understanding guy. And it's been wonderful, Mike, really. OK. So London later this year. And until then no East.'

'No East. Head down. Work. I'm just sorry we couldn't duck through the Wall and take in the *Berliner Ensemble* the other night.'

'The gas station was wonderful, Michael. And all the rest . . . '

They had eaten dinner at one of the most fashionable new places in West Berlin, *Shell* – a converted petrol station on the Knesebeck-strasse. Then Blessed had taken Diane on a tour of other nightspots: the Paris Bar, Chez Alex, Grolman's. He had managed to keep her away from Kreuzberg and the places Erika had taken him to. It wasn't easy; the Kreuzberg *Szene* was one of the things Diane was keen to sample.

Blessed stared back at the fat man in shorts until his victim coughed, looked away.

'Uh-oh,' Diane said, and nodded at the departures screen. 'Pan-Am are making their last call.'

It was a short walk to the gate. Tegel is a small airport. Mutual good wishes, a repeat of the promise to meet in London in the autumn, a chaste kiss. Then Diane shouldered her sensible little carry-on with its dozen useful pockets and hurried towards passport control.

One last turn, a wave, and she was gone. Well, that's the good girl dealt with for now, Blessed thought. Not too difficult. The greater challenge was yet to come. Now came the turn of . . . whatever Erika was, or whatever she was for him . . . He sighed and lit a cigarette. The fat man in shorts had disappeared. So had the woman in the café.

Blessed emerged into the sunlight. *Dark meets light, black meets white, good meets bad.* Everything seemed to be coming to a head. Not just the experiences of a few weeks, but of thirty-eight years. *Welcome to your mid-life crisis, Michael Blessed, and good luck to you.*

He would work all today and most of tomorrow, he promised himself. Tomorrow night, though, he was meeting Erika. He was going to tell her some fine lies about why he couldn't see her again until he had finished work on the memoirs. It was the only safe option, but it was going to be very tough.

Any addictive experience is hard to give up, Blessed reasoned as he made his way towards the taxi-stand. Why, for God's sake, should Erika be an exception? All the same, why was the thought of her eating at him so badly?

FORTY-THREE

BLESSED LOOKED YET AGAIN at the illuminated digits of the alarm clock by his bed. 04:27. It had been a hot, sultry August night. But, of course, there were plenty of other people in Berlin who would have had no trouble sleeping through. People who weren't thinking of Erika.

He lay there, watching the dawn paint pastel shades onto the ceiling. Slowly he became aware that the sheets on his bed were uncomfortably sticky. Time he took them up to the house to Frau Smilovici. *Sit up. Do something*, he thought. Blessed rolled out of bed, naked, shuffled over to the wardrobe, slipped on his light cotton robe. His resolution not to smoke before breakfast lasted about seventy seconds. That was how long elapsed before he found himself glancing through yesterday's work on the memoirs, a lit cigarette between his fingers.

The time was crawling towards day: 04:41.

Blessed wondered what Erika was doing at this moment. What Erika was doing, period. He forced himself to read on, to take his mind off her.

It was during this time that I became personal friends with my direct chief at the HVA, Markus Wolf, Blessed read. *Wolf is known to his friends, and the more intimate of his enemies, as 'Mischa' (he had been brought up mostly in the Soviet Union, son of a German communist émigré). A member of the Central Committee of the Party and Deputy Minister for State Security, Wolf appeared unusually cosmopolitan and sophisticated – his father had been a writer, his brother Konrad, who died some years ago, was a well-known film-director. He was definitely 'liberal' by the standards of most SED bosses. But as a warrior in the secret struggle between East and West he was brilliant, ruthless and cunning in pursuit of his goals – the goals of Communism. It is said that the British spy-writer, John le Carré, based his Russian, codenamed 'Karla', on Mischa Wolf.*

Now, one of Mischa's favourite weapons was the 'honeytrap', the seduction of a western target – male or female, heterosexual or homosexual – by a trained Stasi operative. It's true that spies have gained information in the beds of their enemies since the dawn of history – remember Judith and Holofernes! – but under Wolf this technique was developed into a fine art. Take the example of the bar of the Hotel Metropol in the Friedrichstrasse, where the whores who cruised the bar were Stasi employees and where there were spyholes in every bedroom . . .

Off for another pace round the boathouse. Again the mostly irrational, prickly-physical feeling that he was being observed, recorded, *seen . . .*

Something cracked in Blessed then. His anger, his defiance found an outlet. The observee rebelled, the pawn decided to move like a knight.

OK. They thought they had him taped. So why wait until this evening before the showdown with Erika? Why didn't he, Michael Blessed, start doing the unexpected? Why didn't he himself start doing some watching? Why didn't he start fighting fire with fire?

Blessed went over to the picture-window facing the lake, stuck up his two fingers in a gesture of defiance, just in case there was someone out there. Then he closed the curtains, went into the tiny bathroom, took off his robe, stepped into the shower cubicle.

He dressed, put on his street clothes. He thought of calling a cab, decided against it, just in case they – or, God knows, even Benno Klarfeld – were tapping his phone. Before he went out, Blessed switched on the radio part of the alarm-clock, spun the dial until he got to some likely-sounding insomniac jazz programme. It was playing a floaty Herbie Hancock anthem as he gently closed the door behind him and set off like a hunting animal up the slope towards the road.

A number 18 bus would take him along the Königstrasse to Wannsee Station. From there it was a thirty-minute, lazy rattle in an S-bahn car along with the service workers, the minions, the professional early risers, into the heart of the waking city.

The lights up in Erika's flat had been on for an hour-and-a-half, but no one came out until exactly 08:12.

212

Blessed, in a nondescript grey zipper jacket and jeans, had arrived at 06:20 and gone straight to the pub just down the street, which he had occasionally dropped into with Erika. He knew the place was open almost round the clock, like many Berlin bars. It was one of the privileges of the island-city: not only no military service, but also no licensing-hours, no *Polizeistunde*.

He sat himself by the window, where he could clearly see the street entrance to the apartment block, started with a schnapps and a coffee. By the time he ordered his second coffee it was almost eight o'clock, and the usual characters had started to drop by for their *Frühschoppen*, the German working man's traditional early-morning heart-starter. Not too long after, the lights in Erika's apartment went off . . . and that was when Blessed started to sweat. 08:11 . . . 08:12.

Item: one all-too-familiar, pretty woman in black leather jacket, leggings, wearing a confident, even arrogant smile. Item: a companion, male, mid-forties, bespectacled, wearing a raincoat over a dark business suit and – if Blessed wasn't terribly mistaken – an altogether sheepish-dazed expression, as if he'd just woken up in heaven and didn't know what to do next.

Jesus. They were shaking fucking hands! She was saying something and he was nodding like a schoolkid. The exquisite body-language of the one-night-stand . . . Then a toss of the hair and Erika was moving off away from the man in the glasses and raincoat, tripping away in the direction of the Mehringdamm U-bahn station as if this was just another, normal day . . .

Blessed passed the man on the street. He was round-faced, balding on top, middling-to-senior executive type, almost certainly with a wife and kids somewhere. The man was . . . so . . . fucking . . . ordinary . . . right down to the stupid grin on his face and the fact that – Blessed turned briefly to confirm this – he was making his way towards the pub where Blessed had spent the last two hours.

So celebrate your find, toast your luck, Blessed thought. *I did that too. Stupid, gullible bastard that I am, like you I thought myself a fortunate man . . .*

For a few moments, after she rounded a corner, he lost sight of Erika. For that short time he thought he'd lost her. But no, she had just gone into a hole-in-the-wall that sold newspapers and cigarettes, and there she was again, taking her usual route to the station,

213

the way he and she had walked on other mornings – other mornings when the bedroom light had also been on since early, to enable them to watch each other in the big rattan-framed mirror opposite Erika's bed as they made love – 'my harmless narcissism,' she called it.

Blessed swiftly bought a Berliner Morgenpost from the vendor in front of the station, hung back until Erika was through the barrier. Luckily he had a multiple ticket, which enabled him to quickly stamp one and follow at a safe distance. His assumption was that she must be heading for Möckenbrücke or Hallesches Tor, where a change of trains would take her right into the city. She had said something about taking a temporary receptionist's job at a gallery near the Europa-Zentrum. If so, she would then take one of two lines: either the line that terminated at the Kurfürstendamm or the one that looped off just before that to take itself up to Charlottenburg and the Olympic Stadium. He would have to play that one by ear.

The train that came was for Hallesches Tor/Tegel. Blessed, hiding behind his newspaper at the other end of the platform from Erika, saw her get on, and followed. She got out at Hallesches Tor. He kept well back, felt momentary panic when it occurred to him that she might be aiming north to the Friedrichstrasse and the East. But no, she obediently – if that was the word – ended up on the westbound platform. He watched her covertly as they waited for the train. She looked like a hundred other lively, attractive girls on their way to work, like any woman who had just kissed off a not particularly exciting one-night stand and was now putting a good face on the new day . . .

When he wasn't stealing surreptitious glances at her, Blessed stared sightlessly at the headline in the morning's paper. *What had she told her one-night stand? What had she said? Why didn't he just walk up to her now and ask, demand, in front of all these swarming, bored commuters. Why not?*

From several carriages along, he checked at each station to see if she had got out. But no, Erika kept going all the way to the Kurfürstendamm.

He kept her in view right up to street level. By this stage, Blessed was starting to feel almost insulted at the way Erika failed to see him, pick him out. *Following her is so easy. Could following a spy be so easy?*

Now over to the Joachimstaler Strasse, a hundred yards through the thickening crowds of commuters and tourists. Then an abrupt turn to the Augsburger Strasse. Ah – the finale! Hadn't she mentioned another job at some gallery?

Blessed nearly missed Erika's next move – she swung through some brightly-coloured glass doors. A shop. Her move was so unexpected, Blessed only now registered which particular shop she had entered. And what kind.

Even from the far side of the street, Blessed could not fail to see a life-sized blowup of a pneumatic, pouting, naked girl, positioned as if leaning out of the window to envelop the passer-by, breasts jutting forward, lips pursed in a cold, pink kiss. A starburst covered her crotch. He squinted: it read in German and English: 'Come in and see me! Red-hot!' Beside her in the window was a selection of hardcore videos and magazines, again with the technically obscene bits obscured by spots, starbursts, price-transfers.

The sign above the door Erika had entered read in unmistakably large, bright letters: LOVEMACHINE: SEX-SHOP.

Erika stayed inside LOVEMACHINE for some time. It was impossible to see what was going on, so Blessed crossed the street a little further on, cautiously headed back until he was close to the shop window. He held his newspaper ready, prepared to cover his face if Erika suddenly emerged.

A quick shuffle a little further to the right and Blessed could see quite clearly inside. The shop was carefully decorated in camelia pinks and navy blues. There was nothing in the slightest bit cheap or shabby about it. It could have been a high-class fashion boutique. There were smart, well-designed stands of cleverly named sex-aids, then revolving racks of glossy porn magazines. Towards the back, what looked like an extensive video library. And in the far corner a semi-circular polished steel and brass counter with a futuristic-looking electronic till.

Erika was over there, laughing, idly smoking a cigarette.

There was a man behind the counter. He was leaning over, so close to Erika that their faces were almost touching, talking softly, as if telling her a story.

The man was one Erika had said she would never see again. He was Erika's ex-lover, owner-manager of the Galerie Schnittke . . . Wolfgang.

FORTY-FOUR

ERIKA EMERGED TEN MINUTES later, with Wolfgang. A handshake, and her . . . lover? ex-lover? still-employer? . . . headed back towards the Kurfürstendamm. She went in the opposite direction for fifty or so yards, taking her time, then crossed the street and turned left into the Nürnberger Strasse.

Blessed left the cheap *Stehcafé* from which he had been watching the entrance to LOVEMACHINE, took off after Erika at what he hoped was a safe distance. He had followed people before, during his time in Australia. Politicians reluctant to grant an interview. Crooked policemen setting up rendezvous with drug-dealers. But it had never been like this. He had never known them. He had never been this hot with anger and humiliation, or eaten up by such cruel curiosity.

And, in fact, like every jealous lover, he didn't have the patience for subterfuge. Five minutes of watching and he knew he had to confront her sooner rather than later. When he saw Erika making for the taxi-stand opposite the Europa-Center, he made up his mind that the moment had come. He picked up speed, overtook her some fifteen yards short of her destination, as she was raising one arm to hail a cab.

Erika swung around, obviously thinking she was about to be mugged. Her brow was knit in angry concentration. She was preparing to swing her bag in self-defence. Then she recognised Blessed, and her jaw went slack in amazement – swiftly followed by a still-surprised but convincingly welcoming smile.

'Mike . . . up in the big city on your own. How was . . . my God, what on earth happened to your face?'

'I got attacked. In East Berlin.'

'You are OK?'

'Bloody but unbowed. As you can see.'

'My God. Is the interview with Ziegler still on? If so, afterwards you must tell me all about –'

'I need to talk to you *now*, Erika. That's why I'm here.'

216

'Can't it wait until tonight? I have a job at a gallery in Charlotten-burg, and I'm already late. I wish I could afford to get fired, but –'

Her patter faded out. Blessed was still holding firmly onto her arm.

'We're going to take a walk in the Tiergarten, Erika,' he said. 'Come on.'

'Don't be silly! What's *wrong*, Michael?'

'Come on.'

'That's what you want? This walk and talk?'

'Yes. Absolutely.'

'Then . . . then all right. But five minutes only . . . '

Neither of them spoke until they reached the Landwehr Canal and were almost at the beginning of the park itself.

Erika turned. 'Michael, please tell me what the problem is.'

He ignored her. 'Where are you working at the moment, ac-tually?' he said.

'I told you. At a little place in Charlottenburg. Just for this week and the next. Michael, what is this interrogation suddenly?'

She was acting, Blessed knew that, but she was very good. One part puzzlement, one part concern, one part irritation. Just right. For a moment he felt himself slip into a kind of agonised awe of her. Then he toughened up.

'Easy. I saw you with Wolfgang just a short while ago. In a porno shop. You both looked pretty relaxed. At home, one might say.'

'You're wrong –'

'*I saw you there.*'

'Now come on.' Erika changed tack. Out came the rueful smile. 'A body has to earn money to eat . . . I know I didn't tell you, because I was a little embarrassed, but . . . '

'What was Wolfgang doing there?'

'The gallery isn't his only interest.' She laughed. 'You are sur-prised at this? Really, this is not like England, where sex is dirty, only for gangsters and deadbeats. I mean, is that all?'

'No, it's not all. What about earlier this morning . . . much ear-lier . . . that man I saw coming out of your flat. The one you shook hands with. Also just business, Erika?'

She thrust her accused hands into her jacket pockets. For some time she relapsed into silence.

They had taken a path west along the first of the lakes that covered a substantial part of the Tiergarten. Formerly the hunting preserve of the Prussian kings, this place was Berlin's lung. It was a beautiful morning. Children were busy in the playground that had been built on a little promontory jutting out into the water. On a day like this, Berlin could seem a happy place.

'So. You have been watching me,' she said at last, her expression now one of righteous anger. 'And what has all this got to do with you? I told you, I do what I want, see who I want, sleep with whom I want. I like men. I like you, but you think I like *only* you?'

Blessed's jaw tightened. 'That was the impression you gave, yes.'

'You made me explain. I didn't want to explain. I tried not to hurt you . . . but now . . . '

'Come clean, for Christ's sake! Are you *Stasi*?' Blessed said suddenly, surprising himself with his directness. 'Has someone put you onto me?'

'*What*?' Erika tossed back her head, catching the dappled sunlight in her silky hair, and laughed. Then she shrugged. 'You are such a goddamned prig. So English. I told you, I like to sleep with men. Including you. Don't you believe I would want to fuck with you just because I like it? You poor sap . . . '

It wasn't what he had planned, but suddenly Blessed found himself up close to her, his hands grabbing her shoulders, shaking her. 'You didn't answer my question. You didn't answer my fucking question.'

Erika had gone limp on him. 'You're hurting,' she panted. 'I'll count to three, then I'll yell! Believe me!'

A couple of mothers on a bench in the playground were staring in Blessed's direction. He let go. 'Are you *Stasi*?'

'No.'

In the silence that followed, he looked at her carefully. Her gaze was direct. She stood with her hands on her hips, her eyes narrowed in anger. But then his wife had lied to him too, when he had first confronted her about her late nights 'out with the girls', and he had believed her, because he had wanted to believe her. In Erika's case he couldn't fool himself about her relationships with other men. She made no attempt to deny them. The real question was, had his highly-charged, doomed affair with Erika been a chance thing, or

218

was it all part of a plan? Was Erika working for someone? East, most probably . . . But what about West? It wasn't impossible.

'I don't believe you,' he said quietly. 'You're under orders. This a set-up.'

'Oh, go away. You're crazy, hanging around the street and watching my flat, following me to places where I have a perfect right to go. Get lost, Michael.'

Blessed knew that only violence would get him the truth – and also that violence was the only form of intimacy still possible with this woman.

Erika sighed, looked away. 'Listen, let's just leave it – my life is not for you. It's too *hard* for someone like you to be with someone like me. Just go now,' she added, not angrily as she had before, but sadly, almost gently. 'Let's say the experiment was a failure, OK?'

'For whom?'

'For us both, Michael. For us both.' And she turned and walked away from him.

Blessed hovered outside the porno-shop named LOVEMACHINE for a couple of minutes, making sure Wolfgang was no longer there. He studied the window-display like any curious tourist. The busty beauty with the pout and the come-on message. The sex-aids, magazines and videos in the window. Inside . . .

Inside was one customer. At the counter, next to the fancy till, Wolfgang and Erika had been replaced by a bored young woman in her early twenties. She could equally well have been sitting behind the checkout of a branch of Spar or Aldi. He pushed open the glass door and walked into the shop.

The sales assistant was reading a pop-music magazine. Blessed had to knock gently on the counter-top before she looked up and acknowledged him.

'Yes. You want something specific?'

'Is Wolfgang here?'

The face stayed blank. 'I don't know the name.'

'Erika Winter? What about Erika?'

The girl shrugged. 'Listen, I only started here last week. I don't know anyone called Erika either. This is a shop, not a contact agency.'

The look she gave Blessed was hard, hostile. She had obviously decided that he was trying to pick her up. It must happen all the time.

'They used to work here,' he said. 'Sorry to bother you. I'll just browse, OK?'

'*Bitteschön.*' She was already looking back down at the pop-music magazine.

The only access to the rear of the shop was behind the counter. A single door. Maybe there was a way of getting round there from the other side of the block. Maybe there was some kind of complex behind there, some secret, bizarre *Stasi* world no one knew about.

Blessed wandered over to the display section. Dildos, frilly sheaths, 'ticklers', the usual stuff. A few studded leather items. A crop. The videos seemed to have titles that drew on a quite small store of interchangeable words and phrases: *Sex Party Girls, Party Girl Sex*, and then – to vary it a little – *Housewife Sex Party* . . .

Prominently displayed in the magazine section was a special stand of large-format, full colour material of the hardcore kind. The stand was topped by a sign that said in German: 'From LOVEMA-CHINE'S Own Publishing House'. The magazine was, actually, called *LOVEMACHINE*. Blessed went over, selected an example whose cover showed a young blonde woman posing with her legs spread wide apart, her fingers touching her labia, her tongue lolling with simulated auto-erotic abandon as her half-closed eyes met the camera. Perfect porn cliché.

Blessed flipped through the sex-magazine. The usual. Some out-door exotica. Fellatio in the back of a car. Domestic stuff: husband returns home to find wife in flagrante with the plumber, is overcome with lust and decides to make it a threesome. Blessed put it back. He picked up another, checked the publishing details. In accordance with German law, the publisher was given. In fact, the address was a box number in a suburb of Hamburg. 'Responsible for contents,' it declared in very small type, as was legally necessary, 'J. Brauer'.

The big feature in this issue, running for some pages, was a sequence entitled *Weekend Orgy*! It involved four pairs of men and women – married couples, as the text prissily pointed out before stripping the performers off and getting them down to business – spending an entire weekend in one of their number's apartment, having athletic and extremely varied sex in twos, threes, fours, and . . . yes, in one spectacular image running over the entire centre-spread, definitely in an eight, all gathered on one double-bed in an

220

acrobatic cluster. No trick was left unturned in that picture, no orifice unfilled; the whole ensemble was like some weird, complex sexual leggo-construction that defied not just logic but gravity.

Blessed stared at the centrespread. As he looked, certain details began to disturb him. It wasn't the performers but their surroundings . . . The large, framed print on the wall behind them. It was one of those David Hockney swimming pools, and Blessed knew its every ripple. And those sheets. Pencil-thin red and white stripes. That pannelled door on the built-in wardrobe off to the right, almost out of shot. Finally, the distinctive pattern of the kelim rug alongside the bed . . .

To his deepening horror, Blessed knew the bedroom all this flesh was quivering in.

He knew every damned inch of that bedroom. It belonged to an apartment in Kreuzberg. He had thrashed among those same pin-striped sheets only a few nights ago. And the apartment's tenant was, of course, Erika. Erika Winter.

But there was something even more bizarre, more chilling: because Blessed was so familiar with the layout, he knew for sure that the camera that had taken these pictures couldn't possibly have been in the same room. The orgy had to have been photographed from somewhere else.

Behind the mirror. There was a camera behind the mirror.

221

FORTY-FIVE

THERE WAS A SIGN ON THE DOUBLE doors leading to the hotel's conference room. It read: PRIVATE MEETING – NO ADMITTANCE.

Two security guards with walkie-talkies were stationed along the corridor, to keep away unauthorised members of the hotel staff. They anticipated no problems with the West German general public, because for two days and nights the entire fifty-room mansion, along with its twenty acres of grounds, was booked exclusively for the use of a company named as KINDERWOHLFAHRT KG – 'Kinder Welfare Ltd'. But there were guards on the gates too, just in case.

Granit had crossed the Iron Curtain to be here. He wore civilian clothes, a dark suit and sober tie out of respect for the occasion. As was usual at a plenum meeting of the Kinder, it was his task to read out the names of the members in order and formally check that they were present. The names he announced were, of course, their gang-names . . .

'*Dackel?*'

A clear, ringing reply. 'Here!'

'*Flix?*'

'Here!' The fair-haired man with a deep suntan had come the furthest of all to this meeting, all the way from Adelaide, Australia.

'And *Granit* –' He pronounced his own name, allowed himself a wry smile and added: 'Here!'

'*Gurkel?*'

'Here! Where else?'

Gurkel had already opened the bottle of beer that each man had supplied at his place on the great circle of tables, and it was starting to show.

A swift, withering glance from Granit.

'*Igel?*' he said next.

'Here!' the man growled his formal response. More than forty years before he had rejoiced in the nickname, meaning hedgehog,

222

because of his thick, spiky hair. Now he was bald, and all his prickliness was on the inside.

And so it went, until all twenty-four, from *Banana* to *The Wonder*, had been found present and correct. Only then did Granit address them, explain his reasons for this plenum meeting. God knows, it had taken enough trouble. First sweeping the place for bugs and listening-devices. Ensuring reliable guards. Then getting everyone here – from Germany, Austria, Switzerland, America, Brazil, and Australia. The hiring of the hotel itself was the easiest part, because ultimately KINDERWOHLFAHRT KG owned the place, had bought it via a maze of dummy companies. This hotel was a former Schloss belonging to the Hanoverian royal family. Very elegant, very secluded, inside West Germany but very close to the border with the East.

Granit took a sip of mineral water. Every man in the room was waiting to hear his reasons. He had warned them in advance that this was something big, something fundamental, the greatest threat to their organisation – and the greatest opportunity also – for forty or more years.

'Welcome,' Granit began simply. 'So good to see you.' He grinned broadly. 'Oh yes you beddabelieve it's good . . .' The lapse into the old way of speaking, into the private gang-language they had evolved as children, aroused a ripple of laughter. 'This is one long overdue gaddawlmighdy Kinder-meeting, or what?'

'YOU BEDDABELIEVE!' came the chorus.

Granit always liked to start with some morale-boosting patter, but he got down quickly to business.

'Well, you know, this is historic,' he said. 'Forty-one years and one month ago, we quit the orphanage where we lived together, where we had created the Kinder and a world of safety for ourselves. Everybody remember that?'

Nods. Mutterings of yes, how could we forget?

'OK,' Granit continued. 'At the time we thought this was *bad*. We were forced to do what we did, and it looked like the end of the Kinder. *But it wasn't.*'

No, no, they murmured now. Certainly not.

'In fact, we found ourselves a new place in the East and continued with the old life for a while. Until things got too organised and the *Volkspolizei* got on our trail, and me and Dackel got ourselves

223

arrested.' Granit paused for effect. 'Again, we thought, this is *terrible*. But it wasn't! What happened was, I ended up turning from kid-criminal to kid-cop! And from there I joined the *Stasi* and became a spymaster – which is why we have always had money to spend, passports, businesses, total protection. For all those years we had *everything we needed*. All because I joined the *Stasi* and got my own private group of spies who – guess what – just happened to be *you*!'

His audience roared with laughter. Some thumped their tables, whistled.

'So, out of adversity, out of apparent disaster, came greater and greater triumph! Nothing can defeat us!'

They were all hanging on his words now. In fact, one or two were looking at Granit a little suspiciously. An excess of Goebbels-type defiance here for some tastes, echoes even of the kind of dumb *Durchhaltsparolen* that had blared from the radios in the Nazi-time when they had been kids.

'OK, I'll cut the fancy words,' Granit said, realising he might have gone too far with the rhetoric. 'This is the way we Kinder operate. Through hard work, courage, loyalty to each other, we have lived well. Lately we have also started to create that cushion for ourselves as we grow older, the thing we call the Pension Fund . . .' His face was grave, his voice heavy. 'But this is in danger. Everything we have built up is threatened. Yes, in *great danger*.'

'Get on with it!' said Gurkel.

Granit ignored him. 'As I said, this is a historic Kinder-meeting. You see, we have to face the fact that soon East Germany will be no more. I know this through my contacts. And therefore the *Stasi* will be no more, which means that our network of businesses and accounts and interests could be stripped bare, revealed to the world . . . *And we must make sure that we rise from the ashes of this part of our life together, just as we left the ruins of the old Kinder Garden and prospered even more mightily than before* . . .' Granit leaned forward on his table, resting his meaty knuckles on the polished wood. 'I have been giving my whole attention to this problem. I have already carried out the first part of my recovery plan – aided by Gurkel, Banana and The Wonder. Now we move into the second stage – for which I need the help of all of you, every one. My fellow-Kinder, I have taken every precaution. Now we must strike forward, into a new world!'

FORTY-SIX

BLESSED MUST HAVE STOOD on Erika's landing for a good five minutes, just listening, not so much gathering his courage as convincing himself of the reality of what he was about to do, before he tried the door to her flat.

It was locked. He had been careful to check there was no one up there. Of course it was locked.

Time for application of the criminal lore he had picked up. Once he had interviewed a bunch of professional burglars in Sydney, and one of them had told him, 'Problem with a door? Kick it in. Just kick the bastard in. Unless it's reinforced, you'll get it open eventually. And you know what? No bugger ever hears you. No one.'

Just to the right of the lock, the burglar had said. *Keep hitting it there.*

Blessed put down the carrier bag of tools he had bought at the hardware shop down the street: a screwdriver, a sturdy mallet and chisel. Then he took a step back, lifted his foot and smacked the door hard, with the heel and sole of his right boot. The door shook. Another step back. Another kick. It shook again, gave a bit.

Had that burglar in Sydney been bullshitting him? The noise it made when you did a thing like this. How come the entire building didn't come running?

Blessed put the thought out of his mind. The urgency of his need to get into that flat was as hot and conscienceless as lust. He was sweating. This time he really went for it. The door swung back on its hinges, crashing against the wall of Erika's entrance hall, making more noise than any of his kicks.

Blessed picked up his bag of tools and headed straight for the bedroom.

There was the bed. Tidily made, demurely turned down. The red-and-white pin-striped sheets. But more importantly, the big, rattan-framed mirror opposite it.

225

He and Erika used to look in that mirror when they were naked in bed; they used to watch themselves make love. She had liked that especially. Like a performer. Of course, like a performer . . .

Blessed started to explore how the mirror was fixed to the wall. He felt in the space behind the mirror, testing for the method of fixing. On the left-hand side, his fingers encountered something he assumed to be a bracket. But there was a spinelike ridge down its centre, and he couldn't find the place where the screw ought to be.

This wasn't a bracket. It was a hinge.

Blessed ran his finger up under the rim of the frame, found two more, subjected them to the same test. He transferred his attentions to the right-hand side.

Nothing between the frame and the wall. Not anywhere on the right. Maybe he wouldn't need the tools at all. Maybe . . .

He took hold of the right edge of the mirror frame with both hands, tried to pull it away from the wall. There was resistance. Then the mirror came away and lurched out towards him. It swung open, like a door, and Blessed found himself looking through into the apartment next to Erika's. To be more accurate, he found himself returning the cyclops-gaze of a very high-tech camera mounted on a tripod in the neighbours' living room.

Blessed stepped carefully past the tripod, made his way into the unfamiliar apartment. The curtains were drawn, but slowly his eyes accustomed themselves to the gloom. To say the place was simply furnished would have been flattery. A couple of armchairs. A table. On the table, the remains of a takeaway meal, plastic cups still half-full of a viscous mixture of coffee and cigarette-butts. The room reeked of stale tobacco. There were several ashtrays strewn around the cheaply-carpeted floor, all of them overflowing. He glanced into the bedroom. It was empty except for two unmade camp beds.

No one lived here. This was a workplace, business premises. The two 'quiet gays' next door had been Erika's cover-story.

But what use was any of this to him? Then Blessed's attention was caught by a three-drawer, freestanding steel filing cabinet in the corner of the living room. He advanced on it with his bag of tools. Dear God, he thought, thank you for the inspiration of the mallet and chisel. Thank you.

The opening of the cabinet was just a matter of ruthless application, of hammering away, easing the point of the chisel in until the top drawer eventually weakened and then gave. As it slid open, Blessed felt a peculiar kind of exhilaration, the 'high' that comes from taking direct, physical action. This must be how thieves felt, and spies, and soldiers – all those professions that allowed themselves everything.

Inside everything was arranged with surprising neatness compared with the flat itself. Suspended files in alphabetical order. Names.

Blessed reached in at random, lifted out an envelope, opened it, pulled out the contents.

First several long strips of colour contacts, often too small to see detail without a magnifying glass. But clearly people having sex on a bed, almost certainly next door judging from the pin-striped sheets. Then a sheaf of good-quality eight-by-six colour prints. OK . . .

Erika. An unknown man. A blonde woman. All three of them on the bed. All naked.

Blessed slipped the prints back in the envelope, dropped it back into the file.

'B'. Clearly labelled, B for Blessed.

His hand shook slightly as he took out the envelope. It was quite fat. His eye raced over the contacts. Must have been a couple of hundred. He only needed to look at one or two of the colour prints. It was all he could take, anyway. Some were from his first night with Erika, others from the succeeding weeks . . . months . . .

Jesus, the foolishness he felt. Not anger but just sheer, animal embarrassment. Cuckolded by a camera . . .

At this point Blessed knew he had to get back to the boathouse. Benno was home today. They had to talk, decide what to do. Blessed wavered. Should he return the photographs of himself and Erika to the file? No. He stuffed them all back into the envelope, wedged it into his coat pocket.

No need for anyone to see these. Not even Benno. They could be burned. Now . . . who were these other guys . . .

He began to go through the files alphabetically. Some English names . . . French . . . German . . .

What?

The envelope he picked out now was even fatter than the one he had just pocketed. Blessed went straight for the prints. One shot from behind, an unidentifiable man having sex with a woman in the missionary position.

ELLIOT the label on the file said. It was a common enough name, but somehow Blessed had instinctively known the moment he set eyes on it. The next shot confirmed his suspicions. The man had rolled over, was looking almost towards camera. The woman's face was visible now too . . .

Rockwell and Erika. The wise brother-in-law, the protector, the faithful husband, father and provider. The man on the bed with Erika was Daphne's husband *Rockwell.*

A cold fist tightening slowly in his stomach, Blessed examined a few more of the photographs. Rockwell and Erika. Erika and Rockwell . . . Finally, with great difficulty, he managed to return the prints to the envelope, which joined the other in his pocket. It was time to leave here. More than time.

He pushed the drawer closed, took a deep breath, and turned to go. Then he remembered his bag of tools. Like a robot he bent down to retrieve it. He was just straightening up again when, in the prescient way of such things, he felt the hairs shiver on the back of his neck in warning. He was conscious of hearing the door behind him opening, of careful footfalls in the room.

Blessed swung round wildly, dug into the bag for the mallet.

But there were three of them, young and strong and businesslike. He got one chance to lash out with the mallet, caught one of the men on the shoulder. He saw the man roll slightly to one side on his sneakered feet. Then, still without a word being spoken, one of the others punched Blessed full in the face. He fell back. The mallet was wrenched from his grasp. Then a big, gloved hand went over his mouth, he was dragged backward towards one of the armchairs. He ended up helplessly pinioned on one of the men's laps while another began to pull at his clothing.

The last clear thing he felt was his right arm being wrenched out of its coat-sleeve. Then his arm was held rigid; there was a stinging pain in his forearm. Seconds later, his body became heavy, too heavy to bear. Soon what was left of his consciousness was confined inside his head. He was rushing down a long tunnel. And there was no light at the end of this one – only darkness, solid as a wall.

Then Blessed hit that black wall, at infinite, crazy speed, and there was only the void beyond that darkness. The no-thing-ness beyond everything.

FORTY-SEVEN

'JUST SIGN EACH PIECE of paper in the right place,' Granit ordered. 'Don't worry about what they say. They're nice, legal East German property documents. That's all you need to know. Just trust, boys. For more than forty years we've survived on trust . . . ' He could see some Kinder peering at their neighbours' papers, like children at school. 'You're right, they're all different from each other. That's the whole point, to spread the assets around, have them in as many different names as possible. That's what will ensure our survival – and the prosperity of our pension fund! So come on and sign!'

Granit lit a cigar, leaned back in his chair and watched the smoke drift up to the ceiling. He loosened his tie. It was a hot August day. When this business was over they would throw open the windows and start the party. More than forty years had passed since that violent night in a deserted tyre factory in Lichtenberg when at the age of seventeen he, Granit, had seized the leadership of the orphan gang they called the Kinder. Afterwards, while still remaining leader, he had climbed the greased pole of the *Stasi* hierachy . . . onward and upward . . . until he became General Günther Albrecht of the – soon to be late – Ministry for State Security, God rest its hardworking, sweet, corrupt soul . . .

Granit heard papers shuffling, coughing. He turned his attention back to the meeting. 'Done? Any other questions?'

Banana's voice rang through the room: 'An aspiring writer once asked his old fox of an agent: What can I write that is guaranteed to make me money? Of course, the writer was expecting the man to say, screenplays, scandal-biographies, blockbusters!' Banana paused cunningly, milking the tension. 'The agent looked steadily at the questioner for some time. Then he sighed and solemnly intoned: "*Ransom notes, son. Ransom notes*".' Banana pointed to the documents in front of him. 'So, are these what we're signed here?' he drawled.

Laughter. Gurkel, already quite drunk, guffawed louder than anyone.

'You can leave the extortion to me, Banana,' Granit said, dead pan. 'These papers have to do with something else entirely. They're more like declarations of independence.'

Banana met his eye, nodded. 'Fair enough.'

Granit knew Banana had a conscience to wrestle with. He knew Banana was sometimes troubled. But he didn't worry about his reliability. The one gang-member who had caused him serious concern over the years was Gurkel. Look at him now, pink-faced, clutching a half-empty bottle of beer. A walking, talking security-leak. In times past, Granit had worried that Gurkel might betray the Kinder's secrets in his cups. His fears had been unrealised. Perhaps because, to an outsider, the story of the Kinder was so improbable that Gurkel could have blabbed out the truth in every bar from Konstanz to Kiel, and still no one would have believed him.

'All right. Go fetch 'em, Wonder,' Granit growled to The Wonder *alias* Herr Hildebrandt.

The little man obeyed, scuttled round the table, picking up the signed documents and collecting them into a pile on the table in front of Granit. The stack was eventually several inches thick. Granit picked up the pile in both hands and lowered it ceremoniously into a large attaché case, which he formally snapped shut and locked.

Then Granit rose to his feet, straightened up to his full, impressive height and clapped his hands to gain everyone's attention.

'I declare the business part of this Kinder-meeting *closed*,' he boomed gleefully. 'Party time! *Jetzt wird gefeiert!*'

A cheer went up. Granit walked over to the big double doors behind his seat, flung them back. In the next conference room stood a table laden with cold meats and salad, delicacies from smoked salmon and caviar to guinea-fowl in aspic. Ice-buckets held magnums of champagne. Everywhere the best beers, wines and spirits.

'Guaranteed no lung-soup!' Gurkel declared. 'I mean *guaranteed*!'

Granit opened the first of the magnums, poured champagne into the nearest tulip-glasses, took one for himself, gestured for someone to keep up the distribution. Then he took off his jacket, undid the top button of his shirt and sauntered back into the other room.

Most of the Kinder had gone into the banqueting space. Grateful for the peace and quiet, Granit could also catch up on what was happening out in the world. He looked at his watch, snapped on the large-screen TV in the corner. Some ads. He idly drank some bubbly, looked out over the formal gardens outside the high windows. Granit liked the view. He also liked to check that the guard at the far end of the lawn, a hundred yards from the house, was in place. He was, Granit noted with satisfaction. He'd always hand-chosen the best boys, the élite of what the Stasi offered, and it had paid off. They were his janissaries, his new generation of orphan warriors. He would hate to leave them, too.

The TV news was starting. Several of the Kinder had re-appeared from the banquet room with plates of food and charged glasses.

'Can't you let the world go by on its own for just one day, Granit?' one asked. 'I mean, you think it'll stop turning if you're not there to watch it?'

His companion, the one they called Flix, laughed hard. 'He don't know. And being Granit, he don't aim to find out oh no . . . '

Granit joined in the fun. 'Sure,' he said. 'But this *is* relaxing, because for once I'm not over there in the East and worrying.'

'They really finished, those commies over there?' Flix was slipping into a broad version of the old argot they had used as children, staccato, slangy. 'I mean really really finished?'

As if on cue, the equine features of Egon Krenz appeared on the screen. He was addressing the East German parliament, the *Volkskammer*, about something or other. Maybe the state of General Secretary Honecker's health. The youngest member of the East German Politbüro at fifty-one, Krenz had for many years been the head of the Party's youth wing. He smiled a lot. His teeth worked for their living.

'He any good?' Gurkel asked. He had commandeered a bottle of Gran Reserva Rioja and was knocking it back like soda-pop. 'I mean ol' Krenz? He looks like a dope . . . '

'He's the only one in the Politbüro who's not ripe for his pension. To those old assholes in Wandlitz that makes him "the voice of youth". But he's too small a man for this, you beddabelieve,' Granit said with a shrug. 'Krenz gets to be boss, he'll talk, he'll slither and slide, anything but *do* something. This situation, you need a killer or a real reformer – a Stalin or a Gorbachev. East Germany, God bless it, will get Krenz. That's why the place is doomed. That's why we gotta take drastic measures.'

The phone rang in the other room. Whoever had answered it called out sarcastically: 'Herr *Hildebrandt!* It's for *you* – from deepest Kreuzberg!' The Wonder, who had been hanging around on the fringe of the group of television-watchers, hurried off to take the call.

Granit motioned for someone to refill his glass. He had in mind to drink himself to sleep tonight, something he never normally did. Here, with the other Kinder around him, it was safe. For these few hours, nothing would happen, no one would be listening and watching. Granit could drop his guard, his iron self-control that had brought him – and the other Kinder – all the way from near-starvation in the slums to where they were today.

Then the Wonder was suddenly back at his elbow. There was an anxious look in his big marmoset's eyes. 'Granit,' he muttered, checking to make sure everyone else's attention was still on the TV screen. 'Problem. You gotta come to the phone. *Now.*'

Granit accepted a fresh glass of champagne, took a sip. 'What kind of trouble?'

'Oh, you'll find out, Granit.' The Wonder picked at his sleeve. 'But I tell you it's big, oh yes you beddabelieve *big* trouble . . . '

FORTY-EIGHT

THERE WAS NOTHING SUDDEN about it. The first light inside Blessed's head crept up on him, like fog replacing darkness, one degree of obscurity replacing another.

And there was the soreness in his bruised jaw. The bile thick in his throat, so thick that almost his only thought in those initial moments was that it must be blood, and he must be choking on it. But blood is salty, oddly sweet, and bile is bitter . . .

The headache hit him last, so hard that he threw back his head and groaned before regaining his self-control. When his wrists and legs tensed against the pain, he realised that he was in his underwear and strapped to a chair, a hard, high-backed throne. It bore a sinister resemblance to a torture-frame.

Blessed opened his eyes slowly, like a creature leaving cover. The blackness was complete. Either the room had no windows, or the blinds were so cunning and complete that they excluded every iota of light.

Nightmare. No idea of the size of the room. The darkness had sides, though. Like a box. But there was air coming from somewhere, or he would be suffocating.

Then, without warning, a small point of brightness exploded out of the pitch darkness. Blessed forced himself to focus on it. He realised he was meeting the gaze of another human being's eye, five, seven, ten feet away – impossible to tell, because space meant nothing in such blackness. Then the sliding shutter snapped closed, the outside eye/universe disappeared once more. Blessed was alone with his darkness.

Time passed.

As if in compensation, Blessed found that he was starting to hear things. A door opening somewhere, footsteps. A distant command being shouted. And – no, couldn't be mistaken, though he might be dreaming – a horse neighing and snorting. Then the door closed again, and the sounds of the outside were blotted out, as if murdered.

233

But suddenly there was a German voice, deep and rumbling, only partially comprehensible:

'Mine . . . (inaudible) . . . you assholes . . . '

' . . . found him . . . keep outside Berlin . . . (inaudible) this English journalist . . . (inaudible) . . . check Blessed. But Comrade General, the Minister . . . '

'We'll see! We'll see!'

Silence for some time.

There was an interval, impossible to gauge how long.

Then the spyhole opened once more, and there was the eye again. This time it stayed, feeding on his helplessness – or so it seemed to Blessed. He felt anger for the first time. Before, the eye had been welcome proof of an outside world, of some kind of life. Now it was predatory, emphasising his helplessness. Its gaze was like rape.

Blessed said nothing. Their power lay in their invisibility. His – what power he had – was in silence.

Somehow Blessed fell asleep. Or lost consciousness, for there was no healing, resting quality to what happened. All the pain, the anger, was still coursing through him when he was torn back into the world by a huge irruption of brilliance. It felt like the end of the universe, fire on his eyes, ice in his heart.

Someone had entered the room, bringing the light with him.

Nothing happened for some time afterwards. There was just this eerie, godlike silhouette occupying the middle of Blessed's field of vision, blocking almost the entire doorway, surrounded by a dazzling electric halo, motionless, hands on hips. Slowly, as his eyes accustomed themselves, Blessed began to be able to make out the man's features, his clothes. The man was a little above average height, dressed in a leather jacket and chino-type trousers. His hair was quite short, his features bland. Hard to tell his age. Early thirties, perhaps.

He was smoking. A small, cheap cigar. The perfumed aroma assaulted Blessed's heightened senses, tempting and repellent at once, the syrupy leaf of heaven and the crackling saltpetre of hell.

And – the next realisation – the man was smiling.

'Mr Blessed,' he said softly in German. 'You are all right?'

Blessed said nothing.

'Just nod.'

Blessed shook his head. The man laughed.

'I like your style. Now, we have to move you to somewhere different. A more comfortable place. I'm so sorry. But please, don't worry . . . '

Still smiling, the man took a puff on his cigar, stepped aside.

A man in a white tunic moved past him and came forward into the room. He was carrying a hypodermic. It was then that Blessed broke his silence.

'Piss off, you bastard!' Blessed spat at him in English. He tried to shout, but his voice had gone. It came out as a low, rasping bark: 'BASTARD! PISS OFF!'

Blessed continued to curse and abuse both of them, and to struggle against the straps, even as the man in the white tunic calmly filled the hypodermic, rolled up the sleeve of Blessed's shirt, and searched his exposed right arm for a vein.

SPRING IN AUTUMN

September–November 1989

FORTY-NINE

THERE WAS A PERIOD, he never knew exactly how long it lasted, of half-life, of deep sleep interleaved with dreams. It was a curiously happy, painless time.

Then Blessed awoke, and a strange and painful new existence began.

Once the drugs wore off, he realised that his new prison had one big advantage. Light. Sometimes thin shafts of daylight penetrated the window to his left. They faded and disappeared for what he presumed to be night. So now he could keep count of the passage of time. But what was his starting point? How many precious days – could it be weeks? – had they already taken away from him?

Also, there were cars outside somewhere, sounds of traffic, street noise . . . occasionally the manic tinkle of a tram bell. *They've moved me back to the city*, he thought. *Easier, perhaps, to lose me there?*

The room Blessed was in seemed to be about nine feet by twelve. Not bad, for a cell. The bed he lay on was in the corner. Nearby, a half-open door to a small cubicle containing a handbasin and a WC. The window, off to his right, was all but covered by a blind. The light that seeped in at the corners was Blessed's only indication of night and day. And opposite his bed was the barrier – or rather, the first in a system of barriers – that stood between himself and the outside world. Through this, several times each day, would enter the man he came to know only as 'Werner'.

Blessed was always forewarned of Werner's approach. First by the faint rattle of keys turning in a lock. The outer, steel-lined door would swing open. Then there Blessed's jailer would stand, in a short corridor, visible through a locked, barred gate, like a keeper finding his way into the cage of a desperate wild animal. At that moment, Blessed would be able to catch a strong institutional aroma of disinfectant and floor-polish. Now the sounds of traffic would be a little louder and more distracting. Werner would carefully lock the outer door, cutting off those sounds and smells, before unlocking the cage-gate and stepping into the room.

'Mr Blessed,' he would always say. 'How are you?'

Each time, Blessed would examine him anew. A commonplace face, going a little puffy as he moved into early middle age. An insurance salesman with a taste for late nights and always a couple too many shots of cheap spirit. Was this the same man who had smiled at him, then stepped aside to allow the injection to be administered? Yes. The voice. Above all, Blessed remembered the voice. The man's hair had been cut. (Again that question: how much time had passed?). He was still wearing an insurance salesman's leather jacket. And now – prominently displayed in his waistband – a service pistol. Not standard equipment for an insurance salesman.

Werner would often bring food. Simple cafeteria-type fare. He and Blessed would talk. Then, watching Blessed carefully as did so, he would go back through the cage-gate, lock it behind him, make his way out through the outer door into the corridor and finally lock the outer door too. It was heavy, lined with steel, and always closed with a solid clunk, like the door to an old-fashioned safe or a very expensive car.

Each time, Blessed would sense an extra barrier descending on him, a heavy, stifling curtain of depression. Each time, he had a queasy feeling that jails were among the very few things that the GDR built enough of, and built well.

The prisoner was given a ration of ten cigarettes a day – 'Lord Extra', a West German brand. Werner claimed the credit for this inexplicable generosity, in a transparent attempt to lay the foundations for a special relationship. And he and Blessed really did seem to get to know each other during the days, which would eventually stack up into the weeks, that followed.

Why not? Blessed had expected a succession of turnkeys and interrogators, but in fact Werner was the only human being Blessed ever saw, and since that first overheard conversation the only voice he ever heard. Seven days a week. Efficient, correct, and always with that gun in his waistband, Werner was nevertheless – within his professional limits – friendly and communicative.

Oddly, the business with the cigarettes backfired. Blessed needed and looked forward to the daily (or he assumed daily) delivery of ten Lord Extra – wrapped in a rubber band and tossed to him by

238

Werner with a knowing grin. But the procedure was humiliating. There was the terrible fact of his addiction to nicotine, which Blessed could not ignore. Then his awareness of the control these people exercised over him because of that addiction. The way they could organise the handover as they wished (Why the rubber band? Why only ten a day instead of twenty every two days, in a proper packet?). The entire transaction was fraught with irritation and poisoned by power. Blessed hated Werner at those times.

Except that Werner was his world. Werner was all Blessed had. He could not hate him as savagely, as completely as he wanted to.

'Are you to going to keep me here for ever?' Blessed asked on what by his calculations was the twelfth day.

Werner had just brought in his breakfast. Blessed was sitting on the edge of his iron-framed bed, idly contemplating the meal. A couple of grey socialist rolls, gluey jam, a mug of ersatz coffee. This wasn't the first time Blessed had asked this question. He tried to work in a variation of it at least once a day.

'For ever is a long time. Longer than a life.' Werner grinned craftily.

As usual, Werner stood nearby with his arms folded, but – again as usual – he kept his distance. He had explained carefully to Blessed that this was in case Blessed did anything silly. Werner and his colleagues were taught, you know, always to make sure they had time to draw their weapons.

'I'll rephrase that,' Blessed retorted. 'Are you intending to keep me here for a long time?'

Werner frowned. 'Eat up,' he said. Then he added unexpectedly: 'It isn't my decision, all this, you know. I am very low-grade. A simple operative. This matter of your custody in this place, it's for the very high-up people. Under our law –'

Blessed seized his chance. 'Wait a minute. I haven't done anything against your law. I was kidnapped from West Berlin. I broke *their* law by forcing an entry into that flat. Not yours.'

'This is not for me to say. The executive organs have their reasons. But – as I was going to say – under our law, if you are deemed to pose a threat to the socialist order, then you can be kept in custody for as long as necessary.'

'And the general? What does he think about that?'

Werner smiled uneasily. 'General? What general?'

'The one who came in and had a row with someone – was it you? – the first night I was here.'

Werner had a little gesture he always used when he wanted to avoid difficult subjects. He would simply shrug, then make a child-like wiggling motion with his strong hands.

'I think maybe you are deluded,' he said. 'These drugs . . . off course, they are more humane than violent means of restraint . . . but you know they do strange things to the mind. Our doctors tell me, your memory of that day will be hazy.

'I heard what I heard. I'm sure it wasn't a hallucination. Someone very powerful wanted to take me away from you people. I think that's why you moved me to this place.'

Werner frowned sternly, wagged a finger. 'Now, Mr Blessed, it's rubbish what you say! Delusions! Just delusions!'

FIFTY

'SO. YOU GOT MY MESSAGE.' Granit's voice was heavy with humiliation, reined-in anger.

By contrast, the man on the other end of the line seemed calm, almost casual. 'Of course, old friend,' Benno Klarfeld said. 'Why else would I be calling?'

Granit's tone changed, becoming momentarily softer. 'How strange to hear your voice.'

'Yes. Granit –'

'*Use no names*, please.' The harshness returned. 'I crossed over the border especially, to avoid . . . you know what I wanted to avoid.' Granit sighed. 'I tell you, I can't believe what's happening. You're threatening me.'

'You're right. That's exactly what I'm doing.'

Silence. Crackle of static. Both men wondering if, despite all their meticulous precautions, the line was tapped.

'Believe me,' Granit said, 'this was not at all what I intended at the beginning.'

'Me neither.'

'It's just happened this way, like you're driving along and suddenly there's a tree across the road . . . '

'Yes.'

A pause. Granit broke the deadlock with a question.

'So. What do you want?'

'First things first. Is our friend alive?'

'He is.'

'Do you have him?'

'*I have him. I give you my word on that. All right*?'

'Do you intend to keep him?'

'Not for too long.'

'So, it's a simple question of timing?'

'That's right.'

'Then we have something to talk about.'

241

'Maybe,' Granit snapped. 'But the timing is absolutely critical and must be left to my discretion. And understand one thing. If you betray us this time, then all bets are off. I'll cut my losses and run. I will have no choice . . . I think you know what that will mean for our friend.'

'Oh, don't worry. I'll keep the faith if you do.' Then Klarfeld's voice, though still calm, took on an edge of steel. 'Now listen very carefully, because there's a new deal, and the new deal is this . . . '

FIFTY-ONE

ON THE SEVENTH DAY by Blessed's reckoning, he had received his first change of clothes, on the fourteenth his second, and now, on the twenty-first, his third. One slightly threadbare pair of slacks and one denim shirt exchanged for laundered replacements.

'Do you think of escaping?' Werner asked solemnly as Blessed tucked his clean shirt into his trousers.

'No,' Blessed lied.

'Good. You know why? You are in the middle of the city, in a government quarter. The building is full of our people. And even if you got to the street, you would not get ten yards before someone saw you.' Werner folded his arms again. 'I believe it is important that you know this. Because once you do, you will be able to accept this situation and relax.'

'You're very kind.'

Werner squinted at Blessed shrewdly. 'You don't mean this. You think I am an asshole. Why not admit it?'

Blessed lit a cigarette. Werner looked at his watch.

'I have time for a smoke too, maybe.' Werner took out one of his cheap little cigars and was soon puffing away.

One day, when Werner appeared and handed Blessed his tray, there was, unless Blessed was completely mistaken, a hint of alcohol on his breath.

He noticed the light was beginning to fade in the slit surrounding the window-blind. Twenty-six days, that added up to. If any of the conventional indicators – changes from darkness and light, the way meals succeeded each other, Werner's apparent morning freshness or night-time fatigue – made any sense at all.

'If you're trying to brainwash me, I have to tell you, Werner, that you're the most incompetent indoctrinator I've ever come across,' Blessed said.

Werner walked round the room for a bit. Then he swung around to face Blessed.

243

'See this?' he barked, and slapped the butt of the pistol in his waistband. 'This here is the only indoctrinator that really counts. With a choice between this, and survival, you would change your mind pretty damned quick!'

Blessed studied him for a while. Werner's face was flushed, and his eyes seemed particularly unfocused. Was Werner actually drunk?

'What do you want from me, Werner?' Blessed was surprised, even alarmed, by the real anxiety and passion in his own voice.

Werner had calmed down. 'I?' he said, pursing his lips. 'I? I want us to get along. And maybe I can help you learn some things. About my country and about the world.'

'Listen. I don't care about all that. Or rather –' Blessed corrected himself hastily. 'It's not the most important thing. No. What I really want to know is, why I'm being kept in this place, *and when I'm going to be let out*. Because sooner or later you'll have to let me out. There must be people out there already wanting to know where I am.'

'That is not my department,' answered Werner crisply. 'All the things you ask are answerable only by people very high up, who know all the facts.'

'Sly bastard,' Blessed murmured. 'Sly bastard. I know how sly you are.'

Werner sighed. 'What an evening this has been.'

Evening. The bastard said evening. This is the first time he's actually acknowledged the time of day.

'Now I must go. I tell you, Mr Blessed . . . Michael . . . I need a drink now.' Werner was unlocking the cage gate. 'There is a bar on the corner which will still be open. A beer and a Korn to kick me off. Then I'll take it more slowly. If it's any comfort, I will drink one for you too . . . '

'Don't you have a family?' Blessed blurted out.

Werner paused. Blessed fancied he caught him in a tiny grimace. 'I was an orphan,' he said. 'My family is . . . *die Firma* . . . you know, the firm . . . '

'No wife, child . . . lover . . . ?'

'Once I had a wife. You know how these things go wrong. Now I have no time.' Werner smiled, swung open the iron barrier. 'You are my family these days, Michael,' he called back over his shoulder, eerily like a spouse leaving for work. 'Round the clock.'

FIFTY-TWO

DAY THIRTY-SIX by Blessed's count.

This time when Werner came with breakfast, he was clearly, undeniably drunk.

Werner fumbled the unlocking of the cage-gate. He nearly dropped the keys. His normally well-coordinated movements were clumsy. His face was flushed.

'Mr Michael Blessed, your food,' he announced, kicking the cage-gate shut behind him and stuffing the keys in his pocket with his free hand. It was the first time he hadn't locked up meticulously.

Jesus. Werner's presence stank up the room like a schnapps distillery.

Blessed had been awake for a couple of hours. His mind was clear, almost normal. There was the appearance of light outside. He counted this as the thirty-fifth morning since Werner had first walked into this room and introduced himself.

'How are you, Werner?' Blessed asked.

Werner laughed. He started singing something under his breath. Blessed recognised it as the old German socialist song, *Brothers, To the Sun, to Freedom.*

'Why aren't you speaking to me, Werner?'

'Wassa point?'

'It helps to pass the time, for me at least.'

Werner went on singing softly. Da-da-di-di-di . . . Di-daa-daa . . .

'I'm sorry for you,' he mumbled eventually. It was not good thinking about you last night.'

Werner finally remembered to put down the breakfast tray on the end of the bed. Then he moved out into the room, mindless, as if dancing with an imaginary partner. At one point he almost fell over backwards.

'Why are you sorry for me, Werner?'

Blessed was on his feet now, and possibilities were occurring to him. Wild possibilities.

245

Werner was having trouble focusing on Blessed. He was sweating, too. There was a hint of blond stubble on his normally well-shaven chin.

'Why sorry?' Blessed made himself smile very, very sincerely. He took a step towards Werner.

'Because . . . *ach*, you know, you get attached to someone, you start to identify with him . . . Then . . . then . . . '

'Then *what*, Werner?' Another step. 'They let him go? *What*?'

'Oh no oh no oh no no no . . . Not let him go, oh no no . . . '

Werner was looking at the floor, shaking his head.

'Sit down, Werner,' Blessed said gently. 'Sit down on the bed. Take it easy.'

'You . . . you know . . . '

One more step and Blessed was by Werner's side. He took him by the arm of his leather jacket. 'Come on. It's not so bad, is it?'

'Bad. Oh no no no . . . *bad* . . . '

Blessed began to lead Werner towards the bed.

They were just short of it when Werner tripped over the foot Blessed had put in his way.

'Whooops!'

Blessed reached round Werner's waist as if to steady him.

'OK, Werner. Don't you worry . . . . '

With his right hand, Blessed grabbed the butt of the pistol and pulled hard. At the same time he barged with his shoulder against Werner's, propelling him in the opposite direction. Werner lurched wildly away, toppling off balance.

'WASSAMATTER?'

Werner's slide helped pull the gun completely out of his waistband. With his free hand, Blessed gave him another hard push. Werner hit the ground. Then Blessed back-pedalled rapidly, trying to recall his handgun-drill.

OK. Feet braced apart. Hold gun with both hands. Point it. Lucky this isn't a heavy weapon. Now off with the safety-catch. *Shit*, is there a clip in here? Yes there is, thank Christ . . . and what now . . .

'Don't move, Werner. Just fucking stay where you are,' Blessed said. His throat was dry, his voice a little cracked, but he was surprised how steady his hands were, how completely calm and in control he felt.

Werner was starting to stagger back to his feet when Blessed spoke to him. He stayed in mid-crouch, breathing hard.

'Oh no no . . . ' he panted. 'Mr Blessed, this is so stupid.'

Werner's expression reminded Blessed of a time at school when a bullying teacher had had his bluff called. After endless physical torment, a kid had actually turned round and hit the older man back. And the thing was, the teacher had been utterly deflated. His look had said, *You've found me out.*

There was just the same message of furious submission in Werner's slightly bloodshot eyes now.

'They'll kill you,' Werner said.

'I think they need me,' Blessed said. 'It's certainly worth a bet. Now take off your clothes. Nice and easy. No sudden movements. But no hanging about, either.'

'I think you are crazy.'

'*Strip.*'

Werner took off his leather jacket. While Werner was undoing his shirt buttons, Blessed undid his own. Werner took off his jeans and sneakers. When Werner was down to his underwear, Blessed eased off his own cheap canvas shoes but kept his slacks on. All one-handed, keeping the gun pointed. No simple matter.

For a moment, there they were, jailer-turned-prisoner and con-trariwise, standing opposite each other, one shirtless, the other in his underwear.

'Toss your clothes over to me, one by one,' Blessed said. 'Care-fully.'

Werner obeyed in mortified silence. First the jacket, then the slacks and shirt.

'Now go over to the wall. Put your hands on your head. And face the wall, with your back completely to me. *Move.*'

Werner shuffled backwards, his bare feet slapping the floorboards with a fleshy, slightly squeaky sound. When he reached the wall, he half-turned, then stopped, looking mistrustfully out of the corner of his eye at Blessed.

'Face the wall completely, Werner. No trouble from you, no violence from me. I promise you.'

Werner put his hands on his head and abruptly turned to face the wall. Blessed could see that his whole body was tense. Blessed almost expected him to stamp one foot in childish frustration. It was

247

like that. The whole scene seemed fake, laughably contrived, like a clip from a situation comedy – except that Blessed's fear was real. And the loaded gun he held signalled the total lack of comedy in the situation.

Now that Werner couldn't see him, it was easier for Blessed to slip on the clothes he had decided to steal: the leather jacket, the shirt, the sneakers that were plasticky and a little too big for him but better than the prison-issue canvas ones he had been stuck with for so long. If he was going to sneak around these corridors, avoiding notice, looking for a way out, best to wear a *Stasi* man's clothes. And if – when – he made it to the street, they would come in useful too.

Blessed checked the pockets of the jacket. Keys in the right one. In the inside breast pocket, a pocketbook and a little identity document in a plastic wallet. Could come in useful.

Retreating to the door, Blessed selected the cage-door key, which was the larger of the two. Werner was absolutely silent. No threats, no warnings. Blessed turned the key in the lock of the cage door.

'You don't know what's out there,' Werner said then, and laughed bitterly. 'You just don't know, Mr Blessed.'

The delicate bit was opening the outer door and closing the cage-gate, at the same time keeping an eye on Werner, just in case of any last-minute moves. Blessed's extra problem was that he also had to check the corridor outside, but a cursory glance told him there was no one about. Also, that this might not be at all the kind of institutional place he had expected.

Blessed slammed the outer door behind him, decisively, just as Werner always did, paused for just a moment. From now on he would have to move fast. In case Werner started to yell. In case Werner knew ways of attracting attention, or even getting out of the room, which Blessed had never discovered.

Blessed looked left. A bend in the dimly-lit corridor. To the right, twenty feet away, a graceful, totally uninstitutional staircase going down. And there, centred over that stairwell, an imposing arched window, probably eighteenth-century, disappearing out of sight onto the storey below. Every paned glass in it was painted over black. Above him, Blessed could make out the remains of plaster mouldings, a cornice of grapes and twisting vines interspersed with battered, chipped faces that could once have been either cherubs or gargoyles, impossible to tell.

This building had once been a bit grand, but it was gone to hell now. Making his decision, Blessed began to move quickly to the right, towards the stairs. He realised that the big-city traffic sounds that had filtered through to his cell were still there, but they were booming like a sound track. And as he moved further from the cell door, the louder they got.

His hand rested on the bannister, while his eyes searched the stairs below for a sign of life . . . the traffic sounds were coming from very close by.

Oh shit he thought. Oh shit, there's a speaker up there, mounted on the corner of that wall. All this time I've been hearing a tape, a recording . . . I'm lost . . .

The steps were partly covered in cheap carpet, but underneath they were made of marble. Blessed started to descend, quickly but as quietly as he could. He was still holding the gun at the ready, hoping to God he didn't have to choose whether to use it in cold blood.

No one. There was no-one down on the next level either. Just another softly echoing landing. The place was like a mausoleum. Discounting what had been playing through the speaker, not even distant sounds of steps or voices, doors opening and closing. Nothing and no one.

The great, darkened window descended all the way down to ground level. Here, a dusty entrance hall was dominated by a massive pair of mahogany doors. A couple of low-wattage bulbs were burning on the end of chain-leads suspended from the skeletal corpse of an elaborate chandelier. On either side of the door were further blind windows, every pane blacked out.

'You don't know what's out there,' Werner had said. And he didn't. He still didn't.

Who the hell was Werner? Who did he really work for?

Blessed reached the double doors, panting slightly from tension. There was a large brass handle on each. He chose the right-hand one, pressed it down. Then he passed Werner's gun from his left hand back into his right, pushed open the door with his knee, prepared to meet the day outside.

249

The day?

Yes, Werner had brought him his breakfast half an hour ago.

But through the gap that was opening up between the doors, Blessed saw moonlight pouring onto the grey stone steps. A glance upwards revealed a lightly-clouded, dark-copper night-sky. The breeze was fresh, even a little cold.

Blessed looked out. Six steps down to a driveway. Everything so fucking quiet. He inched his way through the doorway, out onto the wide top step, blinked and looked around. No people. No vehicles. He turned. Behind him the facade of his prison, a neglected country house, probably eighteenth century. In front of him, the drive, lined by elderly, ragged linden trees, curving away to the left after a couple of hundred yards. The full moon hung over it all, bright and insultingly neutral, like a coin wrapped in cellophane.

He forced himself to move forward, down the steps.

Standing on the gravel driveway, Blessed remembered the gun in his hand, and he paused just once more. It was time to make a decision. He had to assume he was in East Germany. There would be no shoot-outs from now on, or at least none he could survive. The weapon he had taken from Werner was a dangerous liability. Blessed weighed it in his hand for a moment, fighting his instincts to keep it. Then he tossed the gun as far as he could. By the time it hit the ground, fifty or so yards to his left, he was already on his way.

There would be hunters to be faced. Aware that any approaching vehicle would pin him in its headlights if he stayed on the drive, Blessed moved into the shadow of the trees on the right-hand verge and began to run. Werner's sneakers were slightly too big for him, and before he had covered more than a few yards the wetness of the uncut grass had begun to soak through them, but the sensuality of movement, and the freedom of the open air, felt good beyond measure.

I hope they come for you eventually, Werner. Not too soon, though. Not a moment too soon . . .

He followed the curve of the drive, for the moment unable to see any further than the shapes of the trees.

First he needed to find a road. He needed a sign, a village name, a river, any landmark, to tell him where he was.

Then he needed some means of transport.

Finally, and above all, Michael Blessed needed a miracle.

250

FIFTY-THREE

THE CURVING, LINDEN-TREE-LINED drive turned out to be about half a mile long.

At its end Blessed confronted heavy wrought-iron gates, all high wall. Very impressive. Except, as he immediately established, the gates were not locked. Perhaps the place's official status was sufficient deterrent. There was a big, peeling sign here that told him most of what he needed to know. It said:

GOVERNMENT OF THE GERMAN DEMOCRATIC REPUBLIC. RESTRICTED MILITARY AREA. ACCESS BY UNAUTHORISED PERSONS WILL BE SEVERELY PUNISHED.

Still no sign of any people or vehicles. Once through the gates, Blessed found himself on a deserted road, lined with woods on the far side. It was cobbled and in poor repair. No place signs in sight, no hints of his whereabouts.

Blessed decided to move right. There the road ran straight for as far as he could see. Less chance of being surprised.

He walked quickly, constantly checking his surroundings. His initial euphoria was quickly giving way to a form of agoraphobic fear. Fear of these sudden open spaces. Fear of the freedom they represented. Fear of those sudden choices – whether to go right or left, whether to walk or run, what to do if a car approached, or if he encountered a stranger.

This strange species of panic must resemble what East Germans felt when they set foot outside their fenced-in country, Blessed thought; when they finally left the big prison cell of the GDR, with all the big Werners lording it over you, telling you it's good when it's bad, white when it's black, day when it's really night . . .

The straight road finally took on a gentle curve, and the trees thinned. Eventually Blessed found himself in open country, looking out over a landscape from a seventeenth-century Dutch painting. Flat polder-like lowland as far as he could see. Moonlight on long, straight ditches, neat ploughed fields. In the distance, maybe a mile away, a village. The moonlight was strong enough for him to make

251

out houses and barns. The conical witch's hat shape of a Lutheran churchspire rose high above the thickly-clustered buildings.

Blessed began to feel a little better. He was in the March of Brandenburg. No mistaking. This landscape was familiar from his trips here in the Seventies, round the perimeter of East Berlin to get to Potsdam – a trip that in pre-Wall days had taken no more than half an hour from the Kurfürstendamm and was now a matter of two, even three hours. It was just possible that they had completed their deception by taking him to some far away part of the country that mysteriously resembled the area around Berlin. If not, then Blessed was no more than fifty miles from the capital, and probably much less.

A couple of minutes later, he saw headlights approaching, in column, coming fast. The leading truck – the headlights were set too high and wide apart for a car – was a couple of kilometres away. Blessed had eighty, ninety seconds in hand, he calculated, before the first vehicle reached him . . .

A wide ditch ran off to his left thirty or forty yards ahead. There was a not very healthy-looking young willow tree clinging to the bank just by the road. Not much to hide behind, but better, infinitely better, than nothing.

Blessed made for the ditch. The fields were unfenced, thank God. He cleared the grassy ridge that separated road from farmland. The willow bowed over, its scraggy trunk curved like a hunchback's spine, its sparse leaves half-immersed in water. He reached it, stepped round to the far side, and crouched, like a child at a game. He was grateful to Werner's leather jacket for its warmth, but also because it was magical, midnight black. A cloak of darkness.

The ditchwater was brackish, sour-smelling. Blessed recalled those adventures in which heroes and heroines would stay under water while the villains searched, breathing only through straws. Fine. Nobody ever mentioned the stink in those stories.

Blessed scooped up a handful of thick mud, smeared it on his face, then hid as much of the rest of himself as he could behind the slender trunk of the tree. The sound of engines was getting louder. The strong beams of the headlights were flicking over the road, scanning the surrounding fields.

The first truck arrived, roaring along the final stretch of road, doing close to seventy . . . tarpaulin-covered, chunky communist-

252

bloc utility vehicles, heavy and noisy. Blessed, with his mud-blackened face, peered cautiously out from behind the willow, watching for the crucial moments when the one truck's lights would illuminate the rear numberplates of the next . . .

Figures and numbers at that speed were an illegible blur. But East German government insignia were very clearly visible. Army? Police? *Stasi*? Impossible to tell. Were they already on his tail? Where else could they possibly be going at this speed and at this time of night? Blessed pulled up the collar of Werner's jacket, went down as far as he could, and waited until they had all passed.

Eventually Blessed straightened up and wiped the mud off his face. He had no choice but to press on to the village and beyond, using the advantage of darkness and hoping the trucks would not be back.

'It's a hell of a lot of trouble you're going to, just for one man.'

'Just one man?' Granit echoed. 'Well, yes. But he's a potential witness to everything, don't forget. And Benno insists we deliver him back in one piece. Nothing is too much trouble for us where he's concerned.'

'All right.' A snort of sardonic laughter down the phone line from Otmar Ziegler, alias Banana. 'He's your witness. And you're the man with the power. Sometimes I forget that. So, where is he now?'

'About three kilometres from the railway line, as he will soon realise. He's approaching a village east of Ludwigsfelde.'

'So, when do the interesting things start to happen for him?'

'We haven't quite decided yet. You see, it's got to *stick*, if you know what I mean. We have to make him feel it was *hard*.'

'No pain, no gain, as they say.'

'Who said that?'

'It's a motto used by exercise freaks in the West.'

'Sounds like Marxism-Leninism to me! See how East and West are getting closer!'

'Maybe. I think we're agreed on the pain. The problem is . . . with Marxism-Leninism it's kind of hard to identify the gain . . .'

Just as he reached the village, Blessed realised that he was travelling east. There, straight ahead of him, were the first hints of dawn.

The sign on the outskirts of the village was old, possibly even pre-war. Unsurprisingly, he had never heard of the village, but underneath its name, as with all German communities, East or West, the sign also mentioned the administrative district. He was in the subdistrict of Zossen, immediately to the south of Berlin. Somewhere not too far away was the railway that encircled the divided city, and also the Transit-Autobahn that led to and from the south of the country.

But he had no passport, no papers except Werner's. He was as thoroughly trapped as any East German citizen. Unless he could reach a western embassy. In other words, unless he could reach East Berlin. And once he got there, were those embassies guarded? Probably. He knew the British embassies in Moscow and Prague were watched. Almost certainly the same in East Berlin.

Forget that. Keep going . . .

Rough farm buildings spilled over into the field nearest the village proper. There was one light on, in a livestock shed off to the right. Blessed heard someone whistling faintly. Should he go towards the sound or avoid it? Sooner or later he would have to risk encountering other human beings, but maybe not yet.

A creaking door swung open. It happened so fast that Blessed had no chance to hide. A fat middle-aged man appeared carrying a bucket. He was wearing a grubby white apron, gumboots, and a battered white hat. Blessed identified him as the whistler. He was still hissing something rhythmic through his teeth.

When he saw Blessed, the man stopped and stared. His gaze was neither hostile nor friendly, just a little suspicious.

'*Na, guten Morgen,*' the man said. 'Looking for something so bright and early?'

'*Guten Morgen,*' Blessed returned the compliment as easily as his rapidly-beating heart would allow. 'My car broke down two, three miles back. I've been under the bonnet but got nowhere,' he said sheepishly, indicating his blackened face and hands, forcing a wry smile. 'I'm looking for a repair workshop.'

The farmhand squinted at him carefully. 'You a foreigner?'

'Hungarian. From Budapest.'

The lie came out smoothly. Blessed had been tempted to claim he was from Prague. Then he reminded himself that the farm-hand might speak Czech. Many of the Germans expelled from their homes in Czechoslovakia after the war now lived in East Germany. Hungarian was far safer. No one spoke Hungarian.

The farmhand grunted. 'You're a long way from home.'

'I'm a salesman. Travelling up to Berlin on business. I hate the Autobahn, thought I'd take the country roads.' Blessed smiled wearily. 'My mistake, eh?'

'What kind of car?'

'Skoda. New one. Listen, I thought I would head for the transit Autobahn. There's always a mechanic on duty at the rest-houses, you know?'

'Nearest one is Michendorf. That's Potsdam-South. It's open all the time. For transit traffic.'

'Yeah. I know. About ten, twelve kilometres from here, isn't that right?'

The farmhand nodded.

Blessed looked hard at his non-existent watch, sighed. 'Better press on. How far to the highway?'

'Keep going through the village. Two, three kilometres. Then you hit Highway 101 going south, and you'll be on the Autobahn in no time. Listen, you wait a while, until seven-thirty or so, I can get you a lift with the milk truck.'

So Blessed was between the Autobahn and the railway. *Even closer to Berlin than he had hoped.*

'It's OK,' Blessed said. 'You're very kind, but I'll press on. I'll hitch a lift when I get to that main highway. Some kind soul's bound to take pity on me.'

'Suit yourself.'

'*Auf Wiedersehen*, my friend.'

'*Auf Wiedersehen.*'

The farmhand took one last, disturbingly thorough look at Blessed and continued on his way. He opened a rusty five-barred gate, disappeared into a farmyard.

Satisfied that the whistling bucket-carrier had gone wherever he was going, Blessed began to walk briskly, with his hands in his pockets, heading into the village.

Crows huddled watchfully along the telephone lines. There was something about the way the farmhand had given Blessed that final once-over that spelled bad news. Natural backwoods distrust of strangers laced with state-promoted xenophobia. No way that man wasn't going to contact the local police, the burgomaster, the collective farm chairman, some link in the chain of power.

When Blessed saw a narrow, straight road, hardly more than a lane, going off to the left, he knew he had to take it. The road Blessed was following at present would eventually connect with a main highway, and once there it couldn't be far to the Berlin transit-Autobahn. It was also, however, on this road that they would come looking for him.

Blessed darted quickly up the lane and broke into a run. He had almost reached a windbreak of poplar trees about half a mile from the village when he heard a sound. He turned, watched a Trabant car in the green-and-white livery of the *Volkspolizei* and with a flashing light on top make its noisy, spluttering way along the main road, following the route he would have taken if he had continued in that direction. The police car then disappeared behind some buildings. It cut its engine. Blessed heard doors slam, the distant voices carrying over the clear early-morning air.

Blessed sprinted for the trees. A cold, grey light had spread over the landscape during the past ten or fifteen minutes. The eastern horizon was glowing pink, ready to burst at any moment into day. He felt terrifyingly visible.

Before long Blessed's heart started to pound, but he kept up the pace. The lane led on through the trees, on a gentle curve. There were more woods . . . small industrial buildings and uncultivated ground . . . and about a mile away, a kind of a high, raised bank, like a dike . . .

It was then that Blessed realised he was looking at a railway embankment, the southern part of the great loop-line that circled divided Berlin. If he caught one of its trains, he could be at the Ostkreuz station in an hour.

At the British Embassy in Unter den Linden before it even opened to visitors.

FIFTY-FOUR

BY THE TIME BLESSED NEARED the railway line, the sun was up, a thin, reluctant presence on the horizon to his right. And Blessed was beginning to feel the combined impact of exhaustion and fear. After so many days cooped up in that cell, his body was in poor shape. But he had to ignore it. He had to find the strength to override the objections of his heart, limbs, head.

Then, cutting into his pain, came the sound of a train.

Rattling its leisurely way from the direction of Potsdam, this was an early commuter service, with old-fashioned doubledecker carriages.

When the train drew close, Blessed threw himself into the damp grass at the side of the road and waited for it to pass. But instead of the clatter of the bogies' fading into the distance, he heard the low, hissing shriek of brakes. The train was stopping.

Was there a station nearby? Blessed got to his feet. Summoning up his courage, he set off at a trot towards the line. The little road made a sharp right-hand curve where it met the railway, and continued alongside it into a large stand of unhealthy-looking trees. Soon he was alongside the tracks.

The train started up again. He heard it pulling away. A station. Yes, for sure a station.

The ground began to rise as the road led him into the trees beside the railway line. An overgrown cinder path led off to the right, losing itself within a few metres among a tangle of bushes. Blessed surveyed the prospect ahead. The station was three or four hundred yards away. He could clearly see the platform.

And there were two men in uniform by the station sign. One of them had a walkie-talkie. The other had a machine-pistol. He couldn't go to that station while those uniforms were there. And there was no going back. Everyone in the village would have heard about the mysterious disappearing stranger who said he was Hungarian – and the Volkspolizei would still be cruising the approach-roads to GDR Highway 101.

You know what, Michael Blessed? You're fucked.

257

The only course of action left to him, was to follow the path through the undergrowth, and try to press on even if the path petered out, because that way he might just find a route out to another road.

Blessed pushed on down the cinder track. There were brambles everywhere he looked. He had gone about ten yards when he felt the first drops of rain, another twenty before the skies opened and the torrent came down on him. Soon Werner's sneakers were a pair of leaky canoes; his prison slacks were already glued to his thighs. At this rate, if the Vopos didn't get him, pneumonia would.

All Blessed could do was put one squelching foot in front of the other and trudge on through the downpour, torn at by brambles, battered by jutting branches. He began to understand why escapers surrendered themselves, even when surrender meant death.

And what was that up ahead?

Blessed stopped. It seemed to be some kind of a shack in a clearing. He moved forward again, very cautiously, until he got to the edge of the space. Here the vegetation had been cut back, the grass mown. There were a few flowering shrubs, long past their summer best, on the far side.

The hut was like hundreds of thousands of other tiny *Gartenhäuschen* found on waste land on the edges of German cities. Each on its own carefully-tended plot, such retreats were traditionally places where working-class families came at weekends to relax, garden and take in the fresh air after being cooped up all week in smelly factories and tenements.

The degree of discomfort Blessed was experiencing can make a man reckless. Without more than a moment's thought, he shuffled up to the door of the hut and tried the handle. Not locked.

Inside was a small table, a chair, a narrow camp bed. Tools were hung neatly from nails on one wall. Hanging on the wall opposite, next to the window, there was a framed photograph of a family – mother, father, two boys and a girl. The father loomed stiffly over his brood, squinting fiercely at the camera. The boys were in baggy shorts and boots, razored thatches of hair. Nineteen-twenties, probably. Rural folk.

Moving like a man in a dream, careless and carefree, Blessed stripped off Werner's leather jacket and hung it on a nail inside the door. He hunched in the chair, began pulling off Werner's sneakers.

There was a blanket on the camp bed, which he could wrap around himself while his clothes dried. Already the rain that was hammering on the roof and coursing down the windows seemed harmless, even comforting to him.

There was only one important thing now, to hide here through the day – real day, not Werner's fake day – and wait for dark – real dark.

And until then to sleep.

FIFTY-FIVE

'HOW ACCURATELY CAN you pinpoint him?'

'To within yards,' Granit said. 'Apparently he's stopped short of the station, which means he saw the men there. Don't worry. My boys will have a precise map-reference within moments.'

Ziegler *alias* Banana was impressed. His voice was that of an excited adolescent. 'So what happens now?'

'We let him stew. Where can he go? If he'd hitched a lift, we might have had to pick him up in East Berlin, which would have been OK. But this is better. Let him stay there a while, feel how it is to be a hunted man behind the Iron Curtain. We have a day or two in hand.'

'Benno is moving forward,' Banana reminded him.

'I know that.'

'Benno is closer to the truth than we'd like.'

'I know that, too.' An irritated intake of breath. 'You think I'm stupid?'

Hastily: 'No. I think you're clever. Maybe too clever.'

'I just know how people's minds work,' Granit said drily. 'I know their *angles*. Benno will mix in, but he won't trouble *us*. He has his own fish to fry.'

A soft, humourless laugh. 'Old, stale fish.'

Pause.

'You know, I never thought the régime would fall so quickly,' Banana continued, changing the subject. 'Honecker gone, right after those famous fortieth-anniversary celebrations of his. Krenz getting the old bastard's job –'

'Sure. And I was right about young Egon's uselessness, wasn't I? What a screw-up! When he hit the television screens, he just parroted the speech he'd come up with after the Central Committee voted him in. Trust me, he said, I can make socialism work. We'll get it right in the end. It was pretty bad the first time. I know. I was there! And the second time, in front of x-million critical viewers, it was even worse.'

260

Banana laughed. 'How long do you give Egon before he's out on his arse?'

'A month. Maybe two or three. Depending on whether the Russians want the changeover to go quick or slow. As stopgaps go, he's harmless. Krenz is just enjoying playing grown-ups, sitting in the big chair.'

Sigh. 'You know something? I'll be glad when all this is over.'

'It'll never be over.' Pause. 'Life's a struggle, you should know that. The price of liberty is perpetual vigilance. It's the price of being rich, too.'

'If you say so. I repeat: so what happens now?'

'We wait.'

'Well, there's a woman in the next room I think I might spend some of the waiting time with, if it's all the same to you.'

'Suit yourself. Personally, I've had a long night. For the moment, a good strong cup of coffee will do me – something our friend out there in the rain would kill for . . . '

FIFTY-SIX

SOMEONE IS STRIKING BLESSED'S HEAD. Perhaps prodding it with a blunt instrument. Like the barrel of a gun . . . No. Surely it's Daisy, trying to wake him up. DADDY! he hears her call, and now Blessed tries to lift his head.

He opens his eyes warily, expecting to see Werner. Instead, he's confronted with a thick stick, and on the other end of it a figure in a thick, military-type coat.

Blessed, suddenly fully conscious, grabs the end of the stick and pulls it violently, first towards him and then to one side. At the same time, he swings himself out of the camp bed and goes into an attacking crouch.

The blankets tumble from him, and so does his attacker, leaving Blessed stark naked, staring at his assailant, who emits a stifled scream and slumps against the far wall . . .

The intruder was at least seventy, and nowhere near as tall as Blessed had thought. About five feet five, in fact, and the oversize coat although of military origin, was old, and had long ago been stripped of any insignia. A mass of grey hair straggled out from beneath a plastic rain hat. Threadbare slacks and gumboots were all that could be glimpsed beneath the coat.

'I won't hurt you,' Blessed said in German. 'Put that stick away.' He reached over, plucked his underpants from where he had hung them on a nail. They weren't quite dry, but never mind. He slipped them on. 'OK?'

The intruder nodded slowly. The eyes in the weatherbeaten face were shrewd.

Blessed picked up one of the blankets, wrapped it around himself like a short toga. 'Who are you?' he demanded, reckoning that attack was the best form of defence.

The intruder's gaze was steady. 'This is my house.' A finger pointed at the blanket Blessed had just purloined. 'That's my blanket.'

The accent was local, with a hint of *Platt* dialect.

'I think this is state-owned ground, grandpa,' Blessed said.

A flicker of amusement. 'Now, maybe. It was my family's once.'

Blessed glanced at the photograph on the wall. 'Your family?' He took a step closer, indicated the two boys. 'Which one are you?'

The intruder made a wry face, gently pointed to the little girl, the one in the dress just like her mother's.

'Ah. Very sorry. Stupid of me.'

'It doesn't matter. At my age, it's all the same.'

'I apologise for using this place without your permission. Only, the rain . . . '

'And the police, yes?'

Blessed made no direct answer. He shrugged. 'They're around, are they?'

'I saw some. Also, a helicopter went over about half an hour ago.' The old woman smiled shyly. 'My name is Bertha, Bertha Silbermann. And you?'

'Michael.'

Blessed pronounced his name the German way, as Mee-kh-ay-ell. He automatically put out his hand, with the other still holding up his 'toga'. Bertha Silbermann and he shook hands like good bourgeois.

'Ask no questions,' she said with a sigh. She turned and indicated a string bag that had been set down just inside the door. 'We can share lunch. I have sausage, cheese and bread.'

The rain had stopped. It was still light outside. Blessed had no idea of how long had passed since he had gone to sleep on the camp bed.

'What time is it?' he asked.

'Two in the afternoon. Somewhere around that. I never carry a watch.'

'And . . . what *date*?'

Bertha had retrieved the bag and placed it on the little table. She looked at Blessed sharply for a moment, then laughed.

'It is the sixteenth of October, young man. Nineteen eighty-nine.'

Sixty-four days. They had kept him there for sixty-four days. He had counted only thirty-six.

'Where have you been? On a desert island? Did you go there without written permission? Is that why they're looking for you in their cars and helicopters?' Her tone was matter-of-fact.

'I'm surprised they haven't searched here,' Blessed said, gently deflecting her curiosity.

'Oh, they don't know about my little house. Hardly anyone knows,' she told him with obvious pleasure. 'It's my secret. Mine and yours.'

Blessed found himself responding to her conspiratorial smile. 'Where do you actually live, Bertha?' he asked. He needed to keep her talking, he decided. He needed to know more about her.

She named a village he had never heard of. 'It's just a couple of kilometres away. In the old days, Pappi used to walk here to his land. We would come with him.'

'Your father was a farmer?'

'No, no. He was a painter and decorator. But like many folk around here, he had land that he worked. Everything between here and the railway. A few fields of cabbages and turnips. And by the hut here, a little vegetable garden.'

'That's a good-sized smallholding.'

'He bought it himself,' Bertha said with pride. 'He started with nothing, worked hard, pulled himself up by his bootstraps. When I was a child, my family owned property. We were all well-fed, well-clothed, well-educated.' She shook her head sadly. 'That made him a petit-bourgeois as far as the communists were concerned. That's why, after the war, they took everything. They even took our house, though they let us rent the basement, out of the kindness of their cold socialist hearts. There was no one left to defend us. What could we do?'

Blessed nodded in the direction of the photograph. 'What about your two brothers?'

'Both fell in the war. In Russia. Heini before Moscow, and Fritzi somewhere terrible in the arctic north, around Archangel. I still have his last letter. He said it was so cold that when they peed their water froze before it hit the ground. I thought that was so strange and so funny. Then we heard he was killed.' Whatever grief all this had cost Bertha, it had long since been faced and dealt with.

Blessed waited while she sliced the sausage and cheese, put the food on a plate she produced from a cupboard by the door. It looked good. Even the bread looked good.

'This I bake myself,' Bertha said. 'I think you will like it. I expect you are hungry, poor boy.'

264

The food was as good as it looked. Especially the bread. He told her so.

She smiled with pleasure, took a slice of cheese for herself. 'I have friends. They make their own, the way they have always made them ... just quietly, you know ... and we exchange good things ... People learn how to keep the old country ways going, despite the collective farm bosses.' She frowned. 'But we are getting old. Many of the young people have gone to the city ... or to the West ... just last week, my friend Frau Warneck's son and his wife took their little girl and drove south. We think they were going to Bavaria. They promised to send a postcard.'

Blessed made a decision. 'I am from the West,' he said. 'I'm English.'

'Ah. I heard a little accent. Not so sure. Maybe Czech, I thought. Maybe Dutch ... '

'And I need to get home.'

There was a silence. Blessed chewed absently on a piece of sausage. He still had to get to Berlin, to the embassy. Nothing had changed. Except that he had been seen by this woman. He wondered if he had already told her too much. Bertha Silbermann might share her lunch with him, but she could walk out of here and report him to the *Volkspolizei* whenever the fancy took her.

In the end it was Bertha who forced the issue. She had been sitting quietly, nibbling a piece of her home-baked bread.

'You are worried,' she said at last. 'You don't trust me.' She paused. 'But I must tell you, I saw you sleeping in here the moment I came in. I watched you sleep for a while, until I got impatient and woke you up. I had plenty of time to sneak off and inform the *Vopos*,' she said, investing the word with a powerful disgust and contempt. 'All the time in the world.'

Blessed knew she was right. And he knew she was his best, perhaps his only chance.

'I want you to help me, Bertha,' he said.

'Any way I can.'

'Thank you. Now, as a pensioner, you're allowed to travel to the West, isn't that so?' he asked softly.

'They gave me a passport a few years ago. I can come and go as I please. It's only the young people the authorities don't allow to leave.'

265

'Is that passport valid for West Berlin?'

Bertha nodded. 'I went over there just last year. To visit my niece, who lives near the American air base at Tempelhof.'

'OK,' Blessed pressed on carefully. 'Once you're through the Wall, can you find a taxi and get him to take you southwest, way down to the Stölpchensee?'

She was smiling. She understood perfectly where his questions were leading. 'Of course. You think I am stupid?'

'Oh no, Bertha. Now I just need to know if you have writing materials to hand.'

Bertha checked through her pockets, came up first with an old pencil-stub and then, after further searching, a single folded scrap of paper. She made a touching attempt to smooth out the creases before handing it to Blessed. 'Last week's shopping list,' she explained apologetically. 'You'll have to write on the back . . .'

'Don't worry,' Blessed assured her. 'I only need to scribble a few words. My friend who lives on the Stölpchensee is clever as well as trustworthy. Once he reads my note, he'll know exactly what to do.'

FIFTY-SEVEN

'WE'RE PICKING UP EVERY second word,' the young man in the headphones told Granit. He was nervous. General Albrecht had just arrived, and had immediately dismissed the other technician so that they could be alone. Now there was just the two of them in the control-van. The big man filled the confined space with his bulk and his authority, making the young man uneasy.

Granit grunted. 'So. Is it enough to work out what's going on?'

'Oh yes, Comrade General. There's an old lady in there with Blessed.'

'What kind of an old lady?'

'A crazy one. Says her family used to own land near the railway. There's a kind of a hut there which has been around since before the war, and she goes there. I guess the local authorities reckon she's harmless.'

'Nobody's harmless. Didn't they teach you that in training school?'

The young man reddened. 'Well, it sounds like she's going to go home, pick up her passport, and hit the border. Blessed's given her a message to deliver to someone in West Berlin. Wannsee.'

'Of course.' Granit smiled unfathomably. 'Now we have a problem. Do you want to know what it is?'

The officer nodded distractedly. He was keeping half an eye on the recording equipment. If anything went wrong, it would be on his own head.

'Well,' Granit continued, 'our friend in the hut there with the crazy lady has a plan. We can counter-act this plan, steer things back our way. But we have to be very careful, because otherwise we'll reveal that we know his every move, and then Blessed might realise that everything he's wearing – his own underwear, the clothes he stole before his escape – is bristling with transmitters. He's got more bugs on him than a Romanian gipsy. *But when we catch him, he's got to think there's another reason why*. That's not easy to arrange.'

267

The technician in the earphones spoke for the first time. '*Wait* . . .
Ah. The old lady's going now. She said she'll get back tomorrow.
Meanwhile, Blessed says he's going to lie low . . . Now she's left
the building. I heard the door close.'

The officer let out a low, disapproving whistle. 'Helping a fugi-
tive. Assisting a criminal in fleeing the territory of the Republic.
Jesus, if those boys at the Normannenstrasse got hold of grandma
there, they'd make her false teeth rattle and no mistake.'

The technician interrupted excitedly. 'Hey . . . Wait a minute.
Blessed's put on the jacket. He's waiting. I think he's on the move.
I think he's following her. This is getting complicated.'

'Keep him tracked,' Granit growled. 'That's all that matters.'

'But he's fucking moving back the way he came, Comrade
General. The exact same way. Would you believe it? He's retracing
his steps, the asshole. What's going on?'

'Who knows? *Just keep . . . him . . . tracked*!'

Blessed judged that about two hours would be enough to test Bertha
Silbermann. That, anyway, was how long he crouched behind
a screen of hawthorn bushes and brambles, watching the railway
line.

Several trains came and went. Eventually Blessed decided that
Bertha had no intention of betraying him. It would have taken a
matter of minutes for her to flag down a car, or contact the cops
down there at the railway station. When another train pulled out,
heading in the direction of Berlin under the bored gaze of the police
platform detail, Blessed made his decision. He headed back, carefully and quietly, towards the shack.

It was good to get back under cover. Before leaving, Bertha had
told him her route: a bus to Genshorn, then on the train, changing
at Ostkreuz for the Friedrichstrasse S-bahn. She chose the Friedrichstrasse crossing because it was always busy. The young men
who controlled the exit queues for GDR citizens were rude – always
ruder to their own people than to the hard-currency-bearing foreign-
ers – but they would be under too much pressure to bother about
one little old lady. Blessed had given her instructions about what to
do once she was safely in West Berlin: pick up a taxi, tell the driver
to take her out to Benno Klarfeld's house on the Stölpchensee, then
ask him to wait while she got someone there to pay him. Never mind

how late it had got. Never mind even if it was the middle of the night.

Blessed settled down beneath the blankets once more. All he could do now was stick it out until dark, then hope for sleep, or at least for the time to pass tolerably before morning came. That was the earliest he could expect any reaction to the message Bertha Silbermann had promised to deliver.

FIFTY-EIGHT

WHEN IT FINALLY HAPPENED, the event was not what he expected, and the way it happened was utterly different from anything he had imagined.

It had been dark for a long time. Blessed had slept only intermittently. An hour or so ago, he had risen from his bed and eaten the last of Bertha's home-made sausage. Since then he had been sitting here in the chair, wrapped in the blankets, wishing for morning. First he had thought about his sister, wondering how he could possibly tell her what he knew about her husband. From there he had started to speculate if she – or Benno, or Diane Kelly – suspected where he was, if *anyone* was worried about what had happened to him ... And for the last few minutes he had been tormented by thoughts of Daisy, by a longing to hear her voice on the phone, to tell her that he was OK ...

A branch cracked outside. Just once. Blessed tensed, then got up and groped his way through the darkness over to the window. No sign of anyone out there.

Must have been an animal. A fox. A badger ... did they have badgers here? Yes, Dachshunds were badger-hounds, that was where the name came from.

Blessed waited there for something like a minute. He had turned, preparing to make his way back to his chair, when he heard a human voice, no more than a whispered command ... and before he could react, a heavy boot kicked the door in. Torchlight flooded the shack's interior, dazzling him.

'Please,' a voice said in English, harsh but strangely calm. 'Please put up your hands. I have a machine-pistol here which I will use if I must. This place is surrounded by other armed men.'

As he raised his hands, Blessed felt sick with disappointment. He had started to believe in Bertha ... perhaps because he had wanted to believe in Bertha ...

The man with the gun kept him covered while another came forward and performed a quick bodysearch. The documents and

270

wallet were removed from the pockets of Werner's leather jacket. The searcher completed his task, confirmed that Blessed was 'clean'. He was young, fresh-faced, and wore cheap cologne. The man with the gun seemed quite a lot older. He wore a dark anorak and a flat cap.

'OK. No funny stuff,' the man with the gun said. His words suffered seriously, but not seriously enough, from having so obviously been learned from old American films. 'They're waiting for you down on the road. It's not far. Please keep your hands up as we walk. So, *move*.'

There were four of them in all. Outside were two other men carrying machine-pistols and torches. The group organised itself quickly and efficiently. Within moments, Blessed was across the far side of the clearing and stumbling down a narrow track through the woods, sandwiched between two pairs of armed men, without a hope of making a break.

It was difficult going, even by torchlight. The path was water-logged from the day's rain, and exposed areas of the men's skin were constantly at risk from wandering thorns and brambles, but the pace was respectable. No one spoke. After just a few minutes, the procession emerged once more into the open, a cinder-surfaced lay-by. None of the dramatic paraphernalia of a largescale manhunt, just three cars waiting quietly by the side of a pot-holed country road. A Wartburg station-wagon. A little Trabi with a man in the driver's seat and its headlights pinpointing the place where Blessed and his captors had just emerged from the undergrowth. Lastly, and distinctly separate from the rest, a large, shiny, top-of-the-range Volvo. Blessed felt a hint of winter in the chilly night air.

His guards fanned out and waited, keeping him covered. Then the original man with the gun started to move towards the Volvo, and said: 'Please follow.'

As soon as they reached the Volvo, its rear door clicked open and swung out to reveal the interior. There was someone waiting in the back seat, on the far side.

The man with the gun made a polite gesture of encouragement. 'Please get in, Mr Blessed. Please.'

Blessed ducked down, started to slide into the back seat. It was upholstered in dark, new-smelling leather. There was music playing very softly from stereo speakers. Bach. One of the Brandenburg

Concertos. He was barely inside when the door slammed behind him. The car's engine started up and it moved forward. Blessed was immediately pitched to the left as the driver swung the wheel and the vehicle began to undertake a reckless getaway turn.

He felt himself collide with a large body dressed in a thick, soft overcoat. A meaty hand grabbed him, steadied him and eased him down into the seat.

'Don't worry, Mr Blessed,' a voice said. 'We're in a bit of a hurry, that's all. Excuse me if I speak German. My English isn't good. I never learned it in school like they do these days ... '

Blessed, still breathing quickly, looked to his left. The big man's hand was still on his arm, but comforting rather than restraining. In the semi-darkness, Blessed could see that this was a massively-built human being, around seventeen stone and six-three or six-four. If he had known this man's nickname, Granit, he would have appreciated it. The profile he glimpsed was rocklike, its expression powerful and sardonic.

'Who are you?' Blessed said. The car had already moved out onto the cobbled country road and was picking up speed.

'I have come to rescue you. If it weren't for me, you would be back in prison by the morning. Instead, you will be in West Berlin. So long as we get out of here before we attract too much attention.'

'I asked, who are you?'

The big man half-turned. The Bach was still there in the background, so civilised, orderly, unreal. He laughed.

'Me? Oh, you know me very well,' he said finally. 'You have spent *months* toiling over the details and secrets of my life – the secrets of this both glorious and wretched German Democratic Republic. You see, I am the writer of those memoirs everyone is so interested in. I am your *Stasi* general, Mr Blessed, your one and only.'

FIFTY-NINE

THE VOLVO RACED ON through the night. Blessed saw from the digital clock on the dashboard that it was 2:49 when they reached the end of the country roads and took a long, looping sliproad onto a four-lane divided highway.

'The Berlin Ring-Autobahn,' the *Stasi* general explained. 'That light you see, high up, many kilometres away, is the East Berlin Television Tower on the Alexanderplatz.'

'What's your name?' Blessed asked.

The *Stasi* general made an apologetic gesture. 'I can't tell you. Not yet. Soon it will be public. But I can't risk premature disclosure. I'll tell you anything you like, but not my name.'

The Bach piece came to an end. The *Stasi* general leaned forward, slid open the glass divide between them and the driver. 'Mozart,' he murmured. 'Let's have the Mozart now.' He shut it once more.

Watching as the driver obeyed, Blessed realised that the object he slid into the stereo deck was a compact disc.

'That's a very expensive piece of western technology you have there,' Blessed said. 'You don't want for much. Just like the people you expose in your memoirs.'

The general shrugged. 'I'm no ascetic, I admit. But neither do I stand up on platforms and tell the masses that they must go without for the sake of socialism. I'm a professional, a manager. These are the rewards for being good at what I do.'

'Which is . . . what?'

'What you also do. Finding things out. Using that information.'

'That's an evasion.'

'It's a certain way of looking at the world.'

The music began again. Mozart's Jupiter Symphony. Like the Bach, lively without being intrusive, redolent of a world of order and culture. Perfect for its soothing effect on a half-crazed escaped prisoner.

For several minutes nothing was said between the two men. The music played on, and the Volvo ate up the kilometres. There were

273

very few cars on the highway, all of them travelling below the East German speed limit of 100 kilometres an hour. Unlike the Volvo. At times Blessed saw the needle on the speedometer touch 160. A police vehicle started to overhaul them, its red light flashing, then took a look, recognised what it saw and fell back. Against his will, Blessed was impressed.

'How did you find me?' he said at last.

'A lot of organisation and a bit of luck.'

'Tell me more.'

'Sure. I tried to get you out when you were first brought over the border, back in mid-August. Then they moved you to that god-damned deserted Schloss there, and hid you. Very successfully. My people couldn't find you. Until you escaped and the alert went out. Then they had to inform the Volkspolizei, among other people, and we have good contacts there. Within hours, we had people in this area. The people you met tonight.'

'You still haven't explained how you found me. How you pin-pointed the hut, I mean.'

'The old lady, Frau Silbermann, lost her nerve, I think. After she returned home to pick up her passport, she tried to phone Benno Klarfeld in West Berlin. We . . . we have that line covered . . . ' The *Stasi* general shrugged. 'Frau Silbermann spoke to Klarfeld's housekeeper. She confined herself to generalities, what time would the gentleman be back and so on. But she stayed on the line long enough for us to trace her. It was too much of a coincidence, the call being made from that particular village, so we got ourselves over there as soon as we could.'

'Is she all right?'

'She's somewhere safe. Until the panic's over.'

Blessed looked at him sharply. 'You've had Klarfeld's phone tapped all this time?'

'Yes –'

'Whose side are you on, General?'

The big man hesitated only slightly. 'Mr Blessed, I . . . I am in an ambivalent situation, half-dissident, half-secret policeman . . . and there was always this fear that Klarfeld would double-cross us . . . ' The general paused, sighed. 'And in this case, our access was vin-dicated. *They* can also listen in to East-West calls, you see. If we hadn't had that line tapped, it's possible *they* would have

274

transcribed her conversation, passed it on in a routine fashion, and someone at the Normannenstrasse would have put two and two together. Then they . . . '

'Wait a minute. Who do you mean when you keep referring to *they*?'

'The die-hard Stalinists in our security forces, of course! The ones who imprisoned you!' The *Stasi* general patted Blessed on the arm. 'Listen, my friend, this is a lot for a man to take on board in so short a time, especially after what you've been through. First we'll get you somewhere comfortable, put some food in your belly and a drink in your hand. Only another few minutes to go, I promise you.'

And the Mozart flowed on delicately like water from some heavenly stream. And the Volvo, so sturdy and safe and comfortable, just like the TV ads said, cruised ever closer to the sparse lights of East Berlin.

They soon came off the East Berlin Ring-Autobahn, drove for some time through darkened suburban streets. Finally the Volvo turned down a driveway, and after a couple of hundred yards arrived at a large, pre-war house surrounded by trees. The lights were on, as if there were a party in progress.

The *Stasi* general took Blessed by the arm and escorted him inside. The hall was filled with pleasant cooking aromas. An elderly man in a dark-grey suit emerged, butler-like, and greeted the general respectfully.

'Fifteen minutes to breakfast, sir. Would you like coffee?'

The *Stasi* general shook his head. 'Later. First get this man a drink,' he said. 'A large cognac. Hennessy. Same for me. This has been a long, hard night. We've both earned a touch of luxury.'

Blessed could have sworn the old man bowed slightly as he first took the general's coat, then his own – or rather, Werner's – leather jacket. But within moments he was already being led through to the comfortable sitting room, where a wood fire glowed in the grate. He could feel his tenuous grip on reality loosening. This was like arriving at an old-established, very low-key English country house hotel.

The *Stasi* general collapsed into a well-padded armchair by the fire. 'Take a seat, Mr Blessed, relax!'

275

The brandies arrived, on a silver tray, complete with soda siphon. The general lifted his glass. 'To freedom!'

Blessed took a cautious sip of his neat brandy. His first alcohol for two months. It was smooth, warming, and it hit his body like a liquid cluster-bomb, spreading out into his brain and his stomach and rocking all the furniture it found there. The room swam before him. After a few moments he had recovered sufficiently to see the *Stasi* general watching him benignly.

'Freedom is heady,' the big man murmured. 'See?'

Blessed could sense the after-glow arriving now. He liked it. He liked it very much. He felt a slow wave of well-being, closely followed by a brisk ripple of defiance. 'Whose freedom are we talking about, General?'

'Ah . . . yours, of course. That's for now. And everyone's. A little later.'

'But I'm still in East Germany.'

'Yes. For a few hours more. Enough time to get some food in your belly, a bath and a change of clothes. This house is where we debrief our best operatives when they come over from the West,' the *Stasi* general explained. 'You'll be back over that border within hours, free to go about your business. It's not hard if you know how.'

'I won't believe I'm back in the West until it happens.'

'And why should you? I could be lying.' The general smiled broadly. 'But, of course, I'm not. You see, you'll realise one thing when you get back and read the newspapers, and that is, the old régime's days here are numbered. While you were imprisoned, Honecker resigned. He was replaced by Egon Krenz, a straw man. There is a power-vacuum at the top in the GDR. The Stalinists are running around like headless chickens. They still have offices to sit in, and they still have the power to victimise bystanders such as yourself. All the same, they're about to be tossed onto the garbage heap of history, and all but the very stupidest among them know it.'

Blessed grunted sceptically. 'And you? What about you?'

The *Stasi* general leaned forward. He was serious now. His grey-blue eyes met Blessed's, drew him in. His was a subtle, slow power, but the charisma in this man was undeniable. 'Me? So far as the communist system is concerned, I cooked my goose some time ago, when I decided to write those memoirs and get them published in the West. There's no going back on that. I still have all the trappings of power, as you see.' He sighed. 'But I shall lose them very soon. When the memoirs are made public. I'll have to resign, naturally.'

'I never quite finished the translation.'

'I know. I don't think it's too much of a problem. Thank God the manuscript survived that break-in, and that almost all the key material has been processed. Klarfeld is ready to go ahead.'

'Does he . . . '

The *Stasi* general nodded. 'Klarfeld knows I'm committed to getting you out. He doesn't know exactly when you'll be arriving – I've had to move fast this last night, and it would have been risky to contact him directly – but he's expecting you to call him the moment you get back to West Berlin.'

Blessed nodded, drank some more cognac. 'What do you get out of this?' he asked.

'It's hard to say with any certainty.'

'You can try.'

'Of course. Well, I have been a major accomplice in what's happened in this country during the past forty years, Mr Blessed,' the *Stasi* general said. Blessed's scepticism must have still been evident. He shrugged his broad shoulders. 'And . . . yes, I will be frank, I hope that perhaps I have earned a few bonus points. Perhaps the fact that I have managed to right a few wrongs during the past year or two will entitle me to ask, when democracy is restored, for forgiveness – a forgiveness that will not be extended to other servants of this régime . . . '

'Is that why you helped me?'

'I felt it was my responsibility to get you out of that mess.' A tiny smile. 'And it was also in my interests, Mr Blessed. A happy marriage between morality and expediency.'

'Quite a mouthful. But I'll drink to that.' Po-faced, Blessed raised his brandy glass. 'Morality and expediency! To a marriage made in a twentieth-century heaven, General. To a perfect match!'

SIXTY

THE UNREAL NIGHT CONTINUED to its end. There was a pre-dawn breakfast of omelettes, dumplings, fruit and excellent coffee. There was more talk of politics. The constant demonstrations in East Berlin and the other major cities. The nation's lifeblood leaking out through Czechoslovakia and Hungary. Krenz's attempts to overcome all problems by PR gloss and promises of reform. The pressure on the Stalinists in neighbouring Czechoslovakia; riots in Prague and Bratislava. The general was, of course, well informed and intelligent. Weren't secret policemen always?

And then the general made to leave. He had so much else to think of. 'Make yourself at home,' he said. 'You have until four o'clock or so, my people tell me. Then they'll take you to the border. You'll be provided with a few Westmarks to make that phone call to Klarfeld.'

They shook hands.

'Good luck, Mr Blessed. Maybe we'll meet again.'

'Oh, I think so. I was promised you by Klarfeld. You're up for an interview when the memoirs go public. It was part of the lure.'

'True. Well, my dear fellow, you can have me. If I'm available . . . and if *you* are . . . '

'And why shouldn't I be?'

'Everything changes. Not just here. Everywhere. *Auf wiedersehen*, Captain Blessed.' The *Stasi* general turned to go.

'*What did you say, General*?' Blessed hissed.

'I'm sorry?'

'I'm sure you said *Captain* Blessed. That was my father's rank when he was in Berlin just after the war. I've never been in the army. Never intend to.'

The smile this time was just a shade too broad. 'Ah . . . a slip of the tongue, Mr Blessed. I am already thinking of my work. Again, *auf wiedersehen*.'

'*Auf wiedersehen*.'

278

The old man in the grey suit showed Blessed up to a pleasant bedroom, with an en suite bathroom and double-bed made up with fresh linen. He invited him to take off his clothes. New ones would be provided.

And so Blessed ran a very hot bath, soaked himself in it for half an hour. He emerged to find a cheap plastic purse containing twenty Westmarks in one-mark pieces and a further thirty in new ten-mark notes. Hanging up outside the closet was a new set of clothes – western-style, with a weatherproof jacket to wear over the top. And a pair of exquisitely unpleasant grey loafers. All in Blessed's size. Average-Joe kind of clothes, fit-in-the-crowd kind of clothes. Sneak-across-the-Iron-Curtain kind of clothes . . .

For the moment, Blessed flopped naked into bed and just slept, deeply and dreamlessly. Just minutes later, so it seemed, he was woken once more by the old man, who told him in the same respectful tone that it was now around three, time for what he called 'the journey'.

Blessed dressed. Downstairs they had prepared a cold snack to keep him going. There were also two youngish types, not unlike Werner in manner or dress, but without the Stalinist spiel. In fact, just a little hip. You could see why they worked for an old closet reformer like the general, Blessed thought. They wanted to be up with the latest thing.

By this stage he was rested, and starting to believe he was really going west. A touch flippant, perhaps. Werner and that cell were fading into memory with astonishing speed.

And nothing went wrong. There were no surprises. They got into a car – the Wartburg station-wagon that had been waiting down by the shack the previous night – drove sedately through the suburbs of East Berlin, heading for the centre of the city. They played Bruce Springsteen tapes all the way. The driver had a thing about that line of Springsteen's where . . . *there's a freight train running through the middle of my head/ooh-hoooo-ho-o-o-h-h* . . . and kept playing the song over and over again. He wanted to know if Blessed thought Springsteen would come to East Berlin sometime, now that things were easing up. He wanted to know if Blessed, as a journalist, could maybe swing them special tickets, maybe even get them backstage.

They arrived at Friedrichstrasse about five-thirty. The general's boys had all the documentation, and they were full of confidence. In fact, the uniformed border guards were very leery of them.

Blessed briefly spotted queues waiting to go west. Then he was whisked away into an office, where the papers were shown again. Finally down a corridor. Through more offices. Identity documents were shown at one more security desk. Finally, a senior transport authority official in a blue-and-red uniform appeared. He led the three of them down some access steps, then along a long, twisting corridor that looked like a maintenance tunnel. Eventually they arrived at a thick steel door. Briskly the official unlocked it, opened up. There was a dim light on the other side.

'*Tschüss*,' said the Springsteen fanatic.

'*Mach's gut*,' said his friend.

The official indicated for Blessed to go through the door. 'Left, right, then left again, understand?' he said. Blessed made to go, but the official tutted reproachfully and restrained him. 'Just a moment.' He presented the Englishman with a small oblong of paper. Blessed stared at it stupidly for a moment, then realised it was a train ticket.

He found himself alone in a concrete corridor. The door slammed behind him. He went left, right, left again, found himself standing on the platform of the Friedrichstrasse U-bahn station, waiting for a border-crossing train along with the usual assortment of tourists, pensioners, and East-West chancers. They ignored the Englishman in his cheap casual clothes, his terrible shoes.

No one had lied this time. The general was on the level. Blessed was going under the Wall. Blessed was going west.

The train eased out, heading south, moving at crawling pace through the two closed and abandoned stations, Französischer Strasse and – bang on the border – Stadtmitte. These were the short-stops, the stations time forgot. Peeling posters. Shuttered refreshment kiosks. Pre-war Gothic script platform signs.

And then, suddenly, Kochstrasse and West Berlin. Even after just a day in the East, it could come as a shock. Densely-peopled platforms, bright lights, magazines and newspapers, sweets and chocolate. Noise and laughter and swearing and rudeness. That raucous western casualness . . .

At Kochstrasse, Blessed just sat and stared. The train moved on to the next stop, Hallesches Tor, and it was only by a huge effort of will that he managed to lurch over to the door and launch himself out onto the crowded platform. A glance at the station clock told Blessed it was six-thirty in the evening. He clambered slowly up the steps, jostled by commuters, stumbled around the perimeter of the station until he came across a row of phone booths.

He had to relearn the whole procedure of making a call. Lift receiver . . . money . . . wait . . . and wait . . .

'Hello. Klarfeld here.'

'Benno. It's Mike Blessed.'

'At last. Where are you calling from?'

'Hallesches Tor U-bahn. There's a phone booth by the post office . . . '

'Listen, I'll come and fetch you . . . just stay where you are . . . '

'Don't worry. I'm not going anywhere.'

'Are you OK? You must have had a hell of a time.'

'I'm fine. I just need a rest. But I've got so much to tell you. Not just the flat. Erika's flat. There's other things. How Rockwell is tangled up in this mess, for instance. Especially that. You're not going to believe . . . ' Blessed had a sudden, cruelly-clear flash of memory: Rockwell naked, with Erika. His explanation trailed away.

'Rockwell.' Klarfeld's repetition of the name was icy, oddly lacking in urgency.

'Yes. You know. My brother-in-law. Rockwell Elliot! I found out something very weird about him, Benno. It's part of the reason I was kidnapped. I . . . '

'Listen to me very carefully, Michael,' Klarfeld interrupted him. His voice was very gentle, like a nurse's or a priest's. He hesitated, then continued in that same firm but kindly tone. 'I'm sorry to have to tell you in this way, but better perhaps now than later. Michael, your brother-in-law disappeared a week ago. Near his home in Connecticut. Apparently, he went out in his boat alone, and he never came back. They found the boat abandoned in the middle of Long Island Sound.'

'*Jesus.*' Blessed's voice was reduced to a hoarse whisper. 'I can't believe this, Benno. Not after everything that's happened.'

'I'm afraid the police are convinced that Rockwell has drowned.'

'But Daphne. Josh. How –'

'We must stay strong for them. And we will. But for now, Michael, just stay *exactly* where you are. I promise you, I'll be with you in a very, very short time.'

SIXTY-ONE

FRAU SMILOVICI PUT DOWN the coffee tray on the desk in Benno Klarfeld's study. She walked over to Blessed and embraced him. Then, slightly flushed and on the edge of tears, she pulled away and left the room.

'There's no question about it. Rockwell was still doing the CIA the odd favour,' Klarfeld said. 'He knew a lot. Perhaps that's why the *Stasi* set a honeytrap operative onto him.'

Blessed shook his head. 'The same one they used for me?'

'Why not? She would have been ready-briefed. A good English speaker with a strong cover. And since she never met you and Rockwell at the same time – and could easily ensure that she never did – there was no risk involved.'

'All right. Let's suppose that. I know what they wanted from me. But what did they want from him?'

Klarfeld shrugged. 'Perhaps information. Perhaps money. Or, most probably, both.' He poured a cup of hot, black coffee, handed it to Blessed. 'I told you the bare facts of the case in the car, Michael. I told you how Daphne and Josh were. Up to a point. Now you're here, and I see you're holding up OK, I'll tell you the rest.'

Blessed nodded slowly. 'Go on.'

'Very well. Your sister is bankrupt. Your brother-in-law's company is bankrupt. In fact, millions of dollars belonging to the family whose money Rockwell held on trust is also missing.' Klarfeld leaned against his sturdy, polished-teak desk, folded his arms. 'The auditors have been in at Elliot, Birnbaum since the weekend. It turns out that when Rockwell went overboard from that boat of his, he was in a hole for a hell of a lot of money, most of it not his.'

Klarfeld's expression was bland-tough. This was his businessman's, his negotiator's face. Blessed chewed the news over for a while before replying.

'How much exactly?'

'That I don't know,' Klarfeld said. 'Only one thing is sure: it's more than your sister can possibly repay.'

282

'Blackmail.'

'The police – and everyone else – has been working on the assumption that he got bled dry by some Mafia loan-sharking operation, or that he spent it all on speculative stock-dealings. What you say about the *Stasi* set-up naturally introduces another aspect.'

'I'm sure the *Stasi* blackmailed him.'

'It's possible. Even probable. But we have no proof. Let's face it, if Rockwell had a secret life where he indulged in one-night stands with strange young women, there's no saying what he left himself open to. Did he gamble, for instance?'

Blessed shook his head. 'I wouldn't have thought so.'

'But you don't know for sure. None of us does.'

'True. The same way no one would have thought . . . ' Blessed let out a humourless laugh of disbelief. 'I know this is no time to dwell on the fact, but I made a complete bloody idiot of myself with that woman Erika . . . '

'It sounds like she was quite something,' Klarfeld said drily. 'Put it down to experience. It's a pity for him that Rockwell can't do the same.'

'I must confess, you don't look too devastated. You didn't think much of him even before all this, did you?'

'No,' Klarfeld admitted. 'Nevertheless, it would help if he was around to answer questions and account for that money.'

'I have to talk to Daff. And Josh. I should be with them.'

Klarfeld glanced at his watch. 'There's another thing I have to tell you, Michael. In a short while I'm going to have to pick up that phone and ring the number of a man who works for the British Foreign Office in West Berlin. You see, I promised him. It was part of our agreement. In return, he has kept everything quiet. His people know how to do that . . . '

'And it's up to him what happens to me.'

'Not exactly. But he'll want to talk to you. And he'll want exclusive rights, so to speak.'

'Which means no phone call to Daff and Josh.'

'Not yet. But . . . she knows you're out, Michael. By agreement with the man from the Foreign Office and his CIA colleagues, we told your family a part of the truth, back in August. We told them that you had become accidentally mixed up with a Stasi operation and that you had been kidnapped. We also told them that, though you were alive and in good health, any publicity would jeopardise your position. In respect of Rockwell . . . he was separately briefed by the CIA, in rather more detail – naturally on the understanding that he kept the information to himself.'

'They *trusted* him?'

'Why not? They didn't know about the photographs you found in the flat next to Erika's. And they had no reason to check Rockwell's business affairs. Not at that time. He was an old boy, he'd been doing them a few favours, and the old boy network is very strong in any intelligence service.'

'Including the West German one. What about you, Benno?'

'Yes. I've talked to acquaintances in the BND as well. I've kept them informed of my contacts with the *Stasi* general who wrote the memoirs, the same man who got you out of East Germany. They approved everything right from the start. Like the rest of us, they didn't quite anticipate how complicated things would become . . .'

'You had more idea than most of us, Benno.'

'Perhaps. That's why I tried to keep you as close as possible.' Klarfeld shrugged. 'I wish you had trusted me more. I wish you had confided in me more. I wish, above all, that when you found out that this woman who called herself Erika was involved in that porn operation, you had not been so impulsive. If you had told me *before* you decided to search her flat –'

'OK. You can come the self-righteous father-figure with me if you like,' Blessed interrupted hoarsely. 'If it makes you feel better.'

'Father-figure, you think?' Klarfeld laughed bitterly. 'Do you know what you're saying. In a sense, we *share* a father, even though he's been dead for so long. Captain Blessed was really the only parent I ever had –'

'*Captain Blessed*,' Blessed interrupted him. 'That's what the *Stasi* general called me, by mistake,' he said. 'Except, he pronounced it in the German way, more like "Kepten".'

Klarfeld stared at him uneasily, thrown off balance. Then he said simply: 'How curious.'

'Oh *yes* . . .' Suddenly Blessed had had enough. 'You know something?' he said sourly. 'I just need to get this debriefing session with you and the man from the Foreign Office over with. Then it's fuck the lot of you. I need to talk to my family – my daughter, my mother, and above all my sister . . . .'

'In a couple of days, I'm sure that will be possible.'

'Great. Sure. There's just one thing I want to know. What's this really about, Benno? *What the hell has been going on*?'

Bland-tough again. The expression came down over Klarfeld's face like a shutter. Then he threw up his hands in an admission of helplessness, and his features softened into a despairing smile. 'I wish I could tell you, Michael,' he said, shaking his head. 'I so wish I could tell you.'

SIXTY-TWO

FOR HIS FULL-DRESS DEBRIEFING, Blessed had been transferred to a small, discreetly-situated villa in Spandau. Klarfeld came with him.

The British debriefer, a man of about Blessed's own age, had introduced himself as 'Bill Prosser'. He was a fluent German speaker, with a schoolmasterly look, a pipe, and functional rather than decorative patches on the elbows of his unfashionable tweed jacket. The only obviously unsettling feature of the interviews was the tape recorder he kept going at all times.

Prosser had been very interested in Erika and Wolfgang and the pornography set-up, much less so in the details of Blessed's imprisonment and escape. The case of the *Stasi* general and what this revealed about the internal problems within the East German security apparatus were, he said primly and with a glance at Klarfeld, an affair for the German authorities to take an interest in if they so wished. Likewise the publication of the memoirs. Whenever Blessed mentioned SIS or MI6, Prosser smiled vaguely and refused to be drawn. The suspicion began to dawn on him that his debriefer was in effect just going through the motions, that he realised Blessed couldn't tell him anything he didn't already know.

For his part, Blessed had wanted to know why the *Stasi* hadn't simply killed him when they had the chance. Prosser's opinion – shared by Klarfeld – was that the 'East German authorities' (he never referred to the *Stasi* by name) were going very carefully these days. Bumping off more or less innocent westerners – especially journalists – had been pretty risky even at the height of the Cold War. These days it was bloody stupid.

Then, after only a little more than thirty-six hours, Prosser let him go, with the solemn advice to leave Berlin as soon as he possibly could. For his own safety.

Klarfeld drove him back to the house on the Stölpchensee and asked Blessed what he wanted to do next. Blessed thought about it, said he wanted to make some telephone calls. Then, he said, he would fly to America, to be with Daphne and Josh.

286

Blessed had feared that Daisy would be hard to talk to. Not a bit. His daughter had completely accepted the cover story, that her father had been called away to the Middle East and wouldn't be back for some months. Now, equally easily, she accepted that he would ring her up, tell her how hot it had been, and how boring, and how much he disliked camels. Blessed repeated his promise to visit her at Christmas. Then he put the phone down and wept with a mixture of complete emotional exhaustion and glorious relief.

His mother had also been told some of the truth by Klarfeld. Blessed's phone conversation with her was calm and dignified, though not especially comfortable. There was a subtle sense of unfinished emotional business between them, but also tacit agreement that it should be dealt with later. Gisela Blessed agreed that, for the time being, his place was with his sister and nephew.

So, then there had been Daphne, waiting for him to call at her house in Connecticut. Brave, calm, devastated. Grateful to have her brother back. She was the typical 'service wife', it seemed to Blessed. Brought up to know terrible things can happen. Brought up not to let on that they hurt. Blessed and his sister did not speak for long. Just enough to arrange for him to fly to the States to be with her and Josh.

The final call was to the phone number in London that Diane Kelly had given him that morning at Tegel Airport. Klarfeld told him she had phoned from London in late September. He had told her that Blessed was away in the East, researching, and he wasn't sure when he would be back. Some fence-mending, then. Some partial explanation.

Blessed spoke to a very nice woman in Elgin Crescent who said that yes, until the end of September Miss Kelly had rented the top floor of her house. She had planned to stay until after Christmas. Unfortunately she had changed her plans, decided that she would do some travelling instead. Between you and me, the very nice woman said to Blessed, she thought there was some man-trouble at the root of it. Miss Kelly, who at first seemed jolly and hard-working, had become unhappy and anxious during September. She seemed to be waiting for something. The nice woman guessed that the decision to go off travelling had to do with a feeling of disappointment, a desire for distraction. She understood this because she

287

as a young woman had once travelled half the way round the world after an unhappy love-affair.

Oh well. He had lost Erika, and now probably Diane too, Blessed thought. The regret was real and hard, but so was the wry acknowledgment of a certain symmetry in the way his life was moving. Bad girl and good girl both deleted from the schema.

Blessed's current relationship with Klarfeld was composed of an odd combination of intimacy and caution. So much remained unspoken.

Not that the German was anything but correct and generous. The memoirs were to be serialised in a major magazine, starting next week, and the book was to be published two weeks later. He aimed for a good sale of the serial rights in the States and in England. And since Blessed understandably wanted to be with his sister in America, he would do two things: pay for an open-ended return ticket to New York, and also give Blessed an increased share of the income. This would help to make up for any professional or financial loss Blessed suffered from not being around to interview the *Stasi* general, if – as seemed likely – the author of the memoirs went public while Blessed was still away in the States. They shook on that.

Klarfeld's office had booked Blessed onto a flight to New York the day after next. The time passed quickly and quietly, recovering in the autumn sunshine, catching up on the news, seeing the East German régime slowly disintegrate. Back in the early summer, they had thought the general's memoirs would destabilise the GDR. Now it was becoming obvious that by the time they and their author hit the headlines, there would be precious little of the Soviets' puppet republic left to be destabilised.

Klarfeld insisted on driving Blessed to the airport in the red BMW convertible he kept for weekends. They headed northwest along the Avus on a crisp, windly October morning, took the signs for Siemensstadt and Tegel at the Funkturm junction, and made it to the airport with a good hour-and-a-half to spare. West Berlin was a city that, until the autumn of 1989, still offered the luxury of free-flowing traffic and easy parking.

After checking in on the Pan Am flight, Klarfeld took Blessed to the bar for a drink.

Blessed thought of Diane Kelly, of the characters he had checked out then, convinced they were watching him – the fat man at the souvenir stand, the woman at the table who never drank her coffee. Ah well, perhaps he had been right.

'I am responsible, I know that, Michael,' Klarfeld said. 'I want to say now: I am sorry.'

Blessed shrugged his shoulders. 'I'm fine. A little bloodied by various experiences, but what the hell.' He lit a cigarette. Cigarettes always made him think of Werner, and that cell, and the humiliation of that rationed ten doled out each day to him, like a dog being fed. 'It's Rockwell I've been thinking about these past few days. I just don't know how much you – and I – had to do with his death. I just don't know. It's not an issue that I'm looking forward to discussing with his widow and his son, I can tell you.'

'If there's one thing I can assure you of, it's that Rockwell Elliot made his own choices,' Klarfeld retorted crisply. 'He was that kind of man. As for Daphne, she will need practical help.' He paused. 'Please . . . please tell her I'll call at the weekend. I'm willing to help her in any way necessary, including financially. But let me find my own way of telling her that, OK?'

'OK.'

'And I want you to know that the boathouse is always available to you. And Frau Smilovici's cooking . . . You don't even need to call first. Just ring the bell.'

Blessed nodded. 'Thanks. I'll be back for a day or two, at least. When I feel I can leave Daphne.'

Neither man spoke for some time. Then Blessed said very quietly: 'Berlin defeated me, the same way it defeated my father. He was a crusader for what was right and made no bones about it. Of course, I fancied myself as something different – all hip self-awareness and sexual curiosity – but really I was just the same as my old man. A straight, down-the-line moralist. For a pair of operators of the quality of Erika and Wolfgang, I must have been the original innocent baby.'

Klarfeld made a small, not especially convincing gesture of amused disbelief.

Blessed looked at him steadily. 'I'll tell you something else. I don't trust that *Stasi* general as far as I can throw him. And that isn't far, because he's a big man. He said to me that his actions were a marriage of expediency and morality. Well, I'd say it's more like they're living together without benefit of wedlock.'

'He's a complicated character, no question.'

'Well, good luck with him, Benno. I'd say the best of British, but of course that wouldn't be appropriate.'

'Don't worry, Michael. I think I can handle the general.' Klarfeld was smiling, but he spoke with quiet deliberation.

Blessed's flight was being called. He looked at Klarfeld and felt affection, respect, even a certain protective care. He could sense the man's loneliness as well as his power. And he still couldn't entirely trust him. Under other circumstances, he would have stayed here, seen this issue through. He knew there was still some key here that he hadn't yet found. But his sister and her son needed him. For the moment he was going where he could give and receive comfort, in a place where he knew trust was unconditional. Blessed got to his feet, picked up his carry-on bag.

'Let me know how the rights sales go,' he said. 'We Blesseds are going to need all the money we can get.'

'Of course. And I'll courier you copies of any new contracts. Plus copies of any magazine or newspaper extracts that come out while you're away. For your collection. Just don't worry about money. That's the least of your problems.'

They shook hands. Klarfeld clapped Blessed on the shoulder.

'I'll be calling Daphne regularly. We'll talk on the phone, Michael. Certainly, we shall see each other again before long.'

'When history's wheel has turned a little further,' Blessed said. 'And crushed a few more minor obstacles in its path.'

'I told you at the beginning of all this. We should envy the country that feels it has no history. It has few complications. And nothing to live up to.'

Blessed walked away quickly. He glanced back as he joined the queue for passport control. Klarfeld was standing exactly where he had left him, hands in pockets, staring after Blessed with a look of sadness. And not just sadness. There was also an emotion that even Klarfeld's careful self-control couldn't hide. So hard to pin down . . .

Envy. That was it, for dear God's sake. *Envy.*

SIXTY-THREE

'FORTY MILLION DOLLARS.'

'*Shit.*'

'That's just the latest figure, Mike. It may not be the final one. They're checking back years. Most of it seems to have disappeared in the last twelve or fifteen months, but . . .' Daphne Elliot bit back the painful words, laid down her fork and put her head in her hands. They were picking at a dinner of cold ham and salad in the glass-vaulted kitchen of her house in Greenwich, Connecticut. Josh had gone out tonight for the first time since his father's disappearance, to a film with an old friend. Daphne and Blessed had both encouraged him. They needed the time alone.

Blessed stroked his sister's hair. 'Does it matter exactly how much money?' he said softly.

Her face still hidden in her hands, Daphne nodded. Then she forced herself to look up. Her cheeks were moist. Her eyes were dark-ringed. Despite the careful make-up, her finely-structured, smooth-skinned face looked gaunt. For the first time in Blessed's adult memory, his sister looked something close to her age.

'I *liked* Rock so much, Mike. Even after the passion wore off. We'd been through a lifetime together. Even before we had Josh . . .'

'I was very fond of him too, Daff. Really. All this has come as a hell of a shock to me too.'

'But . . .' Daphne forced herself to continue. ' . . . I suppose I always knew there was this deeply secret part to him, a part I dared not look at . . . from the early days in the Far East, I mean . . .'

Blessed leaned across the table, took her hands in his. 'He told me about that. The last time I saw him. With you. In Berlin. The way you met. He was delivering secret reports to your boss at the Bangkok embassy.'

Daphne laughed bitterly. 'My boss was second cultural attaché or some such. Read: Head of Station, Bangkok.' She shrugged. 'Can you see how it happened? After the novelty wore off, I got a bit sick of all those posh young FO types. I mean, almost everyone I worked for drank too much, or swapped partners out of sheer boredom . . .' She took a deep breath. 'So, I fell for fresh-faced young Rockwell Elliot, America's finest, a product of Princeton and the Peace Corps – doing a bit of couriering for the Company . . .'

'He claimed to have left the CIA after he met you.'

'That's what we agreed. He said he had gotten tired of the whole organisation.' Daphne still spoke with an English accent, but her speech was full of little Americanisms. 'As far as I could gauge, he *had* left . . . I suppose he was fibbing. When you think about it, real estate development was the perfect cover for a spot of part-time spying . . . flying around looking at buildings and places, talking to local businessmen and officials, finding out who counts and who doesn't, who's bribable and who isn't . . . God! It's always easy to realise these things with hindsight, isn't it?'

'Did you mention this to the police when you talked to them?'

'No. What's the point? I think the cops see it as a straightforward embezzlement-and-suicide case, and I've decided to leave it at that. I talked to Benno about it, and he thought the same way.'

Blessed grunted non-committally, got to his feet. He walked over to the enormous refrigerator in the corner of the kitchen and helped himself to a bottle of Beck's. 'How about you, Daff? There's some Chardonnay in here.'

His sister shook her head. 'No booze for me at the moment. Just open another bottle of Perrier, will you?'

Blessed poured the mineral water, then his beer, glad of the distraction. The Beck's was imported, from Bremen. Surprising how far away Germany felt now, only fory-eight hours after he had left Berlin. America worked like that. Once you had arrived, everywhere else soon began to feel unreal, marginal, and – especially compared with the wealth per square inch here in Greenwich – so damned *poor*.

Given that perspective, it was no wonder the police and the financial investigators were still looking for evidence of an all-American conspiracy – the Mafia, a drugs connection, a money-laundering racket; one of those homegrown scams mounted by any of the usual suspects with the sharp lawyers, the friends in high places, and the billion-dollar turnovers.

Blessed and Daphne had already covered all this ground many times during the past two days. His real problem in helping Daphne

292

come to with terms with the tragedy was the pact he had struck with Klarfeld immediately after his return from East Germany. Unless matters of life or death arose – so the agreement went – they would shield her from the full truth about her husband. This meant saying nothing about the compromising photographs of Rockwell and Erika – not to Daphne, not to Prosser, and not to the American police. The money was gone, they reasoned. Rockwell had taken his final plunge. Revealing that her husband had performed enthusiastically with a professional *Stasi* seductress was not going to help get back either the money or Rockwell, but it would certainly cause Daphne a great deal of extra pain.

Blessed still believed that he and Klarfeld had made the right decision. All the same, the fact that certain things must remain unsaid didn't make his task here any easier.

'Mind if I smoke?' Blessed asked when he returned to the table.

'I give you licence until Christmas. After that, Mike darling, you run out of excuses.'

'Fair enough. When I gave up the last time – for five whole years, let it not be forgotten – it was a New Year's Resolution. I can do the same again. December 31st 1989 will see the last gasp of nicotine pass these increasingly raddled lips of mine.'

'I'll hold you to that. I can be really boring about things when I want to be, as you know.' Daphne paused. 'Do you want to talk about what it was like being locked up over there in the East?' she asked. 'I've been banging on about my own disasters ever since you got off the plane. Now it's your turn.'

'All's reasonably well that ends reasonably well,' Blessed said with a shrug. 'It was pretty awful while it lasted, because at the time I suspected it might go on virtually for ever. It didn't. Thanks first of all to a very careless jailer. Then to the *Stasi* general. And also, I'd guess, to Benno.'

'He's been wonderful. I mean, offering to pay Josh's first year in graduate school. And getting legal advice on the London flat. I was far too devastated to be thinking about anything so sordidly practical as that.'

'Dad helped him all those years ago. I suppose he feels an obligation to us. And especially to you.' Blessed drank some beer. 'I always meant to ask. How serious were you and Benno back when you were a teenager? He told me about his visit to England. Seeing you. Seeing Dad, too.'

Daphne looked away for a moment, then back at Blessed. 'A touch of teenage romance. You know how these things are. When the summer was over, I went to secretarial college in London. He went back to Germany to start his career. We wrote to each other for quite some time. I adored him, but . . . oh, it was my fault, actually.'

'What was your fault?'

'That we didn't stay in touch. I wasn't mature enough for him. He was . . . I mean, it's awful to say so, but when Benno was in his early twenties, he could be a bit of a social embarrassment. He didn't really know how to behave. How could he? And his English was pretty bad too.' Daphne made a helpless gesture. 'Young girls can be such bitches, can't they? They care so much about the surface things.'

'So you never saw each other again?'

Daphne reddened slightly, then shook her head. 'That's not strictly true. I mean, I call Rockwell secretive . . . well, this is the only secret I ever kept from him.'

Blessed looked at his half-sister intently. 'Come on, Daff.'

For just this moment, the sadness had left Daphne's face and she was coyly amused, in another time, an altogether different emotional world. 'It was fifteen years ago,' she said hesitantly. 'By that time, we were living in New York. Josh had just started at school. He was in first grade . . . or maybe just starting second. I had time on my hands. It was autumn. Rock was away on business a lot. Especially then. California, Texas, Vancouver, Chicago . . . We were living in that apartment on 74th Street and Madison. God, I was tired of that endless exec wives' *Kaffeeklatsch*, and I already knew MOMA and the Metropolitan like a guide knows the mountain passes . . .'

'Blimey. You like to fill in the background, don't you just?'

'Shut up, Mike. I'm *getting* there.' Daphne persisted, smiling. 'The phone rang one day, see, and a man's voice asked in good but foreign-accented English if I was Mrs Elliot. And then he said, still in this impeccable English, "I'm Benno Klarfeld. How are you? I'm in town and I'd feel privileged to take you out to lunch". '

'Aha. And what did you say to *that*?'

294

'How could I refuse? He was so polite, asking about Rockwell and Josh and . . . well, you know how he saved me when I was a little girl from the Kinder . . .'

Blessed laughed. 'It's all right. Of course you said yes. Who wouldn't?'

'Right. Well, get this: He sent a *limo* for me. I didn't even know where I was going, but I hastily squeezed into a little black dress and the only Charles Jourdan shoes I had. The limo arrived, whisked me away, and eventually decanted me at the front door of a town house on East Fiftieth Street.' Daphne smiled at Blessed. 'Have you ever heard of a place called Lutèce, Mike?'

'Yes. I've never been there. It's one of the most expensive restaurants in New York, isn't it?'

'Oh yes. But that's not really the point. The thing was, it was such a *tasteful* choice. Lutèce is a simple, comfortable, friendly restaurant that serves absolutely magnificent food and charges prices that accord with this fact. In short, Lutèce is the kind of restaurant where you eat lunch if you've already *arrived*, if you've got nothing to *prove*.'

'He'd obviously learned a lot by then. For a start, that money isn't everything.'

'That's for sure. We had the best lunch – the best I've ever had, I think.' Daphne sighed with the sweetness of the recollection. 'I was shown in. Benno was waiting in the little front room that served as a bar. The barman was a grinning little French cherub, perfectly at home behind his tiny zinc bar. We ate in the covered garden – all pink stucco walls behind white latticework and columns of whitewashed brick topped with palms. I had the Poussin Basquaise, wonderfully earthy sauce with tomatoes and wild mushrooms . . . he had the Cassolette de Crabe . . . It was perfect . . .'

'When do we get to the bit you were supposed to keep quiet about?'

'What?'

'Why the secret?'

'Oh . . . he just made me promise. He was fun and everything, his old self but with the edges knocked off and this perfect English . . . He wanted to know about Rockwell and Josh. I told him about them both. He was very sweet. Jokingly told me that Rockwell sounded such a good husband and father. He gladly stood down in his favour, or so he claimed.'

'OK. And what happened *then*?'

'We said goodbye at about three.'

'That's *all*?'

Daphne reddened slightly. 'Well, yes. Chaste kisses. Vague promises to meet up, maybe introduce him to Rockwell and Josh . . .'

'That's the big secret? You didn't sleep together?'

'Why no. The limo took me home to the apartment. Within minutes I had changed back into jeans and sweater and was at the school gate to pick up Josh.'

'I don't get it. It was completely innocent, yet you never told anyone. Jesus, Daff, which century did you think you were living in?'

'Oh . . . I guess it was my fairytale, my secret assignation. The solitary, innocent secret I kept from Rock.'

Silence fell between them. Blessed got up quietly and fetched himself another beer from the icebox.

'Only one more little thing,' he said a while later. 'Did you ever ask Benno how he found you, fifteen years later, three thousand miles away, married to another man and bearing that man's name?'

'No. I just assumed Benno could do anything he wanted, I suppose. Deep down, that's what I've always believed.'

'Powerful stuff. That gives him quite a hold over you.'

Daphne made no answer. She got to her feet, started to clear the dinner plates and stack the dishwasher.

'I don't trust him, Daff,' Blessed said after a while. 'Just as I don't trust the *Stasi* general we talked about. I doubt very much that he means any of us harm, but I don't trust that he's telling the whole truth.'

His sister paused in her work. 'Well, maybe that's so. Still and all, if Benno's holding anything from us, I'm sure it's because he has to. If he's been dealing with these Intelligence people, there are bound to be some things he's not allowed to discuss. Silence was almost certainly the price he paid for securing their cooperation in rescuing you from that awful place.'

'You have your instinct, Daff, and I have mine.'

Daphne frowned, put the last of the crockery in the machine and pushed the door hard shut. Suddenly she looked angry. She was decades away from the comfort of her dream lunch at Lutèce, back to harsh and frightening reality. 'Mike, why can't you just be grateful you got out of that hideous mess in one piece? Why can't you ease off?'

'Because, as the Americans say, I was suckered, Daff. And I have a nasty feeling that the suckering is still going on.'

'Christ! You're stubborn and you're just like our bloody father!' Half furious, half amused.

Blessed shook his head. 'Wrong. For two reasons. First, after I get back on the other side of the Atlantic I'm going to write a book and I'm having nothing whatsoever to do with any more dirty tricks.' He took another cigarette out of the packet and lit it with a flourish. 'Second, because, again unlike Dad, I'm going to give these bloody things up before they kill me.'

SIXTY-FOUR

LIEUTENANT ALBERT SIMEONI had the eyes of a latin lover and the body of an over-the-hill heavyweight boxer. A working life fuelled by a diet of junkfood had taken its toll – he was stuffed with difficulty into a blue wash-and-wear suit – but Simeoni was polite and articulate, out to show this Englishman that Italian boys from New Haven had class too.

'You knew Rockwell Elliot for ... ah ... twenty-two years. Right?'

'Yes,' Blessed confirmed. 'My sister introduced me to him after she got back from the Far East in 1966. I was only fifteen at the time.'

'Mrs Elliot is actually your half-sister. Right? Just answer yes or no, please. It makes it easier with the transcript.'

'Yes. My father and her mother split up in 1948, when she was very little. He was an officer with the British Army in Berlin. He later married my mother, a German woman he met there.'

They were sitting opposite each other in the family room of the Elliot house. From where Blessed was sitting, he could see the state-of-the-art barbecue out on the deck, the neat lawn, the basketball net fixed to the garage. Daphne's two-seater Mercedes was parked in the drive. That was another little luxury that was going to have to go.

'OK. Mrs Elliot and Mr Elliot met in the Far East?'

'You know they did.'

'Mr Blessed, I need to just check if that is your recollection. For the record.'

'Well, yes. That's my recollection.'

'They came back together, got married. In that order.'

'Yes. There were two weddings, actually. One big one in Cornwall, where Daphne's mother had a house, and the other, a civil ceremony, in Westchester County, where Rockwell came from. I went to the Cornish one.'

Simeoni had a small tape recorder running. He was also taking a few notes. His whole manner was of someone going through the

298

motions, just getting things, as he said, 'for the record'. So, his next question was unexpected.

'Mr Blessed, how did Mr and Mrs Elliot get along?'

'Get along?' Blessed thought for a moment. 'They seemed very fond of each other. They weren't in each other's pockets the whole time. But, God, they seemed pretty damned good to me.'

'OK.' *OK* was a mannerism of Lieutenant Simeoni. It amounted to his stonewall. 'They fight?'

'Hardly ever. They argued good-naturedly. You know, like *I Love Lucy*.'

Simeoni looked sharply at Blessed, as if to check he was serious. 'Yeah,' he said finally. 'They got divorced in the end.'

'Who?'

'Lucille Ball and Desi Arnaz. Kind of a mixed marriage, you know. Conflicting national temperaments.'

'Oh. Like English and American, for instance?'

Simeoni shrugged. 'Mr Elliot travelled a lot.'

'Are we still on the marriage, or on Mr Elliot's travelling?'

'Whatever you think fit, Mr Blessed.' Simeoni paused. 'He travelled to Europe, mainly. Any idea who he used to meet there?'

'Not much. He used to meet developers, bankers, builders.'

'He ever mention any names?'

'The big British merchant banks. A few totally respectable London property companies he did some projects with. Then there were the big German banks and developers. Some stuff in Scandinavia too. He only picked blue-chip companies. Not a spectacular return on capital, but steady and reliable in the long term. He used to say, "It's not my money, I can't throw it around" –'

'Right.' Simeoni was impassive. 'It wasn't his money.'

'No. Mostly it belonged to the Dracoulis family, as we know. Listen, my sister's told me all the bad news.'

'Elliot ever ask for your help or advice?'

'He asked me what I thought of the situation in Australia when I lived there. I said it sucked. Everyone was on the take and living on borrowed money. As proved to be the case. How many of those famous Australian billionaires do you see strutting their stuff these days? He said that was exactly what he'd figured, and he wasn't about to invest there. I quote. When I was in Berlin he also asked me in a vague kind of way about what was happening in Germany.'

'How did he seem in Berlin, by the way?'

'Not too happy, actually. I don't know why. He wasn't specific.'

'OK. You never were active . . . shall we say in any capacity at all on his behalf? On any kind of partnership basis? We can subpoena material, you know . . . '

'Wait a minute.' Blessed took a deep breath. 'Are you asking if I was in on any of this – whatever it was – with him?'

'I'm asking what I asked, Mr Blessed.'

'The answer's no. He was my brother-in-law. Basically I liked and respected him, even though he was a pain in the arse at times. He was good to me. Lent me money when I was down –'

'How much, Mr Blessed?'

'Two thousand pounds. Until I got the money from my divorce settlement at the end of last year. Oh, and . . . ' Simeoni leaned forward, pen poised. ' . . . when I was a student at Oxford, he bought me a bike for Christmas.'

'Huh.' This was Simeoni's laugh. 'Huh. OK.'

Blessed offered him a cigarette. The cop thought for a moment, then accepted. Blessed took one for himself and they lit up. The common addiction gave a new sense of intimacy between them.

'My main aim is to save my sister from any more unhappiness,' Blessed said then. 'And to make sure she comes away from this with her dignity – and some of her property – intact. Whatever Rockwell got up to, she had absolutely nothing to do with it. She's the straightest human being I know.'

Simeoni nodded. 'Worst thing with these guys, the mess they leave behind. You see these nice families suddenly in all kinds of shit. Houses repossessed. Wives out on the street. Kids thrown out of college because they can't pay the tuition no more.' He snapped shut his notebook. 'I'll tell you, you talk to people, they say what a nice guy he was – your Elliot here, or any of 'em – and I think, what do they mean by nice guy? A really nice guy, he doesn't cause this kind of grief in the first place. And even if he does – so he's only a moderately nice guy – at least he stays to face the music when things get tough. Doesn't just leave the family to suffer.' He looked at his watch. 'And anyway, I'm a Catholic. The Church says suicide is a mortal sin. The more cases like this I see, the more I get behind that.'

'Are you – they – sure he killed himself?'

'Maybe eighty per cent sure. We talked to a waitress from the Rusty Scupper in Stamford. She said, when he left to get back on his boat he could hardly walk a straight line. Had at least six large whiskey-sours, and easy on the lemon juice. Witnesses say it took him ten minutes to manoeuvre that thing out of the mooring. Amazing he managed to steer it out into Long Island Sound. Force of habit, maybe.'

'You reckon suicide is an eighty per cent bet. You see other possibilities?'

'A couple. First, he might have been murdered. Someone wanted to get rid of him. Maybe an accomplice, someone who got greedy and wanted all that money. Problem is, at the moment we can't trace any such accomplice.'

'And the second possibility, Lieutenant?'

'Oh yeah. Well, maybe Mr Elliot was so drunk that at some point he just fell overboard into the Sound. Unlikely, but not right out of the question. Wouldn't be the first time.' Simeoni got slowly to his feet. He must have been six-five, probably two hundred and fifty pounds, all that fighter's muscle now softened into layers of fat. 'I have to be back in my office in Stamford in just half an hour.' He thrust out a massive hand. 'Good to meet you, Mr Blessed. Thanks for your help. Tough times for you.'

'Much tougher for Daphne and Josh. Horrific, in fact.'

'OK. Right.'

After Blessed had walked Lieutenant Simeoni out to his car, he joined Daphne and Josh in the kitchen.

'So, what did fatso want to know?' Josh asked.

'Just checking stuff for the record.'

'Is that all?'

'Well, not quite all. I'm the only person they've been able to talk to so far – apart from your mother – who saw your dad in Europe recently. They wanted to hear my impressions.'

'And?' Daphne put the question, very quietly.

'What could I say? He was a bit low when I saw him in Berlin. Or at least that was my impression.'

'I was too busy having a good time there to notice,' Daphne admitted. 'Later in the summer, when I came to think of it, he was more tired, less fun than usual, too. But I thought, he'd been working so hard –'

'Sure. And for what?' Josh cut in. 'I mean, I don't know what my dad did with that money, or why he did it, but what's the goddamn point in the end? He's *gone*.' The boy's face was flushed, his lips pressed tight together so that the flesh showed transparent. 'Work-work-work-*work*! Ever since I can remember, that's all Dad ever seemed to do. It made him crazy in the end! Well, you won't find me living – or dying – for money, like he did!'

Josh got up abruptly and stalked out. They heard him climbing the stairs to his room. For a while there seemed nothing to be said.

'Well, there's another soul saved from capitalism,' Daphne murmured at last. 'If Rockwell did nothing else, he innoculated his son against the lure of filthy lucre. The latest plan is, when he comes out of the graduate film programme, Josh will go and live with the rainforest Indians – and I mean live *exactly* as they do – and make the rainforest documentary to end all rainforest documentaries.'

'Good luck to him. But even if he lives on roots and berries, he'll still need money for film and equipment.'

'I know. He knows it too.' Daphne sighed. 'He's surviving a tragic experience the only way he knows how. He can't really blame his father, because he loved him. So he has to blame the "system".' She walked back and forth for a short while, looking out of the huge, vaulted windows, contemplating the birch trees. Then she turned back to face Blessed. 'I had some good news while you were closeted with Lieutenant Simeoni,' she said briskly.

'What was that?'

'Benno called from Berlin. He said his British lawyers are sure I won't have to give up the flat in London. So at least Josh and I will have a roof over our heads. It's touch-and-go with the cottage in Somerset, though. It was in Rockwell's name. We may have to sell it along with all the other real estate.'

'Could take quite a while. I hear the bottom's fallen out of the property market in England.'

'You hear right, Mike. I want you to know you're welcome to use the place until it is sold – *if* it's sold . . . '

'Thanks. But I don't want to think about that at the moment. I belong here with you and Josh.'

She nodded. 'Benno said something else. He said the first instalment of those memoirs is out, and it's caused a terrific sensation. The *Stasi* general is about to resign, adding to the uproar. He says the East German régime is absolutely reeling from the blow. He says, watch this space.'

Blessed glanced at his watch. 'Speaking of which, I'll go and see if I can catch the news from there on CNN, all right?'

'That's the fourth time today you've checked the update. Do I sense an obsessive interest in events over there?'

'Yes. Why not? You could say I feel very involved in what's happening. You could say I *was* very involved . . . '

'I wish you could let it go, all that political skulduggery,' Daphne said. Then she came up to him and kissed him on the cheek. 'But of course you can suit yourself, darling brother. We're both alone and independent now, aren't we?'

'I suppose we are. There's our kids, of course. But . . . '

'Yes.' Daphne hesitated. 'Mike, do you think Rockwell had other women?' she asked suddenly.

Blessed was thrown off balance. 'I – I – He never gave any hint of it. He wasn't the kind of man who –'

'I think he did,' Daphne said, surprisingly matter-of-factly. 'In fact, I'm sure of it. I think women were like money to him. They were currency in his hands.' She patted him gently on the shoulder. 'Now, get along and catch up with CNN, Mike. I'll start fixing dinner. I got some wonderful shrimp this morning from Bon Ton.'

'You're quite something, Daff. Shrimp dinners at a time like this.'

'You can't go on being miserable for ever. Another good thing happened today. I thought about Rockwell, and money, and the way the world is, and I decided it was time we all got on with our lives.'

SIXTY-FIVE

'YOU UPHELD THIS SYSTEM faithfully for almost forty years, General Albrecht. How come the sudden conversion to democracy?'

'I don't think you should call me General any more. Call me Herr Albrecht. Or Günther if you like.' A big grin from a big man. 'I've resigned from the state's service.'

'You haven't answered my question, Herr Albrecht. How come the sudden conversion?'

'Read the book, gentlemen. It's been translated into English by an excellent writer from London. He worked on the project secretly – at, I may say, no small risk to himself.'

'Is *he* available for comment?'

'He's taking a well-earned rest, gentlemen. I understand he may make a statement later, at a time of his choice.'

'You've been accused of deserting a sinking ship, Gen – Herr Albrecht. Until lately you were reckoned to be close to both Honecker and Mielke. Your critics say you kept your privileges, did as you were told until the last possible moment.'

'Nonsense! I began writing my memoirs almost three years ago. In response to what I could see happening in the Soviet Union. *Perestroika. Glasnost.* I wrote the book in the hope the same thing could soon happen here. And in the meantime, I carried on in my job. I thought I could be of more help from *inside* the system. But the crumbling of this system came even more quickly and suddenly than I – or my publisher – ever believed possible.'

'You say you tried to help. Could you be more specific, Herr Albrecht? What – and whom – did you try to help?'

'It will all come out one day. Maybe. There are individuals in this country and abroad who fought and suffered for the cause of freedom during these past few months. Such brave men and women don't wish – cannot afford – to have their activities made public. I can't be more specific than that.'

'Herr Albrecht, there's talk that the authorities plan to indict you for embezzlement and misuse of state funds –'

304

'Rubbish! Such accusations are always made when the communist die-hards wish to embarrass someone like me!' Another broad, toothy grin. 'Now, gentlemen, excuse me. I am due to address a meeting of Democratic Action in a very short time.'

'Would you call yourself a supporter of Democratic Action?'

'We have a great deal in common, a great deal to discuss. I am still a member of the SED, however, and I wish to remain so. I want to change the GDR, but I want reform, not revolution. Excuse me . . . '

A storm of flashbulbs breaks out. Ex-*Stasi* General Günther Albrecht steps down from his makeshift podium. He makes his way through the assembled press, towering above them all, and leaves the hall. He is wearing a casual jacket, a sweater and slacks. He is tanned and confident, enjoying the limelight. The powerful zoom lenses of the camera crews expertly track him out of the door and into the humble Wartburg station-wagon waiting for him in the street. No sleek Volvo limousine now. Albrecht smiles and waves. He squeezes into the modest, East German-made car and it takes off in the direction of the Marx-Engels-Platz.

Soon the reporters are earnestly spouting their pieces to camera on the slippery cobbles outside the part of the Humboldt University building where Albrecht's press conference had been held. A trenchcoated young American, mike in hand and brows knitted in solemn concentration, launches into his material:

'Last week's publication of General Albrecht's damning attack on the communist system he served so well for so long, and now his resignation, are two more nails in the coffin of struggling East German Party boss Egon Krenz. After less than a month in power, Krenz is facing ever more powerful demands from ordinary citizens for free elections and the freedom to travel. And meanwhile, thousands still pour into the West through Hungary and Czechoslovakia. The question tonight is, how long can the régime stem the floodtide of democracy? This is Gary Chisholm reporting from East Berlin, dateline November 4th . . . '

Blessed pressed the button on the remote, shut off the sound.

'Smooth operator, your general,' said Josh, cutting into Blessed's thoughts. Daphne was in downtown Greenwich, at her accountant's office, effecting the practical steps that would underpin her determination to take on life anew.

'What? Oh, yeah. Sure.'

'He's done what he said he was going to do, you have to admit it.'

'You're right. He has. Or he seems to have.'

Josh laughed. 'Hey, Mike, everything's working out just the way you hoped! General's memoirs all over the newscasts, communism on the skids. Politically sound moves plus money in the bank!'

Blessed nodded. A few days ago, his nephew had been inveighing against mammon. Now he was back on track again. Cash was OK if it was 'correctly' earned. The capitalist instinct was so strong in the American psyche. And when you're twenty-one, you can change your mind as often as you like.

'So why not *happy*?' his nephew persisted doggedly.

'Oh, I don't know, Josh. It's nothing in particular. Just *not*. What more can I say?'

Blessed stared at the silent images on the screen. Demonstrations in Prague now. Many of the pictures he had seen at the last news-update. Teargas drifting around the ancient, eerily beautiful streets of Kafka's city. Cops slugging protesters. Sleek black limousines whizzing in and out of the gates of the Czechoslovak communists' Central Committee building. The Western news-cameras zeroing pruriently in on the drawn, tight-lipped faces of the *apparatchiks* in the back seats. Cut to Vaclav Havel, the opposition leader, tousle-haired, chainsmoking – hunched in a chair in a shabby room and talking, talking, talking. The man of the moment.

'There's a new world coming into being over there, Josh,' Blessed said quietly. 'A far better world. And I still have a problem. Perhaps it's my bruised ego. Perhaps it's because I hate sitting here passively and watching. Anyway, I just wish I could enjoy it – really appreciate what's happening for those people in Eastern Europe – but I can't. Something about it gives me an itch. Something about it causes me worry. *Pain.*'

'Pain? All those people out having a good time and you feel pain?'

'Well, yes.'

'You know, Mike, sometimes you sound just like a Jewish mother.'

'Oh thanks, Josh. I really needed that . . . '

306

SIXTY-SIX

'He's safely in America now. You know how America *envelops* people. They forget the rest of the world. TV and buttered popcorn take over. Soft music and shopping malls –'

'His sister will not be enjoying herself in shopping malls. Not any more. She'll be lucky if her creditors let her eat.'

'True. But all the more reason for him to stay over there indefinitely. He's all his sister has, and he knows it.'

'Christ, you're a cold-hearted bastard.' There was admiration in Banana's voice.

Granit said nothing. His indifferent shrug was almost audible over the line.

Pause. Then: 'Modrow has opened up channels to the more "responsible" members of the opposition.' A laugh. 'People like me. There's talk of a deal. Quiet talk as yet, but it's beginning to look inevitable. If the SED is going to hang on to some semblance of power. And if the GDR is to continue in existence.'

'A *big* if, that second one. Have you seen those crowds out there calling for reunification? Dresden last night. Hard to know how anything can resist a wave like that. We thought we had at least three, four years to play with before West and East formally united. But it's happening faster than any of us could have predicted.'

'Let's hope you're wrong. For all our sakes, but mainly for yours. Not everyone in West Germany believes in your conversion to democracy. I'd bet there are one or two boys at the *Verfassungsschutz* who'd like to get their hands on you in a quiet room somewhere, and if West German law became writ in this country, they'd have a chance to do just that . . . '

'Don't worry about me. I've made my personal preparations. Worst comes to the worst, you and the others will have to carry things through. At least financially everything's taken care of.'

'Likewise the financier.'

'Careful what you say. *Careful.*'

Pause.

'You know what? I'll be glad when this is over.'

'Over? Are you crazy? It will *never* be over. You – we – will always have to fight for everything we have and everything we want, just the same as ever. We've staved off one disaster. That doesn't mean we're completely out of trouble.'

'My God. You can destroy a man's dreams, you know that?'

'A man's illusions, you mean! The kind of illusions you should have lost forty years ago in that damp cellar in the Bernauer Strasse.'

'You were always the realist.' Sarcastically.

In response, with an edge of aggression: 'Realist? You beddabelieve!'

SIXTY-SEVEN

BROTHER AND SISTER AND NEPHEW had driven out to a terrific Mexican place on the Old Boston Post Road for a morale-boosting dinner on Blessed's memoirs money. There had been faces Daphne knew, and even in the lantern-candled half-darkness of the restaurant she had could see their stares.

Two couples had left without acknowledging her. Only one friend came over, separately from her arbitrageur husband, who was feigning last minute business with the bill. She asked Daphne how things were going. To which Daphne replied with a gracious smile and steel in her eyes: 'Thank you for asking, Veronica. Totally lousy, naturally, but bearable. And you?'

'Well, Arnold's still around, as you can see. But these days you never know . . . '

They arrived back around ten-thirty. A brisk wind had risen up during the evening. The suburban darkness carried an abrasive hint of winter, and breeze-blown leaves whipped and scudded around their ankles.

Daphne and Josh each went to bed almost immediately. Blessed, left alone, prowled around the huge goldfish-bowl of a kitchen for a while, listening to the wind. Suddenly he felt as if he belonged back in Benno Klarfeld's boathouse; the almost-bare trees should have been Berlin trees, and the wind should have been coming off the waters of the Stölpchensee. Not nostalgia. Far from it. Just unfinished business.

Get a grip. Get a grip on yourself, Michael Blessed.

He poured himself a drink from Rockwell's still-surviving stock of Bourbon and went through to the family room. Sprawled on the sofa, for the nth time he hit the remote button and the huge TV screen zipped into life. He selected CNN. The world's reality in your living room. And your personal reality right where it belongs, Blessed thought, which was gently numbed with whisky and poised helplessly outside it all, like an orphan with his nose pressed against the window of a sweetshop.

Riots on the West Bank. Israeli conscripts repelling stone throwing Palestinians with tear gas. Cue dusty roads. Angry olive-skinned faces – so hard to tell Jewish from Muslim semites unless they were in uniform.

Germany. Give me East Germany. There was stuff on the last update I saw before we went out. It looked interesting. Give it to me now.

Instead, The Soviet Union. Gorbachev addressing the Soviet parliament. Economic problems. The father of *perestroika* has begun to look tired. His country is in trouble. His empire is falling apart . . .

And now at last: Berlin. More demonstrations against the communist régime in East Germany. Party boss Egon Krenz struggles to control events. Some footage of Krenz having trouble finding the door of a conference room, let alone riding the tiger of history. Faces of opposition leaders – pastors, teachers, feminist spokesmen, environmentalists. The camera lingers for a moment on a familiar face.

The general. Damned if it isn't the Stasi *general. Haven't seen him for a while . . .*

From the sofa, Blessed pressed the remote 'record' button, activating the VCR stacked under the TV set. The recorder eased into operation. He always made sure there was a blank cassette ready in the machine, so he could capture it all on tape whenever some thing interesting came up. Certainly every time he saw the general appear on the screen, or –

Ziegler. Christ. There, right next to the general: Otmar Ziegler. Beanpole-tall, wry, voluble.

'Tonight in East Berlin,' the voice-over intoned, 'men who were once enemies join to call for a new order in this, once the most ossified of communist satellites. Rebel former *Stasi* general Günther Albrecht, whose revealing memoirs recently caused a sensation in East and West alike, joins with a former victim of his own secret police cohorts, dissident writer Otmar Ziegler to address this opposition meeting. They are speaking at a churchyard in East Berlin where recently political demonstrations – and wild, officially-disapproved punk rock concerts – have been the order of the day.'

Blessed urgently checked to make sure the recording light was still on. In case the cassette was somehow full. In case . . .

310

There was no audible sound-track of what Ziegler was saying with such passion to the noisily appreciative crowd. Why should there be? Why should an American station broadcast in German to an English-speaking audience? The brief dumb-show was frustrating only for Blessed. But the main thing was, he could see just a few feet from Ziegler the powerful, bulky figure of General Albrecht. Albrecht was dressed in a light raincoat and a flat cap. He was nodding with approval at Ziegler's words.

'Who would ever have suspected it!' the voice-over quickly returned. 'An alliance such as this – the writer and the secret policeman, both calling for open borders and free elections! General Secretary Krenz must be finding it hard, very hard to sleep at nights these days.'

Sure. Very hard. But . . .

Blessed caught his breath. To the right of General Albrecht on the podium. Two more figures, equally well-known to Blessed. First a very small man with eyes like an opossum. Herr Hildebrandt, the janitor of the apartment block that had housed Erika's honeytrap in West Berlin. And to Herr Hildebrandt's right, another familiar figure. Younger, wearing a leather jacket and stonewashed jeans, uniform of the East-European intellectual. Muscular, handsome, serious.

Wolfgang. The unmistakable Wolfgang, owner of the Galerie Schnittke and habitué of sexshops. Erika's supposed lover and proven co-conspirator, whom Blessed hadn't seen since watching the pair of them say goodbye outside LOVEMACHINE long ago – or so it seemed – in August.

As if in answer to the question forming in Blessed's mind, at that moment General Albrecht turned to the small man, whom Blessed had known in the West as Herr Hildebrandt, smiled and said something. Herr Hildebrandt smiled back at him. So, right at the edge of the frame, did Wolfgang.

They knew each other. All these bastards knew each other!

'So, the supporters of reform mass for a new push on the citadels of power . . .'

Back to a serious-faced reporter, speaking to camera in front of an anonymous grey building on an East Berlin street, wrapping up the story with a summary of the beleaguered communist régime's latest political contortions.

'From East Berlin, where the power is shifting to the streets, and to the people – goodnight.'

Then it was on to a story about China. Blessed sat for a while, stunned. Then he shut off the VCR and got quickly to his feet. He ran out of the family room, through the hall, and up the stairs, heading for the wing of the house where his sister slept.

'OK, Mike. Let's watch it again,' said Daphne.

Blessed played back the clip of Ziegler speaking, General Albrecht standing at his side, then exchanging a joke with Herr Hildebrandt and Wolfgang. He froze it with the last three still in frame, an instant before the camera cut back to the reporter.

'That,' he said, pointing to Albrecht, 'is the general.'

Daphne nodded.

'And that's the man who called himself Herr Hildebrandt – the janitor of the building where the honeytrap was. Where I was found and abducted to East Germany.'

Again, Daphne just nodded. She had been asleep when he had gone to her room to fetch her, but there was something about her now that couldn't be put down to simple tiredness.

'You OK, Daff?' Blessed asked.

Still no response.

'Come on,' he coaxed gently. 'What is it?'

Daphne seemed to be struggling for words. When she did speak, it was quietly, almost inaudibly, quite unlike her normal confident voice. Like a . . . like a terrified small girl's, Blessed thought.

'Just a minute.'

She got to her feet, moved a few steps closer, stared hard at the screen for some moments. Then she turned back to face Blessed, ran one hand through her hair in a nervous gesture.

'You think you know who those people are, Mike?'

'Yes. I just told you.'

She let out a bitter little laugh. 'You don't. I do, though, and I only just realised.' She pointed one finger at the screen. 'Suddenly it all made sense. That man – the tiny one with funny eyes – is the Wonder. I'd know him anywhere. He looks pretty much the same as he always did, give or take a wrinkle or two and some grownup clothes.'

'Daff –'

312

'And that man – the one you say is your *Stasi* general . . . I mean, I never really looked at him before, not properly . . . and well, now I realise that he can only be the one they called "Granit" . . . '

'*The Wonder*? *Granit*? Where did you get those weird names from, Daff? What the hell are you talking about?'

Daphne sat down abruptly. She took a deep breath. 'I'm . . . I'm talking about the Kinder, Mike. That's what. Two members of the Kinder, still together more than forty years later.' Her voice was a little stronger, and her message was a very adult one. 'Get me a nice big slug of what you're drinking, Mike. We have a lot of talking to do tonight. I'm going to need all my strength to say the things I have to say . . . and remember the things I have to remember.'

SIXTY-EIGHT

LESS THAN FORTY-EIGHT HOURS later, in the afternoon of 8 November, Blessed landed once again at West Berlin-Tegel.

For speed, Blessed had crammed everything he needed into one, bulging carry-on bag. He left the terminal ahead of the crowd and within five minutes was installed in a Mercedes cab, heading south-westward towards the lush lakeside suburbs he had come to know so well.

On the morning of the previous day, after that long night's talking with Daphne and before he booked his air ticket, Blessed had got Daphne to ring Benno Klarfeld's house. Frau Smilovici had told her that Klarfeld was away in Hamburg, not due back until the evening of today, the eighth.

Blessed had a few precious hours in hand.

There was no doubt that Frau Smilovici was surprised by Blessed's unannounced appearance at the security gate, but it made no difference to her greeting, or the matter-of-fact way she let him in. Within minutes he was poised on the sofa in the living room of Klarfeld's villa while she busied herself in the kitchen.

You're always welcome here, Michael, Klarfeld had told him, in Frau Smilovici's presence. *For as long as you like, and no questions asked*. He had been as good as his word, in this respect at least. Blessed almost felt guilty for what he was about to do. Almost.

He could hear Frau Smilovici singing to herself in the kitchen, putting on the kettle to fill the French *plongeur* that made the kind of coffee Blessed preferred. Knowing he might have only a couple of minutes, Blessed quickly crossed to the mantlepiece, looked behind the ormolu clock. Yes. The small-calibre Mauser with its clip of ten bullets was still there, exactly where Klarfeld had shown him, back in the summer.

It wasn't easy to do what he did next. There was a moment when Blessed almost succumbed to a powerful sense of his own betrayal. He fought it and won. Blessed reached out and palmed the gun, slipped it into one pocket of his padded windcheater. He dropped the ammunition clip into the other, glanced into the mirror over the fireplace to check that the bulges weren't too obvious. Then he returned to his place on the sofa and tried to look relaxed. Not a moment too soon.

Frau Smilovici re-appeared to tell him that the coffee would soon be ready, and in the meantime here were some chocolate biscuits that he must eat, because he looked exhausted and still maybe a little sad . . . of course, Blessed had been so busy comforting his poor sister, such a nice woman to talk to on the phone, who was going through such terrible times . . .

'Yes . . . ' she continued in her careful but heavily-accented German. 'Such a surprise that you have come. If I had known, I would have put on the heating in the boathouse . . . '

'It's fine. I took a chance. I just felt I couldn't stay away any longer. Too much is happening here. Daphne will be OK for a few days.'

Frau Smilovici nodded gravely. 'She is brave. I can tell. And Herr Klarfeld will be delighted to see you. I think he has been a little lonely since you left. Not that he has been here so much.'

'He's rung us several times in America. Very good of him,' Blessed answered blandly. He finished his coffee, looked at his watch. It was half-past five, rapidly becoming darker outside. 'When will he be back?'

'He told me about eight. So long as his plane is not delayed. He has been in Frankfurt since Sunday night. Business.'

'Right.' Blessed made himself yawn. 'I'm so tired,' he lied. 'Mind if I just crash out on the bed in the boathouse for a couple of hours? Then I'll be fresh to greet Benno.'

'Treat this place as your own house. Dinner at nine, I think.'

'Terrific. Maybe when he gets back Benno could wander down and rouse me. Then we'll have time to talk before we eat.'

'Of course.'

Lugging his carry-on bag, Blessed picked his way down the path to the boathouse, let himself in with the keys Klarfeld had insisted he keep.

Frau Smilovici was right. It had turned chilly in the couple of weeks since Blessed had flown off to the States to be with Daphne and Josh. Otherwise, the place was much as he had left it. The bed was neatly made, with a couple of extra blankets folded on the chest at the foot of the bed, as if Frau Smilovici and Benno Klarfeld had

315

indeed been expecting him and had made preparations. He put down his bag, then flicked the switch on the convection heater in the corner. He kept his jacket on.

Blessed's preparations were thorough, unhurried. First he took from the travel-bag his battery-operated alarm-clock and put it on the coffee-table in the middle of the room. Then he moved one of the armchairs to just beside this table, sat down in it. He was still wearing his jacket. The loaded gun, with its safety-catch on, now rested in his lap.

And he waited with his feet up on the coffee-table, grimly determined not to doze off, relying on the alarm-clock in case he did. He waited for headlights in the driveway. For familiar voices by the villa door. For a footfall outside the boat-house. For the man who once saved his sister's life . . .

For Benno Klarfeld.

Klarfeld arrived back slightly early. The time displayed on the little alarm-clock was 19:47 when Blessed heard the drone of a smooth, powerful engine easing along the drive, glimpsed headlights sweeping the lawns. Half-conscious, Blessed pitched himself to his feet. The gun clattered to the floor. He retrieved it, ran to the sink, splashed some cold water on his face and wrists. Then he began to pace around the boathouse like a madman – he thought of himself *like a madman*. With difficulty Blessed forced himself to stand still. To search for a kind of calm, all the while listening, listening for the expected sounds. To *wait*.

A car door slammed. Silence for two, three minutes. Blessed sweated it out. Then a voice. And a short while after, steps on the path leading towards him. Blessed stood facing the door with the gun in his hand. This was going to be hard. Sometimes it seemed that the terrible things Daphne had explained to him two nights ago in Connecticut must be the stuff of fantasy, of childish nightmares, but of course they weren't. He knew that. And that knowledge made all the difference, all the difference in the world.

To Blessed's numbed surprise, an inner control, a sense, even, of serenity, came over him as the door of the boathouse swung open.

Klarfeld was still wearing a dark business suit, though he had taken off his tie. He walked over the threshold with his arms outstretched, smiling.

316

'Michael. This is terrific. But unexpected. Is Daphne –'

Klarfeld saw the gun in Blessed's fist and stopped, just a couple of feet inside the room. Suddenly he turned terribly pale. Then an unhealthy pink. He swayed momentarily, put his hands to his chest, apparently short of breath. His eyes closed.

Blessed forced himself to stay exactly where he was, and to wait.

Klarfeld recovered quickly. He opened his eyes once more. Automatically he raised his hands slightly and spread the fingers, to show he was weaponless. His face began to return to its normal colour. Its expression went through several rapid and distinct changes. First surprise. Then hurt. Finally a kind of sour curiosity.

'*What*?' Klarfeld murmured throatily.

It was a strange question, strangely put. Not at all what Blessed had expected.

'I want to talk to you,' Blessed said. 'And I want the truth.' He gestured with the gun. 'First move into the room, Benno, and I'll move around behind you. I want us to end up with me between you and that door. All right? Take it easy.'

Klarfeld gazed at him steadily. 'Just know this – I won't tell you anything while you're holding that gun.'

'Please. Come slowly forward.'

The older man obeyed, moving carefully. Blessed himself stepped out in an arc, keeping his distance, holding the gun levelled straight at Klarfeld.

They ended up with Klarfeld facing the door, in front of the coffee table, and Blessed opposite him. They had swapped positions. It was like a weird, silent dance. But this was no dance. It was a duel.

'You can sit down if you like,' Blessed said.

'I'm all right now, thanks. I don't respond well to extreme stress these days. As you know.'

'OK.'

Klarfeld was impassive, apparently back in control of himself. 'OK so far as it goes, Michael,' he said. 'But until you put that gun away, no talking. No truth.'

'Christ,' Blessed snapped. 'How dare you talk to me like that? *You dropped me in the shit. And Daphne. And probably Rockwell too . . .*'

Klarfeld said nothing.

'You and the Kinder,' Blessed said with careful emphasis.

If he expected this to change Klarfeld's attitude, he was disappointed.

'You're wrong in what you say. Otherwise no comment. Please put the gun down, Michael. I know you are capable of using it. You're very angry. And like your father, when you're angry you're formidable. But please put it away. It's . . . inappropriate.'

'You're cool. You always were. But you have to tell me what I need to know, Benno. And if you think I'm about to make myself defenceless at a time like this, you must be crazy.'

Klarfeld sighed. 'Actually, you have no choice,' he said softly.

'*No choice . . .*' Another wave of anger. This was a poker game, and Blessed had to stick it out until his opponent cracked.

'Please take a look behind you, at the doorway,' Klarfeld said calmly. 'Take your time. No sudden movements, I warn you.'

For some moments Blessed refused to respond. Klarfeld just kept staring at him, unreadable, apparently relaxed. Blessed shifted position slightly, pivoting on the balls of his feet, so he could glimpse the door and keep an eye on Klarfeld at the same time.

'*Shit*,' he muttered under his breath in English. '*Oh shit.*'

Frau Smilovici was poised on the threshold of the boathouse. She was till wearing her kitchen apron, but her feet were planted firmly apart, and she was exercising a practised, two-handed grip on a powerful-looking handgun. Her gaze was dispassionate, concentrated. And the weapon was pointed straight at Blessed.

'She never was just a cook, Michael,' Klarfeld said. 'This is a dangerous country these days, especially for a prominent man like me. Terrorists. Kidnappers . . . Didn't you ever wonder why I don't seem to keep a bodyguard around the house?' He paused. 'Put down your gun, and I promise you Frau Smilovici will do the same. Look at it this way. If I wanted you dead, that's what you would be by now. *Dead.*'

Blessed turned his attention slowly away from Frau Smilovici and back to Klarfeld. Klarfeld's look was almost one of pleading now, as if to say, don't make her do it, don't force this upon us.

'One question. Just answer one simple question.'

'A simple question? Are you serious? There are no simple questions!'

'*I want to know if you're involved with the Kinder.*'

318

'I told you. No simple –'

'*Tell me!*'

'You'll put down that gun immediately?'

'If you tell me the truth.'

'Very well, Michael. The simple answer is yes.'

'And now put the gun down or I shoot,' Frau Smilovici's husky voice said from the doorway.

A glance showed Blessed that she meant what she said. He took a deep breath and slowly lowered the Mauser.

'Now drop it,' Frau Smilovici said.

Blessed shrugged and did just that. The Mauser clattered onto the wooden floor.

'OK?' She looked to Klarfeld for instruction.

He nodded. Frau Smilovici immediately lowered her gun and smiled. Klarfeld turned back to Blessed. 'Why don't we both go up to the house and have a drink? A large tumbler of Laphroaig is exactly what I need. Doctor's orders notwithstanding.' He smiled. 'And if Frau Smilovici doesn't get back to her kitchen, we'll get no dinner before midnight.'

'You're on the side of the Kinder,' Blessed said incredulously. 'And you're talking like *this*?'

'Like what? Come on,' Klarfeld said. 'I never said I was on their side. I said I was *involved* with them. There's a big difference.'

'I want the truth, Benno. I told you –'

'And you shall have it.' Klarfeld sighed. He was still smiling, but his eyes were hard, opaque. 'In the end. And if, when the moment comes, you're sure it's what you really want . . . '

'You mustn't let me down.'

'I won't. But you must have patience. There won't be much in the way of revelations tonight, Michael. Just a lot of preparations. Some of which I have to undertake alone.'

In his study, Klarfeld sipped Laphroaig, Blessed gin-and-tonic. Cautiously.

'It's because of my old connection with the Kinder that I was drawn into this affair, I suppose,' Klarfeld admitted, sinking into a leather chair and inviting Blessed to do the same. 'But that is not why I remained involved. Not at all.'

'You'll have to explain in more detail.'

319

'I don't *have* to do anything, Michael,' Klarfeld explained in a deceptively gentle voice. 'I got you into this, and I got you out. You were well paid. I could say my responsibilities ended when you got on that plane to America last month. Instead I am *choosing* to do this . . . but in return you will have to trust me, to trust that the big explanations will come later.'

'That's not good enough.'

'I told you to keep away from Berlin for a while, Michael,' Klarfeld retorted, suddenly altogether less gentle, the man of power. 'You chose not to, which was your right. But now that you're here, we do it my way, or not at all.'

Blessed said nothing. Klarfeld shrugged his shoulders. He put down his drink, got up and walked over to the phone. He dialled, waited. After a while someone came on the line.

'I'd like to speak to Herr Brauer, please,' Klarfeld said with calm authority. 'If you don't know where he is, you'll have to find him. *Yes. Find him. This is an emergency!* And get him to call me back, any time . . . Yes, three, four in the morning, it doesn't matter . . . *Wait* . . . and tell him this, too. Tell him: If he doesn't get back to me tonight, he is finished. Tell him Benno says that, and he knows Benno keeps his promises.'

Klarfeld put the phone down, checked his watch. 'Eight-twenty. I guarantee that our friend will be on that phone to me within an hour. And once he calls back, the machinery will be set in motion.'

'What machinery?'

Klarfeld finished relishing his single malt. 'The machinery of revelation, of course, Michael,' he said eventually. He was back in control, and it showed, but there was no hint of triumph. Just a certain cool solemnity. 'The machinery that should provide you with what you say . . . what you believe . . . is your heart's desire.'

SIXTY-NINE

'TODAY WILL BE A LONG DAY,' Klarfeld said. 'Once Gurkel rings back a second time, we move. Until then, let's try to relax.'

Blessed nodded, took a swallow of Frau Smilovici's strong breakfast coffee. 'Gurkel', he now knew, was the gang-name of the man Klarfeld had spoken to last night – Jakob Brauer, businessman, now of Hamburg. Like Klarfeld, a Berlin war-orphan. Like Klarfeld, a former member of the postwar child-tribe known as 'The Kinder'. And, like Klarfeld, part of this conspiracy, about which Blessed still knew so infuriatingly, so dangerously little.

Klarfeld turned on the radio for the latest news-bulletin from RIAS. Dateline 9 November 1989. The previous night, East German police had shown up at an unofficial rock concert illegally close to their side of the Wall. Some trouble, but the cops soft-pedalling on orders from above. Meanwhile, hundreds more East Germans still crossing from Hungary and Czechoslovakia into Austria, from there into Bavaria. Tearing the DDR nationality stickers from their Trabants and Wartburgs, cutting them down to the simple, West German 'D'. The communist state on German soil was haemorrhaging, constantly haemorrhaging . . . A special meeting of the ruling SED's Central Committee had been called for today to discuss the crisis. Persistent rumours that last-ditch hardliners such as State Security Minister Mielke were planning a Tiananmen Square-style crackdown . . .

The newsreader moved onto the next big story. President Bush meeting congressional leaders to discuss the deficit. Klarfeld killed the radio.

'They're losing control in the East,' he commented matter-of-factly, nibbling on a roll spread with low-sugar jam. 'We'll be lucky to get over there while there's still a chance of finding the people we want to see.'

'You're enjoying this, aren't you?'

'Not really,' Klarfeld said, but there was a shade of an impish grin, the twelve-year-old anarchist inside him momentarily winning out over the responsible middle-aged bourgeois.

321

Blessed couldn't help but laugh. 'Oh, but you bloody well are.'

'Put it this way. I wish this wasn't happening, but there are moments of compensation. Will you buy that?'

'Let's say I'll take it on trial.'

The phone rang several times between nine and noon, but none of the calls were from Brauer alias Gurkel. They didn't talk much. Klarfeld read reports and business magazines, received and sent a couple of faxes. Blessed read the last three copies of *Der Spiegel* from cover to cover. The radio was switched on for each news bulletin. Through it they heard that the SED Central Committee was indeed in all-day emergency session. Discussions were reported to be 'heated'. General Secretary Krenz had presented draft proposals to deal with the emigration crisis. Not for the first time and, so the cynics said, unlikely on past experience to be the last.

The crucial call came at one-forty-five in the afternoon, just after they had finished a sandwich lunch.

Klarfeld sighed as he picked up the phone, obviously suspecting that this might be yet another business call. Then he stiffened, reached for his memo pad and a pen.

'Yes. Gurkel. At last. OK, I understand your problems ...' A pause. '*You got them.* Good ... Fine.' Silence at Klarfeld's end while details, instructions were supplied. 'And my friend here, his safety is assured? ... That's all I need to know ... goodbye, Gurkel. Yes, you've paid your debt, don't worry. But I'd take a low profile from now on ... Oh, and try to cut down on the alcohol ...'

Klarfeld was breathing quite heavily as he replaced the phone in its cradle. He closed his eyes for some moments, then opened them and looked at Blessed with a wry smile.

'OK, Michael,' he said softly. 'Let's go. Let's go East.'

'What if they're after me?'

'Don't worry. No one's after you. You're an honoured guest. A VIP. Gurkel fixed it. Gurkel had no other option.'

'Is he that important, this Gurkel character?'

'The man who works for both sides is always important, Michael. That's why he often ends up dead. And that's why one phone call to Gurkel last night made him do just what I ... what we ... wanted. Now come on. We have business to attend to. Our appoint-

322

ment is not for another six-and-a-half, seven hours, but there are stages that must be gone through first. For security's sake.'

Klarfeld's sporty BMW made it into the centre of the city before an hour had passed.

He dropped Blessed at the border around three-thirty. As a West Berlin resident, Klarfeld couldn't use the Kochstrasse crossing, known all over the world as Checkpoint Charlie, which was for foreign nationals only. He said a temporary farewell to Blessed there and made a detour to Heinrich-Heine Strasse, just a few hundred yards to the east, where his West Berlin identity card would take him through. By the time the Englishman had queued to show his passport, then queued again to change his compulsory fifteen marks into East German currency, and finally emerged onto the southern extremity of the Friedrichstrasse, Klarfeld was waiting for him just across the street.

'I thought about hiring a less conspicuous car than this,' Klarfeld said when Blessed commented on the admiring stares of some passersby. He shrugged, flipped the automatic gearchange into *DRIVE* and pulled away from the kerb. 'Then it occurred to me: maybe they'll think I'm a Stasi boss. Or one of the state's tame artists. You should see the cars they're allowed to buy. So, what we have here is a kind of double-bluff.'

Soon they had moved away from the showcase centre of East Berlin, into the residential areas where few tourists ventured. On the streets of East Berlin this afternoon, there was little indication of momentous events. A few groups standing around official buildings, some freshly-painted graffiti calling for free elections, the right to travel, and – in one or two cases – for reunification with the West.

'Benno,' Blessed said, 'where are we going?'

'Back to your old haunts.'

'*What?*'

'It's all arranged. A little therapy to start with. We're taking you through this day gently.'

'How kind.' Blessed sighed. 'Why do I trust you? Because of my father? My sister?'

'No. You're not that naïve. Shall I tell you why, Michael? You trust me because last night I could have had you arrested. Alternatively,

I could have killed you, and pleaded self-defence. But I didn't. I handed you a gin and tonic and granted you your heart's desire.'

'So it seems.'

'So it is. *So ist das.*'

On they drove. Another fifteen, twenty minutes and they emerged onto the East Berlin Ring-Autobahn. The last time Blessed had driven here was with the *Stasi* general, in that big Volvo with the tinted windows, listening to Mozart on CD. Now he was back, travelling in a Six-Series BMW. One of these days, Blessed thought, I must do this trip in a Trabi, uninsulated from that world out there, the stink and the potholes and the rest.

He saw the back of the big sign looming up ahead, to their left, and craned around as they passed it. The sign, visible to cars coming the other way, read:

WELCOME TO BERLIN – CAPITAL OF THE GDR.

'We're illegal now,' Blessed said quietly.

'You're illegal. Not me. You need a special visa for the GDR proper, I don't. Being a West Berliner brings one or two privileges, even around here.'

'Fair enough. I'm illegal. My visa is valid only as far as the boundary of East Berlin. In the Sixties and Seventies, getting caught outside the city limits could get you into serious trouble.'

'I doubt if we'll be stopped.' Klarfeld pulled out to pass a slow-moving Soviet military truck. 'The *Volkspolizei* has more important things on its collective mind at the moment than checking Western cars.' Once past the truck, he glanced at Blessed and smiled. 'But if we're unlucky after all, I have a number to call. Our friend the ex-*Stasi* general may be technically in opposition – whatever that may mean in the present context – but he still has friends in interesting places. So relax, OK?'

When, just past Schönefeld Airport, Klarfeld suddenly turned off the Autobahn and onto a simple country road, Blessed began to have his suspicions. The BMW pushed on across the flat Vermeer landscape. He kept his own counsel, though with increasing difficulty. Then they passed through the village, the place where he had met the farmworker and tried to convince him he was a Hungarian travelling salesman.

'I know where you're taking me,' he said suddenly. 'You can't do this.'

'But I can. There's nobody there. Yet. Please. I promise you. We needed somewhere private to meet, and then to wait, and this is it. Also . . . '

'Also what?'

'Nothing like revisiting a demon, and finding he's a shadow.'

Resisting a wild impulse to grab the wheel and haul the BMW into the ditch, Blessed sat, sweat beading on his forehead, his stomach hollow, as Klarfeld turned down the same linden-tree-lined drive Blessed recalled from that weird first night of freedom, now almost a month ago. Of course, the distance to the house seemed shorter. And the house itself, in the light of a dull November afternoon, seemed shabbier and greyer. The damage to the ornamental stonework of the facade was terrible, and in parts it had been clumsily repaired with breezeblocks. The effect was somehow both pathetic and irritating. The contempt of the Workers' and Peasants' state for such a remnant of a corrupt, aristocratic past was wrought in cheap building material for all to see.

'There were many mansions such as this all over the March of Brandenburg,' Klarfeld said. 'Built by the gentry of the area in the seventeenth and eighteenth centuries. Not very grand. But too grand for the communists. Many were simply demolished after the war, the bricks and stones used to build workers' housing. A few notable examples became museums. Of those remaining, some have been turned into rest homes for officials of the SED and state-controlled trade unions. Some have been converted into mental hospitals. Others, such as this one, were taken over by the Stasi.'

'It was empty. Except for me and Werner.'

'Yes. Like all large state organisations, east and west, the Stasi has places it once needed but doesn't use any more. Like those other organisations, it's nevertheless reluctant to let go of them. Easy for our General Albrecht to take it over for his top-secret pet project. Remember, he was accountable to no-one one but Mielke. No-one was going to ask any awkward questions, let alone tell him no . . . '

The BMW stopped by the front steps. Klarfeld cut the engine and got out. Blessed stayed in the car, as if rooted to the passenger-seat.

'Come on out. Have a smoke,' Klarfeld was urging cheerfully through the car window. 'We may be here a while. We might as well look round the place! Gurkel told me we were free to wander.'

325

By a huge effort of will, Blessed eased open his door. He swung himself halfway out, then he was standing, shakily, smiling wanly at Klarfeld and fumbling in his pockets for his cigarettes and his matches.

'Not so bad.'

'I don't know about that, Benno. Pretty fucking bad, actually. Pretty bad.'

'Let's explore. Light your cigarette. After you, Michael.' Klarfeld made a slight bow, indicating the door.

Blessed took a drag on his cigarette, shrugged, marched up the steps. He had to do this, Klarfeld was right. Unless Klarfeld was betraying him.

He pushed open the doors. There was the hallway. Empty. High-ceilinged. The staircase visible in the half-darkness, its upper stages lost in gloom. He stepped inside, found an old-fashioned brass light-switch, flicked it down. One bulb in the ceiling, just like before. But enough to make the stairs safe. Turning back to face outwards, he saw Klarfeld waiting just on the threshold.

'You want to do this alone?' Klarfeld asked.

'Thoughtful of you to think I might. But no, I'd like you to come with me. You're corroboration. Proof of sanity. Sort of.'

With the spell of fear and bondage removed, of course the old manor house looked just like what it was: a fallen-down semi-ruin that had been tarted up for use as a stage-set, in the same way television and film companies take over abandoned asylums and TB hospitals to turn them into palaces or prisons.

Nevertheless, it was not easy for Blessed to enter either of the two rooms he had been kept in. The first, the dark one where he had overheard the conversation – contrived, he realised now, along with the rural sounds – must really have been some kind of a holding-cell. It had a small anteroom next door. That was where the voices had come from. As for the second, where he had met Werner and spent so long, Blessed felt nauseous as he crossed the threshold. The place had been left exactly as he remembered it. He even spotted a cigarette under the bed where he must have dropped it some time during his final few hours here.

'OK?' Klarfeld asked. '*Spuk vorbei* . . . ?'

Blessed didn't answer for some time. He took a guilty drag on his cigarette. He felt an urge to give them up. This place reminded him of his slavery, of the way his addiction to nicotine had given Werner such power over him. The ten loose smokes doled out each day . . .

'Hard to come back?'

Blessed nodded.

'This is your free day. Your day of freedom. Michael, I want you to be prepared for everything that happens. Emotionally, I mean. I want your decisions, your choices, to be free. You deserve that, don't you agree?'

Blessed shrugged.

'You understand?'

Finally Blessed spoke. 'Yes. More or less.' He turned away from the room. 'And now I want to go. This place is getting to me. How long until we leave? I might take a walk round the grounds or something.'

Klarfeld looked at his watch. 'They should be here very soon. If you can hold on . . . '

'At least let's go downstairs.'

'Of course.'

They took the stairs back to the ground floor, passing the loudspeakers on the landing. Blessed began to breathe easier even before he reached the hall and saw natural light through the half-open front doors.

Once outside, Blessed stamped on the butt of his cigarette, gazed out over the parkland. And saw a vehicle approaching up the long, wide curve of the drive.

Klarfeld moved to stand next to him. For all his assurances and his appearance of calm, Blessed thought he noticed faint lines of tension around the corners of his mouth.

'It's a Wartburg,' Blessed said. 'Just like the one the General's people use.'

The ageing East German-made station-wagon rattled and growled its way towards them, dwarfed by the huge linden trees on either side. The Wartburg stopped just by where Klarfeld had parked his BMW. The passenger door swung open. Out stepped a male figure. The ponytail had gone now, but Blessed had no trouble recognising the man who stood gazing at him.

'Good afternoon, Wolfgang,' Blessed called out to him. 'You're a man of many parts.'

327

Wolfgang smiled his humourless smile. 'It's in the profession. Goes with the work.'

'Of course. How's Erika?'

Wolfgang made a clown-face that communicated indifference, irritation, how should I know, all in one expression. 'She is busy elsewhere,' he said. 'She travels a lot.'

'She certainly does . . . '

But Wolfgang was already moving round to the other side of the Wartburg. The driver's door was opening.

Blessed recognised the emerging figure too, but for a moment he was tongue-tied.

'Michael. Good to see you.'

Werner. In a neat dark suit, hair well cut and slicked back. Charming smile, fuck him.

'I'm sorry.' Werner was standing, hands on hips, with a look of cheerful apology. 'I am – we are – sorry to spring this on you. Short notice. You know how it is. My colleague here is no longer an art-dealer, and I am no longer a Stalinist jailer. We are here to facilitate an agreement between Herr Klarfeld and our boss. You understand?'

Blessed gave no indication of whether he understood or not. He turned to Klarfeld. 'What do we do now? I know what I'd like to do, but what's *supposed* to happen?' For all his outward calm, he knew that this might be the moment – the moment of betrayal, when Klarfeld showed his hand, casually turned him over to Wolfgang and Werner, the deadly *Stasi* twins. And there would be nothing Blessed could do.

The odd thing was, both Wolfgang and Werner were still standing by the Wartburg, and they were looking at Klarfeld in just the same way as Blessed. It took some time before he realised the reason: they had seen something that he hadn't. In Klarfeld's right fist sat a small-calibre automatic, pointing straight at the two East Germans.

'Just a professional precaution, gentlemen,' Klarfeld said. 'A quick search before we get down to business.'

Wolfgang shrugged. 'Suit yourself, Herr Klarfeld. But remember you are still in our country.' Werner said nothing. His smile did not waver.

Then, without taking his eyes off the two East Germans, Klarfeld turned the barrel of the gun towards Blessed.

The fear came back. Klarfeld, glancing quickly at the Englishman, must have seen the colour drain from his face. Instantly, without comment, Klarfeld handed Blessed the weapon.

'You keep an eye on the comrades here, will you,' he said. 'Just a formality, but you never know.'

Blessed accepted the weapon. 'You brought this thing across the border?'

Klarfeld smiled. 'Plastic casing. Can't you tell by the weight? Doesn't show up on the guards' metal detectors. Our *Stasi* friends are not the only ones to have had intercourse with terrorists and profited thereby.'

Almost nonchalantly, Klarfeld wandered down the steps, performed a quick body search on each of the two East Germans, first Wolfgang, then Werner. Finally he turned back to face Blessed, nodded. 'They're OK. It was part of the deal that they come unarmed.'

Blessed walked down the steps, still keeping the gun trained on the three men by the Wartburg. Just before he reached them, he stopped, eased out the clip. Live ammunition. He clicked it back into the magazine, smiled, returned the weapon to Klarfeld.

'Just checking. I had to know.'

'Come on, Michael,' Klarfeld said. 'The suspicion has to stop somewhere.'

'Sure. I agree. But where?'

'Everything going smoothly?' Klarfeld asked Wolfgang, 'My contact said a few details still had to be sorted out. Whether all the . . . cargo . . . could be got to the docking-place at the right time . . . '

Wolfgang nodded. 'Everything's fine. Spot on,' he added in English in an exaggerated German version of a Woosterish upper-class accent. 'We can confirm the time your contact gave, and the place.'

'Excellent.'

Wolfgang shrugged. 'A deal is a deal.'

Werner stood waiting, smiling broadly but with a tiny hint of anxiety. Close up, his sharp suit lacked shape, generosity of cut. East-bloc tailoring; good, but East-bloc all the same.

Klarfeld clapped Blessed on the shoulder. 'So,' he said. 'We're ready to turn right around again and head back into Berlin. Anything else you need to do around here?'

It was the signal to break up the party. Werner responded by fishing a pack of Marlboros from his jacket pocket and idly offered

329

one first to Wolfgang, who accepted, to Klarfeld, who shook his head, and finally, tentatively, to Blessed.

Blessed let the man's gesture hang. 'Anything else? Yes,' he said, with a glance at Klarfeld. 'I think there's just one more thing.'

Werner, meanwhile, had decided that the Englishman was a lost cause. A cigarette jauntily between his lips, he had fished out his lighter and was preparing to do the honours for Wolfgang and himself. Blessed swung back, put his whole weight behind the punch, which landed square on Werner's jaw. The blow was by no means expert, but there was vigour and venom behind it, as well as the element of surprise. Werner's head tipped to one side drunkenly. He bit through the tip of his cigarette, staggered and almost fell. His lighter flew out of his grasp, hit the gravel with a tinny clatter. He must have swallowed some tobacco. Within seconds, he was clutching his face and coughing like a sick horse. Gobs of tobacco sputtered out of his mouth, along with traces of blood and, most satisfyingly for Blessed, at least one tooth.

Blessed's own knuckles hurt like hell, and he just didn't care.

Klarfeld stared at the scene with open disbelief. Wolfgang started laughing, a kind of loud, machine-gun laugh that was both childishly happy and cruel – maybe happy because it *was* cruel.

Werner, still spitting blood, his eyes blazing, advanced toward Blessed. Quickly Wolfgang, still rocked by his weird, rare laugh, managed to move forward and grab the man by the arm.

'No, Werner!' he ordered. 'Leave the Englishman alone. You know you deserved that? Have you not studied your Pavlovian reactions? Don't you know better than to take a chance like that with an escaped laboratory animal?' And he threw his head back and roared. 'Pavlov! Textbook Pavlov!'

Ten minutes later, the three of them were on their way back up the drive towards the road. Werner stayed behind to clean up and re-secure the place – and nurse his bruises. Wolfgang came with them in the BMW. Blessed transferred to the broad back seat, there to cradle his bruised fist and savour Werner's humiliation.

Wolfgang was still in slightly unnerving good humour. He smiled as he slotted into the passenger seat beside Klarfeld.

'I'm coming along in case there is trouble,' he told them. 'In case, you never know, the sky falls in.'

SEVENTY

GÜNTHER SCHABOWSKI, BERLIN SED secretary and Politbüro spokesman, had been unable to join the other 212 members of the SED's Central Committee for more than a few minutes that afternoon. He had left the management of the meeting to Krenz. For him, there had been incoming news to sift, outgoing news to manipulate, and communications to be maintained with the beleaguered Party leaderships in the provinces. The wry, Walter Matthau-faced Schabowski was now one of the most important men in the East Germany, possibly the most powerful after Egon Krenz. A prime mover in the conspiracy that had overthrown Honecker the previous month, he possessed a sharp intelligence and a ready, streetwise wit – attributes by no means universal in the ageing SED leadership. He was the acceptable face of the new ruling clique, spearhead of the Party's propaganda efforts as it strove desperately to stave off the inevitable.

In a few minutes Schabowski was due to leave the Central Committee building in the Marx-Engels-Platz and travel by car to the studios of East German Television, where the foreign press was assembled for a conference that would also be broadcast live on radio and television. The Central Committee had promised new rules on emigration today – that was what the emergency session had been about – and Schabowski was going to have to say something. He waited nervously outside the plenum hall.

Finally Egon Krenz hurried out, looking tired and anxious. The Party General Secretary thrust a creased piece of paper into Schabowski's hand. 'OK, Günther,' he said, 'can you sell them this?'

Schabowski took the paper and, without examining it, stuffed it into his pocket. Then he made off along the echoing corridor, heading for where his car was waiting.

He slumped into the back of the limousine, gratefully closed his eyes. It was only a few hundred metres to the studios, but he needed all the rest he could get. The piece of paper stayed in his pocket, even more creased now, and still unread.

In the leaden November twilight, East Berlin took on a grainy, unreal appearance, like an old film.

Klarfeld's BMW nosed its way cautiously through the streets. The passing scene was quotidian Eastbloc. A young mother, weary and worn out, wrestling with a toddler and bulky string-bags of groceries. A thick-waisted, pasty-faced middle-aged man in an unidentifiable green uniform, carrying a plastic briefcase. And in contrast, like newly-landed aliens, two East German teenagers in tracksuits, tall and goodlooking; the boy with a canvas bag, the girl toting both a rucksack and a violin-case. They were chatting in an animated, joyful fashion. Creatures from another planet – the planet Youth . . . Just a few years seemed to transform these fresh-faced young products of the communist state's schools and gymnasia into weary, downtrodden socialist producer-consumers. Growing old is always hazardous to the shape and the psyche; here in the East, it seemed catastrophic.

The BMW stopped at a traffic light.

'Seven o'clock,' Blessed heard Klarfeld murmur. 'Let's find out what's happening.'

The crisp, clear sound of the radio filled the car.

'Regarding the situation vis-à-vis permanent exit travel from the German Democratic Republic,' a disembodied voice said, 'it is stated as follows. One: The decree of 30 November 1988 in respect of foreign travel by GDR citizens (GDR Legal Gazette 1. No. 25 p.271) will not be enforced, pending confirmation of new travel regulations. Meanwhile –'

Klarfeld gave a little hiss of exasperation. 'Who needs to listen to that bureaucratic crap? Another Party hack trying to talk his way out of a problem he and his bosses created themselves.' He attacked the tuner, scanned the stations until he found classical music.

Wolfgang laughed. 'That was Günther Schabowski. You know him? Wriggling and writhing. Sure. What choice does he have? Any drastic decisions either way, and Krenz and his clique end up in trouble.'

'So. Suddenly you're referring to your East German government as a "clique",' Klarfeld said sarcastically. 'A few months ago, it was the democratic vanguard of the working class, and its General Secretary, the all-wise, all-powerful hand that guided the destiny of your glorious republic.'

332

'Things have changed, it's true,' said Wolfgang, unfazed. 'Around twenty thousand of our citizens have voted with their feet in the past week, mostly via Czechoslovakia. If the Central Committee decides to seal the borders – no travel to Hungary or Czechoslovakia – there could be civil war here. If it doesn't, then the people will just keep on leaving. After thirty years of the Berlin Wall, the average GDR citizen has had enough –'

'*Ach*, a liberal *Stasi* man. Who'd have thought it?'

'I – *we*, including the general – have at least been consistent,' Wolfgang retorted. 'We have been working for change for years, from inside the government apparatus. But you're right. The final turning-point has arrived. There'll be a lot more like me – if the system keeps crumbling.'

'And will it?'

Wolfgang grimaced. 'The system lost the active support of the masses many years ago. The latest developments, including the smuggling-out of the general's memoirs, will further undermine its hold on ordinary people. But maybe the régime could survive, despite it all . . . Except that now the Party bosses have lost the only real advantage they had left – their belief in themselves. Without that, the system definitely can't survive.'

'So, how long?'

Wolfgang performed a tiny, expressive shrug. 'Who can tell?' he murmured, gazing absently out of the window at the darkening streets. 'Two years? Two weeks? Two minutes?'

Schabowski cleared his throat before he continued reading the announcement from the piece of paper Krenz had thrust into his hand just half an hour earlier.

' . . . The following regulations regarding travel and permanent exit from the GDR are introduced with immediate effect. A: Applications for private travel to foreign countries may be lodged without the need to satisfy the customary preconditions . . . '

Schabowski paused again, sweating under the studio lights, wishing he had taken the time in the car to look at what the paper said. *Shit. He should have thought this one through, prepared himself just a little.* Worse still, he had also just noticed a note typed in bold face at the bottom that said: Press Release Not for Publication

Before 10 November. That was tomorrow. For the second time, *shit*. But Schabowski, ever the professional, pressed on:

'Permission for travel will be granted immediately. Such permission will be refused only under special, exceptional circumstances . . . '

His brow furrowed with tense concentration, Schabowski finished reading out the statement on the soon-to-be-famous creased piece of paper. A loaded silence filled the room. Then a flurry of coughs. The scraping of chairs. The entire room seemed on edge as the journalists sat there, digesting Schabowski's words, wondering . . .

Finally an American raised his hand. 'These . . . ah . . . travel regulations. So, are you saying they're also valid for the border crossings into West Berlin?'

Schabowski checked. Dammit – yes, it did say here, 'including Berlin (West)'. He swallowed hard. 'That is correct,' he said, a little too loudly.

Suddenly Schabowski felt like the loneliest man in East Berlin. Suddenly he wished he'd had a chance to discuss this with Krenz before leaving the Central Committee building. All he could do now was pray that the Russians had approved this, because it played havoc with their military administration's rights and prerogatives in Berlin . . .

When the press had turned up at this latest conference, most had already written their story. This would be yet another attempt by the East German government to defuse the situation without offering real concessions. Even now, most still thought the announcement was merely an attempt to regularise the 'permanent exit travel from the GDR' – in other words, to bring some order to the fact of mass emigration from East Germany. But in fact the wording did something else. The document actually made a statement: *East Germans could travel wherever they liked. Permission would not be refused.*

The silence seemed to last for minutes. By this time, even the least perceptive of the reporters in the room was starting to get the message – the message that the American reporter had been the first to understand, the message that even Schabowski himself had not fully grasped until now.

Then the spell broke, and there was a scramble for the few phones outside. The first journalist to get through to his editor hardly dared to say what he knew to be true, but soon he and a score of his colleagues were blurting out their news: 'Listen. Press conference. Schabowski. Yeah, the usual spokesman. I don't know how to tell you this. The East Germans have basically scrapped all their travel restrictions. Yeah. You know what that means? It means this country is wide open.'

A brief pause. Then the reporter shouted down the line: 'Listen! **IT MEANS THE BERLIN WALL IS DOWN!** Got that? **THE BERLIN WALL IS DOWN** . . . '

SEVENTY-ONE

BLESSED, KLARFELD AND WOLFGANG set foot on the anonymous, wide-open spaces of the Alexanderplatz just before eight. Klarfeld had parked the BMW behind the Red Town Hall. They crossed the Rathausstrasse, aimed themselves diagonally towards the huge television tower that dominated East Berlin's windswept, lego-brick showcase square.

It was dark. There were a few western tourists drifting around in a faintly embarrassed way, like guests who had turned up at the wrong party. Some were looking for places to spend their last few, unconvertible East-marks before they returned home. Groups of East German youths prowled, occasionally tracking westerners for a while and then dropping away. There were a couple of Volkspolizei patrol cars parked over by the St Marienkirche, keeping an eye out for trouble.

The atmosphere was inexplicably electric. Had he glanced that way, Blessed might have seen groups of East Berliners emerging from the Alexanderplatz U-bahn subway, talking excitedly, arguing. He might have heard them mention the name Schabowski and the phrase 'freedom to travel'. But Blessed was too involved with his pressing concerns, mentally preparing himself for this meeting, which he hoped would explain all. He was thinking of the general, of Erika, of Otmar Ziegler and the little opossum-eyed man he had known as Herr Hildebrandt. Whatever he sensed in the air, Blessed put down to his own tension.

They paused at the bottom of the steps leading up to the Television Tower. Twelve hundred feet high with its aerial. Twenty-six thousand tons of concrete and metal, complete with a five-thousand ton sphere at the top of the shaft.

'OK?' Klarfeld said.

Wolfgang nodded. 'So I'm told.'

On ground level in the square was an outdoor café, open in the daytime. From the tower complex a dizzyingly steep, pleated expanse of roof cascaded down to them, fanning out from a central pinnacle. The effect was a cross between a hi-tech Bedouin encampment and a fairground helter-skelter. The comparison had obviously also occurred to the local thrillseekers, because there were prominent signs warning them against using the corrugations as slides.

A bunch of skinheads were fooling around at the top of the steps. As the three men climbed the steps, they were subjected to some routine adolescent abuse, but as they neared the top the kids backed off.

Blessed, Klarfeld and Wolfgang crossed the high, paved plateau. To the north, the great square shape of the 2000-bed Hotel Stadt Berlin. The men arrived at the entrance to the restaurant.

'After you,' said Wolfgang with a smile.

Klarfeld didn't smile back. 'Oh no, my friend. After *you*.'

There was the usual maitre d' in dinner jacket and black tie, waiting by his bookings list, which was perched on an ornate lectern – they were keen on the social proprieties in the First Workers' and Peasant's State on German Soil. The maitre d' frowned, levelled a stare of unconcealed distaste at Blessed's casual jacket and jeans. Then Wolfgang said, 'Booking in the name of Herr Albrecht,' and the man was all smiles, welcoming and deferential.

They must all be in the Stasi's pocket, for God's sake, Blessed thought. *Of course. He had always suspected it with these places, and now he knew it must be true.*

'The rest of the party are already here,' the maitre d' said. 'May I take –'

'No,' Klarfeld said crisply. 'We'll keep our coats on. It's not a warm night.'

A nod. A thin, frozen gash of a smile. No comment.

They walked on through, still allowing Wolfgang to keep ahead. Blessed next . . . Klarfeld at the rear.

A waiter held open a thick velvet curtain and they passed finally into the dining room itself. There was a just discernible odour of cooked chicken mixed with that of sparingly-applied floor-polish. The lights of the Hotel Stadt Berlin glinted dully through a picture-window at the far end. The restaurant was not at all busy. In fact, at first glance it seemed all but deserted. A squat, bearded man in a dark suit was seated at a piano, playing what after a few moments Blessed recognised as a version of the Beatles' *Strawberry Fields*.

337

At a table nearby, two men in suits were seated, paying little attention to their food, apparently deep in conversation. They looked like very unsuccessful travelling salesmen – or quite successful informers.

The only other customers were way at the far end: a man and a woman sitting side by side at a table for six, talking and drinking. A bottle of champagne nestled in a fake-silver icebucket between them. As Wolfgang entered the room, the woman smiled and waved.

Blessed froze. He felt a hand on his arm, Klarfeld gently steadying him.

'I'm fine,' he said quietly to Klarfeld. 'I'm in perfect working order. Let's just do this thing. OK?'

Klarfeld nodded.

Blessed started to walk down the aisle between the closely-arranged, white-clothed tables. He had taken only a few steps when the man at the table turned and saw him. The man's smile faded. With obvious effort, he let go of the woman's hand and raised himself to his full height. By the time Blessed arrived at the table he seemed to have recovered, and was standing with his hands in his pockets – not exactly nonchalant – but to all appearances in control. A familiar, wry half-smile playing over his puffily handsome features. Ever the realist, ready to accept the way the cards were dealt and to act accordingly . . .

Their eyes met.

'Hello,' Blessed said in English. 'Hello, Rockwell.'

'Mike. Hi! This is unexpected. And, well, I have to admit it kind of knocks some of the fun out of the evening.'

'Not enough. Never enough.' Blessed turned to his left, made a brief little half-bow to Rockwell Elliot's companion. 'And Diane. What could be *more* unexpected – and less of a pleasure.'

Diane Kelly lacked Rockwell's self-possession – she was trying to sip at her champagne, show her indifference, but the crystal rim of her tulip-shaped glass refused to dock neatly with her lips. To compensate, she drew on a cold instinct to wound: 'The human race is divided into two kinds of people, Michael: those who've figured out the way the world works, and those who're still operating in the dark. Seems to me, you belong in the latter category.'

'Let's sit down.' Klarfeld pulled out a chair for Blessed.

338

Rockwell looked up as if to heaven and let out a whistle. 'Boy, I really fell for this one.' His tone was conversational, as if some guy at the office had just played a practical joke on him. 'The trouble is, all Germans sound alike to me on the phone. My friend General Albrecht included. I thought, hey – kind of nice of him to ask us to dinner!'

'I said sit *down*!' Klarfeld hissed. Blessed saw that the veins in his forehead were standing out, his face taut with fury.

'C'mon, who actually made the call?' Rockwell pressed on. 'Was it you, Benno? No. Then maybe the one they call Gurkel, the porn-merchant.' He shook his head. 'Or maybe old Wolfgang here –'

'*Sit!*'

There was a scraping of chairs as everyone sat down. With the white tablecloth, the champagne on ice, the waiter gliding over to take the newcomers' drinks orders, the careful way everyone was moving, the scene was apparently civilised. Apparently.

Rockwell gulped down some champagne, refilled his glass. Then he took Diane's hand. She was young, blonde, clever . . . Rockwell's pride in his conquest of this woman was visible to everyone else at the table. He had betrayed kith and kin; he was scared; he was fighting for survival; but he had won a rare and enviable prize, and to him that still mattered.

'This is all very entertaining,' Rockwell said. 'But you people have no rights in this country. I, on the other hand, certainly do.' He put his arm around Diane's shoulder, just to emphasise his proprietorship once more. Blessed suspected, just suspected, that she flinched. And a glance passed between . . . Was it her and Wolfgang, of all people? Meanwhile, Rockwell was still setting out his hand. 'Yeah. I'm Herr X, GDR citizen. And Frau X here – also possessor of all the documents you could wish to have – we're privileged immigrants in this country. Top-grade ideological refugees. We got the papers to prove it.' He switched to a Bronx-landlord grunt. 'And naturally, everything's in da wife's name.'

Blessed cut into the silence. 'I want to know how you did it, Rockwell. More important, why.'

'Hey. Marriage doesn't always work out. You should know that! People leave people, Mike.' Rockwell's gaze was direct, guiltless. The look of a psychopath who, when it comes to moral qualms, has all the exits covered. 'We all change our lives sometimes. Wives, husbands, kids – someone's always walking out on someone. *It happens all the time.*'

'You could have got a divorce, then moved in with this woman.'

'You don't understand the way these things work. And you know what? I don't really have to explain . . . '

'You had more than enough money, Rock. Enough for ten men, for Christ's sake –'

Rockwell's only answer was a tight shrug.

Benno Klarfeld moved in on Blessed's thoughts.

'Shall I tell you how the system works, Michael?' Klarfeld said dispassionately, as if Rockwell was no longer in his presence. Except that, as he spoke, his eyes never left Rockwell's face, and his gaze was filled with hate.

'Oh yes. Please do.'

'All right. It's like this: Directly and through front organisations, all various departments of the *Stasi* control billions and billions of dollars' worth of land, property, and industrial facilities in this country. And one particular, very special *Stasi* department, run by our brave General Albrecht as his private fiefdom, has spent the last few years systematically ensuring that a great amount of this real estate – specially-selected prime sites that before the war were among the most valuable in Germany – is now effectively its property, to dispose of as it – or rather the general – wishes. Are you with me so far?'

'Oh yes. Absolutely.'

'But that's not all. There's an extra twist. You see, all General Albrecht's friends, and many of his *Stasi* employees, were once members of the orphan gang called "the Kinder". These men, twenty-three in all, bound by a loyalty that has nothing to do with the communist régime, have been invested with rights to property formerly controlled by Albrecht's department. Cast-iron, apparently unassailable rights, protected by a labyrinth of documents prepared at the general's orders by the *Stasi*'s best lawyers. And I can assure you, the *Stasi* employs the cream of the legal profession in this country.'

Klarfeld paused for a sip of water. Rockwell was staring into space, idly stroking Diane Kelly's hand. Blessed said, 'I'd never thought such a thing was possible, even here.'

'Oh yes,' said Klarfeld. 'The legal situation is complex. But in many cases, they have carefully chosen properties and assets

340

originally confiscated on behalf of their East German communist friends by the Russians between 1945 and 1949, when the country was technically under their military rule. Unlike real estate taken into state ownership by the East German government after 1949, such properties are not recoverable by their original owners under either German or international law. Or maybe ownership documents have been forged going back well pre-war, and forged so skilfully that no one will be able to challenge them. In other cases . . . '

'All right. How many properties are we talking about?'

'I don't know exactly. Hundreds, certainly.'

And you used to be one of the Kinder too, Blessed thought. *What's your angle?* He put that question aside for the moment. 'OK, Benno, so what's Rockwell's part in all this?' he asked instead.

'Simple. He's the man with the dollars, the hard currency. Very little of it his own, actually – mostly other people's –'

'All the missing money from the accounts controlled by Elliot, Birnbaum. Around forty million dollars,' said Blessed slowly.

'Absolutely,' Klarfeld confirmed. 'Most of this has already been fed, through a maze of dummy companies in Switzerland, Panama and other safe havens, to an organisation called *Kinderwohlfahrt KG* – the Kinder's Pension Fund, as they jokingly refer to it . . . '

'Two million each for the poor old Kinder, eh?' Blessed said.

Klarfeld sighed, paused while the waiter set down drinks. Beers for Blessed and Wolfgang, mineral water for himself. 'Yes. In return for granting the Kinder that guaranteed lump sum in hard currency, Rockwell Elliot receives his new identity, as does the inscrutable Miss Kelly here, plus control of these extremely valuable assets. The idea is that if – or as seems to be becoming inevitable – *when* – capitalism returns to East Germany, and the free market is restored, then these assets' value will skyrocket. Elliot and Miss Kelly here will offload when the moment is ripe and end up sitting on a nest egg of . . . I'd say at least a hundred million dollars.'

Again something electric passed between Diane and Wolfgang. There and gone in a second, easy to miss. A signal? Was Wolfgang about to do something dangerous? No, he was sitting patiently to Blessed's right, apparently listening carefully, in that impassive, faintly supercilious way of his.

There was silence. Blessed had lit a cigarette to chase down his beer. 'It stinks,' he said simply. 'Of course, it's illegal.'

Klarfeld nodded. 'But very hard to prove. You should bear that in mind when you're considering what to do. Because that's what this meeting is about. It's up to you, Michael. Now you know the truth.'

'Come on!' Rockwell erupted. 'What is this self-righteous bull-shit? Nobody died! Did I shotgun a little old lady in a bank? Did I poison anyone's well? Did I plant a bomb on a 747?'

'Klaus Hammerschmidt.' Blessed's whisper was hard, metallic. 'And who knows who else?'

'Never heard of the guy you mentioned. Listen, it was me who made sure they didn't rub you out, those *Stasi* guys, you know that? They'd happily have totalled you. Wouldn't have given it a second thought. It was me, sentimental jerk that I am, who had you spared. I'm sorry to fucking say . . . ' He turned to Diane Kelly. 'You were there. You know . . . '

'He likes you, Michael,' she said reluctantly. 'I even like you myself.'

'You're a lousy liar,' Blessed said.

'You think so?'

Diane smiled. That smile said, *Lousy? Not world class, OK, but good enough to get by. Good enough to fool an amateur like you for as long it took. And that's what matters.*

'What was your problem?' Blessed said. 'Too long paying lip-service to the pursuit of truth?'

'It got boring, Mike. The kids were dull, and the money was terrible. And I got tired of pretending to be nice. Does that help to explain?'

'The parents' weekend, was it? I mean, where you and Rock-well got together? You already had a scene going strong when we met . . . '

She looked away. In any case, Rockwell was impatient to keep centre stage.

'Listen, I'm just a creature of the times, gentlemen,' he said. 'Like Gorbachev. Like Lech Walesa. Like that guy Havel in Cze-choslovakia. You know?' Rockwell leaned forward earnestly, press-ing for his audience to listen, to take him seriously, to – Blessed thought with sickened astonishment – even to *like* him. 'For me, the important, freeing realisation was that ideology doesn't matter shit. When the time is ripe, when the buyer and the seller are ready,

nothing gets in the way of a deal. It's a force of nature, like sex –
way beyond anything so trivial as communism or capitalism.' He
smiled suavely at his brother-in-law. 'You want some free advice,
Mike? Some survival notes for the years ahead? Then forget all that
crap they taught you in school! History? Politics? Ideas? Bullshit!
It's all about *real estate*! It's never been about anything else! Those
three dudes who carved up Europe back in '45 – Churchill, Stalin,
Truman – they knew that. Commies got the eastern bits of the
property; capitalists the west. That meeting over the river there in
Potsdam was to put the boundaries between.' Rockwell laughed,
like a huckster at a business seminar who knows he's got his audience by the balls at last and loves himself for it. 'We know-nothing
civilians, we called the result the Iron Curtain, the Berlin Wall . . .
we kidded ourselves it was some kind of a spiritual barrier, a place
of the mind. Hah! You know what the Iron Curtain amounted to? *A
fence. It was just a fucking fence!* . . . and you know what fences are
for? They're for marking off real estate!'

There was a deep, chill silence.

'People like me oil the wheels of history, and at the moment
history's going in the right direction,' Rockwell persisted. 'I'm
helping manage the changeover from communism to freedom, from
war to peace. Hell, I'm just a broker, got that? *A peace broker!*'

Blessed said softly but very slowly and clearly: 'I didn't know
peace was for sale.'

Rockwell turned abruptly to Klarfeld. His face was a little too pink
now. He looked tired. 'OK,' he said angrily. 'Now, c'mon, Benno.
What's your percentage in all this? I never heard of you doing a deal
that wasn't worth your while. You've gotten off pretty much scot-
free in this little truth-telling exercise so far.' He glanced around the
table for support. 'Why don't we hear Benno's reasons, what do you
say? Tell me you didn't figure yourself in for a cosy two million
along with the rest of those urchin-turned-*Stasi* pals of yours!'

Klarfeld simply laughed, furious and triumphant at the same time.
'You don't understand anything, do you? I'm in love,' he hissed.
'In love with the woman you were lucky enough to be married to
for more than twenty years and whom you tossed away like an old
coat! I've loved Daphne since I was a teenager! Of course, such a
simple emotion would never occur to you as a motive for risking
one's life!'

For the first time, Rockwell was struck dumb. This was not at all what he had been expecting to hear. Not from a man like Klarfeld. Diane seemed embarrassed, pained. Blessed couldn't take his eyes off Klarfeld. There was a volcano inside this man. Glorious. And dangerous, both to others and to himself.

'Go on, Benno,' Blessed urged. 'I want to know about this too.'

Klarfeld drank from his glass and then continued. 'I was determined to protect Daphne, Michael. That's all I cared about. I wanted this creep here out of her life for ever, but I didn't want Daphne hurt. That's why, when Gurkel came to me with the memoirs project, I decided to handle it as far as possible on my own, to keep control. Sure, I could have passed the general's memoirs on to my contacts within West German Intelligence and washed my hands of the whole affair. Or I could have simply sold the German language rights, made a quick killing.' He shrugged heavily. 'Either of these would have been a practical, rational course of action. But my old feelings got the better of me. If I involved you, Michael, I would be in a position to help Daphne. Love can be stronger than ideology or politics.' He eyed Rockwell. 'It's even more powerful than owning half a country.'

'How did you know that the Kinder organisation still existed after all this time?' Blessed asked.

'I had my suspicious. I knew that apart from Gurkel, the gang-leader known as Granit had become a high-ranking *Stasi* official, and that the one we used to call Banana was now a supposed dissident in East Germany. It seemed likely to me that the gang had held together in some as-yet-undefined way . . . So, I decided to make a few more enquiries, and . . . '

Klarfeld took out a handkerchief, mopped his forehead. The strain was starting to tell. Blessed was tempted to ease off, let certain things remain unsaid, unsolved, but he knew he could not, dare not. This was his only chance, and it had to be seen through to the bitter end.

'When did you realise he was involved in the conspiracy?' Michael asked brusquely, his gaze shifting between Rockwell and Klarfeld.

'In April. I sent some men over to England. They reported that your brother-in-law had been meeting with this man here, who calls himself Wolfgang. That was when I knew Rockwell was intending to do terrible things, and that I had to keep control of this business by any means whatsoever . . . '

'So, you let me walk into a trap,' Blessed spelled out his conclusion coldly.

Klarfeld didn't flinch at the indictment. 'You were a pawn who wandered into the big pieces' game,' he said. 'But be honest, Michael. No one forced you to get involved. You were feeling unfulfilled, unimportant. You saw this project as an adventure, the answer to your problems. It gave some meaning to your life.' He shrugged. 'I did my best to protect you, Michael. I know Albrecht's *Stasi* people had you under surveillance all winter in England, awaiting the right moment for Erika and Wolfgang to establish contact – but once you had become involved, the watchers who followed you were mine, not theirs.'

'Including the one in the States, on the goddamned Robert Frost Trail!'

Klarfeld's gaze flickered over to include Diane Kelly, testing her reaction. 'Oh yes. Even him. Listen, I like you, and I also respect you very much. But it's Daphne I *love* . . . She always came first for me. She still does.'

The silence was broken by Rockwell. He leaned back in his chair, frowned like an attorney considering the evidence. 'Well, Benno . . . kinda looks like everyone's gotten what they want. Me and Diane here, you and Daphne . . . '

'But you're forgetting me, Rockwell,' Blessed cut in. 'I've had very little for my trouble. Above all, I don't have what I want from you.'

Rockwell contemplated his champagne glass for a moment or two, then looked back up and met Blessed's gaze. 'Which is . . . ?' he said quietly.

'It's simple. I want to see you punished.'

Rockwell smiled pleasantly. 'Maybe you do. But there's no extradition from this country, Mike. And I'd guess that by the time there is, you'll be too late to get your pound of flesh.'

'We'll see about that.'

'Mike, come on!' Rockwell threw up his hands in mock despair. 'Isn't all this a little unenlightened? Don't you realise that you've just been through what our therapist friends would call "A Major Growth Experience"?' He followed up with a fatherly chortle.

'People pay a fortune to experience this stuff! Hey, where's your sense of humour!'

'You put your wife and son through hell this autumn. I know. I was there. Keep talking, Rockwell. Tell me why you shouldn't be sent to hell too.'

Blessed's stubbornness was beginning to unsettle Rockwell. Now Rockwell decided to ditch the chummy act. He was still smiling, but there was a sharpness in his tone: 'Well, you know what, Mike? If I was in the States, from now on I wouldn't say another thing without my lawyer.' He turned to Diane. 'Honey, do you think there's such a thing as the fifth amendment in this country?'

'No, but I'm sure there soon will be. Things are moving fast.'

Suddenly their attention was drawn to the big picture-window facing the Alexanderplatz. The waiters had moved in a body to that side of the restaurant, abandoning their tables, and for the past few minutes had been engaged in a lively discussion. Now, one of them turned to face the diners and burst out: 'Everyone's going to the West! The border posts have been opened! Do you hear me? *The Wall is finished – the border is open!*'

The effect on everyone in the room was explosive. The two men at the other table hastily scrambled to their feet and hurried over to join the waiters. Klarfeld went so pale that Blessed feared for his blood-pressure. Wolfgang's gaze started darting around the room as if searching for exits. His fingers began drumming on the table. Diane Kelly's eyes widened, and Rockwell began to laugh, loud and long, with an edge of hysteria. Everyone else had half-risen from the table. They paused, stared at him in astonishment.

'Don't you *understand*?' he eventually stammered. 'You get the irony? I must be the only guy in East Berlin tonight who hasn't the faintest intention of heading for that Wall and going west . . . '

The group moved over to join the others at the window. They looked down over the Alexanderplatz towards the St Marienkirche and the Statue of Neptune. Crowds were streaming across the Alex, choking the Karl-Liebknecht-Strasse in the direction of the Marx-Engels-Brücke. The tide of humanity was swelling even as they watched. And the traffic, which earlier had been nothing much, was building up minute by minute, clogging at the junctions, threatening jams before the evening progressed much further. Everybody was heading for the border crossings with West Berlin.

Blessed, mesmerised by the spectacle, felt a burden lifting. He remembered his father's death, now almost thirty years in the past. He recalled the ominous black-and-white television pictures on that day of the superpower confrontation at Checkpoint Charlie. The painful loss of his own father, together with the violent imprisonment of a city. Now the wheel had come full circle. Now the imprisonment of half of this city was over. Perhaps this could mean a new freedom for Michael Blessed too.

Rockwell was positioned alongside Blessed, still with that possessive arm round Diane Kelly's shoulder.

'What an evening,' Blessed commented, apparently to no one in particular. 'I wonder what Erika's doing tonight?' He felt Rockwell's eyes suddenly concentrated on him. 'You do *remember* Erika, don't you?' Blessed added.

For a moment Rockwell tightened. Then he managed a casual-looking shrug and turned away. Just the reaction Blessed would have expected. But he hadn't really been watching Rockwell; Blessed had been looking out for a repeat of that tiny but powerful electric flash between Diane and Wolfgang, and he was rewarded. *Diane knows all about Erika. The realisation sent a shiver down Blessed's spine. And she doesn't mind at all. In fact, she's bloody delighted.*

This is very weird, he thought. *Even weirder than I expected. And, thank God, none of my business any more.*

The decision about Rockwell was suddenly easy. He had seen what he just saw, and he remembered that the property was in Diane Kelly's name. All Blessed had to do, he knew now, was relax and let nature take its course . . .

As for Daphne, she's safe. Already over the worst. She'll be OK.

He turned to Klarfeld. 'Let's go.'

Blessed wanted out; out of this room, with its reek of intrigue and betrayal and greed. In the open air was where Blessed wanted to be, with the rest of the human race, flowing with the warm, happy tide of history.

Klarfeld, spellbound by the sight beneath them, failed to register Blessed's words.

'I said, let's go, Benno.'

Finally Klarfeld reacted. 'Go? Now? Don't you want to know more . . . don't you . . . '

'I know enough. You can fill in the gaps for me later.'

'And punishment? What about the punishment you were so determined to inflict, Michael?'

Blessed allowed himself a bitter smile. 'Oh, I think the punishment will fit the crime. Really. Let's go.' Rockwell was looking at him intently. Blessed shrugged. 'Keep what you think you've gained, Rockwell. Enjoy it! While you still can.'

And then he walked out of the restaurant, with Benno Klarfeld behind him. He kept going, brushing by the waiters and the other customers. At the heavy curtain, he stopped, turned and glanced back, as if to capture the tableau in the room for the album of his memory.

Rockwell was staring after him, open-mouthed. As if . . . as if he was offended, hurt, at being dismissed so easily . . .

Diane had left Rockwell's side; she stood halfway between him and Wolfgang. She was also gazing after Blessed. But there was no hurt or confusion in her eyes. Only triumph.

And Wolfgang? Wolfgang stood at the window, expressionless, with his muscular arms folded, calmly observing the crowds as they swarmed towards the open border crossings. A man without worries.

When they reached the top of the steps, Blessed paused. 'One thing, Benno. Promise me that Daphne and Josh will never learn that Rockwell's alive. If you really do love my sister . . . '

'That's something we have to discuss. That and many other things.'

Blessed buttoned his jacket against the cold. They began to descend towards the square. As they reached ground level, beneath the sweep of the tentlike roofs, they stopped again for a moment to contemplate the crowds.

'My God, Michael! This is –'

The rest of Klarfeld's words disappeared in a screeching, screaming *whoosh* as the first of the skinhead assailants came careering down the great corrugated roof-slide. The human missile hit Klarfeld smack between the shoulderblades, knocking the breath from him and sending him sprawling forward onto the hard cement. Within seconds, others followed. Five, six in a row, crashing down with a chilling, co-ordinated whoop, as if they were a single, vicious organism.

The Müggelsee skinheads who had attacked him when he had been with Diane – the skinheads who had kicked Klaus Hammerschmidt to pulp . . .

Blessed barely had time to make the chilling connection – the *Stasi*, General Albrecht, a final reckoning – before he was fighting for his life against a pack of shaven-headed assailants.

Blows landed on Blessed's unprotected face. A fist struck his jaw. He reeled back, tasted blood. Ducking another punch, he caught a quick, terrible glimpse of where Benno was sprawled just a few feet away. *Just like that poor bastard Hammerschmidt. Just like . . .* The older man was pinned to the ground, with a group of young thugs kicking him savagely.

'*Helft ihm!*' Blessed croaked. 'Help him!' His mouth was slowly filling with blood. The cry came out, again and again, no more than a strangled choking sound, but by the third or fourth attempt it had some effect. Finally passersby began to peel off from the moving crowd towards the violent mêlée at the foot of the steps, including a few who looked as though they could handle themselves in a fight.

One of the skinheads bawled an order. As quickly as they had come, the pack withdrew. One final steel-capped lunge at the sprawled body of Klarfeld and they were off, whooping and yelling, heading north across the Alex towards the U-bahn station on the far side. The crowd parted all too willingly before them.

Blessed, aware now of a piercing pain in his ribs as well as swellings on his face, paid no attention. He hobbled grimly, swallowing blood, to where Klarfeld lay. He had to get Benno to the West. To Daphne. He had to.

Two Berliners were already kneeling over Klarfeld. At least he was alive. His face was a mass of bruises, and his breath was coming in short gasps, but he was aware of his surroundings. As Blessed neared him, Klarfeld painfully struggled to rise. Blessed, almost weeping with relief, made to help him up.

Klarfeld waved him away. 'I'm OK . . .' he mumbled between panting breaths.

And he began to make it to his feet, unaided. First onto his knees. Then slowly, with savage determination, hauling himself upright. Blessed insisted on taking Klarfeld's right hand.

'Easy, Benno,' he said thickly. 'I'm here . . . '

'I . . . am . . . OK –'

349

Without warning, the hand Blessed had been holding was no longer gripping his. For a moment it tensed around Blessed's, then whipped away. Klarfeld toppled back onto his knees, with both hands now clutching his chest. Then his head slumped forward and he collapsed, hit the ground with a sickening crack of skullbone striking concrete.

'Oh Christ. Benno –'

History was being made. The people of East Berlin, of the whole of East Germany, had been sprung, like caged birds, from their prison. Here at the core of Europe, after half a lifetime of Cold War, peace was breaking out.

Meanwhile, in a corner of the Alexanderplatz at the bottom of the tower steps, someone was already pushing through the crowd, looking for a phone to call an ambulance. A man who claimed to be a doctor was frantically massaging Benno Klarfeld's chest. And instead of joining the celebrations of his own and a people's freedom, Michael Blessed knelt with tears in his eyes – tears of grief, anger, and loss.

THE SPOILS OF PEACE

February 1990

SEVENTY-TWO

IT WAS A CRISP, COLD DAY. A wicked north-westerly, sweeping the platform of Taunton station with its icy broom, had sent all but the most hardy scuttling for the warm fug of the snackbar.

The train was fifteen minutes late. Michael Blessed clapped his gloved hands together, executed another little shuffle to keep his feet from freezing. The huge, colourful hoarding on the middle platform invited industry to do itself a favour and move to Somerset. The poster depicted this corner of the West Country as a perfect hybrid of high-tech wonderland and lovingly-preserved heritage park: Silicon Valley meets Doone Valley.

Not for the first time this winter, Blessed congratulated himself for investing in thermal underwear. Even the beard on his chin was a response to the rigours of country life; it meant less time in that chilly bathroom each morning, and insulation against the cold. Maybe he would shave if off when the spring came; then again, maybe not. There was no one to consult, and no one to give his or her opinion. Only Daisy, his daughter, who had spent ten days here at Christmas. 'It makes you look like the son of Santa.' she had told him, which he guessed was approval of a kind.

Blessed saw the sharp beak of the westbound Intercity Express appear around the wide final curve in the track.

This was the kind of moment that would once have had him reaching automatically for a cigarette. Instead Blessed's hands burrowed deep into the empty pockets of his quilted jacket, and stayed there. Not a puff of nicotine since the night of 9 November 1989. No regrets, but always a keen sense of the way the craving could surge back at times like this.

A couple of station staff had appeared, reluctantly leaving the cosy parcels office to greet the train. The express eased alongside the platform, letting out one final, surprisingly thin squeak. A tiny, animal shudder travelled along its entire length. Then the doors began to fly open. There was banging and voices and the usual indecipherable announcement over the P.A.

Blessed scanned the length of the train, looking for the first class section. Ah. There, towards the rear, a tweedy-looking matron with a Harrods bag. A couple of gents who looked like upper-grade execs. But that seemed to be that. Doors were being slammed shut again now. Blessed felt a stab of concern. Then a familiar figure stepped down onto the platform and began waving in his direction.

'Mike!'

'Daphne!'

By the time he'd reached his sister, the train was pulling away from the station, and at Daphne's side there was another face Blessed knew well. Thinner. Browner. Perhaps more relaxed . . .

'Benno.'

'Michael. Wonderful to see you.'

And they embraced, the three of them, on that rural station platform, thoroughly un-English and not giving a damn.

'So,' Blessed said to his sister. 'How's life in the London flat? Settling in?'

'Very well, Mike darling.' A slightly secret smile. 'Fashionable as it might be to divide one's time between several homes, it's actually a relief to have all my things in one place.'

'And you, Benno. How are you?' Blessed looked Klarfeld up and down, nodded his approval. 'Two months in Tunisia have transformed you.'

'Ah, I'm a lucky man,' Klarfeld said with a wry smile. 'Very lucky to be alive, and determined to take full advantage of the fact.'

Klarfeld owed his survival to a combination of chance and science. The East German doctor who had appeared from among the crowd on Alexanderplatz that night last November had turned out to be a coronary specialist from the Charité Hospital. His prompt action had almost certainly made the difference between life and death.

'I look forward to a good talk,' Blessed said.

'Of course. Exactly as I promised, Michael, when we were in Berlin. Before I was so rudely interrupted . . .'

Blessed smiled, accepting the coded message. *Later* . . . 'Right. Let's get out of here shall we?' he said briskly. 'I found a spot in the station car park, so we don't have far to go. Daff, you bring that little bag there. I'll take the suitcases. No, I insist . . .'

353

The following afternoon, the two men stood beneath the FOR SALE board outside the cottage and waved goodbye to Daphne as she drove off down the lane in Blessed's second-hand Ford. The car hiccoughed once or twice as she experimented with its unfamiliar controls, then pulled away and disappeared.

Benno glanced up at the estate-agent's sign. 'A lot of these around in England, Michael,' he commented.

Blessed nodded. 'The property boom's gone bust. No more gloating over how much we're all worth, and how much more we're going to be worth a week or a month from now.'

'No. Well, these are serious times. Maybe in the 1990s the English, like everyone else, will have to roll up their sleeves and get their money by making things.'

'Perhaps. We'll certainly have to find more interesting topics to discuss at dinner parties, thank God.'

Klarfeld laughed. 'So, it seems you have a certain security of tenure here . . .'

'I think so. Only two people to see the cottage since Christmas, and not a single offer. Young guy from the estate agent dropped by the other day. Told me we'd be lucky to shift the place before the summer – if then. I think he wondered why I looked so pleased.' Blessed led the way back into the cottage, ducking under the low lintel and motioning for Klarfeld to do the same. 'Should have time to finish the book. Then I'll see.'

Blessed set about building a fire. Before long they were settled down, each with something to drink, in front of the blazing logs.

'Explanations?' Blessed began.

Klarfeld nodded. 'As much as I can, yes.'

Blessed took a thoughtful sip of his whisky and launched in: 'So what's happening to our friends in East Germany? Have you managed to monitor the investigations?'

Klarfeld, confined these days to one measure of his beloved Laphroaig before bed, was hugging a hot lemon tea.

'Michael,' he said slowly, 'you must understand that there is massive confusion all over East Germany. Although the *Stasi* has been formally abolished, free elections have been ordered, and the communists will soon be giving up power, the German Democratic Republic is *still* a sovereign state.' Klarfeld shrugged. 'And the hands on the levers of power in the country are *still* those of the old

354

régime's bureaucrats. Including official, and unofficial, agents of the old *Stasi*.'

'Who are capable of obstructing justice indefinitely.'

'Yes.'

'But what about the people who were supposed to have taken over? What about the priests and the civil rights lawyers and the writers? I mean, every day I read about ex-dissidents being appointed to government posts in East Berlin.'

'Sure. Ex-dissidents like the member of the Kinder you knew as Otmar Ziegler . . .'

'Oh Christ.' Blessed's mood turned sombre. 'Go on,' he said quietly.

'You're not going to like this, but if you promise to hear me out, I'll tell you what I think is going on. Do we have a deal?'

'All right. Yes.'

'So. All change in the GDR. Dramatic reforms. That's the story the outside world hears . . . .' Klarfeld breathed in hard and began to explain. 'Now, let's take the example of a company that went in the old communist days by the name People's Own Factory "Komputron". The factory is on a huge, very modern greenfield sight not far from Weimar. Well, it's already switched from making material for the *Stasi* to producing computerised home and business-security equipment. Not a big step! The firm is already employing western salesmen to sell their wares. Business is holding up well. There are BMWs instead of Wartburgs in the car park . . . And meanwhile, the old personnel files have mysteriously gone missing, as have the old inventory files. The new management – which is mostly the same as the old management – claims that "anarchic elements" got at the records during the revolutionary disturbances last November . . .'

'I get the picture, Benno,' Blessed interrupted. 'But what my enquiring little journo's mind wants to know is, precisely who owns the company at the moment?'

'Technically, nobody! The *Stasi* no longer exists. And its involvement was in any case kept indirect. They were very careful about that. But that situation won't last long. You see, East Germany now has a new, clean government, and that new government desperately needs hard cash. A committee has been set up to offload state properties and companies. It's already approved Komputron's privatisation.'

'Ah yes. So will there be bids? And if so, who's up for it? I think I can guess . . .'

'In fact, the sale has already been agreed,' Klarfeld said calmly. 'To a Liechtenstein-based company. I should tell you that the committee that made the decision is chaired by an erstwhile hero of the anti-communist opposition well known to us. Otmar Ziegler . . .'

'And the Liechtenstein company is one of the dummy corporations set up by Rockwell, right?'

'So we suspect. As I said, the problem is to prove it.'

Blessed went over to the cupboard and recklessly topped up his almost-empty whisky glass.

'There I was, thinking I'd stumbled into an old-fashioned spy-thriller,' he growled, slumping back into the wingchair that had always been Rockwell's favourite perch. 'I expected there'd be an end to this, a logical conclusion . . . maybe not white-hats beating black-hats – I mean, nothing so terminally unhip, but . . . a resolution of some kind . . .'

'You're right about one thing,' Klarfeld said. 'The espionage aspect was basically a false trail,' he said finally. 'To keep you and other minor players off the scent. You were *supposed* to think this was a Cold War saga. Rockwell, in particular, played it up shamelessly, with his dark hints and his subtle accusations. The general's memoirs were . . . shall we say . . . the icing on that particular cake.'

Blessed moodily sipped some whisky. 'And . . . speaking of false trails . . . will you be honest about something else, Benno?'

'Of course. That's the purpose of this weekend.'

'OK. Since that night in Berlin, when you first hinted that the watchers were yours, I've had time to think.' Blessed held Klarfeld's gaze and didn't let go. 'It was you who made those tapes of Daisy, wasn't it? It was your people, not the *Stasi*, who made those phone calls to me?'

'Yes . . . It's the one thing I did that still haunts me. But you see, I needed to make you nervous, suspicious of everyone – and especially of Erika. She was getting things too much her own way. I needed you to do something irrational, Michael – to upset the apple-cart. Though exactly how irrational, I could never have predicted . . .' Klarfeld shrugged uncomfortably, tried without success to read Blessed's reaction. 'I can't ask you to forgive me for that

356

part of what you went through, only to put other things in the balance with it . . .'

Blessed gazed into the fire for a while, then shook his head. 'I suppose I've already forgiven you. After all, Daisy was never actually in danger. But now you mention it, I still don't fully understand why they bothered to put Erika onto me in the first place.'

'Well, she was an extra inducement for you to stay in Berlin and take on the job. Plus, of course, once you were regularly sharing her bed, the relationship provided an effective way of keeping an eye on you.' Klarfeld seemed to be wondering how to go on. 'Also . . .'

'Also what?'

'I'll be frank. The fact is, your involvement with Erika meant that if at any point the general's boss, Minister Mielke, got wise to the financial scam that was going on under his nose, you could be thrown to the wolves.'

'*Me*? Why me?'

'Simple. Your father was in the military police and later involved with British Intelligence. Any problems and they could feed something to the press – "SON OF BRITISH INTELLIGENCE BOSS IN *STASI* SEX-TRAP", that kind of thing. So, if necessary, the whole story of the memoirs and your part in them could be presented by the *Stasi* general, alias my childhood companion Granit, as a cunning propaganda coup designed to discredit the West. In this way he would be able to cover his tracks with his superiors.' Klarfeld laughed drily. 'Espionage as cover once more. The Cold War as a diversion from the hot money, you might say.'

'And in the end, trying to repair my bruised male ego, I ended up at Erika's flat that day last August – and threw everyone's schedule. Granit's. Rockwell's. Yours, too.'

'It's just a pity I had no watcher on you the morning you went over to confront Erika. The early shift hadn't turned up. We could have stopped you getting into that terrible mess at Erika's flat and ending up in East Germany.'

'That's nice to know. On the other hand, if I hadn't screwed up everyone's plans, I might never have got to the truth.' Blessed's lingering resentment of the older man flared up briefly. 'You should have told me about those people. When I finally levelled with you about Erika.'

357

'I thought you might panic. I didn't know you then the way I do now . . . And listen, the whole thing had got very complicated. At some points I even organised my people to bug me! When Gurkel visited me in Tunisia, for example, to finalise the details of our supposed business arrangement. I wanted everything on the record. I knew from the start I was mixed up in something very big and very illegal. You didn't. Not even when you started having suspicions about Erika. How could you?'

Blessed sighed. 'But I should have realised I was out of my depth. God knows, I've seen some corruption in my life – though maybe not on this scale. I mean, it's hard to get to grips with a scam that involves a whole country . . .'

'Oh, it's a unique historical situation. When the state owns everything, and the state collapses . . . nothing belongs to anyone, so everything's up for grabs . . .'

Blessed said nothing. He was still thinking about Erika. The one aspect of the affair he still found hard to take. *Sexual pride. You can hurt me as much as you like. Just leave me my male sexual pride . . .*

'If it's any comfort,' Klarfeld said softly, 'when you were shafted, as the Americans say, you were at least shafted by experts. Michael, I think you'd be surprised how many people in the West were compromised over the years, forced to work for the *Stasi* and the Russians. That was the aim of operations like Erika's "honeytrap". Her job at Wolfgang's gallery was just a cover. Her real work took place in the evenings, when she picked up the potential victims – Western businessmen, officials, politicians, military men. Always, naturally, she would insist they came back to her place, which they were usually delighted to do . . .'

'The *Stasi* blackmail setup dovetailed perfectly with Gurkel's commercial pornography business,' Blessed contributed. 'Erika's flat as porn-studio. Shared facilities. That made sense. A perfect example of capitalist-communist cooperation,' he added drily, 'until I happened to browse through one of Gurkel's hardcore magazines in *Lovemachine* and found the set-design for one particular orgy oddly familiar.'

'Gurkel owned the apartment building. There's reason to believe that Granit's *Stasi* department advanced him the money to buy it . . .'

'Don't tell me: but it will be impossible to prove it!' Blessed got up, tossed another log on the fire. 'So many people involved,' he said. 'So much to go wrong. Extraordinary that Granit's plan held together the way it did.'

'Oh, not so surprising! Because of the nature of the Kinder as an organisation, and the way they operated. Never any paperwork that could be traced. Only favours given and received, verbal orders and confirmations – and unquestioning loyalty.'

'We're talking Mafia.'

Klarfeld nodded. 'With Granit the boss for forty years, the gang's constant protector and guiding hand, insurer of everyone's future . . .'

'The Godfather and his soldiers, nestled happily in the corrupt fabric of the *Stasi*.'

'You see, all those years, Granit had been arranging everything, including access for all the Kinder to a secret hard-currency fund controlled by his *Stasi* department. This was fine while he was Minister Mielke's blue-eyed boy, pretty much accountable to no-one . . . but very risky once the régime began to crumble, new brooms started to sweep, and other people started to look critically at the account books . . .'

'Then, suddenly, he and his friends urgently needed a "legitimate" income that would outlast the communist régime.' Blessed shook his head in wonder. 'Granit had us convinced that it was the old régime he was frightened of, that the reactionaries were out to get him and his liberal friends, whereas in fact his real fear was of change . . . But that doesn't explain why his skinheads attacked me that day out at the Müggelsee and stole my keys, so that someone could get into the boat-house and destroy the English version of the memoirs. After all, it wasn't in Granit's interests for that material to be lost.'

'Of course not. But he knew it wouldn't be.'

'How? There's no way he could have known that I kept a spare, updated set of computer disks in your safe.'

'You don't think so?' Klarfeld smiled. 'Did you ever discuss your working habits with Diane Kelly, as one writer to another? I mean, that would have seemed natural, wouldn't it?'

'Ah . . . We talked about all that shortly after we got across the border into East Berlin. Actually, I remember she wanted to know exactly . . . I remember telling her how I insured myself against loss of disks by making copies and putting them elsewhere . . .' Blessed shrugged. 'But she never had the chance to tell anyone. We were together the whole time . . .'

359

'And what,' Klarfeld said gently, 'does the Komputron company manufacture, Michael?'

'Christ. *Bugs. Listening devices.*'

'So, Granit is listening in. He sets the skinheads onto you, then has his people smash up the computer and destroy the manuscript, knowing it will make no difference. You, quite logically, think it is his enemies who did it . . . and he has further shown his impcccable, persecuted liberal credentials . . . Just as he did by "rescuing" you after you had been kidnapped!'

'You think the whole kidnap operation was deliberate too? Give me a break –'

Klarfeld laughed. 'Oh no. You caught him by surprise, I think. Now, once you had stumbled across the set-up at Erika's apartment, the easiest thing would have been to kill you. But he knew I would be after him for that. And having carefully built up a "nice-guy" image, he didn't want a potentially embarrassing corpse on his hands. So, he decided he might as well turn the potential disaster to his advantage. What he did –' Klarfeld stabbed the air with his forefinger '– and this I have to say was *inspired* – was to conduct an elaborate charade over a period of two months, aimed at convincing you that he'd saved you from the same wholly fictional evil Stalinist *Stasi* clique that you thought had tried to destroy the memoirs. He could also convince you that it was they who were behind the entire honeytrap operation. And he could eventually release you back to the West to provide yet more evidence of his supposed humane, pro-opposition credentials. Meanwhile, of course, he had successfully kept you out of the way while his people faked Rockwell's "suicide" and spirited your brother-in-law over to East Germany.'

'Rockwell. My God, Rockwell. I'd almost forgotten him.' Blessed looked around the room. 'Amazing how quickly his spirit has disappeared from this place.'

'Perhaps, in a way, he was only ever here in body – no more,' Klarfeld observed, almost to himself.

'Granit must have thought old Rock was the perfect go-between.'

'Oh yes. Well-connected, outwardly completely respectable, and absolutely amoral . . . I'd guess Erika targeted him a quite some time ago when he was on a business-trip to Berlin, but blackmail turned out to be unnecessary. A simple approach through a Swiss intermediary was enough. Rockwell was already involved with Diane Kelly and thoroughly dissatisfied with his life. He leapt at the idea.' Klarfeld waved one hand in contemptuous dismissal. 'He provided the cash Granit needed by stealing it from trusted clients. In exchange Rockwell got the factories and the real estate at a knockdown price. Plus the means for himself and his poetry-quoting blonde to "disappear". A second chance at youth. Every middle-aged Mr Average's fantasy.'

'So our *Stasi* general turned out to be a *fairy* Godfather!'

'There you have it. Using the normal Stasi channels, Granit fixed up Rockwell with all the relevant documents and papers. Then he had the file dealing with the case removed from the department's archives and destroyed. The *Stasi* officer who removed the file on Granit's orders was killed in an explosion at a filling station shortly afterwards. Experts – probably selected by Granit, we don't know for sure – duly declared this an accident.' No joking now. Klarfeld's face was set in a solemn mask. 'Thus, no evidence. No witnesses. Except the other Kinder . . .'

'And Rockwell's new identity can't even be traced through the secret *Stasi* archives, when and if they're opened up, am I also right?'

'Yes.'

'So Granit was a murderer, after all. Even if we give him the benefit of the doubt about that poor bastard Hammerschmidt. That secret policeman may have been just a *Stasi* hack, but he was a human being. Granit and his friends murdered him, whichever way you look at it.' Blessed looked searchingly at Klarfeld. 'The same way they sent those skinheads to murder you, on the night of 9 November . . .'

'No!' Klarfeld said sharply. Then he became calmer, more thoughtful. 'I . . . I don't think they intended to kill me, or that's what they would have done. The beating-up I got was Granit's reckoning with me, the price he demanded from me for having forced his hand over Rockwell, for marring the perfection of his beautiful plan . . . And, yes, also a warning – to leave him and the Kinder alone in future . . .' He shrugged gently. 'Granit couldn't know that my heart would give out.'

'Which reminds me. Where is Granit now?' Blessed asked. 'There was the big splash for the few weeks after the memoirs were published. I heard he'd gone to Bavaria. Then there were stories

361

that he might be prosecuted, for corruption and murder, along with the other *Stasi* chiefs.'

'Unlikely. He knows where too many bodies are buried.'

'Listen,' Blessed cut in. 'This is all very interesting and pretty depressing. But you still haven't given me a solid, good reason why Granit and all the rest of them can't eventually be prosecuted. Unless there's something you haven't yet told me.'

Klarfeld nodded, conceding the point. 'There is something else, yes. The situation is complicated. Granit was never one to rely on just a single insurance. He was always running scams within a scam . . .'

'OK. Let's hear about them. I can be very patient when I want to be.'

'Very well,' Klarfeld said. 'Now, as we know, the main aim was to provide financial insurance for the Kinder, through the sale of those assets and properties to Rockwell. But there was also a need for cast-iron political insurance – especially for Granit. He had made plans to switch sides, parading his "liberal" credentials through the memoirs and so on, but he was – and is – no fool. He knew that, despite this, when the communist régime collapsed he could still end up in the dock along with the rest of the régime's bully-boys. After thirty years in the *Stasi*, Granit's hands were not of the cleanest, as you can imagine.'

'Easily. Very easily.'

'Yes. Well, I know these things I'm about to tell you only because of my relationship with Gurkel, who got very scared after you were kidnapped and decided to treat me as his father-confessor. The fact is that by the time you and I became hooked into his activities, Granit had already set up this alternative insurance scheme, running in parallel with the Rockwell scam and the memoirs. And . . . well, when I said that the espionage aspect was just a cover, this was true so far as your role was concerned. But the Cold War – or should I say, the leftovers from the East-West conflict – did play a part in this personal plan of Granit's.'

'Go on. Turn things on their head just one more time, Benno. Surprise me . . .'

'I'll try. Here goes. For some time, Granit had been busily transferring top-level *Stasi* material onto microfiche and smuggling it out of East Germany, using Gurkel's film-processing business.'

362

'Ah. This business of Gurkel's was legitimate, presumably?'

'Absolutely. But the labs in East Germany which had the contract to develop his bargain-price photographs were, of course, ultimately controlled by Granit's department of the *Stasi*. They shared the Komputron site, in fact. Anyway, it was easy to arrange for a few extra "special" packages to be sent back to West Germany, concealed among the shipments of ordinary developed photographs being returned across the border to Gurkel's customers. In the average truckload, the huge majority of the material was quite genuine – thousands of envelopes containing West German citizens' harmless holiday snaps. Only a few discreetly but – if you knew what to look for – unmistakably coded envelopes contained contraband microfiche. Once the delivery truck arrived at Gurkel's depot outside Hamburg, the precious microfiche was picked out and spirited away – to a Swiss safe deposit box registered under one of Granit's false identities.'

'And what did these rolls of microfiche contain?'

'Ah. Gold dust,' Klarfeld said. 'Files listing the *Stasi*'s best agents and sources operating in the West. Hundreds, even thousands of names. Information any foreign intelligence service would pay millions for. And which many governments in the West would rather not saw the light of day . . .'

Blessed whistled softly. 'Those lists are Granit's protection against prosecution. A blackmailer's dream. Shit.'

Klarfeld sighed wearily. He ran the back of his hand across his forehead, closed his eyes for a moment.

'Yes,' he said eventually. His voice was bleak, harsh. 'You know, Michael, peace is not a simple business. It can be just as morally complicated as war. To that extent, Rockwell, the so-called "peacebroker", was right.'

'Sure. And if what you say is true, then Rockwell was right all along! Peace *is* up for sale! Which means he's bloody laughing!' Blessed suddenly saw the man opposite him quite differently. He glimpsed his weakness, he understood, and his own anger evaporated. 'I think you should leave the prosecution of the Kinder to others – if it ever happens,' he said softly.

'Oh yes?'

'Because deep down you have more loyalty to the friends of your youth than you think, Benno. More than is good for you.'

Klarfeld sat impassively, absorbing Blessed's words, then conceded with a nod of assent. 'I know how they suffered as children. I know the terrible experiences that made them what they are. And I also know that everything Granit did, no matter how terrible, he did to protect the only human beings who really mattered to him . . .'

Blessed nodded, weary now of revelation. It seemed as if there was no more to be discovered. And probably no more to be done. Then Klarfeld surprised him by pressing on.

'Michael,' he said. 'It hasn't been at all easy telling you these things. It certainly doesn't help me to feel proud of myself. I have made mistakes. But coming clean with you is my . . . my duty.' Klarfeld hesitated. 'You see . . . there's another good reason why I came down here for the weekend with Daphne – and another reason why I wanted to speak to you in private.'

'Please, Benno. I know I said I could be patient. But I think I've had enough revelations for a lifetime.'

Klarfeld spoke quietly and deliberately: 'You don't understand. I'm here to tell you that Daphne and I plan to marry. As soon as it can be arranged.'

Blessed's mood swung in a moment from exasperation to sheer disbelief. 'Benno!' he exploded. 'You just can't do that! There are *bigamy laws* in Europe. I mean, I'm sure one day Daphne really will be legally free, but –'

'She *is* free,' Klarfeld interrupted. He got to his feet. 'Wait a moment.'

Klarfeld went over to the foot of the stairs, where he had left his leather briefcase. He opened it up, extracted a manilla folder, and returned to his place by the fireside.

'Read this, Michael,' he said, handing the folder to Blessed. It contained just a single piece of paper, a clipping from an East German newspaper, dated three weeks ago. The headline read: *POLICE ISSUE DESCRIPTION OF BODY IN LAKE*. The body of a man, around fifty years old and one metre eighty tall, fair haired and in good health, had been discovered floating in one of the lakes that surrounded Berlin. So far, the identity of the corpse remained a mystery. Suicide was suspected. Suicide had become commonplace. Many East Germans, especially former communist loyalists, had been unable to live with the huge political and social changes of the past few months.

364

Blessed looked up at Klarfeld. *'You're sure?'*

'There's no question, Michael. The body is Rockwell's. I saw it with my own eyes just a couple of weeks ago. I had to, for everyone's sake.'

Blessed replaced the clipping in the folder, handed it back to Klarfeld. 'Amazing,' he murmured. 'Two successful suicide bids in one lifetime. Maybe some expert assistance on the second occasion, just to make absolutely sure. A little help from his friends – the muscle-bound ones with the special *Stasi* training.'

'But you saw it coming, didn't you, Michael? That's why you were able to leave that restaurant the night the Wall came down, to walk out on Rockwell.'

Blessed nodded. 'After what I'd heard and seen and noticed, I sensed that between Diane Kelly and the man we call Wolfgang, Rockwell was dead meat. I reckoned they'd carve him up far more cruelly and effectively than I ever could.'

'And as the twice-late Rockwell Elliot so rightly said, "it's all in da wife's name". My latest estimate is that the assets Diane Kelly now controls will eventually be worth between two and three hundred million dollars. If she can hold onto them – which I'm beginning to think she can . . .'

'Especially if she's got Wolfgang on her side. And she must have done a deal with the Kinder, or she'd have ended up at the bottom of that lake too.'

Klarfeld nodded. 'I'd imagine the Kinder Pension Fund has profited twice, taking a hefty extra rake-off from Diane Kelly's potential fortune, as well as keeping the hard currency that Rockwell originally handed over.' He let out a grim little laugh. 'You think some kind of double-cross like this wasn't planned from the outset? You think they were just going to let Rockwell enjoy his gains? Granit and the Kinder don't work like that.'

'But my sister should have been the rich widow,' Blessed said. 'Not Diane Kelly, or whatever she intends to call herself.'

'Ah, but Daphne *will* be a rich widow, now that she has me!'

Blessed toasted the couple's happiness with another whisky. Klarfeld accepted his good wishes with a freshly-poured tumbler of mineral water. A few minutes later there was the sound of a car pulling up in the lane outside . . . Daphne returning from her trip to Taunton.

'How can you ever tell her the things you've told me?' Blessed asked Klarfeld. 'Where would you start?'

Klarfeld smiled. 'She's already heard the truth. And faced up to what it implies.'

'*For Christ's sake! When?*'

'She had always half-suspected something of the sort, of course,' Klarfeld said calmly. 'You think she didn't know Rockwell for what he was? But the crucial moment came last November, when she called from the States to tell me you were jetting across the Atlantic to Berlin, hell-bent on confronting me. It was then that I had to come clean about everything. Daphne was absolutely furious. She cajoled and she threatened, and she said if I let anyone hurt a hair of her brother's head . . .'

'Shit. I wondered why you were so well-prepared for me. My God, but Daphne must have been sure of you.'

Klarfeld nodded slowly. 'And that was also the moment I was finally sure of her . . .'

Sounds of a car door slamming.

'How did she take it?' Blessed asked quickly. 'The news about Rockwell's deception, I mean.'

'She wept,' Klarfeld explained matter-of-factly. 'Then she got down to practicalities. We discussed the options, decided that exposing Rockwell would only cause more trouble than it was worth. Arrest, extradition, trial . . . disgrace. Daphne's tougher than you think, Michael. You forget what she – what we – went through as children.'

'Benno – does Josh know everything too? I mean, Christ, *Diane Kelly* – Robert Frost, Vermont, all that Yankee integrity!'

'Daphne explained as much as she felt able. He's now a more cynical young man than he used to be, I suppose. And maybe, in the world he is about to enter, that's not such a bad thing.'

The front-door key turned in the lock. Daphne appeared, carrying two plastic shopping-bags in each hand.

'Hello, men,' she said. She looked at Klarfeld and then at Blessed. 'Ah. I can see you've heard the whole truth, Mike.' Her manner softened. 'You look as though you're still in a slight state of shock.'

Blessed nodded.

'It takes time for it to sink in, doesn't it?'

366

He nodded again.

Daphne continued on into the kitchen with her bags. Some opening and shutting of cupboards. Then she returned with three flute glasses and a chilled bottle of champagne. Nominé-Renard, *Cuvée de Réserve. Very special.*

'And the truth shall make ye free! Isn't that right, Mike?' she said.

'Of course You're absolutely sure of that, are you?'

'Never more so, no matter how unpalatable that truth, it's what you do with that precious freedom that matters.' Daphne expertly uncorked the bottle, poured champagne into the glasses. 'A fact of life that we in the world-weary, decadent West have known . . . and struggled with . . . for quite some time. And one which all those newly-liberated people in Eastern Europe, God help them, are about to find out.' She handed a glass to each of the men. 'Cheers!'

'To freedom!' said Benno.

Blessed smiled sourly. 'Perhaps . . .'

And so the three of them – Blessed, his sister, and Benno Klarfeld – raised their glasses in a somewhat sober toast, a qualified toast, a toast appropriate to the uncertainties of the heady but imponderable 1990s:

'To freedom! Cheers! . . . Perhaps . . .'

THE END